"WHO ARE YOU?" LUCIUS WHISPERED . . .

"I told you, I am a mystic," the voice said. "And this night I have been visited by a vision."

"You've had no vision!" Lucius snarled. "You're just as much of a fake as I am!"

The voice came closer, so close that Lucius shuddered at its cold intimacy. *"I am your father. Do you like that one any better?"*

Lucius closed his eyes tightly, as if trying to elude some hideous pain.

CHILDREN OF THE RIVER

By William Lavender
from Jove

Chinaberry

WILLIAM LAVENDER

**VOLUME ONE OF
THE HARGRAVE JOURNAL**

A JOVE BOOK

First Jove edition published January 1980

10 9 8 7 6 5 4 3 2 1

Printed in the United States of America

Jove books are published by Jove Publications, Inc., 200 Madison Avenue, New York, NY 10016

To Patience
... for more than can be said

AUTHOR'S PREFACE

This book is the first in a three-volume series entitled THE HARGRAVE JOURNAL, which traces the history of an American family from the frontier wilderness of the Ohio River Valley in the early 1800s to booming post-Civil War California.

It is followed by
Journey to Quiet Waters, Volume Two,
and
The Fields Above the Sea, Volume Three.

PROLOGUE

April, 1836

This is an end, and a beginning.

I am Lucius Hargrave, and I lie in my bedroll on a sandy hill in western Louisiana and stare up into a resplendent sky. The stars are gaudy jewels on black velvet, crackling with electricity. A lonely wind sweeps unhindered across a thousand miles of plain to the west and flows over me like a deep transparent river. I listen to its far-off moaning song, and wait for dawn.

By ordinary standards I am a very young man—it is only a few days ago that I passed my twentieth birthday—but I have traveled far and seen much and lived with abandon. At twenty my youth is behind me. Yet I know that my past is but an empty prelude; only the future holds meaning. The windswept ridge on which I lie tonight is the major watershed of my total existence; the shadowy lowlands behind me no more than a prenatal dream; this place the moment of birth; and the plains ahead, shining with virginal newness—true life.

In a more literal sense, I came into this world in 1816 in a tiny village of southern Indiana on the banks of the Ohio River, departed from there at the age of sixteen to make my own way, and have been a wanderer ever since. Now I dare to hope I am at last beginning to approach a condition of stability, and a place I can call home.

9

It is a time made for reminiscence, though I am not naturally inclined to that form of diversion. And because I am not inclined to it, I have recently begun recording a few personal memoirs, lest the events of my life—the impressions, the scenes, and the people who appeared in them—be forgotten and lost. I call this collection my Journal, though I write only when the mood strikes me, not on a regular basis. Nor have I attempted to construct a continuous narrative, but merely to set down from time to time a few isolated observations on things that have become part of me, for good or ill.

My sleepless eyes are attracted by a subtle change in the night. There is a tint of color in the east, a glow of dark rose brushing along the horizon, throwing the spires of the pine forest into black silhouette. Soon it will be time.

Quietly I sit up, grope in the folds of my bedroll, and bring out a leather satchel. It is scuffed and battered, the once-elegant scroll design on its front almost worn away. It is older than I by far, older than I can know, and it is the most precious object I will ever possess. It is a gift from my lost father. I open it—carefully, not to strain the old lacings—and take out my Journal. I leaf through the book, squinting at the slightly slanted lines of my laborious handwriting. It is too dark still to make out the words.

There are pleasures in these pages, and pains; profound experiences and frivolous ones; encounters I care for no more than the snap of a finger, and encounters I treasure as deeply as life. I have tried to include all things of consequence, and exclude the meaningless. Everything I have put down I have represented with candor and, I swear, with truthfulness, as best I can.

If no other eyes than my own ever fall on these lines, I hope my feeble efforts will have served a useful purpose nonetheless; perhaps one day the contemplation that has gone into them will help me to know myself. If strangers should read my scribblings, I beg to be judged with kindness and charity, for I stand revealed here, probably more than I know, with flaws I cannot dream of.

I seek not so much to be loved, as to be known and understood.

10

Part One

1

IN THE YEAR 1800, William Henry Harrison, lately the Secretary of the Territory of the United States Northwest of the River Ohio and presently territorial delegate to Congress, took notice of a disturbing fact: the territory wasn't being settled very rapidly, and the few people it was attracting were mostly the wrong kinds—land speculators and squatters. The reason for this was easy enough to perceive. None but the wealthy could afford the minimum purchase of 640 acres, to be paid for in a lump sum. Harrison proposed to Congress a plan that would reduce by half the minimum purchase, and give the buyer the privilege of paying for his land over a period of four years.

The proposal was adopted, and immediately resulted in the first land rush along the Ohio River, as settlers moved into the area, coming from the North and East down the river, and from the South via the Cumberland Gap and along Daniel Boone's Wilderness Road through the forests and meadows of Kentucky.

One of those men who came down the river was a Connecticut farmer named Samuel Gilpin. He brought with him his wife Matilda and his two children, George and Sarah, four hogs, a cow, a flock of chickens, an iron stove, some miscellaneous farm tools, several sacks of potatoes, a barrel of dried apples, and a huge trunk full of books. Samuel Gilpin was one of those rarities among the pioneer settlers of the American interior—an educated man.

Samuel landed his barge on the north shore of the river a day's journey below the town of Louisville, and after inspecting the area for half an hour, he announced to his family: "This is where we will live."

The place where he landed was a jutting promontory formed by a sharp bend in the river, with dense forest along the banks and more open rolling land behind. There was a huge sand bar in the river at that point, and this, coupled with Samuel's mistaken notion that he was at the southernmost point of the river's course, prompted him to name the place South Bar.

George was a boy of fifteen when the Gilpins settled in their wilderness home, and the girl Sarah was a two-year-old baby. These two, the firstborn and the youngest, were the only survivors out of a brood of six. The death of children was one of the natural facts of life, to be endured with fortitude and pious resignation. In a few years George had attained maturity, married a daughter of a neighboring family, and established his own farm not far from his parents'.

Sarah grew into a strong, buxom girl, dutiful, sensible and industrious—though in the opinion of her traditionalist father a trifle too inclined to independent thought. By the time she was thirteen years old she had taken over more than half the household responsibilities from Matilda.

Her parents watched her grow, saw the lumpy child's body expand into the fullness of young womanhood, knew that they must soon lose her to some ardent suitor, and dreaded the day.

14

2

EARLY AFTERNOON of a day in late summer, 1815.

The Reverend Oliver Hargrave, dressed in starched white collar, broad-brimmed hat, and neatly pressed black cloth coat, sat in splendid dignity in a wicker chair on the foredeck of his little keelboat, as regal as Cleopatra in her perfumed barge of the Nile. His crew consisted of three: an old man with jet black skin as tough as uncured leather, his face worn and lined into an ageless mask; a younger man, broad-shouldered and powerfully built, also of the black race but with creamy nut-brown skin; and a small boy no more than six years old, with a shock of dark brown hair and skin almost as dark, which, if scrubbed, would have shown him to be white. The first two members of the crew were indispensable, the third an ornament.

The young black man was poling the boat in toward the river bank. He was naked above the waist, and as he labored under the merciless August sun, his great muscles rippled across his broad shoulders, and his smooth skin gleamed. At his feet, crosslegged on the deck, the little boy sat wide-eyed, watching the approaching shoreline. At the rear of the boat the old man squatted, handling the tiller.

The younger man paused in his work and glanced over his shoulder at the white man sitting on the deck. "Don' see no peoples here, sar," he said.

Reverend Hargrave grunted. "You know better than that, Camus. You know the pioneering folk are social misfits by nature, else they wouldn't have become pioneers in the first place."

The reverend leaned back in his chair and crossed his long legs. "They are skulking in the woods like Indians," he said. "They will come out when they are coaxed."

The poleman went back to work. With superb skill he nosed the clumsy craft into the muddy shallows for a feather-soft landing, leaped out, and hauled on the line. After him came scurrying the boy, splashing muddy water on himself as he flopped overboard.

"Careful, Isaac!" the reverend snapped. "Don't get yourself soiled the first minute!"

Little Isaac scrambled up the bank and grasped the taut mooring line and pulled on it, as if to help. The big black man did his work, and ignored the boy.

The master of the vessel sat motionless, waiting placidly until the boat was completely secure. Then he rose, walked leisurely forward, stepped off onto the north shore of the Ohio River, and gazed at yet another stretch of the vast shadowy forest wilderness that was the Territory of Indiana.

He looked up and down the lifeless landscape, and frowned.

"It is evident," he announced, "that the heathens hereabouts are too sunken in lethargy to investigate the arrival of strangers on their shore, or they are insufficiently observant to notice it. They are blind men or dullards, or both."

No one listened to or responded to the reverend's remarks. Little Isaac had run off to inspect a gurgling brook a short way downstream. The younger black man was examining a path that led into the forest. The old man was stretched out motionless under a canvas lean-to at the stern end of the boat deck.

The reverend summoned the younger crewman with a snap of his fingers. "Camus! Go and inform the people here that the Gospel of the Lord will be spoken unto them at this place an hour before sundown today. All are welcome, women and children and the aged and infirm, as well as the able-bodied menfolk. The Lord's message is no less for the weak than for the strong. Go."

"Ain't no peoples here, sar," Camus said.

"Of course there are people here, fool!" the reverend growled. "I was informed of this place at our last stop. It is the Gilpin settlement. About a hundred people live within a one-mile radius, I'm told. And, Camus, be sure and find out which is the house of Mr. Gilpin, and describe it to me."

"We ain't never been here befo'," Camus said, frowning.

"No, but we are here now. Go!"

"Yas, sar." The black man went off at an easy trot up the path into the woods.

Reverend Hargrave turned toward the boat and bellowed, "Cicero! Cicero, come here!"

Under the canvas at the rear of the boat, the old black man stirred, groaned softly, and got slowly to his feet.

The reverend became impatient. "Hurry up, Cicero!"

The old man climbed painfully off the boat and came to stand at his master's elbow, awaiting further instructions.

Without looking at him, the master said, "Keep an eye on Isaac, Cicero. I'll be in the cabin, preparing my text for today's sermon."

The old man mumbled, "Yas, suh."

Reverend Hargrave returned to the boat. He took off his hat and coat and loosened his collar, in private admission that he was not so spiritual as to be unaffected by the stifling August heat. Stooping low, he entered the squat rectangular cabin that occupied the center of the deck, deposited his hat and coat neatly on a peg, and sat down on one of two bunks built against the walls of the tiny room. From the semidarkness there, the square of daylight through the doorway was dazzling.

For a little while the reverend sat very still and gazed out at a patch of the rich green forest of southern Indiana. There was no sound except the soft gurgle of the little brook nearby, and the droning of a million invisible insects, so faint as to be almost subliminal. The world was asleep on an August afternoon.

The reverend stretched out on his back, folded his hands across his chest, and stared at the low-planked ceiling above him.

17

"Dullards," he mumbled. "Nothing but blind men and dullards."

He sighed, and within two minutes fell to snoring.

In another life Oliver Hargrave could have made a career as an actor, a salesman, or a hawker of carnival curiosities. In any pursuit, his instincts would have been those of a showman. As a self-styled itinerant preacher, his stock-in-trade was awe and terror, his medium stark melodrama. He could describe the hideous fate that awaited the sinful unbeliever in the next world—nay, could act it out, could *illustrate* it—with such realism that the poor wretches in the congregation felt the hot breath of Satan on their necks. Oliver depicted it all, he performed it with abandon; in his piercing black eyes shone hellfire and brimstone, on his contorted features the agony of damnation burned.

That was when he was preaching. When he was, so to speak, offstage, he was soft-spoken and subdued, with manners polished and controlled to perfection. In appearance he was a puzzle. Not quite thirty years of age, he looked much older—or somehow ageless—because there was nothing of youthfulness in his manner. He was of average height, but his thin angular frame and his immense dignity made him seem uncommonly tall. His frame was a loosely assembled skeleton held together by a sallow, wind-roughened skin. Between skin and bones there appeared to be nothing much except a few bits of cotton padding here and there.

Yet there was power in the resonant voice, and something that seemed like nobility in the gaunt, expressive face, a sense of tragedy hanging about the deep-set eyes, bringing forth from men respect, and from women an urge to take his head upon their bosoms and stroke the troubled brow.

Oliver accepted respect with quiet confidence, as his due. And on many a trembling bosom did he lay his head.

18

3

LATE IN THE AFTERNOON the people came, straggling along the forest path in small groups, the men walking ahead, the women and children following. And as they gathered, waiting in the lengthening shade of nearby trees and staring in cautious curiosity at the little boat, the two black crewmen brought forth a homemade podium and set it up on the ground a few feet from the water's edge. The local people watched in silence; no one spoke except in an occasional whisper close to another's ear. And when the preparations were done and the crewmen had retired, the crowd edged forward and formed a tight semicircle, and in the expectant hush, even the whispering ceased.

From within the boat cabin the Reverend Hargrave had watched and waited, and scowled as he appraised his congregation. There were no more than twenty people—a disappointing turnout, even though he had not expected much. Quickly he made a last-minute adjustment in his plan of action. Then he stepped out onto the deck. His coat was on again and his collar was buttoned, and in his hands he held his Bible. With graceful ease he swung himself off the boat onto land, mounted his little platform, and gazed out over the assemblage, and the people gazed back at him. The hush was total.

"My dear friends," the reverend began, and the rich vibrant voice cast an immediate spell. "I cannot find words to express how deeply it gladdens my heart to see so many who have torn themselves away from their many pressing tasks in order to gather here to receive the word of the Lord. Yea, I am gladdened, but more importantly, He whose divine eye above sees all and knows all is gladdened, for it signifies that the old and venerable faith you brought into this wilderness frontier from the far-off homes of your birth has not faltered and died, but lives on in your hearts. Oh yes, my friends, it is a glad sight for this weary, wandering servant of the Lord; verily, it is just cause for rejoicing . . ."

But instead of looking rejoiced, the reverend now closed his eyes, frowned as if in pain, sighed heavily, and placed a trembling hand over his brow.

"Forgive me, my friends . . ." The dark, tragic eyes looked out pleadingly at the entranced audience. "I am weary and famished, both in body and in spirit. Of late, in my travels in the service of Our Lord, I have sojourned among the Hoosiers. They are our brothers, of course—all men are brothers, in the Lord's eyes. The Hoosiers have come from the south side of the river to settle in the Indiana wilderness, along with you who come from the North and the East, and they are worthy men, God knows, they are men of honor for the most part, and deserve our respect.

"But oh, my friends, I must confess to you, I am comforted mightily that in this place today I have come among my own kind again. Your clear eyes, your bright, intelligent faces, your clean, sturdy limbs, yea, the proud way you stand upon the ground—all these things assure me that once more I am among my people, true-blooded Yankees."

The little congregation reacted precisely as the reverend had planned. The stony faces melted, the men chuckled quietly, and the women smiled discreetly behind their hands. A soft ripple of amusement and understanding passed through the gathering. Reverend Hargrave observed this and moved to consolidate his advantage. He placed his Bible unopened on the podium, gripped the sides of the wooden structure, and leaned heavily on it.

"My friends, bear with me. I must beg your pardon. We have fallen upon hard times in our travels. Our foodstuffs have run low. The hospitality we have been offered by our Hoosier brothers has been warm and gratefully received,

20

but we are Yankees, after all, accustomed to Yankee fare. Oh, my dear friends, I do not complain for myself, believe me. But even now my poor little motherless son, aged six years, lies in the ship's cabin, pale and faint from hunger and from the lack of a mother's smile, and the soft touch of her hand . . ."

The reverend's voice choked, his face contorted with emotion, and a murmur of sympathy welled up from among the women in the congregation. The reverend struggled to control himself, and continued.

"I crave your indulgence, good friends, your patience, your forgiveness for my having summoned you here when I am so ill-prepared to perform my duty toward you. I implore you to excuse me, and to come again tomorrow. Pray let me now have your leave to go and search in the woods for some scrap of food with which to feed my poor sick child . . ."

He could not go on. He trembled, swayed, seemed in danger of falling. His listeners broke ranks and surged forward. Concerned faces were lifted, toward him, hands reached out in compassion.

Moments of crisis always bring forth the natural leaders of any group. Now the people instinctively made way for the most prominent man among them, and he stepped to the front of the crowd. He was about fifty years old, stockily built, of medium height, with florid skin and completely white hair, eyes watery-pale but strong and level, and a rugged, lined face that seemed chiseled from the hardwood of the forest around him.

He grasped Reverend Hargrave by the arm and said, "Take heart, sir. You are among your kind, indeed, and we will look after your needs, you may be sure."

The reverend had known very well which of his listeners would prove to be the leader. His sharp eyes had found this man in the crowd at the beginning, and had kept him under secret watch.

"I thank you, sir," he mumbled. "You are most kind."

The stranger held onto the reverend's arm and helped him down from the pulpit, while the other members of the local populace formed a circle around them.

"My name is Samuel Gilpin," the white-haired man announced.

The reverend feigned surprise. "Ah! I had heard there

21

was some stretch of the river along here under the able stewardship of one Samuel Gilpin, but I had no idea—"

"This is that place," Samuel said. "Though I don't claim jurisdiction over any part of the Good Lord's river, I do claim to own a parcel of fine land on its banks, and a house that has ample room for guests, where you will be made welcome."

The reverend was almost inarticulate with gratitude. "You are most generous. The Lord will bless you . . ."

"May I have the honor of your acquaintance, sir?" Samuel Gilpin said.

The reverend pulled himself together. "Forgive me. I am the Reverend Oliver Hargrave, minister in the service of the Lord and of His earthly children. And the honor is mine, my dear Mr. Gilpin."

Surrounded by admiring faces, the two men clasped hands.

4

IT WAS a big, fine house; Camus had reported as much to his master earlier—even so, Reverend Hargrave was surprised. Though constructed of rough-hewn logs from the forest around it, the Gilpin house far exceeded in dimensions and comfort the average settler's hovel.

In the huge combination kitchen and dining room, Samuel Gilpin sat at the head of the table and looked down a ten-foot length of board. On his right was the guest of honor, the Reverend Oliver Hargrave. To his left sat the guest second in prominence, Rufus King, a neighbor.

22

Next to King was the hostess, Matilda Gilpin, a big-boned, sallow-faced woman; and next to Matilda sat the Gilpins' pride, their thirty-year-old firstborn, George, broad-shouldered and broad-chested, with a tendency to glower. On the other side, after Oliver, was Mrs. King, a wasted, nervous woman, and then George's wife Emily, with large doe eyes and delicate features and, at thirty, a glow of prettiness still.

There were children: ten-year-old Susan Gilpin, demure and silent, sat next to her mother Emily; at the foot of the table the elder Gilpin's seventeen-year-old daughter Sarah kept watch over two boys—on her left, her nephew Henry, eight, and on her right, little Isaac Hargrave, bright and cheerful, showing no signs of the afflictions his father had so movingly ascribed to him a few hours earlier. Sarah was golden-haired, brown-eyed, rosy-cheeked, and plump. She was out of her seat as often as in it, for it was her duty to serve the meal and minister to the needs of the adults.

The center of attention was the Reverend Hargrave, who basked in its glow. He was bombarded with questions, and gave back amiable and ready replies, full of detail. Well he knew that the isolated inhabitants along the wilderness river wanted two things from him: a sense of continuing connection with the old, established religious tradition—and news. To many the second was more important than the first.

"What news from downriver, Reverend?" Samuel Gilpin asked.

"The population grows," Oliver said. "Settlers continue to move in. I find many stretches of shore that I remember as unbroken wilderness in previous years, now dotted with cabins. The axe rings in the forest, my friends."

"Mostly Hoosiers, I suppose?" Rufus King said.

The reverend nodded. "Yes, mostly Kentuckians, I'm afraid."

"Damned scum!" George Gilpin muttered. "Populating the territory with their dirty degenerate young'uns and their illegitimate mulatto slaves!"

"Not many of those, thank the Lord," Oliver said. "I see very few slaves."

'They're a-scared to bring 'em in," Rufus King said.

23

"They're a-scared the territory might join the Union as a free state."

"It will," Samuel Gilpin said. "Let no man doubt it— Indiana will go in free."

George continued to fume. "Just try and convey that news to the lace-cuffed Virginia dandies in Vincennes, who think they're going to establish slavery here and turn this place into another Virginia!"

"Your compassion for the poor, oppressed black man is most admirable," Reverend Hargrave said.

George glowered across the table at the reverend. "You misunderstand me, sir," he snapped. "I have no interest whatever in the nigger, except to keep him the hell out of Indiana."

The reverend smiled, and Samuel Gilpin hastened to turn the conversation in another direction.

"How far downriver do you venture, Reverend?"

"Usually down to the Wabash. But this year, one of my crewmen is ailing, so out of consideration for him I turned back at the settlement of General Evans."

Here the reverend was distracted. The girl Sarah was standing at his elbow, holding a steaming pot. Her broad, sunny face smiled down at him.

"Excuse me, sir. Could I serve you a bit more stew?" Her voice was soft and shy.

The reverend turned his gaze up at the girl, and returned her smile several times over. "Why, yes, I believe I might have a morsel or two more. Thank you, my dear. You are very kind."

"Sarah made the stew herself, Reverend," Matilda Gilpin said. "She's a better cook than I am, I must admit."

The reverend's eyes feasted on the girl. "Lovely, lovely," he murmured.

Sarah turned scarlet, served the reverend's plate, and withdrew hastily.

"You were saying, Reverend?" Samuel prompted. "About General Evans?"

With difficulty, Oliver recaptured his previous line of thought. "Yes. He is platting a town at the site of McGary's ferry. Plans to call it Evansville."

"Splendid!" George Gilpin said. "No doubt the principal industry of this new town will be a bigger and better

24

ferry, to fetch the ignorant Kentuckians across in a flood rather than in trickles, and their niggers with 'em."

Rufus King entered the conversation. "I think, in all fairness, George, we should recognize that not all Southerners are slaveholders."

"Of course they're not," George shot back. "Most of 'em are so poor they don't own shoes, let alone slaves."

"I think it's wrong to condemn people just because they're poor," said a childlike voice, and everybody turned to gaze at young Sarah Gilpin.

Mrs. King, hands fluttering nervously, contributed, "But Sarah dear, we were all born with equal opportunities. The reason the Kentucky Hoosiers are poor is because they're lazy and shiftless."

"I don't believe that," Sarah said firmly. "I think being poor makes people shiftless, not the other way around—"

"Hold your tongue, Sarah!" her brother George barked. "You know nothing of such things!"

Sarah compressed her lips and looked defiant, but was silent.

"My host and hostess are to be congratulated," Reverend Hargrave announced. "They should feel a glow of pride in that charming maid their daughter, who in her tender years has spoken words of wisdom and Christian charity, and shamed us all."

George Gilpin expelled his breath noisily.

"We are remiss, Reverend," Samuel said hastily. "We have done nothing about providing those men of yours with some supper. We must rectify this."

"Ah, do not trouble yourself, sir," said the reverend. "They have their own foodstuff, which they will augment by foraging in the woods, and by fishing. They are near-savages, you know, incapable of learning the ways of civilized men."

George Gilpin leaned forward and fixed a hard gaze on the guest of honor. "Those niggers of yours, Reverend. Are they slaves?"

The reverend recoiled in horror. "Slaves? I should say not, sir! As I said, they are not far removed from savagery, but the truth is they are as free as you or I."

"Let them be free somewhere else," George said grimly. "Let them not think they are free to live in Indiana."

25

Reverend Hargrave's eyes narrowed slightly. "No danger of that, sir. No danger at all."

Very soon after dinner, Rufus King and his wife said good-bye and prepared to return to their home, half a mile away through the woods. Reverend Hargrave announced that he would be preaching late in the afternoon of the next day at the site of his boat mooring, and the Kings promised to be there. Shortly, George Gilpin summoned his family for departure also.

Reverend Hargrave extended his hand to George. "Will I see you at the preaching tomorrow, sir?"

"I'm afraid not." George shook hands perfunctorily. "I'm on my way to Corydon tomorrow. I'll be gone several days, so I will probably not see you again. I wish you fair sailing on the remainder of your journey."

"Thank you, sir. Most kind, I'm—"

"Come along, Emily," George called to his wife, and turned to say goodbye to his parents.

Emily Gilpin stood before Reverend Hargrave, and he blinked in surprise to notice that there was depth and intelligence in her clear hazel eyes.

"*I* will be at the preaching tomorrow, Reverend Hargrave. I look forward to it with the greatest pleasure." Her voice was warm and vibrant.

She offered the reverend her hand, and he took it and held it for a moment while he gazed at her and contemplated another surprise—the realization that those were the first words this woman had uttered during the entire evening.

"It will be *my* pleasure, madam, most assuredly," the reverend breathed.

"I must say I regret I did not have the opportunity to converse with you this evening. I hope there will be other opportunities."

"Come along, Emily," her husband said again, more sharply.

Reverend Hargrave and his son were given the use of a spare bedroom, small but comfortable, at the rear of the house. Little Isaac had formed a warm attachment to Sarah, and begged that she put him to bed.

26

"I will," Sarah said, and ruffled the boy's hair. "After I give you a bath."

"A bath!" shrieked Isaac. "What for?"

"Because you're dirty," Sarah said.

Isaac howled his outrage, but was soon having the bath, and enjoying it.

The boy's father observed, and beamed his approval. "Beautiful child, beautiful," he said to his host and hostess, as they sat together before the fireplace. "The young man who wins your Sarah for his bride someday will be most fortunate indeed."

Matilda fluttered with pleasure. Samuel looked thoughtful.

In the quiet of late evening, after everyone else had retired, Samuel and Oliver sat together. Samuel poured two measures of whiskey and lit his pipe, and Oliver opened his Bible and held it near the single candle that provided their light.

"Will you excuse me, sir?" Oliver said. "I always read just a few lines before retiring. Restores my serenity of mind."

Samuel nodded, and puffed his pipe. After a few minutes he cleared his throat and spoke.

"Reverend . . . I would like to apologize for my son George's blunt manner this evening. I hope he didn't offend you."

"Not at all, sir," Reverend Hargrave smiled. "Banish it from your mind."

The reverend resumed his reading. Samuel puffed on his pipe and regarded his guest through clouds of blue smoke. Soon he spoke again.

"Excuse me, Reverend—it didn't come clear to me what your religious affiliation is, exactly."

"I am an ordained minister in the Methodist Episcopal Church," Oliver announced solemnly.

"Good. Most of us hereabouts are Methodists, though there are some Baptists, and a few Presbyterians."

With a finger marking his place, the reverend closed his Bible. "Precisely why I try not to mention affiliation. I prefer to fill my role as a personal minister of the Lord, carrying the divine message to all His children, excluding none."

27

"Admirable!" Samuel exclaimed. "A true servant of the Lord!"

The reverend sipped his whiskey, and looked at once modest and saintly. "I try to be," he murmured, and returned to his Bible.

5

WORD SPREAD mysteriously through the wilderness. In the late afternoon of the next day, people came for miles along the forest trails, and by boat from remoter places along the river. When Reverend Hargrave stepped up to the portable pulpit beside his flatboat, he found an eager audience, tripled in size from the day before. Nearly everybody looked freshly scrubbed. Most of the people wore crisp, neat, spotlessly clean clothes. The reverend sniffed the air and picked up the faint smell of camphor, and though his outward expression remained grave, secretly he was pleased. The smell of camphor in a frontier audience was a sign that these were Sunday clothes, fancy dress-up attire taken out of trunks and storage boxes and worn for special occasions only. The Reverend Hargrave's appearance had clearly been adjudged an Event.

The reverend gave one of his most inspired and impassioned performances, lasting nearly an hour, and the people quailed before the fire and brimstone conjured up before them. Strong men turned pale, women gasped and trembled, and children whimpered in terror.

At the front of the congregation Emily Gilpin stood en-

28

tranced, her face shining. From farther back in the crowd, Sarah Gilpin fixed her brown eyes unwaveringly on the minister. It was Reverend Hargrave's habit, when preaching, to pick two or three of the most attentive and responsive faces in his audiences, and concentrate on them. Now he divided his attention equally between Samuel Gilpin and the two Gilpin sisters-in-law, Emily and Sarah.

Afterward people surged forward, flushed with emotion, and vied with each other to clasp the preacher's hand. From all sides they earnestly beseeched him to remain among them and preach again, and yet again.

The reverend remonstrated: "My friends, I have a long and arduous journey ahead still, and the summer draws to a close."

His admirers were insistent. "There's a good four weeks before the first frost, Reverend," someone said. "You can afford to tarry a few days."

The reverend was moved. "You are all so kind . . ." He was plainly wavering.

Samuel Gilpin provided the decisive comment. "Of course, sir, you know you are welcome in my house for as long as you care to honor us with your company."

The reverend capitulated, consented to stay awhile, and promised to preach every day. A great cheer arose. Through the milling crowd around him, Oliver caught sight of the round, rosy face of Sarah Gilpin, watching him. He smiled at her. She smiled back, blushing, and turned quickly away and disappeared.

After the crowd had thinned somewhat, Reverend Hargrave scanned the area again and found Emily Gilpin standing alone, somewhat apart from the others. Seeing that he had noticed her, she came quickly toward him and extended her hand.

"It was a magnificent sermon, Reverend Hargrave. Most eloquent."

Again he took the opportunity to hold Emily's hand distinctly longer than necessary, and to gaze soulfully into her eyes.

"Your kind words make me very happy, my dear Mrs. Gilpin."

Emily delicately retrieved her hand. "Reverend Hargrave, it would give me—" She hesitated, seemed suddenly ill at ease, glanced hastily left and right.

29

"Yes, madam?"

"It would give me great pleasure to have your company at supper one evening."

Oliver's eyebrows lifted slightly in surprise. "Why, I'd be delighted, madam. However, to be perfectly frank . . . it seemed to me I detected in your husband a distinct coolness toward me, for some unknown—"

Emily's laugh was quick and strained. "Well, that's why I hoped you'd come soon, while George is away. That is, of course, unless you'd consider it somehow improper—" Emily was twisting her hands together nervously, betraying an inner tension.

The reverend chuckled his reassurance. "Oh, good heavens, no, by no means! I'm sure a lady of your obvious refinement is quite above reproach hereabouts."

Emily took heart. "Actually, you see, George does not share my interest in theology. I thought we might have a discussion without risk of . . . of boring him." Nervousness flitted around her mouth, but her hazel eyes held on Oliver steadfastly.

"I see." The reverend smiled broadly. "That is an enchanting prospect indeed."

"Would tomorrow evening be convenient?"

"Entirely convenient, madam."

"Our house is the first one beyond my parents-in-law's place, on the path that leads away from the river. It's less than a mile. Can I expect you directly after preaching?"

"Directly."

"Bring little Isaac too, of course. My Henry has grown quite fond of him."

"I will. I thank you, madam, and I must say I look forward to it with the utmost—"

Other people intruded, seeking the reverend's attention.

"Tomorrow, then," Emily said, and was gone.

6

AT SUPPER in the evening, Matilda was uncharacteristically effusive. "My, my, it was such a wonderful sermon, Reverend. I don't know when I've felt so uplifted!"

"Surely not since we left Connecticut, fifteen years ago," Samuel declared.

Matilda looked at her husband with a trace of a smile. "You know, Samuel, I do believe even Sarah was impressed."

Reverend Hargrave looked up curiously. Sarah was bringing a platter of corn muffins from the stove. She set the muffins on the table, heard her name mentioned, and realized that her parents and Reverend Hargrave were looking at her.

"What's that you said, Mama?"

"Did you enjoy Reverend Hargrave's sermon, Sarah?" her father asked.

The girl glanced at the preacher and met his eyes, beaming up at her.

"Yes, Papa, I did. I love to hear Reverend Hargrave preach. But . . ."

Sarah backed away a few steps. Her rosy cheeks became flushed. Oliver's smiling eyes followed her.

"Yes. Sarah?" He coaxed her gently. "But what?"

The girl hesitated, casting an apprehensive look at her father. Then she summoned up her courage and replied,

31

"I just don't believe in all that . . . that awful talk about hellfire."

Her mother looked shocked. "Why, Sarah!"

"Don't you believe that God punishes sinfulness, girl?" her father demanded.

"Yes, but . . . not *that* way. I just can't see—"

"It is written, Sarah! It is written in the Lord's book! Reverend Hargrave has told you so—"

The reverend held up a hand. "Please, my dear friend," he said to Samuel. "Questions of this sort should be discussed dispassionately, or not at all."

Samuel subsided. "Well, I think the child is altogether too opinionated," he grumbled.

"Nevertheless we must respect her beliefs, sir. She is wise beyond her years, I've already discovered that."

In the silence that followed, Sarah looked shyly at the preacher beneath lowered lashes and said, "But I do love to hear you preach, Reverend Hargrave. I like it very well indeed." She turned away abruptly and went back to the stove.

Later in the evening Sarah put little Isaac to bed again, and crooned to him a soft lullaby. And much later still, Samuel and Oliver sat before the hearth again and Samuel poured their small bedtime measures of whiskey. Oliver held his Bible in his lap, but this time he did not seem eagerly inclined to read in it. He watched Samuel light his pipe, then he cleared his throat and spoke.

"By the way, Mr. Gilpin, tomorrow evening I've been invited to sup at the home of your daughter-in-law." The reverend kept his eye on the face of his host, watching for a reaction.

Samuel puffed his pipe and nodded. "Yes. Emily told us."

"But since your son won't be there, perhaps you might not consider it entirely proper . . ."

Samuel chuckled. "Nonsense, Reverend! You're a man of the cloth, a pillar of virtue. Besides, Emily is amply chaperoned by her mother."

Oliver's face fell. "Her . . . mother?"

"Emily's mother lives with them. She won't be much company, though. Mrs. Morrow's old as Methuselah, and fairly well gone in the head."

"I see." Oliver stared glumly into the fireplace.

32

"But Emily will give you a lively discussion," Samuel went on. "She's a mighty quiet woman when George is around—hardly opens her mouth. But when she's on her own, she can talk right smartly."

"Yes, I'm sure."

"It's an easy walk up the trail out back here. And I'll leave the door unbolted for you."

"Thank you." Oliver turned his attention to his Bible.

After a moment Samuel spoke again, hesitantly. "Uh, Reverend . . . could I ask a question or two?"

"Why, certainly."

"Don't mean to be nosy, mind. And if I am, just stop me and tell me to stick to my own business—but we've all been wondering about little Isaac. Well, not about the lad, exactly. About his mother."

Oliver closed his eyes and put a hand over his brow.

Samuel went on hastily, "Excuse me, now, Reverend. If you'd rather I didn't ask, why—"

"No, no. It's quite all right." Oliver had recovered his composure, though his face was strained. "But the thought of my beloved late wife stabs me with a pain that is very nearly unbearable. You must forgive me. May God rest her soul."

"Amen to that, sir."

"My poor Caroline passed away quite suddenly, just a year ago. I left her healthy and cheerful when I departed on my annual journey down the river that spring, and when I returned in September, she had . . . she had . . ." The reverend's voice broke. He was unable to continue.

"What a terrible thing," Samuel said dolefully.

"The boy could be left with relatives, of course, but naturally I prefer to have him with me. He is my joy, the only thing I have left . . ." Again the reverend struggled to control his emotions.

Samuel leaned forward and spoke earnestly. "Well, Reverend, what I'm getting at here is, if you don't have strong ties elsewhere, why not settle here in South Bar? Why not be our permanent minister? We need you here, Reverend. Why, you just say the word, and we'll turn to and clear a piece of land for you, and build you a church and a house to boot. Say the word, and it'll be done before the first frost hits."

33

The reverend smiled. "You tempt me, my dear friend. Indeed you do."

Samuel pressed his advantage. "Why, Reverend, you could do more of the Lord's good work here in a year than in a whole lifetime of roaming up and down the river, wasting your breath on Hoosiers and squatters and the like. Stay with us."

Still smiling, Oliver held up a hand. "Desist, my friend, I implore you . . ."

Samuel would not desist. "Reverend, we have sore need of your wisdom and guidance. There are unbelievers among us. Why, even here under my own roof, I—" Samuel paused and examined his pipe.

The reverend looked quickly at him. "What is it, friend?"

"It's Sarah. She has a waywardness in her head, Reverend. She has no piety, and no respect for established authority. Even tonight you heard her impudence, telling you she disbelieves in the word of the Lord."

The reverend pondered. "She has an independence of mind that is rare in young maidens, that is true. Channeled in the proper direction, it can be an asset. Uncontrolled, it can be a curse."

"The worst thing in a maid is lack of piety," Samuel declared. "Sarah just won't take to religious teaching a'tall. I was surprised she went to your preaching today, and I'll be surprised if she goes to another."

"Hmmm." The reverend pondered further. "I will have a talk with her."

"Would you, sir?" Samuel said eagerly.

"Of course. Perhaps I can find a way to . . . strike a responsive chord in her heart."

"I'd be much obliged if you would. It's a burden on you, I know—you're a busy man, with all your sermons to prepare."

Reverend Hargrave's long, sharp face took on a serene nobility as he gazed over the head of his host.

"My first duty, sir, is to look after the souls of my flock," he said softly. "And I *never* neglect my duty."

34

7

FROM THE JOURNAL of Lucius Hargrave:

My father, Oliver Hargrave, was a minister of the Gospel, an ordained pastor in the Methodist Episcopal Church of America, and much more, a messenger of God whose selfless love for his fellowman drove him repeatedly to forsake the warmth and comfort of a permanent home, and to journey at great peril in the vast wilderness of the Ohio River Valley, carrying the divine word to the hardy pioneer folk who dwelt and labored there.

For a number of years during the decade between 1810 and 1820, he would set forth in the spring from his home port of Cincinnati in his little keelboat, which he had built with his own hands—somewhat crude perhaps, certainly modest, but a brave and sturdy craft—and float down the Ohio waterway, dispensing inspiration and spiritual renewal and, I believe, many a piece of sound advice of a practical nature as well, to all he encountered. My father was not only a pious and learned man, but a sensible one who understood that the hungering mouth must be fed and the aching body eased with balm before the heart can be opened to receive the spiritual message.

After a time, when it became apparent that settlers were venturing in great numbers farther down the river, pushing the frontier ever westward, the Reverend Hargrave moved his base from Cincinnati down to Louisville, so that he too

35

could penetrate farther west each summer, and thus remain in the vanguard, where, he well knew, he was most needed.

The good Reverend's task would not have been easy even for an unencumbered man. But during the middle years of this period he was the sole parent and protector of his firstborn, my older half-brother Isaac, whose mother had died at a tragically early age in Cincinnati. Isaac was a lively boy, full of mischief and healthy curiosity, and must have been a terrible burden of responsibility to a wifeless man without an established home. But our dear father would never have conceded it to be a burden; to him the tender care of little Isaac was but a joy, as were all his other forms of human succor.

Reverend Hargrave was the despair of the officials of the church, who in their pinched and narrow view considered the establishment of as many church sites as possible to be of greater importance than the spreading of the Divine Word among the greatest number of people. They remonstrated with the reverend, they implored him in vain to renounce his annual journeying and to settle down to a permanent location. He listened patiently, but turned them firmly aside; he hearkened to a higher voice than theirs, he told them.

The voice to which he hearkened was the voice of compassion, and it was that quality in him that inspired confidence in the simple backwoods folk whom he had chosen to serve. Wherever he went, members of his hastily assembled congregations, usually utter strangers, would come to him seeking his friendship, and welcome him to their homes for as long as he cared to stay. Immediately thereupon, they would pour out their hearts to him, divest themselves of their innermost secrets, and implore his help and guidance in their personal lives, often on matters of the most intimate and private nature.

This instinctive trust that people invariably placed in Reverend Hargrave was entirely justified. Never did he betray a confidence or turn away a troubled soul without providing aid and comfort, sound advice, and, if need be, positive action, sometimes at great personal risk. Indeed, if the truth were known, it would be seen that the number of lives the reverend saved through kindness and practical wisdom fully equalled the number of souls he retrieved from heathen darkness and brought into the shining grace of the Lord. And of course, his acts of quiet heroism went largely unrecorded.

Thus it is that men who are blessed with extraordinary gifts are not permitted to live lives of limited scope and modest achievement, but are called upon by their fellow-man to pour out their God-given talent with prodigious generosity, even as an ungrateful world absorbs it all and clamors for more.

The Reverend Oliver Hargrave accepted his burden of greatness gladly, and gave of himself without stint, oblivious to the terrible drain on his energies. He was a man at once noble and humble, profound and simple, of the highest personal standard of morality but understanding and forgiving toward sinners. While others far less capable climbed the ladder of fame and wallowed in ill-gotten luxury and wealth, he labored in obscurity, endured hardship and peril with sublime indifference to his own comfort and safety, and dedicated his life to performing an arduous task for no other reason than that he believed God wished it done. In him were embodied the qualities that have made this nation great.

I am proud to claim him as my father.

8

IN THE LATE MORNING Reverend Hargrave took a walk down to the river, where his boat was moored. Camus was swinging an axe, chopping firewood, and punctuating his swings with a low, rhythmic chant. He stopped abrupt-

37

ly when he saw the reverend, flashed a grin, and bobbed his head rapidly.

"Mornin', Massa, mornin'."

Reverend Hargrave glanced around. "Where's Cicero?"

"In he bed, Massa. He ailin' agin."

The reverend climbed aboard his boat and made his way past the center cabin to the stern, where he stooped and peered under a canvas awning that was strung two feet above the deck.

"Cicero? What's the matter with you?" His sharp manner bespoke annoyance.

He was answered by a feeble groan. "Got de fever, Massa."

Reverend Hargrave stood up and frowned at the top of the tattered old canvas. "Cicero, you come out of there immediately, do you hear me? I want you off the boat. If you don't do as I say, I'm going to speak to the devil about you."

Cicero's groan turned to a piteous whine. "Oh no, Massa, no! Don' speak to de debbil! Don' speak, Massa . . ."

The reverend turned away, returned to shore, and again approached the younger crewman. He planted himself squarely in front of the black man and issued a stern order: "Camus. This afternoon I'm coming on board with one of the lambs of my flock, who is in need of counseling. I want the boat cleaned up. And I want you and Cicero off and away, out of sight. That is, I want you to *stay* out of sight. I must have absolute privacy, do you understand?"

Camus's grin reappeared. "A lady lamb, Massa?"

The reverend's eyes flashed with anger. "Do you understand me, Camus?"

"Yas, sar. Camus understand, Massa. We be gone."

The reverend's temper was not soothed. "Goddamned insolent bastard!"

Camus looked injured. He hung his head in shame. " 'Scuse, Massa. Camus good boy. Don' talk to de debbil, Massa. We be gone, sho'."

"Well, see to it!" the reverend snapped. He stalked away, going back up the path from whence he had come.

Camus stood still and watched until his master was out of sight. Then his grin broke out again. He swung his axe,

38

and timed his strokes to a new song, which he sang in a low, mellifluous voice:

"Massa got a little lamb,
Sweet, tender, juicy lamb,
Massa got a little lamb,
Hey, hey, ho . . ."

In the afternoon, Reverend Hargrave came down the path again. This time he was strolling, and at his side was Sarah Gilpin. They came to the riverbank and stood looking at the squat little flatboat lying low in the water. The reverend propped his foot on the low gunwale, and smiled at the girl.

"Made it with my own hands, Sarah."

"It's mighty pretty," Sarah said.

"Rather crude, I'm afraid. But it serves me well. It's my home five months out of the year."

"I'd love to go on a boat ride sometime," Sarah said wistfully. "I've not been on the river since we came here, and I was a baby then."

"Would you like to see the inside?" the reverend asked.

Sarah's eyes opened wide. "Would it be all right?"

The reverend chuckled and held out his hand to her. "Perfectly all right."

Gallantly he helped her to climb up onto the deck, putting his arm around her to steady her, causing the color to rise in her cheeks again. Then he took her by the hand and led her to the entrance of the little cabin. She peered into the dark interior.

"Step inside," the reverend coaxed.

"But it's . . . it's your *bedroom*, sir!"

He laughed. "It's my home, my dear. My parlor, my bedroom, my study, my . . . sanctuary." He gazed at her with a gentle smile, bowed, and gestured for her to enter.

She hesitated for a moment longer, then stepped across the threshold. He followed. She stood in the center of the tiny room and looked around, open-mouthed. The rough board wall at the opposite end was hung with a profusion of religious pictures, and supported a bookshelf loaded with old books and stacks of papers and pamphlets. On the two bunks that occupied the walls on the left and right

39

were thick bearskin rugs, and another covered the floor-space between.

Sarah was enthralled. "Oh, my . . . it's beautiful!" she breathed.

"Thank you." From behind her, the reverend watched her closely.

She edged toward one of the bunks, let her fingers move lightly through the soft bearskin fur, and smiled with child-like pleasure.

"Mmmm. I think a body could be happy, living here."

"Sit down, my dear," the reverend said. When he saw that she was unwilling, he sat down on the bunk and took her hand and pulled her down beside him.

She extracted her hand from his and sat prim and stiff, and said, "I oughtn't to sit on a gentleman's bed."

He smiled. "It's all right, dear child. You're sitting on Isaac's bed."

She was amused; a peal of charming girlish laughter escaped her.

Suddenly Reverend Hargrave was gripped by an intense earnestness. "Sarah . . ." He took her hand and held it. "Sarah, I would like you to feel completely at ease, because I want to talk to you about something of the deepest importance."

The brown eyes widened again. "What is that, sir?"

"Your spiritual life."

Sarah hung her head. "I'm sorry I was so impudent and disagreeable, sir. My father has spoken severely to me about it."

"No, no, child, I don't mean that."

She raised resolute eyes to him. "But I just can't believe in a God who punishes poor sinners with cruel torture, sir. I can believe only in a kind, merciful, and forgiving God."

The reverend smiled with affection upon her. "Dear Sarah . . . would it comfort you to know that I consider your views quite as valid as my own?"

"*Do* you, sir?"

"Indeed I do. None of us has looked upon the face of the Creator, nor ever shall while living on this earth. We are as the poor blind shellfish that crawl in the black mud at the bottom of this river. We know no more of Him than the mindless crustaceans know of us. Like them, we are forever prisoners of our own ignorance."

The wide brown eyes were staring at him. "But, sir . . . how can you preach those horrid things if you don't believe with all your heart—"

"Tut, tut, child." Smilingly he patted her on the cheek. "It is not my place to speak *truth*. I cannot deliver what I am not in possession of. It is my duty merely to give comfort and succor to the lost and wandering lambs that I encounter along the way."

"Comfort, sir? That is *comfort?*"

"Yes! It is what the pioneer, who lives uneasily in the raw wilderness, needs. It gives him the sense of universal order that his spirit longs for. I see that hunger there, and I feed it. *That* is comfort."

Sarah was entranced. "Why, sir . . . that's wonderful!"

The reverend enclosed the girl's hand in both of his own. His voice went low and soft.

"But theology is not our subject this afternoon, Sarah. There is something far nobler, far more inspiring, than theology. A tender and fragile thing, in the presence of which the crusty old theologians must close their weighty tomes and slink away."

"And what is *that,* sir?"

He fairly whispered it. "Love."

Sarah sucked in her breath.

"Love of the gentle Savior, and of the heavenly Shepherd whose little lambs all of us are. Love, without which life is meaningless and empty."

He moved closer to her, and held her hand a little tighter. "Sarah, that beautiful thing lies sleeping within your maidenly breast, and I want to awaken it. For until that is done, you cannot be fully known to the Lord, nor receive His blessing. You cannot become that most glorious of God's creatures, a woman, but must remain a callow child. Oh, Sarah, my sweet Sarah, I want to awaken your love . . ."

His hand hovered over her, touched her hair.

She recoiled. "Oh, sir! It sounds so *wicked,* what you say."

"It's according to Scripture, Sarah."

"No! That cannot be!"

"It is, my dear, it is. God . . . is love."

He crept closer still. His hand stole over her back. He murmured dreamily, close to her ear, "Thou hast ravished

41

my heart, my sister, my bride. Thou hast ravished my heart with a glance of thine eyes . . ."

Sarah squirmed. "Oh, *sir!*"

"Thy lips are like a thread of scarlet, and thy speech is comely. Thy two breasts are like two young roes that are twins . . ."

Sarah put her hands to her ears. Her cheeks were burning. "Oh, *sir!* Wicked, wicked!"

". . . which feed among the lilies."

Sarah tried to rise. The reverend's hand on her shoulder pulled her back, and held her.

"Of course, it is spiritual love of which Solomon sings. Divine love." His hand moved up and down caressingly on her shoulder and upper arm.

"But you must understand, dear Sarah, divine love is a lofty thing. It is the topmost mountain peak of human experience. It can be attained only by stages. And the first great step toward that attainment, my adorable one . . ." His hands now grasped her firmly by the arms and pulled her into a close embrace. ". . . is love between man and woman."

"Oh no, sir, I can't—"

His lips were upon her mouth. She pulled back; he pressed forward. She leaned back farther, pushing futilely against him, and found herself lying flat on the bearskin bedcover, with the weight of the preacher's body pressing down on her chest, and his open mouth covering hers.

She struggled, fought free from his devouring kiss, and gasped for breath. "Stop it, sir! It's sinful, it's—"

"No, Sarah, no! Not sinful!" The reverend was panting, staring wildly into her eyes, and holding her helpless. "Oh, Sarah, pity my grief, my loneliness. I have suffered so much since the loss of my beloved wife, just one year ago. Oh God, Sarah, that a poor man could endure a year of such misery!"

His hand, which had found its way under her clothes, groped among the folds of her petticoat and found smooth skin along the rounded hips. Sarah's struggles became feeble.

"And the cruellest thing of all, my sweet girl, is that you remind me of her. You are so *like* her . . ." The reverend sobbed convulsively. "Oh, Sarah, as you believe in a kind and merciful God, be kind to me!"

42

He buried his face in the soft curve of the girl's neck. His hand, under her garments, had worked its way up to a breast, and squeezed it gently.

Sarah stared at the ceiling. Her chest rose and fell in gulping breaths. The reverend's lips roamed over her neck and throat, climbed to her chin, her cheeks, and returned again to the trembling mouth, murmuring, "Oh, Sarah, Sarah, my beautiful. Today you will become a woman, and blessed in God's eyes . . ."

Sarah reached a sudden decision. With a quick surge of strength that took the reverend by surprise, she pushed him upward and rolled out from under him and free of his grasp. By the time he had recovered and reached for her, she was standing in the center of the room, adjusting her clothes and smoothing her hair, and looking coolly down at him with only the burning color in her face betraying her agitation.

He sat up and held out a hand toward her, pleadingly. "Sarah . . ."

She stepped back. Her big brown eyes were clouded under a frown.

"Reverend Hargrave, we are taught that the Lord chose a virgin to be the mother of His Son. I can't believe He loves me any less while I preserve my *own* virginity."

She started for the door. He was up like a cat, and caught her in the doorway, and held her fast by the wrist.

"Sarah . . . you have injured me grievously. From the depths of my anguish I have held out my hand to you, and you most cruelly spurned me."

Sarah tried to pull free, evading the preacher's gaze. "Please, sir, let me go."

He held on. "You are cruel, Sarah. And the Lord abhors cruelty." With his free hand, he lifted her chin and looked deeply into her eyes. "But I will return your cruelty with kindness. I forgive you, Sarah. And I will pray for you."

"Might I go now, sir?"

"Have you a Bible, Sarah?"

"Yes, sir."

"Then open it to the Song of Songs, which is Solomon's, and read therein of the raptures of love, which God, *through me,* has offered you."

"I will, sir."

"And Sarah . . ."

43

She cowered before him. "Yes, sir?"

"Promise me you will keep that which you read, and our conversation here today, locked . . . *locked* . . . in your secret heart."

"Yes, sir. I will. I promise."

Suddenly he smiled. "Bless you, my sweet child."

He released her, and she fled like a wild thing, and disappeared up the winding forest path toward home.

Reverend Hargrave stood in his doorway and watched her go. Then he walked to the edge of the foredeck and spat with anger into the rippling water.

"Damn the little strumpet!" he muttered. "I will *have* her, by God. I swear it!"

9

THE HOUSE of George and Emily Gilpin was far less fine than that of George's parents, and the fare laid out on the table was scanty by comparison. But when Reverend Hargrave arrived at dusk, he was in an expansive mood, and praised everything he saw. He bowed low to his hostess and kissed her hand, bowed even lower to the ancient crone Mrs. Morrow, Emily's mother, and congratulated her at some length on her lovely daughter, her admirable son-in-law, and her beautiful grandchildren. The old woman's watery eyes stared at him fiercely. She did not appear to understand what he said.

The children, Henry and Susan, were scampering about on the floor, playing with a kitten. Little Henry timidly

44

asked about Isaac, and was told that Isaac had been feeling tired, and wished to stay, as he had put it, "at home" with Sarah.

"Remarkable what a talent Sarah has with children," the reverend said to Emily. "Isaac has become totally devoted to her. She will make some fortunate man a splendid wife."

"I wonder," Emily said dryly.

The reverend raised his eyes in curiosity. "What do you mean, madam?"

"She has an unruly mind, I'm afraid. George worries constantly about her."

"So does her father, apparently. Only last evening he begged me to have a talk with the girl."

"And did you?"

"Briefly. With very little result, I'm afraid. I can see a certain . . . obstinacy in her. Most regrettable."

The children were given their supper and sent out to play, after which the adults sat down at the table. At Emily's request, the reverend said grace. He made it brief, then smiled at his hostess as she served his plate.

"I'm sorry your husband isn't here," he said. "What business takes him to Corydon, may I ask?"

"Officially he has gone to buy some household supplies. In truth, his purpose is to talk politics."

"He is interested in the movement toward statehood for Indiana, I believe?"

"Intensely interested. Talks of nothing else. As for me, I find the entire matter a bore. I'm afraid politics is a hopeless mystery to me."

Reverend Hargrave chuckled. "And I must admit I agree with you. I consider people much more interesting than political abstractions."

Emily's severely dignified expression softened with a small smile.

The reverend turned his attention to his plate. "Delicious cabbage, madam. You're a fine cook."

"Not so fine as Sarah, I'm afraid."

"Every bit as fine. I might say a trifle finer. Don't you agree, Mrs. Morrow?"

The old woman was nodding in her chair. At the mention of her name, she started, opened her pale eyes wide, and looked in confusion around her.

45

"Hmmm? Wha'zat, Em'ly?"

"Reverend Hargrave was speaking to you, Mama."

Mrs. Morrow looked vaguely in the guest's direction. "Rev'rend who?"

The reverend smiled. "I was saying, madam, I think your daughter is a fine cook."

"Yas," Mrs. Morrow said. "Em'ly's a good girl. That she is, indeed." She smacked her lips vigorously several times, in preparation for further vocal effort.

"Yas, I mind how Em'ly was one o' my best chil'run, one o' my very best. Her and Robert. My very best chil'run."

"My brother Robert," Emily explained to the Reverend. "He lives in Corydon. George will be stopping there."

"Yas, George is a fine man," Mrs. Morrow said. "Em'ly married well, that she did. Robert married well too, yas. Cordelia's a fine girl. Edward, though—" Mrs. Morrow smacked her lips and frowned, remembering. "I mind how Edward always said he'd never marry. Won't be tied down by women and chil'run, Edward always said. He went off and joined the army."

"And promptly married one of those fancy Virginia girls at Vincennes," Emily said.

"Fought with Harrison at Tippecanoe, Edward did," Mrs. Morrow proclaimed.

"Mama—" Emily began.

"Fought and fought, till every last one o' them damned Injuns was—"

"Mama!"

"Died there too, Edward did," Mrs. Morrow finished softly.

"Mama, Reverend Hargrave doesn't want to hear all that old family history!"

Mrs. Morrow turned her eyes on the reverend and squinted. "You a married man, Rev'rend?"

"Mama, don't be so personal!" Emily protested.

The reverend's smile was full of sadness. "I regret to say, madam, I am since last summer a widower."

Mrs. Morrow smacked her lips and studied him. "You don't want to be without wife too long, Rev'rend. A man needs a woman's body to comfort himself with. Helps drain the meanness out of 'im."

"Mama!" Emily gasped.

"There's a right good number o' single females right

'round South Bar here, Rev'rend. You might keep yer eyes open—"

Emily rapped sharply on the table with her knuckles. "Mama, that's quite enough! I have *never* heard you talk so! Finish your supper, please, so I can get you ready for bed. It's very late for you."

The old woman stiffened her frail back and glared at her daughter. "I ain't a'goin' to bed with the chil'run tonight, Em'ly. We got company." She smiled at the reverend, revealing toothless gums.

The reverend's responding smile was faint and half-hearted.

Afterward, when the purple late-summer twilight had deepened to blue night and the children were asleep, Emily and Reverend Hargrave sat on opposite sides of the hearth and engaged in quiet and dignified conversation. Old Mrs. Morrow sat in a rocking chair and listened for a while, then began to nod. Outside, the invisible legions of frogs and insects sang their endless night-song. Inside, Reverend Hargrave fixed his eyes on Emily and expounded with some fervor on his religious philosophy.

"Indeed, madam, my differences with the church go deeper than the mere fine points of theology. We are at odds over the question of what the central aim and purpose of the church should be. My view is that the saving of souls is our primary duty. My superiors seem to be interested only in the building of a profitable business organization."

"It seems to me," Emily observed, "that you are the true man of God, while they are no better than moneychangers in the temple."

Reverend Hargrave slapped his knee. "Precisely! I must say, madam, your ready grasp of ideas is astonishing. Seldom have I seen such a keen intellect combined with such feminine charm, and—if I may say—attractiveness."

Before Emily had time to become embarrassed, the reverend himself squirmed with discomfiture. "Forgive me, madam. It is most unseemly. I should not speak so to you."

Emily glanced quickly at her mother, and saw that her gray head was resting on her chest. The rocking chair was still. Emily gave the reverend a fleeting smile. "Your words

47

are not unpleasant, Reverend Hargrave. Not unpleasant at all."

The reverend clasped his hands between his knees and bowed his head, and appeared to be deeply troubled.

"Madam . . . last evening your father-in-law made a suggestion to me that warmed my heart. He suggested that I settle here in South Bar."

Emily's face lit up. "What a wonderful idea!"

The reverend ground his hands together, reflecting inner struggle. "The truth is, madam, I could not possibly . . ."

Suddenly he was distracted by a new sound. Mrs. Morrow was snoring. Emily stood up.

"If you'll excuse me, Reverend Hargrave, I'm going to put Mama to bed now."

The reverend rose immediately. "Perhaps I should be on my way—"

"Oh no, please don't." Emily said quickly. "I'll only be a few minutes. Then we can . . . we can talk."

The reverend smiled.

Emily got Mrs. Morrow to her feet. "Say goodnight to Reverend Hargrave, Mama."

The watery blue eyes drifted for a moment before coming to rest on the Reverend. A small, gnarled hand was extended toward him.

"Oh, goin' so soon, Rev'rend?"

"Very soon, madam. I have much work to do in the morning." He shook her hand. "It was an enormous pleasure to make your acquaintance, dear lady."

"Mind now, you keep yer eyes open like I told you, Rev'rend. South Bar is full o' likely young maids to—"

"Come along, Mama," Emily said sharply, and led her mother away.

When she returned, her guest was pacing the floor. Instead of going back to her chair, Emily sat down at the end of a small wicker-backed settee.

"Please sit down, Reverend." She pulled her skirt close to her to make room.

The reverend sat gingerly on the edge of the settee, and gazed intently into Emily's face.

"You were saying, a moment ago?" she prompted.

"I was about to say, madam, I could not possibly undertake to settle here. It would be sheer madness."

"I don't understand, sir."

48

"The reason I say that, madam, is simply . . ." The reverend faltered, struggling with himself.

"The reason, sir?"

"The reason—forgive me, madam—is you."

"Me?!" Emily's hand flew to her cheek.

"It is the strangest phenomenon. I cannot tell you with what a tumultuous stirring of emotion I beheld your lovely features at our very first meeting, and saw in you a virtual replica of my adored late wife. I could barely believe my eyes—a miracle, no less! Perhaps you noticed that I kept my gaze steadfastly averted from you that evening. It was a desperate attempt to calm my racing heart— I could not trust myself to look at you!"

Emily was aghast. "Mercy, sir! I had no idea!"

The reverend's face was contorted with deep anguish. "You see, dear Emily—oh, pardon me, I become so reckless —the feelings that stir within my breast when I am in your presence are not feelings that a man of the cloth can permit himself to feel for a married woman."

"Oh . . . Reverend!"

Suddenly he seized her hand and held it between both his own.

"Oh, pity me, my dear sweet lady. I suffer the tortures of the damned! For a year I have carried the ache of loneliness imprisoned within me. The great Milton spoke of his talent as 'lodged with me useless, though my soul more bent to serve therewith my maker'—and thus I speak of mine, for my greatest talent, I confess to you, is my vast capacity for loving."

Emily shuddered—whether from horror or delight could not be told. The reverend tightened his grip on her hand, and moved a little closer.

"Sweet Emily, that is why I cannot stay. I could not bear to be near you unless I could know the heavenly raptures of your love." His hands were suddenly on her shoulders, pulling her toward him.

"Reverend Hargrave, please!" she hissed. "Mama lies in her bed, wide awake!"

This only served to intensify the attack. He pulled her closer, bringing his mouth close to hers. "Oh, please, my dearest Emily, forgive me, I have quite taken leave of my senses. Your ravishing beauty has destroyed my sanity. I am *mad* for you . . ."

49

His lips touched hers, and found them soft and trembling. She held herself rigid, but did not struggle. He slid an arm down to her waist, encircling it, felt her back arch slightly, and pulled her body tightly against his own.

For an instant her rigidity held, and the kiss remained tentative. Then, with a deep languorous sigh, she melted, wound her arms around his neck, and opened her mouth, receiving him fully.

And from her bedroom across the central hallway, Mrs. Morrow called out in a shrill voice, "Em'ly? Has the rev'rend gone yet?"

They came apart with the suddenness of a whiplash. Emily smoothed her dress and tried to regain her composure.

"Yes, Mama," she called. "That is—no, Mama, not yet."

"It's gittin' right late," Mrs. Morrow said. There was a querulous tone to the raspy old voice.

Emily leaned close to the reverend. "Oliver?"

He was startled by the sound of his first name. "Yes, my dear?"

"You must bid me goodnight now, so that Mama will know you are gone. Otherwise she will lie awake for hours."

He stared glumly at the floor. "I cannot bear the thought of parting from you," he murmured.

"And Oliver?"

He looked up quickly, catching a special tremor in her whispering voice. Her hand stole softly into his.

"If you should so much desire my . . . my company . . . as to be willing to brave the dark forest in the deep of night . . . I would be most . . ." She struggled against embarrassment, her eyes downcast. "I would make no objection."

He was transfixed, gazing at her demure face. "Oh, Emily, my sweet love," he breathed. "I would brave the fires of hell—"

Suddenly she was all urgency. "Go," she whispered. "Return in two hours. Be silent, and use no light. I will leave the door unlocked for you, and I will receive you—" she nodded toward a doorway at the far end of the room— "there."

In a loud voice, the reverend said goodnight to his hostess at the front door, thanked her profusely for her

50

hospitality, spoke of looking forward to seeing her at his sermon the following afternoon, and departed. Emily slammed the heavy iron sliding bolt into place, and very slowly, silently, eased it back into the unlocked position. Then she went into her mother's room to say goodnight once more, before retiring.

10

THE AIR of the August night lay hot and stifling, and heavy with the damp fragrance of the earth. The house was still; the silence, except for an occasional animal sound in the forest, was complete.

Reverend Hargrave was stretched out naked on his bed, staring up into the darkness. Beside him, on the inner side of the bed, the boy Isaac lay motionless in sleep, his face turned toward the wall. A shaft of light from a late-rising moon slanted in at the window and cast a pale glow on the tiny room.

The reverend held his large gold watch in his hand. He raised it to his face, squinted at it in the dim light, then put it down on the bedside table. Another half-hour yet. He sighed softly, and thought of Emily. He tried to imagine her lying in her bed, staring at the darkness just as he was doing, her bosom rising and falling a little more rapidly than normal in the excitement of anticipation. Perhas she was a tiny bit frightened, too; probably she had never before dreamed of straying from the safe and comfortable paths of fidelity.

51

And, thinking of Emily, he thought of the dark, mist-filled forest path that lay between them. There are bear in those woods, he knew, and wildcat, even panther—the wilderness along the Ohio is but a few years removed from its primeval state. One does not venture into it at night without so much as a lantern for protection. The reverend smiled to himself. Well, yes, one *does*, if one is drawn by the sort of prize that awaited him.

He thought of stiff-necked, belligerent George, who for some perverse reason had taken an instant dislike to him. This would be a good joke on George. He smiled again. An excellent joke—too bad it had to be hidden away in secrecy. There were probably a good number of people in the vicinity who would find it hugely amusing. Could any-one—the Good Lord even—possibly blame Emily for stray-ing, married as she was to that glowering ass?

Then he thought of Sarah. Virginal, voluptuous beyond her own knowing, indescribably soft and yielding to the touch, her wide child-eyes staring at him in astonishment at the revelation that a minister could have carnal desires. A flicker of regret crossed his mind as he realized that he would prefer this tryst tonight to be with the nubile maiden rather than with the worn and weary housewife. Ah, well, one must keep free from the sins of greed and ingratitude. Pluck those tender grapes in the Lord's vine-yard that are available for plucking, and pine not after those that are out of reach. The reverend chuckled to him-self, thinking: I could make a fine sermon on that text.

He checked his watch again. Fifteen minutes. He glanced at the sleeping child beside him. Isaac's breathing was soft and regular. Oliver slid his legs over the side of the bed and sat up. Suddenly he frowned, listening. There was a faint, indeterminate sound coming from somewhere. Prob-ably a mouse; these frontier houses were always alive with field mice. He started to rise, then froze. There was another sound—a soft click. Faint also, but recognizable. It was the lifting of a door latch.

Oliver twisted quickly and stared at the door of his room. He sensed rather than saw the beginning of the dark crack at the edge of the door, watched fascinated as it grew slowly wider, and knew that someone was there. Hardly breathing, he waited. His jaw dropped in genuine amazement as Sarah entered the diffuse glow of moonlight in the room, and stood there like a vision from a dream, gazing at him with her large eyes shining, her golden hair loose and resplendent on her shoulders. She was in a long white nightgown, and on her face was a look that made the reverend think of the word *exaltation.*

In his astonishment Oliver did not for an instant lose his poise, his presence of mind, or his practical sense. He lifted a supplicating hand toward the girl and breathed soulfully, "Sarah . . . Sarah, my beautiful . . . close the door."

She reached behind her and closed the door very quietly, then moved around the end of the bed and came toward him, seeming to float rather than walk, so otherworldly did she appear. She took no notice of his nakedness, but stood before him, swaying slightly, and looking steadily down into his eyes. She spoke, and her speech was a murmur, faint and dreamy.

" 'I sleep, but my heart waketh: it is the voice of my beloved that knocketh, saying, Open to me, my sister, my love, my dove, my undefiled . . .' "

"You have read the Song of Songs," he whispered. He was on his feet, his hard male nudity tall before her, and his hands moved deftly along the string lacings on the front of her nightgown, untying.

" 'I am my beloved's,' " she said, " 'and his desire is toward me.' "

Oliver pushed the garment off the girl's shoulders, and it fell loose to the floor. His gaze drifted down over the young body, full and pink and bursting with life. His right hand covered a breast, his left hand slid around her waist and, with the open palm against the curve of her back, pulled her against him.

"My sweet one, you have read God's message, and you have understood it. I can see the heavenly light of love aglow in your eyes."

She turned her face up toward him, and her brown eyes were large and liquid and solemn. " 'Let him kiss me with the kisses of his mouth: for thy love is better than wine.' "

And obediently his lips roamed over her neck and throat, wandered back to her mouth, and pressed against it. Slowly he pulled her down onto the bed and brought her body over his own, and her long hair spread over the pillow and covered them both. Against his ear, her murmuring whisper sounded soft and intimate once more: " 'Let my beloved come into his garden, and eat his pleasant fruits.' "

After a while little Isaac sighed, rolled onto his back, and opened his eyes. Something had penetrated his rest, and brought him gradually up to a fuzzy half-wakefulness. It was movement, but not the gentle rolling motion of his father's boat on the river, which never disturbed him; it was more erratic, a jarring, complex action. And as his mind grew clearer, he realized that the movement was accompanied by sounds—creaking of the bed, heavy puffing and blowing, and a delicate whimpering—and comprehension quickly came to him.

He looked toward the other side of the bed and saw his father's long torso heaving and rolling between the widespread legs of the girl Sarah, whose plump nude body lay pressed beneath the man's, her mouth locked to his, her arms around his back and clutching.

Isaac raised himself on an elbow and watched. Gradually his father's breathing became heavier and more rapid, the workings of his body more frenzied, and the girl's little whimper grew tight and tremulous. Soon, Isaac knew, the game would be over, and he could go back to sleep. And soon it was over, indeed. The rocking and blowing and whimpering subsided, and his father and Sarah lay still and limp in each other's arms.

Isaac quietly lay down, turned his face to the wall again, yawned, and drifted back into peaceful slumber. He had seen it all many times before.

11

IN THE AFTERNOON of the following day—Saturday—
a community project, undertaken in secrecy and accomplished in feverish haste, was completed. For the second
consecutive morning, Samuel Gilpin was out at first light,
supervising a work force of fifteen or twenty men, and
for two days the forest had resounded with the thud of
axes. The site of the activity was a small grassy clearing
in the woods near the junction of several forest paths, a
half-mile from the Gilpin house. First the clearing was
enlarged by the felling of a number of trees around its
perimeter. Then thongs were strung taut on poles across
the area at a height of ten feet, over which branches were
spread for shade. Makeshift benches were made of logs,
and another short log section was mounted upright, to
serve as a pulpit.

The structure was Samuel's idea. He wanted it to be a
surprise for Reverend Hargrave and, he hoped, a strong
influence toward the idea of permanent residence for the
reverend at South Bar. Saturday evening would be a
festive time, Samuel thought. In addition to the sermon,
several weddings would take place; the reverend had been
besieged by requests. And afterward, Samuel would be
the host at an open-air supper to which all comers were
invited. A side of venison and a whole hog were already
roasting over a deep-pit fire for the occasion.

So in the afternoon, Samuel led the reverend through

55

the forest on some pretext, and smiled as he saw the look of astonishment on Oliver's face when they came to the secret structure.

"What in heaven's name . . .?" the reverend breathed.

"We call it the tabernacle," Samuel said. "I hope you're pleased."

The reverend *was* pleased; more than pleased, he was overwhelmed. He walked all around under the wide canopy, inspecting. Then he went to the pulpit, gripped it with both hands, and turned his eyes upward.

"Lord, this is Thy temple, as fair, as holy, and as worthy as the mightiest cathedral. Let Thy blessings fall upon it, and upon Thy faithful servants here, who have built it out of love for Thee."

Then the people came, in greater numbers than ever, and formed a congregation of several hundred. Reverend Hargrave stood near his pulpit, and his eye roved ceaselessly, watching. Matilda and Sarah came in, with Sarah holding little Isaac by the hand. They sat in the front row. Sarah fastened her eyes on the reverend, and on her face there shone some wondrous secret knowledge that seemed ready to burst forth at any moment in a hymn of joy. Reverend Hargrave looked at her once, gave her a faint smile, and looked away quickly, wishing that her inner feelings did not surface so readily on her broad, expressive face.

Finally the tabernacle was filled to overflowing, and the reverend stepped up to the pulpit. An expectant hush fell. The preacher began by expressing his deep gratitude for the tabernacle, and pronouncing it beautiful in his eyes and in the eyes of God. Then he delivered his sermon, and scaled heights of impassioned eloquence the like of which few in the congregation had ever heard.

And through it all, the reverend had only one thought: *Emily is not here.*

Afterward the members of the wedding parties took their places, and the reverend performed the multiple ceremony with gentleness and charm, spoke feelingly of God's love of those who come into His grace through the love of each other, and quoted briefly from the least sensuous passages of the Song of Solomon. And as he spoke, Reverend Hargrave felt the attentive eyes of Sarah Gilpin upon

56

him, received the warm vibrations of her silent communication, and, to his consternation, began to perspire.

Then, later still, when the day was falling into dusk and the fields beside Samuel Gilpin's house were within the long shadows of the low hills to the west, the crowd gathered there for feasting, singing, dancing, and game-playing. A bonfire was built, and all was merriment.

Reverend Hargrave stood chatting with Samuel Gilpin and Rufus King and several other prominent men of the community, and as he watched the happy activity, the thought that had obsessed his mind all afternoon continued to prey upon it.

Where is Emily? Why didn't she come?

At length he turned to Samuel and said casually, "I don't see your daughter-in-law among us, nor her charming mother. I trust they are not indisposed?"

Samuel made a face, and laughed. "Pray forgive me, sir. In the confusion, I entirely forgot to mention it—this morning Emily received word that George is returning today, and she awaits his arrival. She sends her regrets."

Simultaneously, Reverend Hargrave felt relief and a tinge of apprehension. "Ah, I see. Is it a long trip?"

"A full day. But Emily insisted on remaining at home to receive him."

The reverend nodded his approval. "She is a good, dutiful wife."

"That she is."

The reverend strolled a bit and chatted with people, smiling his geniality on all sides. Young Sarah Gilpin was prominent in the merrymaking, he noticed. She performed in a vivacious country dance with a group of other young people, acompanied by a banjo and a homemade fiddle, and her great brown eyes sparkled. The reverend watched her covertly. She was a trifle heavy, and lacked the natural grace of a good dancer, he thought, but her buxom, pink-cheeked charm was undeniable. Constantly she sought the reverend's eye, and smiled at him. He acknowledged her, finally, with a slight nod and a faint smile, cloaked in the stiffest dignity.

Two other young couples approached the reverend and inquired timidly about having marriage ceremonies per-

57

formed in the near future. The preacher smiled upon them and told them it could be done next Saturday.

Samuel Gilpin, listening, smiled to himself. Clearly, Reverend Hargrave was beginning to think of South Bar as home.

Later in the evening, when the people had gone and quiet had descended over the forest and fields, Samuel and Oliver sat together like old friends and sipped their bedtime whiskey, and basked in a warm and comfortable glow.

"You understand, sir, the tabernacle is a temporary structure, unfit for bad weather," Samuel said. "But the site is a good one, I believe—"

"The site is an excellent one," the reverend readily agreed.

"And there is plenty of time to put up a permanent building there. The land is part of my own holdings, and I stand ready to donate it to the community for the establishment of a church. The decision is yours, Reverend. As I say, I stand ready—"

The reverend nodded, looked gravely thoughtful, and sipped his whiskey. "You are a good friend, Samuel," he said. "A good, good friend."

Presently there was a knock at the door. Reverend Hargrave started.

"That will be George, come to bring us news from Corydon," Samuel said, and went to the door.

George Gilpin greeted his father with an affection that barely showed though his immense reserve. Matilda, hearing his voice, appeared from her bedroom, wrapping herself hastily in a heavy, quilted house robe. She embraced George warmly, and for her he managed a weak smile.

Then he turned to Reverend Hargrave, who was on his feet, waiting, and extended his hand.

"Good to see you again, Reverend," he said dryly.

"Indeed, my pleasure, sir," the preacher answered. "I trust your journey was fruitful?"

"It was. Interesting things are happening."

"Sit down, George," Samuel urged. "Tell us."

George sat down at the table, where his mother had already set a plate of cold venison. Samuel poured a glass of whiskey for him.

"Well, first off, the statehood issue is moving forward rapidly," George said. "Everybody feels sure Mr. Jennings will introduce a bill in Congress very soon for the enabling act, and that it will pass immediately. By spring we'll hold our constitutional convention, I'm sure of it."

"Fine, fine," Samuel said.

"Second, the goddamned pro-slavery—" He glanced at Reverend Hargrave. "Excuse me, Reverend—the pro-slavery people are hard at work. It'll be a fight, all the way."

"Ah, the Vincennes crowd," Samuel said.

"It's an unholy alliance, Father. The lace-cuffed Virginians, in league with the foul-smelling Hoosiers from across the river. Strange bedfellows, eh? 'Twas ever thus. If a man is fanatical enough in his desires, he will lie abed with anybody . . ."

Again George glanced at Reverend Hargrave. "I trust I don't offend you, sir."

The reverend smiled and waved a casual hand. "Please speak freely. Do not imagine that I am unacquainted with the sordid realities of life."

"I don't." George gazed steadily at the reverend.

The reverend's smile faded.

"George, I believe you're taking it all too seriously," his father said. "The slavery people don't have a chance in Indiana, and they know it."

George frowned. "Well, I think you don't take it seriously enough, Father. And by the way, a number of people I talked to are wondering if you intend to campaign for election as a delegate to the convention."

Samuel's eyebrows went up in surprise. "Do I need to campaign?"

"George, your father is the founder of this community," Matilda said. "He's the natural choice, isn't he?"

George shrugged. "They're also wondering if you plan to make your anti-Negro sentiments sufficiently well known."

"My sentiments are not anti-Negro, George," Samuel said carefully. "They're antislavery."

George looked hard at his father, and hesitated a moment before continuing, "And a lot of people are wondering if, all things considered, you are the . . . well, the best possible delegate from this area—"

"George!" Matilda was shocked.

"And who might they have in mind instead, pray?" Samuel asked quietly.

"The suggestion has been put forth that *I* become a candidate."

There was a short, strained silence.

"George, you *wouldn't!*" Matilda exclaimed.

"Of course not," George said. "I would never consider campaigning against Father. Still, the general consensus is that this movement is going to be mostly in the hands of . . . well, younger men."

The silence grew deeper and even more strained. Samuel sipped his whiskey.

"Well, we'll see how it goes," he said placidly. "Springtime is a long way off."

"Not so long," George said. "Not so very long."

He lifted his own glass toward his father, and toward Reverend Hargrave. "Here's to a short winter."

The three men drained their glasses. George got up abruptly.

"I must go. I promised Emily I'd be back in a wink." He kissed Matilda on the cheek. "Good night, Mother. Tell my little sister I brought her a present from Corydon."

"Oh my!" Matilda exclaimed. "What is it?"

"Red ribbon for her hair. But don't tell her. I want it to be a surprise."

Matilda put her hands on her son's shoulders, and beamed up at him. "I do declare, George . . . sometimes you act so fierce I think your heart is made of stone, then you do something like that, and I know that, underneath, you're still my good, sweet boy."

"Stop it, Mother," George said in a gentle growl.

"You should have seen your little sister at the outdoor supper this evening, George," Samuel said. "Dancing like an angel! Seemed to me some kind of joyousness was welling up in her that I'd never seen before."

"The child wore herself completely out," Matilda said. "Came home and went right to sleep."

"I'll see her tomorrow," George said. He shook hands with his father, turned to Reverend Hargrave, and bowed. "Reverend?"

The reverend was on his feet. "Goodnight to you, sir," he said stiffly.

60

"I look forward to one of your uplifting sermons tomorrow," George said.

"Most kind of you," the reverend mumbled. He sat down again.

George went to the door. With his hand on the latch, he paused and pondered something. His gaze returned to Reverend Hargrave.

"By the way, I had some news for you, and I almost forgot. I met a man who knows you."

The reverend's eyes narrowed imperceptibly. "Indeed?"

"Yes. Last evening I attended a social gathering at the house of my brother-in-law, Robert Morrow, who's a prominent merchant in Corydon. One of the guests was a distinguished gentleman from Cincinnati. I happened to mention your name, and the gentleman declared that he knows you well. In fact, he's a professional colleague of yours. He is the Reverend Jacob Nellis, of the Methodist Episcopal Church."

It seemed, in the silence that followed, that Reverend Hargrave had turned somewhat pale, though his face was a blank mask. Then he frowned in thought.

"Nellis, Nellis . . ." he murmured. A glimmer of light came. "Ah yes, seems to me I recall. He's been retired from the pulpit for a number of years, I believe."

"I understand he's high up in the church organization," George said.

The reverend produced a small shrug. "That, I think, is something of an exaggeration."

George stepped closer to Reverend Hargrave. "The point is, Reverend Nellis knows *you* well, and is most eager to see you again. He became very excited when I told him you were here. He wanted to come with me today, but unfortunately, business detained him."

"Too bad," Reverend Hargrave said. "I would have been delighted—"

"That's why I wanted to tell you—" George was smiling an odd smile, without warmth— "he's coming tomorrow. He's starting out hours before dawn, to be here in time for your evening sermon."

George had spoken with an unnaturally slow and deliberate enunciation, as if he wanted to be doubly sure Reverend Hargrave understood the message fully.

Reverend Hargrave understood. He was gripping his

61

empty whiskey glass with a pressure that made the tips of his fingers whiten. As if suddenly becoming aware of this betrayal of tension, he quickly put the glass down on the table. He stared up into George Gilpin's eyes a long time before replying, "It will be an honor to have Reverend Nellis in my congregation. I look forward to it with the utmost pleasure."

"Reverend Nellis was sure you'd be pleased," George said, with that strange deliberateness.

Then he turned away, nodded briefly to his parents, and left.

"Well!" Samuel said, and rubbed his hands together enthusiastically. "Another gala day tomorrow!" He picked up Reverend Hargrave's glass, and his own. "Shall we have another whiskey, Reverend, to celebrate?"

He turned to Matilda. "Will you join us, my dear? Just this once?"

Matilda was deeply flattered. "Why, thank you, Samuel, I—"

"No more for me, thank you." Reverend Hargrave got slowly to his feet. "It has been a long and strenuous day. And tomorrow will be another." He went toward his room, paused in the doorway, and looked again at his host and hostess. His deepset eyes seemed sunk in melancholy.

"My dear friends, your kindness has moved me as profoundly as ever I have been moved by anything. Your generosity is boundless, and so, too, is my gratitude. May the Lord's blessings rain down upon you. Good night."

"Good night, sir," Samuel said, and Matilda echoed him feebly.

Reverend Hargrave went into his room and closed the door softly behind him, and Samuel Gilpin stood for a few seconds holding the empty whiskey glasses and staring in bewilderment at his wife.

Later, deep in the night, the last-quarter-moon rode high in the sky above skittish, fast-moving clouds, and a soft wind moaned through the dark branches of the forest. Somewhere in the distance a wild animal barked. And little Isaac was again awakened from a sound sleep, this time by the sensation of being lifted from his bed. He

62

opened his eyes wide in sudden fright, stared into the darkness, and murmured, "Sarah?"

"Shhh." His father's husky whisper sounded close to his ear. "There now, my boy, do not fret." The man hugged the child, and patted him soothingly. "We are going for a little walk now."

Instinctively Isaac wrapped his slender legs around his father's waist, nestled his head on a shoulder, and went back to sleep.

12

SUNDAY came up cloudy.

Samuel Gilpin walked slowly along the banks of the river under the humid sky, at the place where Reverend Hargrave's boat had been moored. Idly he picked up stones and tossed them, and watched the ripples spread and fade and die on the muddy shallows and in the outer reaches of open water.

George came and stood beside his father. Samuel stared out over the river, glittering gray under the constant breeze, and empty.

"I don't understand," he said softly. "I just don't understand."

"I think I can explain it, Father," George said.

"Explain it, then," Samuel said. He sounded angry.

"Last night when I arrived home, Emily told me that she had had Oliver for dinner the night before."

"I know that," Samuel snapped. "And?"

63

"And she said that after spending several hours listening to him talk, she became completely convinced that he was an impostor."

Samuel glared at his son. "You call that an explanation? The babble of a silly woman? That means nothing!"

"I think it does—in the light of the information I got from Reverend Nellis in Corydon."

Samuel exhaled in exasperation. "Well, stop being so damned mysterious, George! What is this information?"

George took a deep breath. "Oliver Hargrave has never held credentials in the Methodist Church, or any other. He is wanted for a wide variety of unpaid debts in a number of places along the river from Pittsburgh to Louisville. Some years ago he married a well-to-do widow in Cincinnati, squandered away her money, then deserted her. Isaac is Oliver's only issue from that marriage, and when Oliver left his wife, he took Isaac with him— primarily to spite the lady, it is said. She died suddenly last year—that is the only true thing Oliver has told you, though he neglected to mention that he hadn't seen her for more than a year before that. The dead woman's relatives are after Oliver with blood in their eyes—they hold him morally responsible for her death. His debtors are after him. And the church authorities have been trying to catch up with him for years, because of this thing of impersonating a minister. In short, Father, the man is a fraud. And you have been taken in."

Samuel's face was livid. "You got all this from Reverend Nellis, did you?"

"Yes."

"And you believe it?"

"Yes, Father, I do. Reverend Nellis is a prominent church elder, highly respected—"

"Then why didn't you speak up last night? Why didn't you confront Reverend Hargrave with these things, so that we might have heard *his* side of the story? Were you afraid of him?"

George's jaw muscles worked furiously. His face was dark and grim, but his voice remained calm.

"I chose not to create a painful scene in your house, Father. I didn't want to embarrass you. I thought just a hint to your distinguished guest would be enough—and it

64

was. He acknowledged his guilt by slinking away like a cowardly cur in the middle of the night—"

"Enough!" Samuel roared. "I am ashamed of you, George!" He trembled with rage.

"Father—"

"What you are doing is spreading malicious rumors against an innocent and virtuous man!"

"Father, look there." George swept an arm toward the empty river. "Hargrave has gone. Doesn't that prove—"

"Of course he has gone! A man can sense it when that kind of vicious hostility is growing against him! Reverend Hargrave freely admitted that the Methodist authorities disapprove of him, and it is only because he is more dedicated to the Lord's true work than they wish him to be."

"Is that a reason to sneak away in the middle of the night, without a word?"

"Why, George, the man has been hounded and harassed, and driven from pillar to post until he—he—" Samuel sighed, slumped, and gave up. He stared down at the muddy water at his feet.

George spoke with gentleness. "Father, Reverend Nellis is coming here today. And you will hear the story of Oliver Hargrave from his own lips."

Samuel looked up reluctantly, and studied George's face. "This Reverend Nellis—his credentials are beyond question?"

"Absolutely. He is a widely known and honored man."

Samuel nodded gravely. "I will receive him. I will hear what he has to say. But I will not . . . like him."

"I'm sorry, Father."

George turned away, and left Samuel alone by the river.

And a quarter of a mile upstream, in a secluded cove that had been a favorite spot since she was a little girl, Sarah Gilpin sat on an old log and fixed bleak, staring eyes on the iron gray surface of the water, and wept, soundlessly and without tears.

65

13

FROM THE JOURNAL of Lucius Hargrave:

The pitfalls that threatened my father at every turn took many forms, but the most insidious of these was the weakness of the flesh. It beckoned him from all sides, tantalized him with treacherous smiles on pretty faces, and worked ceaselessly to pull him away from his true goals and toward the dark paths of lust.

Reverend Hargrave was a handsome man, tall and striking in appearance. This, together with his magnetic personality and immense charm, refined by the most cultivated manners, made him the unwitting object of countless amorous advances.

It may be that the reverend (inadvertently, to be sure) contributed to the arousal of sinful passions in the breasts of the female members of his congregations by emphasizing the concept of spiritual love as one of the strong themes running through his sermons. And it must be an ageless axiom that women—particularly lonely women—tend to translate this idea of divine love into a *romantic* notion, to which the physical aspect is quickly added, and thus their purity of thought is corrupted.

Temptation, then, which rears its seductive head but a few times in the lives of ordinary men, floated before Reverend Hargrave's eyes constantly, wherever he went. A weaker man would have been crumbled before it, and slid inevitably down to ruin. It is to my father's everlasting credit that he remained staunchly unyielding against these invitations to sin, and limited his carnal knowledge of women, as God had intended, to the sanctity of the marriage bed.

Yet great men must inevitably inspire the enmity of lesser ones, and this melancholy truth became a wellspring of sorrow for that kind and gentle man. His humanitarian efforts in the Ohio River Valley frontier were consistently crowned with spectacular success, and as success is bound to do, it caused a number of his colleagues to burn with professional jealousy. They hounded his footsteps, sought to discredit him with filthy lies and sordid rumors, and at every turn to blacken his good name with all the disreputable devices their envious and evil minds could invent.

The result of these relentless attacks by his enemies was that Reverend Hargrave was forced to follow an existence not unlike that of a wild animal driven before the hounds —or worse, that of a hunted criminal. But through all his trials, his innate saintliness never dimmed, nor did bitterness ever taint his tranquil nature. Not once did he stoop to the level of his cowardly tormentors, or dignify their contemptible charges with reply. His example shines like beauty upon me across the years, shames me in my own moments of weakness, and perpetually renews my spirit.

Such is the legacy of love from father to son. May God grant its continuing blessing into the next generation.

14

SUMMER DIED and gave way to autumn, the time of blazing copper-and-gold adornment in the frontier wilderness that was Indiana—the time for crop-gathering, for slaughtering, for harvesting the apple orchards and bleeding the maple trees, for collecting hickory nuts—the time of the sharp smell of the woodsmoke that hung like a blue mist in the chill air. Then winter, and the edges of the Ohio River glinted with icy lace, and for weeks the shorelines were hidden under a frozen crust that bordered lifeless snowfields, blinding white and empty.

In January, 1816, Jonathan Jennings, representative in Congress from the Territory of Indiana, introduced a bill for an enabling act that would start the ponderous machinery moving in the direction of statehood for the territory. The bill passed the House on the thirtieth of March, the Senate on the thirteenth of April, and six days later was signed into law by President Madison. It stipulated certain conditions under which a petition for statehood would be considered, and authorized the election of constitutional convention delegates on the second Monday in May, and the meeting of the convention four weeks later, on June tenth.

In Indiana the pro- and antislavery forces girded for battle.

15

TOWARD THE END of June a New York newspaper reporter, sent to observe the political developments in Indiana, wrote a dispatch in the form of a letter to his editor, and sent it off on its slow journey to the East.

Corydon, Indiana Territory
Monday, June 27th, 1816

This place is a crude and rustic village, and a mere infant besides, having been laid out only eight years ago by the then territorial governor, William Henry Harrison. For all its modest dimensions, Corydon is the center of commerce in this part of the territory, and will doubtless go on to greater prominence as the capital of what will apparently soon become the nineteenth state of the Union.

The activity here for the past two weeks has been feverish, and of a degree of excitement almost unheard of for so remote a place. The limited facilities of the inns and taverns have been overwhelmed. Adding to the general discomfort has been the onset of intensely hot weather, most unusual for early summer, which arrived with the convention delegates and seems determined to match them in staying power.

Owing to the heat, many of the sessions of the convention have been moved outdoors, to the shade of a magnificent old elm that spreads its wide branches conveniently nearby. There the honourable delegates, forty-three in number, loll on the grass and shout out their approval or disapproval of every speaker who addresses them and every proposition that is put forth. They appear more like a gathering of backwoods rabble than a convention of responsible political leaders.

It is a young man's affair. The average age of the delegates is probably no more than thirty-five; Jonathan Jennings, the chairman of the proceedings, is thirty-two; another delegate whose acquaintance I have made, one George Gilpin, is barely thirty-one; other delegates, I am told, are not yet thirty. George Gilpin tells me that it is a young man's business for the very good reason that the molding of new states out of the frontier wilderness is a vigorous and hazardous undertaking that requires the blood and stamina of youth, and for which comfort-loving old men have no heart. Gilpin, like many of these men gathered here, is clearly a hot-eyed visionary. He tends to grasp your lapels and impale you with a fiery glare when delivering his pronouncements, and you tend to nod in ready agreement to whatever he is saying.

One of the hottest points of controversy here has been the question of slavery. The pro-slavery men are badly outnumbered, but have been devilishly determined in their resistance. Time after time they have attempted to insert clever escape clauses into the constitution text; time after time they have been shouted down. They seem at last to have exhausted their resources. It appears certain that Indiana's state constitution, complete with the slavery-exclusion article, will be adopted within a day or two.

A postscript, dated three days later, was added to the letter.

Yesterday the delegates of the Indiana state constitutional convention met in final session, formally adopted their brainchild, the constitution, and adjourned. Their work is done. The constitution will quickly be submitted to Congress, where its acceptance is regarded as a formality. Indiana will enter the Union as the nineteenth state, and this little town rings with the exultant cries of the victorious opponents of slavery: "She comes in free! She comes in free!"

As for me, I intend to depart this shabby town not

later than tomorrow morning, and make my way farther westward. In a week or so I will send you some observations on what effect the Indiana statehood affair has had on the political thinking in the wilds of the Illinois Territory.

The letter ended thus, but the correspondent committed a somewhat fuller account of the events to his own journal.

Last evening I was invited to a victory celebration at the home of a prominent Corydon citizen, Mr. Robert Morrow. Present were several delegates of the antislavery faction, including the man I mentioned in my dispatch, Mr. George Gilpin, who also happens to be the brother-in-law of the host. Among the celebrants, only Gilpin seemed unable to bask in the glow of victory, but tended to scowl over prospects of vengeance to be exacted against slaveholders in Indiana.

"Just wait till they find out what happens next!" he said. "Wait till we run their niggers out of the state altogether, *then* you'll hear a bit of hollering!"

Mr. Morrow waved a casual hand. "Oh, now, George— just between us friends, it's not that big an issue, when you get right down to it. I'll warrant there are no more than two or three hundred Negroes within our borders, all told."

"That," declared Gilpin hotly, "is two or three hundred too many!"

Morrow laughed, and turned the conversation in another direction.

Were I to eschew these political discourses, and become instead a gatherer of gossip and recorder of social foibles, I could perhaps have offered my readers a lively account of last evening's affair. I could wax lyrical, for instance, on the charms of my hostess, Mrs. Cordelia Morrow, a lady of some beauty and refinement. Also attracting my attention was a curious fellow identified as a nephew of Mrs. Morrow—a tall muscular youth, perhaps twenty years of age, dressed in the crude buckskins of a backwoodsman. This young man, Cyrus Thacker by name, is a professional huntsman. Throughout the evening, as the convention delegates talked, young Thacker wore an uneasy expres-

71

sion, as if he were thinking: These men mean to bring civilization to Indiana, and destroy my means of livelihood.

There was, moreover, an undercurrent of something else going on, some private concern that seemed to be shared by the Morrows, their nephew Cyrus, and their brother-in-law, George Gilpin. I tried to attune my ears to it, but succeeded only in whetting my curiosity in vain.

At one point I overheard Mrs. Morrow inquiring in low, confidential tones of Mr. Gilpin, "And how is Sarah, George? You have spoken so little of her."

To which Mr. Gilpin shrugged and replied enigmatically, "As well as can be expected, I suppose."

And Mrs. Morrow shook her head sadly and murmured, "Poor child."

Then, a bit later, my sharp ears picked up a fragment of confidential conversation between Mr. Morrow and Mr. Gilpin:

"So, George," Mr. Morrow says, "any word yet on your, uh, private investigation?"

"Nothing yet," says Gilpin, "but we're closing in. Morton King is in Louisville now. I might hear from him at any moment. And if I do, I'm ready to move."

Mr. Morrow lowers his voice still further, and I have to listen even harder. "You know, George, Cyrus and I stand ready to go with you, if you think we could be of help."

Mr. Gilpin nods, and looks exceedingly grim. "Good. I may need an extra strong right arm or two."

All in all, it was an interesting evening, if somewhat puzzling.

This afternoon I have been out strolling, and have noticed that, the convention now being over, Corydon is rapidly beginning to look like the small country town it is. I encountered Mr. Robert Morrow on the street, and immediately inquired after George Gilpin. Mr. Morrow informed me that his brother-in-law had already left Corydon.

"For home?" I asked.

"For Louisville," he replied.

"A rather abrupt departure," I remarked, fishing for information.

"I intend to make an abrupt departure myself, and follow him within the hour," Mr. Morrow said.

"Oh?" I said, and waited expectantly.

"We have some pressing business in Louisville," Mr. Morrow said, and added—somewhat pointedly, I thought—"of a confidential nature."

After a bit of general conversation, he tipped his hat and bade me good day.

And if the truth were known, I myself would rather be off to Louisville, snooping after George Gilpin, and discovering what dark and devious adventure he is about, than following the path of duty.

Ah, well.

16

ON a blazing blue summertime afternoon, when Samuel Gilpin was in his orchard inspecting the apple trees, a young man came off the little road adjoining the property and approached him, hat in hand. Samuel saw him coming, and waited, grim-faced.

"How do, Mr. Gilpin," Morton King said.

"Afternoon, Morton. You're back, I see."

"Just docked the skiff this minute, Mr. Gilpin. Only six and a half hours from Louisville. River's high, water's movin' fast."

Samuel's face showed a trace of impatience. "What's the news, Morton?"

"We've got him, sir. George and Mr. Morrow and another fella came from Corydon yesterday, and last night we went right to the place and took him."

"Any trouble?"

"Not a bit, sir. George didn't tell him anything, just said he was wanted in South Bar. The reverend was very pleasant—seemed like he was glad to see us."

"What kind of a place was it?"

Morton shook his head. "Strange kind of a place, Mr. Gilpin. A big canvas-covered shack, with a sign on it saying, 'The Temple of the Eternal Light.' Another sign said, 'God's Eternal Truths, Transmitted Through the Mystic Secrets of Ancient Egypt.' And the reverend was wearing a long white robe and a turban. I almost didn't recognize him at first. Mighty strange."

Samuel took a low-hanging branch of an apple tree in his hands and studied the small green knobs that would soon be apples. "The Lord works in many and wondrous ways," he said.

"George sent me on ahead to tell you," Morton King said. "He figures they ought to be getting in here late tomorrow afternoon."

Samuel nodded and went on inspecting the apple blossoms. "We'll be ready."

The next day, lookouts were stationed on the river, their watchful eyes trained upstream. Around four o'clock in the afternoon, Oliver Hargrave's little keelboat hove into view. Immediately a hue and cry was raised, and fleet-footed young messengers raced along the forest trails, carrying the word.

By the time the boat was moored, a crowd had gathered at Samuel Gilpin's house. The people were dressed in their best clothes, as if for festivities, but their faces were tense. They stood in the small yard before the house and waited, strangely quiet. Many of the men carried arms.

In a little while four men came up the path from the river: George Gilpin; beside him Oliver Hargrave, dressed in his familiar black suit and wide-brimmed hat; Robert Morrow, with a long rifle in the crook of his arm; finally the tall, lanky Cyrus Thacker, who walked in a crouch, dodging overhanging branches. Cyrus also carried a rifle, and he led little Isaac Hargrave by the hand.

At the Gilpin house Oliver's eyes roamed over the people gathered there, the former lambs of his flock. They regarded him with hard, unsmiling eyes. No words were

74

spoken. George Gilpin escorted Oliver into the house while the others remained outside.

In the front room Samuel Gilpin stood waiting. George stepped toward his father, and the two men embraced lightly.

"Welcome home, George," Samuel said in an undertone.

"Thank you, Father. It's good to be back."

"You have much to tell us, I know."

"Yes, but that's for later. Is everything ready here?"

"Everything is ready."

George nodded. "I will go speak to Sarah, and to Mama. I leave our guest of honor in your hands."

George disappeared into the back of the house, and Samuel turned to face Oliver Hargrave. Unhesitatingly, Oliver stepped forward and held out his hand.

"I am glad to see you, my friend," he said.

Samuel studied the other man's face intently. Then he took the proffered hand and clasped it.

"Welcome, sir. Welcome."

Oliver smiled. "I trust I find you well? And your dear wife, and Sarah?"

Samuel's eyes continued to search Oliver's face. "Tell me, sir, has George acquainted you with the situation here?"

Oliver sighed. "As you may know, dear friend, your son and I don't enjoy close rapport. He informed me of nothing, except to indicate that my presence was urgently desired. I came as quickly as I could, of course, hoping that I would not find trouble or grief among you . . ."

"Trouble?" said Samuel, raising his eyebrows. "Grief, sir? I should say not, and I hope *you* will not consider it such. Fact is, we aim to have a wedding here today."

"Capital!" Oliver exclaimed with a show of enthusiasm. "You wish me to officiate, I take it."

"No, sir," Samuel said pleasantly. "We wish you to stand as bridegroom."

Oliver stared. "As bridegroom?" he repeated faintly.

"As for officiating," Samuel continued, "we have a permanent minister here in South Bar now, I'm proud to say. Reverend Jonathan Daniels. A young man, quite capable and very well liked. As you know, I had hoped it could be you, Oliver, but Reverend Daniels is doing well, so we're content. You'll meet him shortly."

75

Oliver's gaze was drifting around the room. He noted that the people who had been standing outside were now filing into the house and forming a circle of silent spectators. Oliver turned back to Samuel.

"I don't quite understand, sir."

Samuel smiled. "You see, Oliver—I hope you don't mind my using your first name, since you'll soon be my son-in-law—you are the father of a fine baby son, born to Sarah in this house on the thirty-first of March last."

The muscles of Oliver's jaw worked furiously. His breath came in quick, shallow gulps. He seemed to shrink in stature, to recede visibly within himself. He did not notice that Sarah had come into the room, was not aware of her until she stood before him. Then he started, and turned wide, incredulous eyes upon her.

"Sarah . . ."

She was dressed in a long, straight gown of deep pink that seemed to be reflected in her soft brown eyes. She held a little bouquet of white rosebuds. As Oliver had seemed to shrink, Sarah appeared taller than ever, so that her eyes were almost on a level with his. Her face was thinner, the tawny hair pulled back more severely, and the cheeks that had been the color of ripe peaches were pale. She stood very still and gazed with a solemn expression at Oliver, and he returned her look, oblivious to all else.

"Sarah . . ." he repeated breathlessly.

"Hello, Oliver," she whispered.

George had returned with Matilda, who took her place beside Samuel, and with them also was a thin young man in clerical garb, carrying a Bible.

Samuel touched Oliver on the sleeve. "Here is Reverend Daniels, Oliver. He will perform the ceremony, whenever you and Sarah are ready."

Oliver gave no indication of having heard. His eyes remained on Sarah. He stepped closer to her.

"May I see our son?"

Without a word, Sarah took him by the hand and led him out of the room, toward the back of the house.

The child lay sleeping in a small trundle bed. Oliver knelt and leaned down close, and studied the fat little face for a long time. Then he carefully lifted the baby and

76

held him in his arms. The child opened his eyes, squirmed, and uttered a cry of protest.

"There now, little one," Oliver murmured. "Do not fret. Your father is here." He held the infant close against his shoulder and walked slowly around the room. The baby gurgled softly several times, and went back to sleep. Oliver stopped in front of Sarah and looked hard at her.

"You are sure he is mine, Sarah?"

Sarah's eyes were steady on his. "He is yours, Oliver. I have been with no other."

"What is his name?"

"He has no name as yet. I wanted to wait for his father to come and name his son himself."

Oliver stared at her for a moment, and a kind of wonderment came into his eyes. He lifted the baby off his shoulder and looked into the little face, and again the child wriggled and voiced his displeasure.

Oliver smiled. "A fine boy," he said. "He is a seven-months baby, isn't he, Sarah?"

"Yes, he came very suddenly. The midwife said she'd never seen such a strong baby, and such a quick . . ."

Oliver was not listening. He was running a finger over the baby's puffy cheeks and dimpled chin, and his smile was growing broader.

"You know, Sarah, according to ancient Egyptian philosophers, the number seven carries with it certain mystical blessings. For that reason the seven-months baby is regarded as especially fortunate. His mind and his body are charmed, Sarah. He will meet with nothing but success, wherever life takes him."

Sarah smiled weakly. "I'm glad, Oliver."

The father nestled his child on his shoulder again, took Sarah's hand, and returned to the front room. He led the girl to the center of the room and looked around at the faces of the assembly. He stood tall and straight, full of confidence again, and when he spoke his voice was powerful and secure, as it had been in the past.

"My dear friends! I am deeply grateful that you have done us the kindness to gather here today, to share with me and my beloved bride this joyous occasion. Lesser people than you might have harbored suspicions against me, thinking my intentions had been other than honorable. Perish the thought, friends, may God be my witness!

77

Though the pressure of urgent duties called me away at a most inopportune time, nevertheless my prayers, my thoughts, and my heart were ever here, nowhere else."

Oliver beamed at Sarah and squeezed her hand, and she responded with a charming blush. In a voice quivering with emotion, he continued his speech.

"Oh, my friends . . . rejoice with us in the pride and happiness that every loving parent feels at the birth of a beautiful child."

He held the baby up for all to see. "My little son is fair, he is splendid, he is good to look upon. Surely, surely, my cup runneth over today."

The people were moved. There was a stirring and murmuring among them. A few dared to smile.

Oliver chuckled. His spirits were soaring. He gave his son a playful little bounce, and the child opened his watery blue eyes wide, and stared at the man. Then Oliver spoke again, in his deepest, most resonant voice, and the baby's eyes opened wider still, in alarm.

"Thou shalt be called Lucius," Oliver proclaimed. "Thy name shalt be Lucius, Bringer of Light, for thou hast brought light into our darkling world."

The murmuring in the audience swelled, and the sternness faded from many more faces, replaced with smiles of approval. Sarah smiled too, and put out her hand to touch her baby's downy head.

And Oliver, holding the child in one arm, took Sarah by the hand again and turned toward Reverend Daniels, and his face was flushed and triumphant.

"We are ready, Reverend," he said. "Commence the ceremony." It was a command, and the young minister hastened to obey.

The bride's parents and brother gathered behind the couple, the spectators crowded in closer, and Cyrus Thacker kindly lifted little Isaac Hargrave in his arms, so the boy could see his father's wedding.

Only Emily was absent.

78

17

IN THE CALM of early morning on the day following the wedding, George Gilpin went down to the river where Oliver's boat was tied. He stood on the slope above it for a few minutes, looked down at the dilapidated old craft, and scowled. The black man Camus was squatting before a little fire on the bank, a few feet from the water's edge. He was cooking something in an iron skillet. George went down toward him.

Camus stood up, flashed a grin, and began his incessant head-bobbing. "Mornin', sar! Mornin'!" he called out heartily.

George came close to the fire and sniffed at the smoke curling up from it. He made a sour face.

"What in God's name are you cooking, man?"

"Eel, sar. Eel from de river. Mighty fine eatin', sar."

George made another face, and moved a few steps away from the fire. "I want to talk to you, Camus."

"Yas, sar. Camus listenin'."

"Camus, I want to know the exact relationship between you and Oliver Hargrave."

Camus looked blank. "Sar?"

George reworded his question. "I want to know what you are to Mr. Hargrave. Are you his employee? Are you his servant?"

The black man chuckled good-naturedly. "Camus a slave, sar."

79

George's face darkened. "I thought so," he muttered.

"Yas, sar. Camus good slave, sar. Rev'rend Hargrave good massa. Git along fine, sar."

"Camus, there is something I must tell you."

"Yas, sar."

"Recently a number of men in this territory, I among them, took steps to obtain statehood for Indiana. And one of the laws we adopted for the new state is a law that prohibits slavery."

The black man's eyes were straying toward his pan of food, which was beginning to smoke heavily.

" 'Scuse, sar." Camus quickly removed the skillet from the fire and set it on the ground, then returned his attention to his visitor.

"Camus, do you understand what I said to you?" George demanded.

Camus grinned. "No, Sar."

"I'm saying that very soon Hargrave will not be able to hold you as a slave. It will no longer be allowed."

Camus's face grew solemn. "Rev'rend good massa, sar. Camus don' want no other massa."

"Why, man, you don't need to have any master at all!"

"Sar?"

"Camus—what you should do is, you should take this boat and leave. Nobody will come chasing after you."

The black man shook his head. "Camus don' know whar to go, sar. Rev'rend Hargrave, he my massa. He always tell Camus what to do."

"He can't be your master any longer, Camus. Nobody can, in Indiana. But you can't *live* in Indiana either, because there will be a law to prevent that too, I can promise you. So run, man. Hargrave will not be able to stop you."

Camus's face clouded in misery. "Can't do dat, sar."

"Why not?"

"If I runned away, Rev'rend Hargrave, he speak to de debbil 'bout me. He give my soul to de debbil!"

George snorted loudly. "No, no, he will not! He can't do anything like that. He has filled your head with lies!"

Camus backed away, shaking his head. Fear shone in his eyes. "Yas, sar, yas, he can. Rev'rend Hargrave, he got much power. He give ol' Cicero's soul to de debbil—"

"He did what?" George followed Camus as the black man retreated. "What did he do to Cicero?"

"I dasn't speak on it, sar . . ."

"Speak, man, speak!" George growled. "What did he do? Tell me!"

Camus cowered and trembled. "Cicero very sick. Lie on de deck, wouldn't do no work nor nothin'. Rev'rend, he say, git up, Cicero. Work. Cicero wouldn't git up. Two, t'ree days, Cicero lie dere, won't git up. Rev'rend, he curse terrible, use de Lord's name bad. He tell me to land de boat, tell me to carry Cicero into de woods and lay him under a tree. Rev'rend, he stand and look down at Cicero and he say, Cicero, you are bad man. Tonight you will die, and de debbil will come and take yo' soul. An' ol' Cicero, he cry lak a baby, and say, no, Massa, no! Don' let de debbil git me! We leave him dere, cryin' lak a baby. Nex' day we come back. Lo and behold! Cicero dead, just lak Rev'rend say. De debbil done come and tooken his soul . . ."

George glowered. "Damn you!" he roared. "Damn you for the stupid, ignorant fool that you are!"

"No, sar, Camus no fool—"

"Fool, fool, fool!" George spat. "Hargrave fills your head with witchcraft and superstition, and you believe every ridiculous word!"

"He speak de truth, sar."

"He speaks damnable, evil nonsense! He tells you to help him kill an old man, and you *do* it, without blinking an eye!"

"Rev'rend my massa, sar."

"Hah! And a good master, too, you say!"

"Yas, sar. Rev'rend good massa."

George expelled his breath explosively. "Damn you, Camus. *Damn* you!"

Camus hung his head.

George turned abruptly and strode back up the slope to the river bank. A short distance away he paused and looked back.

"Run, you ignorant fool!" he shouted. "Run away, run away before it's too late!" He went on up the path, walking rapidly.

Camus stood very still watching the white man until he

81

was out of sight. "Camus no fool," he mumbled softly. "White man fool. White man big fool."

He squatted down before his pan of food and began to eat.

18

EMILY had been indisposed on the day of the wedding, it was said. She was expecting soon. Oliver and Sarah went to see her immediately, Oliver bringing her a large bouquet of wild primroses he had gathered in the woods. Emily received the visitors with cool reserve, which appeared cordial in comparison to George's stony silence. Emily encouraged her garrulous old mother to gabble endlessly, and all other conversation was stifled. The guests departed after a very short stay.

As a wedding present Samuel Gilpin gave Oliver and Sarah a plot of fine fertile land, near the river. And in keeping with the pioneer tradition, all able-bodied males in the community turned out and set to work building the newlyweds a house and quantities of crude but serviceable homemade furniture for it. With such massive manpower applied to the task, the work went quickly. In two weeks, Oliver moved his little family out of the single room they occupied in the elder Gilpins' place, and into their new home.

Oliver lost no time in ingratiating himself with the people of South Bar, and made miraculous progress in restoring his former good name. He quickly made friends with the Reverend Daniels. A permanent church had been built on the site of Oliver's old tabernacle, and Oliver and Sarah were there every Sunday, sitting in the front row, and after every service Oliver shook the young pastor's hand and congratulated him warmly on the excellent sermon.

Meanwhile, Oliver plunged energetically into domestic chores. He cleared land, planted a garden, started an orchard from seedling apple trees donated by Samuel, built a beautiful rocking cradle of maplewood for little Lucius, and a tall swing, suspended from a huge walnut tree, for Isaac.

Seven-year-old Isaac was ecstatic in his new life—a permanent home; a new mother, loving and kind; a little brother who would soon be old enough to play with; in the meantime, his old playmates Henry and Susan Gilpin not far away; and now, a swing in a walnut tree.

And the people of South Bar watched, whispered among themselves, and grudgingly acknowledged admiration for a man who could so skillfully turn shame and humiliation into a kind of triumph.

Soon after the Hargraves moved into their new home, Samuel and Oliver resumed their old habit of sitting together over a glass of whiskey in the late evening for a bit of quiet conversation, sometimes at Samuel's house, sometimes at Oliver's. On the very first of these occasions, Oliver made bold to speak with candor.

"In me, Samuel my friend, you see a man who was proud, and who is now humbled."

Samuel was packing his pipe. "How so, Oliver?"

"Once I considered myself a teacher of Christian ethics. But here in South Bar I have seen a display of the spirit of forgiveness that puts my old pretensions to shame. I have sinned, and I have been blessed for it. Verily, it does seem passing strange."

Samuel smiled. "Now, Oliver, you needn't carry on about that. I've told you, Sarah explained everything to us. She was entirely frank and honest."

Oliver shook his head. "I cannot allow her to take the blame."

"Nonsense, man!" Samuel paused in lighting his pipe. "She went naked into your room in the middle of the

83

night, and lay down beside you, and woke you out of a sound sleep, and bewitched you with temptations that the holiest of holy men could not have withstood."

He chuckled, and slapped Oliver on the arm. "Anyway, it's all for the best now, isn't it?"

Oliver hung his head. "You are a good friend, Samuel. A better friend than I deserve."

On one occasion, when the late-evening ritual was being held at Samuel's house, George came and brought with him the young man Cyrus Thacker.

"I have contracted for Cyrus, here, to stay with me in permanent employment," George announced to his father. "He is building himself a cabin in the woods, near Stone Creek."

"Good!" Samuel said. "Glad to have you with us, Cyrus."

Cyrus twitched with embarrassment. "Thank you, sir," he said shyly.

"He'll be a great help to me in the fields, of course," George went on. "And he will keep us supplied with game. Cyrus is a crack huntsman, you know."

"Yes, so I've heard," Samuel said.

George continued. "Then too, if I'm elected to the new state assembly, I'll probably be away from home a good deal during the next year or so. It will be a comfort to Emily to have Cyrus on the place, keeping an eye on things. She doesn't feel safe when I'm away."

"Doesn't feel safe?" said Samuel in surprise. "Why, South Bar's as safe as any place on earth."

For the first time during the conversation, George looked directly at Oliver. "When a man leaves his wife alone," he said quietly, "he should take precautions."

Oliver's fingers drummed silently on the tabletop. He said nothing.

Samuel picked up his whiskey jug and poured four glasses. "Well, anyway, it's good to have you with us, Cyrus." He held up his glass. "Here's to our new neighbor."

After everyone had sipped in response to the toast, George said, "I'm afraid my main purpose tonight is not convivial, Father." Again he turned his gaze on Oliver.

84

"I'd like to discuss a matter of some seriousness with my esteemed brother-in-law."

Oliver looked surprised. "Indeed?"

"The question concerns your, uh, your man, Camus."

"Yes?"

"He seems to be setting up a homestead at the river. Apparently he thinks he is going to live there permanently."

"That is at my invitation, George," Samuel put in.

George scowled. "You can't do that, Father."

"Why not? It's my land."

"Father, I don't think you realize the exact nature of the relationship between Oliver and his boatman. Camus is a slave."

"What!" Samuel turned horrified eyes on Oliver. "Is this true, sir?"

Oliver sipped his whiskey and smiled. "Of course not."

"Why does he call himself a slave, if it isn't so?" George demanded.

"Ah. You have been questioning him, I see," Oliver said coolly. "And no doubt he has filled your eager ear with all manner of preposterous tales."

"You haven't answered my question," George growled. "Why does he call himself—"

"Quite simple. He is an abject primitive. He speaks glibly, but understands nothing. The fact is that Camus *was* a slave for the first twenty years of his life. It was the only condition he had ever known, and he is utterly unable to comprehend that it ceased at the time I purchased his liberty, two years ago. Camus and Cicero—poor Cicero passed away recently, God rest his soul—Camus and Cicero were slaves of a traveling merchant, and when I first saw them, they were half dead from starvation. Out of sheer pity, I bought them. They needed employment, so I put them to work as boatmen, constantly reminding them that they were free to leave me anytime. They never would."

Oliver chuckled, with a wry look. "To my regret, I must say. They were incurably lazy, both of them. Incapable of being trained."

George was not satisfied. "Then why didn't you turn them out, if they were so useless?"

85

Samuel frowned at his son, and answered the question for Oliver.

"Why, because he is a kind and Christian man, George. To turn such poor helpless souls out is to condemn them to death!"

Oliver nodded. "Exactly."

"What about Cicero?" George went on relentlessly. "How did he die?"

Oliver arched an eyebrow at his questioner, and sipped his whiskey for a moment before replying.

"I must tell you, sir," he said finally, "I find this interrogation somewhat tedious."

Samuel's disapproving frown grew darker still. "I can't understand this strange behavior of yours, George. You admit you have no love for the black race. Why this sudden interest in the death of an old Negro man?"

George kept his eyes on Oliver. "I'm not interested in the death of an old Negro man, Father. I'm interested in the veracity of your new son-in-law."

Samuel huffed indignantly. "I consider that very ill-mannered of you, George, I must say."

George fixed a belligerent look on Samuel. "Father, as a delegate to the constitutional convention, I helped see to it that slavery would be barred from Indiana. Now I expect to gain a seat in the general assembly, and I can promise you, I intend to introduce a bill to exclude Negroes from the state altogether."

"That's disgraceful, George!" Samuel growled. "We are in agreement on slavery, but beyond that our paths diverge!"

"So it seems. Since you have taken to providing free homesteads to every illiterate black that wanders along—"

"Enough!" Samuel rapped on the table. Anger burned in his pale blue eyes. "I allowed you to persuade me to step aside in your favor as a convention delegate. Maybe I made a mistake. If you are going to use hatred between races as the foundation of your political career, then you will not have my support!"

"As you wish, Father," George said evenly. "If things continue to go well with me, maybe I won't need it."

He drained his glass and got to his feet. "Come along, Cyrus. We have much work to do tomorrow."

After George and Cyrus had gone, Samuel lowered his

86

head for a moment, and shielded his eyes with his hand. "Forgive him, Oliver. I don't know what's come over George. His political ambitions are making him fanatical, I'm afraid. Why doesn't he realize what a strong friend a dynamic man like you could be?"

Oliver sipped his whiskey and gazed placidly into space. "Or what a dangerous enemy."

Seeing a look of consternation come over Samuel's face, Oliver went on quickly, "But put it out of your mind, my friend. I have naught but Christian thoughts toward your son." He produced a kindly smile. "Naught but Christian thoughts."

19

ONE MORNING Camus returned to the river from a hunting foray into the woods. Over his shoulder he carried the carcass of a huge jackrabbit. He vaulted on board the boat, and flung the rabbit onto the deck. He was humming to himself as he went to the cabin door, opened it, and started to enter. The he stopped abruptly and fell silent.

From the cabin's interior, Oliver Hargrave said quietly, "Come in, Camus, come in."

Oliver was reclining on one of the bunks. He looked coolly at Camus as the black man stood before him.

"Mornin', Massa, mornin'." Camus's head bobbed rapidly up and down.

Oliver sat up. "Where have you been, Camus?"

87

"Checkin' my traps, sar. Got me a fine rabbit. Good huntin' in dese woods, sar."

"You like it here, do you, Camus?"

"Yas, sar. Lak it fine, sar. Only—"

"Only what?"

"Camus got no woman here, sar. In Louisville, plenty woman for Camus." The man's white teeth flashed in a quick grin.

"Well, don't fret," Oliver said. "One day you and I will go to a great city where there are more women than you have ever seen, black or white."

"More dan Louisville, sar?"

"More than Louisville."

Camus's eyes glowed. "When we go, sar?"

"Content yourself. I will tell you when."

"Yas, sar. Hope it be soon, sar."

"I brought you vittles," Oliver said, and pointed to a large bag on the floor. "Flour, bacon, some fruit. Mrs. Hargrave wanted you to have it. She won't believe me when I tell her you live off the forest and the river."

"She good lady," said Camus. "Bless her, she good lady."

With no change in his casual tone, Oliver said, "Camus, you've been waggling your tongue again."

Camus looked horrified. "Sar?"

"What have I told you about that waggling tongue of yours. Camus?"

Camus hung his head. "Someday, sar . . . someday you take a knife, an'—" His head hung lower. His face was twisted in misery.

"Go on," Oliver said.

"Take a knife an' . . . cut it out o' my head."

"That's right."

Camus whined. "Camus good boy, sar, don' mean no harm—"

"Camus is an idiotic tale-teller, and an ungrateful wretch."

"No, sar, no! I always say Rev'rend Hargrave good massa."

"Do you know George Gilpin, Camus?"

"No, sar, don' know—"

"Of course you do! He's the man who brought us here

88

from Louisville. He's been here questioning you, hasn't he?"

"No, sar, I don't see 'im—"

In a lightning-like movement Oliver lunged upward, grasped Camus by the ear, and pulled. Camus wailed and dropped to his knees. Oliver's eyes were pinpoints of ferocity as he glared down into the stricken face of the black man.

"He has been here, hasn't he?"

"Yas, sar. He bad man. He beat Camus, make Camus tell t'ings—"

"You're lying. He did not beat you, he questioned you. Didn't he?"

Camus wailed again, and trembled as Oliver's grip tightened on his ear. "Yas, sar. He bad man, sar. Camus scared."

"What else did he say?"

"Don' remember, sar—"

Oliver squeezed the ear harder, and Camus screeched and bent low to the floor.

"Remember, damn you!" Oliver growled. "What did he say to you?"

Camus was whimpering like a frightened child. "He say . . . he tell Camus to run away. He say Rev'rend not Camus' massa no more."

"I see. Very interesting. He said that, did he? Do you believe it, Camus?"

"Oh, no sar, no sar, you good massa, sar! Camus don' want 'nother massa . . ."

Oliver leaned down close, and spoke in a low voice. "Listen to me, Camus. Listen carefully and understand this, because your very life depends upon it. George Gilpin is our enemy. He is the most villainous man you and I have ever met, and the most dangerous. If he ever comes here again, you will speak to him only in the language of your African ancestors. No matter what threats he utters, you will never speak another word of English to that man. Do you hear me, Camus?"

"Yas, sar, yas, sar."

Oliver suddenly released Camus's ear and struck the crouching man hard in the face with the back of his hand. Camus crashed against the opposite bunk and sat still, with his hands clasped over the side of his face that had received the blow, and his exposed eye staring in terror at his master.

Unhurriedly, Oliver got to his feet. "You know what would happen to you if you tried to run away, Camus?" he asked quietly.

Camus nodded.

"The devil would have your soul," Oliver said. "He would get it just the way he got Cicero's."

Camus shuddered. His hands spread over his face, covering it completely.

"You mind yourself, Camus," Oliver said. His voice was gentle now. "Mind yourself, and hold your tongue. And one day we will go to the great city, and you will have your reward."

"Yas, sar."

Oliver left, and Camus sat on the floor of the boat cabin for several minutes, rubbing his bruises and mumbling softly to himself.

20

FROM THE JOURNAL of Lucius Hargrave:

In the midst of the melancholy procession of trials and torments that dogged my father's footsteps through this merciless world, the story of his wooing and wedding my mother stands in blessed contrast, like a fragile rose among cruel thorns. The circumstances, as I learned of them in later years, were so imbued with a soft and dream-

90

like quality that a stranger might have been inclined to dismiss them as a concoction of romantic fiction.

During the years of Reverend Hargrave's travels on the river, he chanced one summer to stop at a tiny settlement in southern Indiana, called South Bar. He found the inhabitants there, with a few exceptions, to be so sunken in heathenish depravity that he resolved immediately to prolong his stay for a week or longer, in order to minister to their spiritual needs.

The exceptions I mentioned were certain members of the family of a man named Samuel Gilpin, who had brought his family west from Conecticut in 1800, and had founded the town of South Bar.

Samuel Gilpin, a man of some educational attainments, instantly recognized in Reverend Hargrave an intellectual equal (not to say superior), and eagerly sought his company, taking him into his house as a guest. There the Reverend beheld the Gilpin's lovely young daughter Sarah, and was immediately smitten. And Sarah, in most becoming modesty, let it be known by blushes and soft smiles that she would not be averse to the Reverend's suit. Meanwhile my father's little son Isaac had developed a touching devotion to Sarah, clinging to her skirts as if she were his natural mother, and she, in the warmth of her heart, returned his affections fully. Her parents, seeing all this, were delighted, and did all they could to nourish the delicate flower of romance blossoming in their midst.

After several idyllic weeks, during which Reverend Hargrave found himself curiously unwilling to face the thought of leaving, his ardent desires were transformed into firm resolve: he would seek the young woman's hand in marriage. Sarah readily expressed willingness, and with pardonable pride the Gilpins announced their daughter's betrothal. But the Reverend's wide-flung responsibilities as a traveling minister could not be lightly dismissed and forgotten; his unrelenting sense of duty prevented that. Moreover, his enemies within the church were once again yapping like curs at his heels, evermore threatening to disrupt the tranquility for which he so wistfully longed. So with a heavy heart he bade his tearful love fearwell, and soothed her with the promise that he would return in the spring, and they would become man and wife.

The ensuing winter was a long and lonely one for both,

91

as Sarah waited while the Reverend went about the painful process of severing the ties that bound him here and there. But when the first rain-dampened flowers of springtime adorned the verdant hillsides along *la belle rivière*, he again stepped ashore at South Bar and enfolded his beloved in his arms. Their love had stood the test of time and separation, and had grown even stronger by the trial. A few days later, in the home of the bride's parents, the two were joined in holy wedlock.

In the spring of the year following—on the thirty-first of March, 1816—Sarah gave birth to me. It was said that I was an unusually robust infant, though born prematurely, and I confess I have ever since considered myself profoundly fortunate to possess a faint reflection of the comeliness of that beautiful woman, my mother, and at least a tiny portion of the sterling qualities of that splendid man, my father. Surely no prouder heritage could any man boast than I of my parents, Oliver and Sarah Hargrave. For so long as this brutal world permitted it to exist, theirs was a perfect love.

21

EARLY IN AUGUST were held the first annual elections for the officials of what would soon become the new state of Indiana. George Gilpin offered himself as a representative to the general assembly, his chief opponent being a local merchant named Nelson Hall, whose campaign was halfhearted and lackluster compared to George's intense ef-

92

forts. George was elected overwhelmingly. Nevertheless he made no plans to move his family to the new state capital of Corydon. The coming year, he said, would be his trial plunge into the turbulent waters of politics. After that initial experience, a long-range decision would be reached, and arrangements made accordingly.

By October the time for the birth of Emily's baby was upon her. She was living virtually alone except for her children, Henry and Susan; old Mrs. Morrow had been taken away by her son Robert to his home in Corydon, while George was already deeply involved in political maneuvering in the capital, and spending less and less time at home. Sarah tried to be helpful, to visit her sister-in-law often and keep her company, but was continually rebuffed by Emily's icy reserve. Baffled and hurt, she gave up the effort.

One day in the midst of a spell of balmy weather, when Emily was taking advantage of the warm sunshine and sitting in her garden, Oliver came. He approached her diffidently, almost timidly, and gave her a formal bow.

"Good afternoon, Emily."

Emily was knitting. She glanced up at her visitor, nodded gravely, and went on with her work.

"May I sit with you for a little while?" Oliver asked.

"If you wish."

He sat down. For a minute he watched the movements of Emily's knitting needles. Then his gaze drifted up and down her swollen body, finally coming to rest on her face. It was a mask.

"You're looking well," Oliver said.

"Thank you." She did not look at him.

Oliver glanced around the little garden. Fallen leaves made a carpet of speckled gold and copper on the warm ground.

"Splendid weather, isn't it?" Oliver said.

"Indeed it is."

"Do you know why they call it Indian summer, Emily?"

"I haven't the slightest idea."

"In earlier times, when settlers hacked out the first homesites in the wilderness, they would look forward eagerly to the coming of autumn, because Indians became

93

inactive during cold weather. But during warm spells, the braves would often launch surprise attacks. Consequently, this kind of weather became known as Indian summer. It was considered a dangerous time."

"How interesting," Emily said, without detectable interest. She kept her eyes on her work.

Oliver observed her in silence for a while. "Remarkable," he said at length. "I've noticed that most women tend to lose their attractiveness quickly from the rigors of childbearing. In your case, it seems the reverse is true. I've never seen you look so lovely."

Still she did not look at him, or make any response.

Oliver leaned forward and gazed at her intently. "You are very beautiful, Emily," he said softly. "The most bewitching woman I've ever met."

The knitting needles were stilled. Emily raised her eyes to Oliver's and held them there steadily.

"Oliver, why are you here?"

He reacted with surprise. "Why, to pay a social call, my dear. I thought you must be lonely, with George away so much of the time. Besides, I . . . I have been yearning for an opportunity to talk to you. Alone."

"I'm sure I cannot imagine why, or what about," Emily said coldly. "And I am not lonely at all. Susan and Henry are all the company I need. I am quite content."

She turned back to her work. The knitting needles began to fly.

"Don't be cruel, Emily," Oliver said.

It was her turn to be surprised. "Don't be . . . *cruel?!* The master scoundrel of the world is sensitive to cruelty!"

"Please, Emily. You don't know the tortures I've been through—"

She laughed. "Poor Oliver! It appears your entire life has been a constant parade of tortures!"

"Oh, Emily—"

He tried to grasp her hand, but she shrank from him with hostility snapping in her eyes. He noted that she was gripping a knitting needle like a weapon.

"Emily . . . that night . . . that night would have been the most perfect experience of my life . . ." Oliver's voice shook with emotion. His speech came haltingly. "But I was . . . prevented. Believe me, I was prevented—"

94

"Yes, I know, Oliver. You were detained with the business of impregnating Sarah."

"Emily, stop! You cannot understand how it was!"

"Oh, but I do, indeed. Sarah told us all, in the most frightful detail, how she went into your room and shamelessly seduced you. She even mentioned how, at the height of the proceedings, she noticed little Isaac, wide awake, calmly watching."

Oliver recoiled. "Oh . . . *God!*"

Emily smiled. "I pity you, Oliver. You are married to a witch."

Oliver was choking with anguish. "Emily, I beg you . . . spare me! Were it not for that evil, scheming female, you and I might have— Oh, Emily, my darling . . . it is too cruel!" He buried his face in his hands.

Emily's stern face softened. After a moment she reached out and put a gentle hand on Oliver's arm. He looked up at her, his eyes full of suffering.

"Never mind," she said. "It is all long past now, and had best be forgot—"

Suddenly she sucked in her breath in a sharp gasp, and stiffened.

"Oliver!"

Instantly he was on his feet, looking down at her in alarm. "What is it, Emily? What's wrong?"

She was gripping the sides of her chair, and trembling. Her face was deathly pale.

"Is it . . . the baby?" he stammered.

She nodded. Perspiration stood out on her brow. "I think it may be my time," she said with difficulty. Blindly she held out a hand to him. "Help me, Oliver."

He hovered over her awkwardly, uncertain what to do. She clutched at him.

"Help me to my bed, please."

"Yes, Emily."

He tried to get her to her feet. Half-rising, she froze suddenly and gasped again, and her face contorted. Her arm crept around Oliver's neck.

"Carry me," she whispered.

He lifted her in his arms with ease, and carried her toward the house. Twelve-year-old Susan met them at the door, and her eyes went wide with fright.

"Mama, Mama, what's the matter?"

"Hush, Susan, it's all right," Oliver said. "Run to my house quickly, and tell Sarah to—"

"Not Sarah!" Emily said fiercely. "Matilda. Go to your grandmother, Susan. Tell her the baby is coming. And find Henry if you can."

The girl flew.

Oliver carried Emily into her bedroom and laid her down on the bed with careful gentleness, and knelt beside her. One hand remained spread under her back. The other went to her face, moved tenderly over her forehead, and came to rest on her cheek. His lips came down close to hers.

"My beautiful," he breathed. "My adored."

She murmured something incoherent and stirred feebly, but made no move or sound of resistance.

"Emily, darling Emily! Would to God it were my child you carry! Oh, then how gladly I could endure the world's abuse, for that would be glory, glory . . ."

He grasped her hand and planted fervent little kisses in the open palm. Her feverish lips were parted and straining toward him, and he took them, pulling her up into an embrace that half-lifted her from the bed. Her arms wound tightly around his neck, her hands dug into his back.

It was a full minute before he released her gently, and she sank back down on the bed with another low moan, and the light of ardor in her eyes turned again to pain. →

Cyrus Thacker rode all night to take the news to George in Corydon. George arrived home at nightfall of the following day, accompanied by Cyrus, and Emily's brother, Robert Morrow. He found Emily lying weak and pale, a newborn baby boy shriveled and near death, and Samuel Gilpin poring desperately over an enormous book from his library called *Household Encyclopedia of the Medical Art,* the only source of medical knowledge in the area.

"The little fellow seems to have some kind of membrane covering the esophagus," Samuel explained. "He can't take nourishment. When he tries to suckle, he only chokes."

Though bone-weary from his long journey, George climbed back into the saddle. His little son, securely wrapped in blankets, was handed up to him. Accompanied

96

by the faithful Cyrus, he started back to Corydon, where lived the only physician within fifty miles.

At dawn they returned. In his arms George clutched the body of his dead child.

22

ONE GRAY AND GLOWERING DAY in early winter, Oliver was in the forest chopping firewood when George came looking for him. Oliver leaned on his axe and smiled amiably.

"Ah, George! What a pleasant surprise!"

George planted himself in front of Oliver without responding to the pleasantry. His face was grim.

"Sorry to interrupt you. But I was curious about something, and I thought perhaps—"

Oliver laughed gently. "Ah, George, curiosity is something that just won't leave you alone, isn't it?" He sighed. "Well, what is it this time?"

George took a small step closer. "The other day I happened to be talking with my daughter Susan, and I learned, quite by accident, a very odd thing. I learned that on the day Emil went into labor, *you* were in attendance to her."

Oliver's facial expression quickly passed through astonishment to amusement. He laughed.

"Oh, good Lord, George! *'In attendance'* is hardly the way to put it! By chance I had passed your house and, it being a fine day, Emily was sitting in the garden. Purely

97

out of neighborly courtesy, I stopped to inquire after her health, and we chatted for a few minutes. Precisely *then* she was seized with her pains. I helped her to her bed, and sent Susan running to fetch your mother. Of course I remained with Emily and comforted her as best I could until help arrived."

"Peculiar," George said.

"My God, man, what would you have had me do?!" Oliver's mood had changed from amusement to indignation.

"I mean it's peculiar that neither Emily nor anybody else ever mentioned your having been there. Too bad. I would have expressed my gratitude for your . . . kindness . . . long before now."

Oliver was fuming. "You're a suspicious man, George, and evidently an insanely jealous one, as well. Someday it will get the better of you."

"You think so?"

"I predict it. You think it odd that Emily never mentioned it to you? Not in the least—just plain good sense on her part. She knew well enough that you would take a trifling thing like that and find in it all manner of sinister meaning. She *knows* you, George."

"And I know *you*, Oliver."

Oliver's eyes hardened. "Sir?"

"I know more about your past life than you realize. And every farmhand in South Bar knows that you accepted my father's hospitality, seduced his young daughter right under his nose, and then fled into the night. Why shouldn't I look upon you with suspicion?"

Oliver blustered in anger. "It was *her* doing, George! She admits it herself!"

"I don't believe that. I think she said it only to protect you."

"I *married* the girl, and I'm a good and faithful husband!"

"You married her, yes. At the point of my gun." George stepped closer still, and his glinting eyes impaled Oliver.

"And speaking of trifles, let me acquaint you with another one. When it was discovered last winter that my little sister was pregnant, there was a family meeting, attended by Sarah and our parents, and Emily and myself. I announced my intention of moving heaven and earth to find you and bring you back. The meeting then moved on

98

to its principal purpose—to decide your fate. If I brought you back to my father's house, what ceremony would we conduct. A wedding? Or a funeral?"

Oliver took a step backward. George moved forward, closing the distance again, and continued, "In accordance with the democratic process, which we all hold dear, the issue was settled by a vote. Would you care to know how that vote went, Oliver? *Exactly* how it went?"

"Yes," Oliver breathed. "Yes, I would."

"I will tell you. You were saved by a vote of three to two. Sarah and both of our parents voted for a wedding. I voted for a funeral. And Emily—know this, Oliver— Emily voted with me."

Oliver swallowed. He stepped backward again, and leaned heavily on his axe. This time George did not follow. A smile appeared on his face, glassy hard, and as icy as the biting winter air.

"Interesting, eh?" He reached out and tapped Oliver lightly on the shoulder with his finger. "So do not toy with us, my friend. Emily and I stand together. Offend either of us again, and I will use my own private judgment, and the democratic process be damned."

He turned and strode rapidly away, and left Oliver alone.

Oliver lifted his axe, and stood for a long time with the thick oaken handle gripped rigidly in his hands. He stared down at the log he had been chopping. Then he muttered a curse and lifted the axe as high as he could, and buried the iron blade with shuddering force in the wood.

99

23

EMILY REGAINED her health slowly, remaining in seclusion through the long winter, mostly in her bed, while George spent half his time on horseback commuting frantically between Corydon and South Bar, trying to pursue his career in the capital without appearing to neglect his family. Cyrus Thacker took over a large share of the farm duties, but his limited experience produced poor results. The fields and barns began to take on a dilapidated look.

In the spring Emily seemed to be fully recovered. She became compulsively industrious, as if to make up for lost time, and assumed the management of the farm in her husband's extended absences.

And the Gilpin family's attention shifted away from George's wife and settled on Oliver's. Sarah was herself beginning to move slowly, and to grow heavy again with child.

On a damp morning in April, after a light spring rain had washed the young green leaves and made them glisten, Emily walked through her orchard, inspecting the new blossoms. At the far end of the grounds she suddenly came upon Oliver. He was standing there as if confident that she would come to him at an appointed hour. Emily uttered a little cry of surprise and alarm, and drew back.

"Oliver! You should not be here!"

He took a quick step toward her. "Emily, my dearest, I had to see you—"

"No!" She recoiled. "You mustn't—"

"I *must*. Because of you I am sick unto death. You have infected my blood, Emily. I will never be free of you again. Never."

He approached her slowly, and she stood still and allowed him to come near. He reached out and laid his fingers lightly on her sleeve.

"Since the day I held you in my arms—"

"Hush, Oliver. Stop it! You must not speak of that!"

"Emily . . . how can I remain silent about something that torments my soul every waking moment, and intrudes upon my sleep as well?" Abruptly he seized her and pulled her close. "Sweet Emily . . ."

She resisted. "No, no, Oliver! There are spies . . . I'm being watched!"

She wrenched free of his grasp, retreated a few steps, and stood with her back to him, trembling.

He stared at her. "Watched? What do you mean?"

"George has become distrustful of me, and deeply suspicious of you. He has instructed Cyrus to keep me under observation. He has even tried to enlist Susan and Henry in the conspiracy, and poison their minds against me."

She turned toward Oliver, and her eyes entreated him. "Go, please. Leave me alone. If you are seen here, your . . ." She struggled with herself. "Your life will be in danger."

He laughed quietly. Her eyes flashed at him.

"How can you laugh! Don't you realize—"

He came toward her again. "I will not be intimidated by that bumbling simpleton, Cyrus Thacker."

"But, Oliver, he is an informer! He will run to George, and George will kill you! Please—stay away from me, for my sake as well as yours."

She started to walk away from him, but he grasped her by the wrist and held her.

"What do I care if George kills me?" he muttered.

"Oliver!"

"My angel . . ." He took her other wrist and again pulled her toward him. "If I cannot have you, I will die anyway."

His arms were around her, his lips on her neck. For

101

only a moment she strained against his embrace, then her open mouth turned toward him, searching, and found his. She clung to him while his hands moved in a slow caress up and down her body.

After the long kiss ended, his lips went to her ear, and he whispered, "Tell me when, Emily. Give me a time."

She shook her head. "I can't. George is on his way from Corydon today. He will be here tonight."

"For how long?"

"Until Saturday."

"Then on the Sunday following—"

"Oh, you are *mad*, Oliver!" She struggled in his arms, but he held her tenaciously.

"On that Sunday, Emily, that night, my dearest love, on that night I will know the supreme moment that will make my life worth enduring—or death, if that is the price, acceptable without regret."

With a little cry she broke away from him and ran toward the house.

He watched her go, and smiled.

24

ON SATURDAY MORNING George Gilpin appeared at the Hargraves' door. Oliver saw him coming, and rushed out to greet him with effusive cordiality.

"George! Good to see you!" He seized his brother-in-law's hand and shook it vigorously. "Heard you were

102

going back to Corydon today. I hoped we'd see you before you left."

George gave him a sharp look. "Where'd you hear it? I thought only Emily knew, and she has spoken to no one. So she says."

Oliver laughed. "Come now, George. South Bar is full of gossips, and you, sir, are something of a celebrity. Your comings and goings are talked about. That's the price of fame."

Oliver laughed again, took George by the arm, and led him into the house.

Sarah was overjoyed to see her brother, and embraced him warmly. George gave her an affectionate pat on the cheek.

"How are you feeling, little sister?"

Sarah laughed and clutched her swollen belly. "Please, George! Whatever I am, I am certainly not little!"

George observed her wonderingly, and shook his head. "My, how fast the time goes . . ."

"It wouldn't go so fast if you'd spend a little more time at home." A little pout came on Sarah's face. "Really, I'm quite vexed with you, George. I see you so seldom, you're a perfect stranger."

Oliver quickly spoke up. "George is an important man, Sarah. You know, a member of the state assembly has little time—"

"Pshaw!" Sarah was scornful. "He should have time for his family! And Emily—she's even worse! I go to see her, and she's cold as an iceberg. And she *never* comes to see me. What have I done that she should treat me so?"

"Forgive her, Sarah," George said. "She is not herself. I think she never fully recovered from the baby's death. She needs quiet and rest, and has very little of either. As for me, I'm trying to live two lives—one in Corydon, one here. It's hard on both of us."

Oliver, hovering nearby, made another interjection.

"Also, Sarah, you must consider that George's term expires this summer, and he will face another election. And you know how it is in politics. Better he should neglect his family than appear to neglect his official duties. Especially before an election."

"That's nonsense," George muttered.

Oliver went on, unabashed. "By the way, George, have

103

you heard? Nelson Hall intends to oppose you again this year."

"Of course I've heard. It's very uninteresting information."

"I was talking to him about it the other day. He says he's convinced your infatuation with the idea of Negro exclusion is political poison—"

"More nonsense!" George growled. "Next year I intend to introduce a bill—"

"You said that *last* year, George."

"The time was not yet ripe."

"Hall says such a measure, if it should ever be passed, would be immediately struck down by the U.S. Supreme Court, and you'd be left looking very foolish."

"Hall is an idiot. I will dispose of him again, just as I did before."

Oliver laughed softly, and George's dark visage grew darker.

"Don't be too sure," Oliver said. "There are many who agree with him. Including your father."

The muscles in George's jaw were working dangerously as he glared at Oliver. "If you don't mind," he said in a carefully controlled voice, "I came here to visit with Sarah, not to seek your political advice."

Oliver smiled and looked apologetic. "What could I be thinking of? A nonentity giving advice to a recognized master!"

He kissed Sarah lightly on the cheek, and went to the door. "I think I'll go down to the river and discuss politics with my Negro friend Camus," he said. "I like to be neighborly, you know. And after all, Camus *is* our neighbor."

He smiled again, bowed slightly, and went out.

Sarah looked at George, and her eyes were grieving. "You and Oliver will never be friends, will you, George?"

"No," he said. "Never."

104

25

ON SUNDAY Oliver and Samuel came to church together and sat in the first row, where Oliver usually sat with Sarah. Matilda and Sarah did not come. Emily appeared, accompanied only by her son Henry, and sat in the rear. After the service, Oliver and Samuel spoke to Reverend Daniels, and while Oliver remained to chat with the minister, Samuel made his way through the crowd to Emily, bade her good morning, and playfully ruffled young Henry's hair.

"I don't see Matilda here," Emily said.

"She's staying with Sarah," Samuel replied. "Or rather, Sarah is staying with us. She moved back to our house until the birth of her child."

"A sensible arrangement."

"It was Oliver's idea. He thought of it quite suddenly, yesterday afternoon. Sarah wanted to stay at home, but Oliver insisted—said she'd be better off with her mother. He's a thoughtful man, Oliver."

Emily looked away.

"I suppose George got off all right?" Samuel said.

"Oh yes. George always gets off all right."

"Pity he couldn't have stayed a little longer. Sarah's baby is so close, I thought—"

Emily uttered a hollow little laugh. "Dear Samuel! George was too busy to be here when *my* baby was born. Surely you don't expect—" She broke off and turned her attention to the boy at her side, who was impatiently shuffling his feet.

"Do be still, Henry."

"Can I go, Mama?"

"Go where, dear?"

"To find Isaac."

"Isn't he here, with your Uncle Oliver?"

"Naw! Isaac never has to go to church!" Young Henry seemed exasperated by the gross injustices of the world.

"Well, go along, then," Emily said, and the boy fled.

"Strange . . ." Samuel mused.

"What is, sir?" Emily asked.

"About George. I hardly saw him at all this trip. Why does he drift away from us like this?"

"I think—" Emily was suddenly uncomfortable. "Maybe he's a little resentful that he no longer has your political support."

This touched a nerve. "Well, damn it all, Emily!" he growled, and immediately checked himself. "Forgive me. I mean to say . . . how can a man of good conscience, which I am, support the kind of bigotry that George is now—"

"Please, sir!" Emily raised a limp hand and waved the discussion off. "These political issues are beyond my poor comprehension."

Samuel shrugged and smiled. "Well, be that as it may. Will you come to dinner tonight?"

"Oh no, thank you. I think not."

"Sarah hoped you'd come. Oliver will be there too, of course, and I'm sure he'd be glad to walk you home."

"No, no, no—" Agitation erupted briefly in Emily's voice. Quickly she brought it under control. "Thank you just the same, Samuel. I really don't feel up to it."

"A pity."

"I think I'd better get home," Emily said abruptly. "I left Susan doing chores, and she needs supervision. Give my love to Matilda, will you?" She started away.

"And to Sarah?" Samuel said.

Emily paused. "Of course. To Sarah."

When she had gone a short distance up the path toward home, Oliver overtook her.

106

"Emily?" he called, and she stopped and went rigid, and turned slowly to face him.

"We can't talk here, Oliver." She spoke in low, urgent tones as Oliver came up to her. "Cyrus is wandering about. He'll be following me."

"Emily . . . tonight?"

She stared at him, wild-eyed. The tense muscles of her face failed to conceal the turmoil within her.

"Oliver . . . how can I *trust* you?"

He was aghast. "Emily! How can you *not* trust me? You mean more to me than life!"

The struggle inside her continued, grew more apparent in her eyes. "Oh, Oliver . . . what are we to do?"

He grasped her by the arms and pulled her close. His lips were against her ear. He whispered, "I will come for you at midnight, and take you to the boat."

She looked at him in quick panic. "The boat? Oh no, I dare not! There are the children—"

"They sleep soundly, don't they? You will be home again in an hour. They will never know."

Emily strained against him. Her voice trembled in desperation. "Oh . . . this is madness."

"Not yet, my darling. But it will be soon. If we try to defy the great force that grips us, it will destroy us both."

He pulled her closer, and his fingertips caressed her cheek. "Don't torture me any longer, Emily. Or yourself. Please."

He kissed her. With a muffled sigh, she sagged in his arms, accepted the kiss, and returned it fully. Afterward she pulled back and gazed dully at the ground, and her breath came in quick little gasps. She spoke in an almost inaudible whisper.

"At midnight, then."

Oliver smiled. "At midnight. Precisely."

"Make certain you are not observed," she said, and her whisper was now fierce and commanding.

Oliver stepped back. His smile broadened. He bowed. He spoke in a loud, amiable voice, from which all trace of conspiracy was gone.

"So pleasant to have chatted with you, madam. Good day to you."

"Good day, sir." She wheeled and walked rapidly away from him.

107

Oliver turned and strolled back toward the church, where people were still standing in scattered groups, socializing. When he was almost there, he met Cyrus Thacker hurrying up the path.

"Good morning, Cyrus!" Oliver called out cheerily.

Cyrus's narrowed eyes telegraphed suspicion. "'Scuse me, Mr. Hargrave. Have you seen Mrs. Gilpin?"

Oliver rubbed his chin and pondered the question. "Well now, yes and no. That is to say, it depends on which Mrs. Gilpin you mean."

"Mrs. George Gilpin."

Oliver's face lit up. "Ah yes, Mrs. George Gilpin. As a matter of fact, I just left her. I met her on the path, and we spent almost five minutes chatting together. Alone. Shocking, isn't it?" Oliver's eyes twinkled as he gave Cyrus a playful little pat on the arm. "You won't forget to tell George, will you?"

He went on his way, and Cyrus stood staring after him with a befuddled frown.

26

THERE WAS a festive air in the elder Gilpins' house that evening. Sarah was in a jolly mood. She bounced the year-old Lucius on her lap and beamed with motherly pride as the child's grandparents exclaimed over his phenomenal growth, praised his beauty and intelligence, and professed to hear good English words in his baby prattle. Oliver looked on and beamed, and readily agreed when

Matilda predicted that the second child would be fully as beautiful as the first. And Isaac, who, at eight, was already beginning to shoot up tall and thin like his father, stood by Sarah's chair and watched and listened with quiet solemn eyes.

Sarah suddenly handed little Lucius to Matilda, grasped Isaac, and smiled up at him. "No matter what they say, my darling Isaac is the handsomest, most intelligent, most splendid one of all!"

She pulled the boy close to her and gave him a huge hug, and he smiled a smile of deep joy.

When Lucius began to nod and doze, Oliver took the baby in his arms and kissed him, and carried him off to bed. And when it was Isaac's bedtime, Oliver went along with him, his hand on the boy's shoulder. Isaac climbed into bed and his father sat down beside him.

"Well, Isaac, how are things with you? Seems to me we haven't had a good talk in a long time."

"I'm fine, Papa," the boy said.

"Are you keeping up with the lessons Grandpa Samuel gives you?"

"I try, Papa. I do the arithmetic all right, but the readin' and writin' is terrible hard for me."

"It doesn't matter how hard it is, boy. What matters is that you have a desire to learn, and a willingness to work at it. You have that, and someday you'll make a name for yourself. The opportunities are out there, just waiting for you to grow up and come after them."

Isaac gave a little shrug. "All I want to do is stay here with Mama Sarah."

Oliver looked down at the boy for a moment. "You love Mama Sarah very much, don't you, Isaac?"

"I sure do. She's the best mother in the world."

"You wouldn't ever want to be taken away from her again, would you?"

Isaac's eyes filled with alarm. "Oh no, Papa!" The boy raised himself on an elbow. "We're not goin' away from her, are we?"

Oliver chuckled. "No, no, no, of course not." He patted Isaac on the head and settled him back down in the bed.

"You know, Isaac, as you grow older, you will have a responsibility toward your brother Lucius, and to the new little brother or sister you will have soon. They'll

109

watch what you do, and imitate it. You'll want to be strong and resourceful and self-reliant, to set a good example for them."

Isaac's eyelids were growing heavy. "Yes, Papa," he murmured sleepily.

"I know I can count on you to do that," Oliver said. He leaned down and kissed the boy on the forehead.

"Good night, my son."

"G'night, Papa."

Oliver got up and went out quickly, and closed the door.

When Sarah had retired, Oliver sat beside her as he had sat with Isaac. She reached out and clasped him around the neck.

"Stay with me," she murmured.

"No, dear, I'll go home. I'm a restless sleeper, as you know. I want you to rest undisturbed."

She continued to hold him, and gazed dreamily into his eyes. "Do you remember, Oliver?"

"Remember what, dear?"

"The first time. Right here in this little room where you were sleeping, and I came to you in the night, and our love began."

Oliver smiled faintly. "Yes, of course I remember."

"Oliver, did you know that sometimes women talk among themselves about . . . lovemaking?"

"Mmm. I hadn't thought of it."

"I've heard other women talk. They say it takes years to learn to enjoy it. Some say they never do, at all."

Sarah's arms crept farther around her husband's neck. "I feel sorry for them, because for me it was wonderful from the very beginning. Of course, I can't claim to be an unusual woman. Just a lucky one, to have such a fine lover . . ."

She giggled, drew Oliver down to her, and kissed him on the lips. He was unresponsive.

"You're cold toward me, Oliver," she complained.

"Not at all, silly girl, but it's time for you to go to sleep now. You must take care of yourself." He patted her protruding belly. "And the little one."

She smiled at him. "Soon I will be back to normal. Then you will love me again, won't you, Oliver?"

He pulled her hands from around his neck and kissed

110

the palms, one after the other. His thin face was dark and brooding.

"Sarah, my dear, you are the kindest, gentlest, most virtuous woman I have ever known. No man could wish for a better wife than you. I am unworthy of you, I know that full well."

Her laugh was scornful. "Oh, Oliver! How you talk!"

He tucked the covers around her, kissed her on the cheek, and got up.

"Goodnight, Sarah." He moved to the door.

"Will you come back early in the morning? I'll want to see you the minute I wake up."

"Don't worry about the morning," he whispered. "Go to sleep now. With every rising of the sun . . . life begins anew."

He closed the door slowly, smiling at her as his face disappeared from her view.

Later in the evening, when they were alone, Samuel poured the traditional measure of whiskey for himself and Oliver, and they sat together, sipping quietly.

"Well, Oliver, your family grows apace," Samuel remarked.

Oliver nodded absently.

Samuel fell to musing. "Strange, as George has grown distant from us, you have become closer. It's been less than two years since you first set foot on our shore, yet I can barely remember the time when you were not a member of our little family circle."

"Yes," Oliver said dreamily. "Time plays tricks on us."

Samuel raised his glass toward Oliver. "To your unborn child. May it inherit the best qualities of us all."

Oliver touched his glass to Samuel's. "Thank you, sir. A noble sentiment." He gulped the whiskey, and got to his feet.

"I must be off," he said curtly.

"Off? It's early yet."

Oliver looked around the room. He frowned as if troubled by something elusive that was teasing his imagination.

"There are times, sir, when the darkness weighs heavily on my mind. I long for daylight."

111

Samuel stared up at him. "You're in a strange mood, Oliver."

Oliver's eyes fell on the other man, and suddenly burned like hot coals.

"Good night, Samuel," he said in a husky whisper. "Good night, my friend, and . . . God keep you."

He strode to the front door, went out, and closed the door heavily behind him.

Samuel sat still, gazing blankly at the door, listening to the sound of Oliver's footsteps receding in the darkness outside. Then all was quiet.

Samuel sighed. "A strange mood," he murmured.

He poured himself another whiskey.

27

IN THE NIGHT a dismal wind arose, and wailed through the dark pathways of the forest.

Samuel had heard a banging noise for what seemed like a long time, but his mind was submerged in sleep and tried to dismiss the disturbance as something flapping in the wind. Then he became aware of Matilda shaking him.

"Wake up, Samuel! Somebody's pounding on the door!"

Samuel arose, hastily pulled his pants on over his night-shirt, and groped his way through the darkness toward the front of the house. His wife started to follow, but hung back fearfully.

"Who could it be at this hour? Be careful, Samuel!"

112

Through the cracks in the heavy oak boards of the door, Samuel could see the yellowish glare of a lantern outside. He stood close to the door and shouted, "Who's there?"

"Camus, sar. Open de do', please!" The voice of the black man sounded sharp and urgent.

Samuel unbolted the door and flung it open. Camus stood there holding a lantern high above his head. In the dim light, the shining brown face and wide eyes seemed like an African mask, transfigured by some mysterious passion.

Samuel spoke gruffly. "What the devil do you want, Camus? It's way past midnight!"

Camus recoiled in horror. "Oh, sar, don' speak o' de debbil! Not on such a night!" His eyes darted about frantically, and there was awe in his whispering voice.

"Listen, sar!" he said. "Do you hear dat sound? Dat howlin' and a-wailin' in de woods? You know what dat sound is, sar? Dat's de voices o' de dead and damned, a-cryin' out fo' mercy."

Matilda had come, and was standing at her husband's side. "What's the matter with him, Samuel?" she whispered.

Her appearance seemed to startle the black man. He shrank back.

Samuel advanced a few steps toward him. "What is it you want, Camus? Now don't waste my time, man. Talk sense, do you hear me?"

Camus seemed to struggle to bring himself under control. "Sar, Rev'rend Hargrave in de grip o' de debbil tonight. Yas, sar. Rev'rend, he tell me to fetch some people dat he name, and bring dem to a place where he will be, fo' de debbil has a message fo' de people o' South Bar, an' he will deliver it to you—"

Sarah's voice, tight with anxiety, sounded from within the house. "Papa? What is it? Is something wrong?"

Samuel turned to his wife and spoke hurriedly, in a low voice. "Go to her. Tell her it's only Camus, drunk and acting the fool. I'll get rid of him."

Matilda disappeared into the house, and Samuel turned back to the visitor.

Camus's face was hard and defiant. "Camus not drunk, sar," he said with dignity.

Samuel stepped closer to him. "I know it, Camus. Now

113

go on. Where does Reverend Hargrave want you to bring these people?"

"Dat I cannot say, sar. You follow Camus. He lead you dere."

"So. And what people did he name for you to fetch? Can you tell me that?"

"Sar, he say fetch you an' Mr. Thacker. Den he say, fetch de Rev'rend Daniels. Den Mr. Hall an' Mr. Tibbetts—"

"Hall? You mean Nelson Hall?"

"Yas, sar, de same. An' den de widow Jemison—"

"What on earth is he talking about, Samuel?" whispered Matilda, who had returned to the door.

"He says Oliver wants him to fetch this strange collection of people—"

"Did he say Nelson Hall? George's opponent?"

"Yes. And John Tibbetts, who is surely one of Hall's chief supporters, and the widow Jemison, the most notorious gossip in the state of Indiana. I can't fathom what this is all about."

"Send him away, Samuel! He's a madman!"

Camus stood silent and held his lantern high. Samuel's eyes had never left his face.

"I doubt that," Samuel said quietly.

"De other people be gatherin' at de crossroads close by de church," Camus said. "Dey be waitin' fo' us. Will you come, sar?"

Samuel stared fixedly into Camus's inscrutable face.

"Just give me a minute to get my boots on," he said.

The others were waiting at the crossroads in front of the church, huddled in a tight group within the circle of light provided by the lanterns they carried. As Samuel and Camus approached, Nelson Hall stepped forward to meet them.

"What is the meaning of this, Samuel? What's your peculiar son-in-law up to now?"

"I have no idea, sir," Samuel said stiffly. "I thought maybe somebody else could shed some light on it."

"All *I* know is, Oliver came to my house this afternoon and told me to expect a summons tonight, through his man Camus. He said I should pay heed to it, that it could profit me. The others here say very much the same."

114

Samuel studied the faces of the group: Reverend Daniels, somber in his clerical garb; Cyrus Thacker, confused and anxious, with his rifle balanced in the crook of his arm; the widow Jemison, an elderly gray-haired woman wrapped in a heavy shawl, her eyes darting eagerly; John Tibbetts, a thin, nervous man, keeper of a small trading post in South Bar; and portly Nelson Hall.

"Well, let's git on with it, then," said the widow Jemison in a cackling voice that was shrill with impatience.

"And at this ungodly hour, it had better be good," Nelson Hall muttered.

They all turned their eyes to the black man.

"Lead on, Camus," Samuel said.

"One moment, sar," Camus said. He stepped up to Cyrus.

"'Scuse, sar. Leave yo' weapon behind."

"What?!" Cyrus bellowed.

"No weapon, sar. De Rev'rend Hargrave, he be angry. Dere will be no message if you come wid a weapon."

"The hell you say!" Cyrus growled. "I don't go nowhere 'thout my gun!"

"Why don't you leave it by the church, Mr. Thacker?" Reverend Daniels said. "It will be safe there."

"No," Cyrus said stubbornly.

Camus stood before him, unyielding. "You don' go wid de weapon, sar," he said quietly. A hush of astonishment came over the listeners.

"Leave it, Cyrus," Samuel said. "Do as he says."

"Let's git *on* with it!" squeaked the widow Jemison.

Cyrus backed off, grumbling, went to the church, and leaned his rifle in a corner by the front entrance.

Camus smiled at his little group. His head bobbed up and down. "Now den, good people, Camus lead you to de place. Follow, please."

He started toward the river, and the others fell in behind him.

Oliver Hargrave lay naked, flat on his back on one of the thick bearskins that covered the bunks in the tiny cabin of his keelboat. At his side, Emily Gilpin lay facing him, her nude body close against his. One of her arms was flung loosely across his chest. Her head rested on his shoulder, and her eyes were closed as if in slumber.

115

Oliver was wide awake. He stared upward in the darkness, listening. He heard the soft footfalls on the trail as the people approached, and saw through the cracks in the cabin wallboards the glow of their lanterns. He lay motionless, barely breathing, and waited.

Suddenly there was a jolt—someone was pulling on the mooring rope—and immediately Camus's voice rang out.

"Hal-loo! Rev'rend, sar!"

Emily's head jerked up from Oliver's shoulder. Her body went instantly tense.

"Oliver!" she whispered. "Someone's here!"

"It's all right, my dear, don't be alarmed," Oliver said. His voice was calm.

"Hal-loo, sar!" Camus called. "De people here, sar, fo' to receive de message!"

Oliver was up and pulling his pants on. Emily gasped, reached out and tried to cling to him.

"My God, Oliver! We're discovered!"

Oliver disengaged himself from her grasp. "It is nothing, my dear. Just a few friends, come to wish us happiness in our newfound love. I will see to it."

Emily sat up and stared wildly at him, and at the cabin door. Her eyes shone with terror in the darkness.

"Oliver, what do you mean? I can't believe . . . *Oliver!*"

He had turned from her and gone to the cabin door and flung it open, and his face and bare chest were lit by the glare of lanterns.

Cyrus arrived back at the church on the run, panting. He grabbed his rifle and started back, but paused when he heard someone call his name. Sarah Hargrave, wrapped in a house robe, was coming toward him from the opposite direction.

She was trying to hurry, but her efforts were clumsy with the burden of her unborn child. Matilda followed behind her, clutching at her, trying to hold her back. Sarah rushed on, ignoring her mother.

"Cyrus!" she cried. "Wait for me!"

Cyrus groaned as Sarah came up to him. "My God, ma'am, you oughtn't to be here!"

"What's happened, Cyrus? Where is Oliver?"

116

"Why, he's down at the boat, ma'am, and he's . . . he's got somebody with 'im."

"Who?"

Matilda was at Sarah's side, pulling at her. "Sarah, love, come home, please! Think of the baby!"

"Who, Cyrus?" Sarah demanded. "Tell me!"

Cyrus swallowed hard, and fidgeted with impatience. "Emily Gilpin, ma'am," he blurted.

Sarah staggered back. *"Emily . . ."* she whispered.

The women clung to each other and stared at Cyrus.

Then Mrs. Jemison appeared, hobbling up the path from the river as fast as her ancient legs would carry her, mumbling to herself.

"You ask the widow Jemison about it, ma'am," Cyrus said. "I ain't got time to stand here talkin'. I got to go." He started to run off.

"Cyrus, what are you going to do?" Sarah cried.

He was gone without answering.

Sarah rushed toward Mrs. Jemison, and clutched the old woman by the shoulders. "Mrs. Jemison! What's happened?"

Mrs. Jemison tried to pull away. "Oh Lor', child! Heaven forbid I should be the one to tell ye!"

Matilda was beside Sarah again, pleading, "Come home, Sarah. You'll ruin yourself!"

Sarah held the widow Jemison in a fierce grip, and shook her. "Speak, woman, speak!" she hissed.

The old woman held up a hand. "All right, child. Ye might as well hear it now, ye'll hear it soon enough. Yer husband comes out o' the boat, half undressed, smiles at us, and says, 'Welcome, friends! I'm glad ye're here. I want to tell ye that Emily Gilpin and I be runnin' away together—' "

Sarah released the woman and stepped back, swaying. Matilda held her.

Mrs. Jemison went on, " 'Runnin' away together,' he says, 'on acount o' we love each other mos' wondrously.' Well, we all jes' stood there a-rooted to the ground. An' then, Lor' help me, Emily herself appears from out o' the boat cabin, lookin' like a wild woman. She's a-strugglin' to git her dress on, an' she screams at us, 'No, no, it's a lie! It's a lie!' She runs to the edge o' the boat an' holds out her arms to Cyrus Thacker, an' she screams,

117

'Save me, Cyrus, save me! I'm betrayed!' Cyrus an' yer father, they run to the boat, splashin' their feet in th' water, an' they catch pore Emily jes' in time afore she swoons dead away. Her dress falls partway down an' exposes her shamefully. They lift her out an' lay her on the bank and cover her."

Sarah had closed her eyes and was leaning against her mother. Mrs. Jemison rushed on, heedless. Her narrative had become an uncontrolled torrent of words.

"Then, Lor' bless me, child, yer darlin' husband looks plumb distressed. He says, 'Emily! Ye be a treacherous woman!' An' he turns to us an' says, 'Friends, *I* be the one betrayed! She gave me the promise of her undyin' love.' Well, Cyrus Thacker delivers a blasphemous oath an' rushes toward the boat, lookin' as if to strangle yer husband with his bare hands. Mr. Hall an' Mr. Tibbetts start to follow him. But then the big black buck, Camus, jumps in front of 'em an' pulls forth a pistol an' yells, 'The first one sets foot on the boat is a dead man!' Then he jumps like a monkey up onto the deck, grabs a hatchet, and chops the rope that binds the boat to shore. Then, like a fiend o' hell, he waves his pistol in th' air an'—"

A single sharp report shattered the night, and rolled echoing away through the forest. Sarah flinched as if struck, and stared into the darkness toward the river.

"Then it was that Cyrus run to git his rifle," the widow Jemison said in hushed tones. "An' I went runnin' after 'im, on account o' my old eyes ain't hankerin' to see a killin'."

Sarah wrenched herself free from her mother's grasp and ran wildly toward the river, oblivious of Matilda's frantic entreaties, and screaming, "Oliver! Oliver!"

She got halfway there before she fell on a steep slope, uttered one piteous cry as she rolled on the ground in the darkness, and then lay still.

The boat whirled and spun like a fallen leaf on the dark surge of the river. In the middle of the deck, Oliver Hargrave stood naked to the waist, with feet wide apart, staring at the night sky. The wind roamed unhindered over the open water, and whipped his hair around his face. At his feet the black man Camus knelt, gazing raptly up at his master.

118

When the crack of Cyrus Thacker's rifle reached their ears it was a feeble pop, from a shore that was hidden in darkness and rapidly being left behind. Nevertheless the ball whistled menacingly in the turbulent air and splashed into the river not far away.

Camus instinctively ducked at the sound of the shot. Oliver sneered.

"The blithering fool! He knows not what else to do, so he fires bravely at the river."

Camus timidly tugged at Oliver's pants leg. "Rev'rend, sar? Did Camus do good? Did Camus do de job, sar?"

Oliver looked down at the man at his feet, and his smile grew broader.

"Camus, my boy, you were splendid! I have never seen you perform so well!"

Camus grinned. Oliver leaned down and slapped Camus on the bare shoulder.

"And you will be rewarded. Yes, you will. Your master always rewards good work, doesn't he?"

Camus's head bobbed rapidly. "Yas, sar. You good massa, sar."

Oliver straightened, and turned his smiling face upward again. "Yes, I'm a good master, and my boy Camus is a good slave. He will have women soon. Many, many women."

Camus lay flat on his back on the deck and laughed. "Oh, good massa, sar! Camus have many womans!"

Cyrus Thacker's rifle cracked again, now faint in the distance, and futile.

Camus continued to lie on the deck and laugh and kick his legs like a delighted child. Oliver, watching, began to laugh with him—at first softly, then louder, and louder still, and finally he threw back his head and flung his laughter into the teeth of the wind.

"By God, Camus!" he shouted, and his shout rang with exaltation. "It is done, man, it is done! *I have defeated George Gilpin!*"

28

AT DAWN Sarah's baby was born. Elizabeth Daniels, the reverend's wife, emerged from the bedroom and moved quickly to where Samuel Gilpin sat hunched over the big table. Samuel raised his eyes and searched her face for some hint of news. She gave him a wan smile.

"The Lord has been kind, Mr. Gilpin. The child lives. It is a girl. Sarah seems to be resting well."

Reverend Daniels, sitting next to Samuel, clasped his hands and turned his eyes upward. "Thank thee, Lord," he murmured.

Samuel seemed confused. "I had thought the worst," he said. "I heard no cry, no sound. I was afraid . . ."

"No," Mrs. Daniels said. "Strange to say, the baby doesn't cry. But she does live."

By the time Matilda came out of Sarah's room and sagged wearily into a chair, it was full light. The night wind had ceased; the day was balmy and springtime-gentle.

In her arms Matilda held a small burden, wrapped in a blanket. Samuel came and stood beside his wife, and peered down into a tiny, wrinkled face.

"She lives, Matilda?"

"For the present."

"And Sarah is all right?"

"As far as I can tell."

"Well, that's good, that's good." Samuel leaned down

and looked closely at the sleeping infant. "I think Sarah wanted to name the child Martha, after your mother, if it was a girl. Isn't that so?"

Matilda did not answer immediately. Gently she rocked the baby.

"I don't believe it's worthwhile to name it," she said at last.

Reverend Daniels gasped audibly. "Mrs. Gilpin, don't say such a thing!"

"What do you mean, Matilda?" Samuel asked quietly.

"The skull is cracked. Probably when Sarah fell. Poor little head was pushed all out of shape."

"But maybe it will mend," Samuel said hopefully. "Stranger things have happened." He looked toward Reverend and Mrs. Daniels for help.

"Indeed they have," Elizabeth Daniels said brightly. "How well I remember my younger brother Clarence. Absolutely nobody thought he would survive. And today he's . . ."

Matilda wasn't listening. Her sad, drooping eyes were gazing off into some distant place.

"Martha," she said softly. "I don't remember Martha, my mother. She died when I was a little girl. They say she was very beautiful. I don't know, I never knew her."

Her eyes returned to the fragile little thing she held in her lap. With one finger she touched the tiny chin.

"And I will never know this Martha, either."

Tears gushed, rolled down Matilda's gaunt cheeks, and fell on the infant's covering.

29

FROM THE JOURNAL of Lucius Hargrave:

My father and mother was rapturously happy together, as was evident to all observers by the unwavering devotion they displayed toward one another. Indeed, I think it no exaggeration to say the only true peace and happiness my poor father ever knew was that which he enjoyed during those early days of idyllic bliss with his beloved Sarah, in the house he built for her with his own hands.

But it was not to last. Life is so ordered in this world that such an island of tranquility could not long remain unbuffeted by stormy seas. The torment that had forever dogged my father's footsteps soon returned in a most unexpected form. I refer to the mystery of my uncle, George Gilpin.

My mother's elder brother George, for some unaccountable reason, had developed a hostility toward my father. It was a thing that must have begun from some weightless seed too small to be detected, to flourish in the fertile soil of his dark, suspicious mind until it had grown into a poisonous tree, bringing forth fruits of hatred. I call it a mystery because, for all the earnest efforts of my mother and her father Samuel, and of my father himself, to reason with George and determine the basis of the man's animosity, no inkling of its source could ever be discovered.

My belief has always been that it was simply the result of jealousy, fed by a naturally cold and unfriendly heart. Uncle George had ambitions for a political career, but was seriously hampered by a stern visage and a gruff, taciturn style—truly grievous handicaps in a profession that demanded the opposite qualities. In contrast, my father's ability as an orator and the natural warmth of his personality were known far and wide, and must have nurtured the bitterest envy in his brother-in-law's breast. For whatever reason, that malevolent man showered upon my father's head a string of insults and abuses that had no end, and grew increasingly vicious. A lesser man would have lashed out in retaliation. The Reverend Hargrave bore his misfortune as he bore all his life's sufferings: quietly, uncomplainingly, and with the serene patience that so distinguished his nature.

Yet no man is completely invulnerable. At last George Gilpin had the evil satisfaction of seeing the idyllic happiness of his imagined enemy disrupted, and that of his sister as well. And, since Justice never sleeps entirely, he felt the chill hand of ruin upon his own miserable head, in the bargain.

The strange and melancholy story was a favorite subject for the loose tongues of gossip in South Bar for years afterward, and the details of what really happened were argued about endlessly. According to my own investigations, conducted secretly but with careful thoroughness a long time later, the events actually transpired in this manner:

George's wife, a not unattractive but somewhat hard and haughty woman named Emily, developed a sinful desire for the Reverend Hargrave, and began to make subtle advances toward him—which, needless to say, were gently but firmly turned aside. Gilpin, being a deeply suspicious man by nature, promptly commissioned a hired hand on his farm to spy on Emily and to report to him anything—even a casual exchange of good mornings—that transpired between her and my father. This hireling, an oafish rustic named Cyrus Thacker, became a veritable Iago, filling his employer's ear with lurid tales of assignations where none existed, tales that his muddleheaded Othello was all too eager to believe.

Gilpin's suspicions, had they been directed solely toward

123

his discontented wife, would not have been unjustified (in this case, Desdemona was innocent only because her chosen lover refused to cooperate). But he was blinded by righteous rage; the truth escaped him; he heaped his malice upon the head of an innocent man, and his hatred grew.

Likewise grew the illicit passion in the breast of Emily Gilpin. The wretched woman's husband was neglecting her shamefully, which only added fuel to the smouldering fires within her. Gradually her advances toward my father became bolder. As considerately as possible, he attempted to discourage her. She persisted. The devil had possessed her, and would not be denied. My father went to extreme lengths to avoid the pathetic creature—in vain. She sought him out and threw herself at his feet, all dignity abandoned. In desperation, my father confided in his dearest friend, my mother. They concluded that there was but one course of action open to them as decent Christian people: they must leave South Bar forever. He would depart first, to select a suitable location for a home somewhere farther west. This done, he would return to fetch his wife and children. (Unwilling to add to his worries, my mother bravely kept from him the knowledge that she was at that time again beginning to sense the stirring of a new life growing within her.)

One night in the spring of the year 1817, my father prepared his trusty old riverboat for departure. He was assisted by his long-time faithful employee and boatman, Camus, a primitive Negro whom the Reverend had once rescued from slavery.

Somehow, word of my father's plans reached Emily Gilpin. Some people believe it was the Negro Camus who informed her, for no other reason than his own amusement. This may be so. But my own inquiries led me to the conviction that it was the snooping Cyrus Thacker who brought Mrs. Gilpin the news, wishing, no doubt, to observe her reaction and report it to her husband. That reaction must have exceeded the simpleton's furthest reckonings. Emily became a madwoman. Shrieking my father's name at the top of her voice, she rushed wildly through the night, alarming the entire community. They found her lying in a faint on the banks of the river, at the point from which my father had but a little while before launched his boat. Her clothing was rent to shreds,

124

attesting to the violence of her distress. They lifted her up and took her home, where it is said she lay in her bed for days, alternately weeping and mumbling incoherently.

I never personally knew my uncle George Gilpin. Throughout the years, I have constantly marveled at the things I have heard about him—all, without exception, stern and forbidding, unrelieved by the slightest hint of humanity. Alas for the poor wretch, the poisonous hatred he carried in his heart contained the seeds of his own undoing. The scandal surrounding his wife's shocking behavior utterly wrecked his budding political career, and left him disgraced and ruined.

Relating such a mournful tale should cause sympathy to well up in even the coldest heart, I know, yet honesty compels me to admit I can feel but little of it. As ye sow, so shall ye reap, it is written. George Gilpin reaped a hideous harvest of ironic justice—but at what a cost to innocent people!

May God have mercy on him.

30

AFTER A FEW YEARS, the traveling journalist from New York returned to Indiana for a second look, and sent his editor a series of reports and letters.

Corydon, Indiana
June 10, 1821

I trust you received my last communication, sent last week from New Albany. I have now journeyed on to Corydon, curious to see what has transpired here in the five years since a group of backwoodsmen met under an elm tree to struggle with the tedious business of fashioning a state constitution.

Corydon's day of greatness (such as it was) seems already to be drawing to a close. The site of a new capital has recently been chosen, farther north, more nearly in the center of the state. It is a place called Indianapolis. I am told by the numerous critics of this selection that Indianapolis is Nothing, situated in the middle of Nowhere, and can never hope to become the substantial city that a state capital ought to be. But the decision has been made, plans for the move drawn up, and that is that. Presumably Corydon will revert to its old status as a sleepy little village, to dream forever of its past glory.

Here the journalist paused. Corydon might merit no more space in his dispatch, but the strange tale he had heard there deserved a retelling in his personal journal.

As is my custom, I have been prowling about the taverns that are known to be the favorite haunts of local politicians, striking up acquaintances and asking questions. Today I had a drink with a certain assemblyman from one of the southern counties, a rotund gentleman named Nelson Hall. When I heard the name of his district, something tugged at my memory.

I said: "I seem to recall, sir, that when I was here covering the constitutional convention, I met a delegate from that area. Gilpin was his name, I believe. Do you know him?"

Hall looked at me in a strange way. "George Gilpin," he said. "Yes, I knew him well."

"Is he no longer in politics?" I inquired.

"He is no longer in Indiana," Hall replied. "Picked up and moved away several years ago."

"Oh?" I said. "I would have thought he had a promising career going."

"Many people thought that." Hall seemed to grow philosophical. "But politics is a perilous game."

"Evidently so," I agreed.

126

Hall hesitated a moment. I waited, knowing my patience would be rewarded.

"Well, seeing that you are curious about Gilpin, I will tell you the story," Hall said finally.

"Please do," I said. I ordered a fresh round of drinks, and he began:

"It happens that I was George Gilpin's opponent in the election of 1817, and I defeated him so overwhelmingly that it was almost embarrassing. But, truthfully, I can't take much credit. Gilpin was done in by a scandal in his own family. Seems he had begun to neglect his wife, and she had retaliated by developing a devilish passion for his brother-in-law, of all people. Just before the election, the lovers were discovered together. It was the most sensational tidbit the local gossips had ever had to chew on.

"Well, Gilpin went home and barricaded his family in their farmhouse, refused to set foot in public, refused to talk to anybody, refused to have anything more to do with his election campaign or anything else. They say he kept his wife locked up against her will, kept her a virtual prisoner. Meanwhile, I won the election by default, you might say. The next thing anybody knew, George had secretly sold his farm, packed his disgraced wife and their children and all their worldly goods into a couple of wagons, and departed."

Hall shook his head solemnly as he ruminated on these extraordinary events.

"A sad case, sir," he said. "A tragic case. I took no pleasure in that election victory, believe me. Especially since I've known Emily and her brother, Robert Morrow, all their lives. We practically grew up together."

At this point I remarked, "Yes, I remember Robert Morrow. I spent a pleasant evening at his home when I was here before."

"A fine fellow, Robert," Hall observed. "He could easily have believed that I was involved in a plot to ruin George Gilpin. But thank God he did not."

"A plot?" I asked, puzzled.

"Oh yes, there was a plot, all right. On the part of Emily's lover, the brother-in-law. I know. I was there, and saw it all. But I was only an innocent bystander, entirely without blame."

Hall tapped me on the arm. "If you write this story

127

for your Eastern readers," he said, "please be sure and make that clear."

"Yes, of course," I replied, having no intention of writing it.

"Have you heard of Gilpin since?" I asked.

"Robert is in loose touch with him," Hall said. "He went to northern Illinois and bought a small farm, to try to make a new beginning. Poor fellow. I hear he squandered all his resources, and went heavily into debt besides, in the pursuit of one burning purpose: to find his wayward brother-in-law and exact vengeance."

"Find him?"

"The man ran away, deserted his family. Vanished. Seems he was a fallen-by-the-wayside minister who had been in plenty of other trouble before this episode. They say Gilpin had armed agents roaming up and down the river for years, looking for the rascal. To no avail."

"Extraordinary!" I remarked.

"Yes, indeed," Hall agreed. "Politics is a perilous game," he said again.

"So is that larger game, Life," I murmured profoundly, and immediately regretted having uttered such an inane remark. But Mr. Hall liked it.

He nodded gravely. "You are right, my dear fellow. So very, very right."

The journalist then related a much abbreviated version of the story to his editor, concluding:

I can't help feeling that this tale, trivial though it is, illustrates something interesting about our national character. The Westerner thinks of himself as a new breed of man. Out here in the great inland river valleys, taming the wilderness and forging a fearless society, he sees himself as forward-looking, lionhearted, independent-minded, unfettered by the conventions that shackle his more tradition-bound brother in the East. But in reality he is as thoroughly enslaved by the rigid old morality as any strait-laced New Englander.

The puritanical spirit still lives in America, no less in the West than in the East, no less now than when it was brought to these shores two hundred years ago. I imagine it will still be thriving here two hundred years hence. Some things never change.

128

Part Two

1

IN 1824, when Isaac Hargrave was fifteen years old, he put on his only suit (a hand-me-down from his adopted grandfather Samuel Gilpin) and his one good white shirt, and went out looking for a job.

At fifteen Isaac was tall and thin and gangling. In this, as in his narrow face and the slightly aquiline hook to his nose, he bore a resemblance to his father that was disconcerting to many people. His disposition was warm and sunny. He was gentle, kind, thoughtful, both trusting and trustworthy, and his dark eyes were honest and level and without a trace of guile.

"He resembles Oliver in ways that don't matter," Sarah said of him. "In ways that do, thank the Lord, no two more different people ever lived."

Isaac liked people, and people liked him. But most of all he adored his stepmother, whom he thought of as his own mother, though she was only eleven years his senior. It seemed to Isaac that Mama Sarah's energies were boundless, her kindness and generosity inexhaustible. She took care of her own house and family, and in addition helped regularly at her parents' house, since Matilda was ailing, and aging rapidly. And yet our house is in perfect order, Isaac thought proudly, and Mama Sarah is always cheerful, even though her days are filled with drudgery and she has to contend with an eight-year-old son who is a constant trial, and a seven-year-old daughter who can't

131

be left unattended for one minute. But after all, it's natural for a boy like Lucius to be lively, Isaac told himself. And Martha—well, little Martha is loved, and always will be as long as I'm around. That was Isaac's secret vow.

Sarah had made a few vows, too. After Oliver had gone, she swore to be done with men and marriage forever. Men were nothing but a source of trouble and grief anyway, she decided. A woman was better off without them. She was strong and resourceful, and could perfectly well make a home for the children without a husband. This she resolved to do, and she was doing it.

She also vowed to love Isaac no less than her own children. This turned out to require no effort at all, for as the seasons turned and the children grew, it was Isaac with whom she developed the strongest bond of affection and understanding.

Samuel had never quite given up on Oliver. He kept saying Oliver would come back as soon as he could, and would explain everything. There was a perfectly logical explanation, if only people would keep calm and wait for it to come to light, instead of poisoning their minds with vicious gossip. Yes, Oliver would come back eventually, and make everything right.

Sarah would smile emptily, and keep silent. Once she said, "Papa, why don't you stop trying to deceive yourself like that? Why can't you admit there was one time in your life when you made a wrong judgment about somebody?"

"Because it's not true," Samuel said indignantly.

"It *is* true, Papa. We were all deceived. All except George."

"Don't be impertinent, Sarah!" Samuel growled, trying to sound fierce.

"Oliver will never come back," Sarah said flatly. "And if he does, he will not set foot in my house. Not while I can draw a breath."

And that was the end of it.

So when Isaac was fifteen, he looked at his beloved Mama Sarah and saw that her life was hard, and he decided it was time he earned some money so he could buy things for her. He observed other women of the village, the wives and daughters of prosperous men, sitting prettily in

132

the church listening to the bland sermons of Reverend Daniels, and afterward chattering like sparrows in the churchyard. He saw that they wore fine clothes and fancy bonnets made of brightly colored fabric, and carried parasols and rode in carriages. Sarah wore plain homespun, worked from sunup to dark every day of the week, and hardly ever went anywhere, even to church. Isaac brooded on the matter for a while. Then came the day when he put on his best clothes and went out to do something about it.

The business area of South Bar was strung out along a half-mile-long thoroughfare called River Street. At the upper end was a blacksmith's shop, and at the lower end, at the river, a sawmill. Between these were a general store, a handful of smaller establishments, and the Methodist Church. Isaac started at the upper end and worked his way down. In half an hour he stood discouraged at the river, having received nothing but negative responses.

One possibility remained: the sawmill. Isaac could hear very plainly the grinding of the saws at the millyard a short distance away. It would mean long hours and aching muscles if he could get work there, he knew. But that was all right; that was not the reason he hesitated. The reason was that the sawmill was owned and operated by a man whom Mama Sarah had forbidden him ever to go near.

Isaac picked up a few pebbles, tossed them idly into the river, and thought about the mill. He stood still for a while, listening to the grating sound of the tireless sawteeth eating into a tree trunk. Well, he told himself, there are times when a man has to make decisions on his own. Even when a man is only fifteen years old.

He took a deep breath and walked across the road toward the little shack that served as the sawmill office.

Late in the afternoon Isaac came to the house of Samuel and Matilda Gilpin, because he knew he would find Mama Sarah there. Samuel was in the backyard, unloading a wagonful of corn and stacking it in a storehouse. Samuel paused in his work and frowned at the boy.

"Sarah's been looking for you, Isaac. Where've you been?"

"I've been workin', Grandpa," Isaac said proudly.

133

"You've been working! Well, what do you think this is I'm doing, eh? I could have used a bit of help with this corn."

"But I been workin' for money, Grandpa. And soon's I get paid, I'm gonna give you some of it."

Sarah had come out of the house, carrying a load of wet wash. When she saw Isaac, she stopped and stared at him, horrified.

"Isaac! Look at you, you've ruined your good clothes!"

"They're not ruined, Mama Sarah, they're just dirty. I've got a job, and if I do good work I'll make two dollars a week, and I'll be able to buy things for you."

"A job! What are you talking about? A job where?"

It took Isaac a moment to summon the courage to answer. "At the sawmill," he said.

"*What?!*" Sarah shrieked. "You're working for Cyrus Thacker?!"

Isaac had a little speech all prepared for this moment.

"Mama Sarah, you remember when you and Papa got married? Cyrus lifted me up and sat me on his shoulder so I could see. And when it was over, he put me down and he said, 'Young feller, your pa sure is lucky to have such a beautiful lady for a wife.' He said that, Mama Sarah, honest he did."

"Hmph!" Sarah snorted. "Don't quote me ancient history, boy. I can't remember that far back."

"Mr. Thacker's a nice man, Mama Sarah. He asked how you were, and all. And he asked about Grandpa and Grandma too, and Lucius and Martha and everybody."

Sarah looked at her father, and her face was twisted with bitterness. "Did you hear that, Papa? He even asked about Martha. Isn't that thoughtful of him?"

"Well now, Sarah," Samuel said mildly, "I've got no more use for Cyrus than you have, but let's be fair. He wasn't to blame for you running through the woods in the pitch black darkness, like some kind of demented—"

"All right, Papa," Sarah said wearily. "Never mind." She started to walk away.

Isaac followed her. "Mr. Thacker said he's jes' been lookin' for a young fellow like me," he said. "He told me I could start at somethin' real easy, like stackin' wood, and work up to handlin' the saw."

Sarah increased her pace. "I don't want you working for

134

Cyrus Thacker. I don't want you having anything to do with—"

"But Mama Sarah, I'll make two dollars a week! We'll be rich!"

Isaac grasped Sarah's arm and pulled her to a stop. "It don't mean I won't be helpin' *you* anymore, Mama Sarah," he said gently. "I'll never stop helpin' you."

He took the load of wash from her and carried it away.

"You should have been here today, helping your grandpa, instead of hanging around that sawmill!" she called after him.

"Leave him be, Sarah," Samuel said from behind her. "The boy has to make his own way in the world. He might as well start now."

Sarah transferred her attention from her stepson to her own son, who was coming toward the house from the orchard.

"Now here's Lucius," she said. "And I can tell just by looking at him that he's been daydreaming again, instead of watching after Martha the way he's supposed to."

In contrast to the tall, lanky Isaac, eight-year-old Lucius was sturdy and thick-chested. As Isaac was dark, the younger boy was sandy-haired, with light gray eyes and fair skin. Isaac moved quietly, with an almost catlike grace; Lucius churned along like a miniature steam engine.

Sarah compressed her lips as she watched the boy approach. Then she called, "Lucius, where's Martha?"

"Down in the orchard, eatin' apples," Lucius answered with an air of nonchalance.

Sarah stamped her foot. "Lucius, you *know* she's not allowed to eat those green apples, and you know you're not supposed to leave her alone! Now go back and bring her here!"

"She'll be along in a minute," Lucius said, and kept coming.

"Lucius!" Samuel barked. "Go and fetch your sister here, immediately!"

Lucius stopped, glared at his grandfather, and turned back. On his way he passed Isaac, who was hanging out the wash on a line near the edge of the orchard.

"I don't see why *I* got to watch after the idiot all the time," Lucius muttered. "She ain't no more my sister'n she is yours."

135

"She is too," Isaac said. "She's your full sister, and just my half-sister. Besides, I got a lot of other things to do. I got a job now, anyway." A trace of smugness had crept into Isaac's voice.

"I don't keer!" Lucius grumbled, and went on into the orchard.

In a few minutes he emerged again, leading by the hand a pretty, tawny-haired girl a little younger than himself. She was dragging her feet along clumsily, kicking up dust, and was gnawing on a small, rock-hard green apple.

Lucius pulled her along impatiently. "Come on, idiot. Pick up your feet, can't you?"

"Nah, nah, nah," the girl crooned cheerfully.

When they passed Isaac, she held out the green apple toward him and smiled. "Nah, nah, nah?" she offered.

Isaac smiled back at her. "No, thank you, Martha."

Lucius led his sister into the house and set her down on a wooden bench by the hearth, where Sarah was now working.

Sarah came quickly to the little girl and took the apple out of her hand. "No, no, Martha! You mustn't!" she scolded gently.

"Nah, nah, nah, nah!" Martha complained, and tried to reach her apple.

"Can I go now?" asked Lucius, with exasperation.

His mother looked at him with eyes heavy with weariness. "Lucius, everybody in our family has to help, some way or other. You're not asked to do very much except look after Martha a few hours a day. I know it's tiresome, but it has to be done."

"Why can't Isaac watch her sometime?" Lucius demanded.

Sarah tried to be patient. "Isaac does, Lucius. For years he watched her practically all the time, before you were old enough. He watched over you too. He always kept both of you from harm, and he never complained, not once."

Lucius was fuming. "Well, I ain't gonna spend *my* whole life watchin' no idiot! That ain't no fair—"

"Lucius!"

The boy jumped, and turned toward the door. Samuel was standing there, and the look on his face was ferocious.

136

He strode quickly across the room and gave Lucius a cuff that sent him staggering.

"Oh, Papa, no!" Sarah wailed.

Samuel took Lucius by the arms and held him dangling off the floor. "Don't you ever let me hear you use that word again!"

Lucius gulped and said bravely, "What word?"

"You know what word!" Samuel bellowed. "If I ever hear you call your sister that again, I'll whale the daylights out of you!"

Sarah was trying to pull Lucius out of Samuel's grasp. "Papa, don't! Please!"

Martha began to cry.

Matilda's voice, weak and quavering, sounded from her bedroom. "Sarah? What's all that commotion?"

"Nothing, Mama," Sarah called. "It's all right."

She swept little Martha up in her arms and soothed her with soft sounds. Samuel had sat down heavily in a chair by the table.

Lucius stared at his mother. His face was blank.

"Can I go now, Mama?"

"Yes, yes! Go!"

Unhurriedly and with immense dignity, the boy walked past his grandfather and went to the door. He turned and looked back.

"Idiot!" he screamed, and fled.

Samuel went deathly pale and grasped the sides of the table. Sarah released Martha and rushed to her father's side.

"Don't, Papa, don't. Just . . . be calm. I'll take him home and punish him later."

Samuel was staring at her with fierce eyes, and breathing heavily. "Sarah, it may become necessary for you to keep that boy away from here."

"But . . . what about his lessons?"

"Damn the lessons. He may just have to do without education."

Sarah wrung her hands. "I can't come here and help unless I can bring my children, Papa. What am I to *do* with them?"

"I don't know what anybody is ever going to do with *that* boy," Samuel growled. He got up slowly and left the room.

Little Martha was whimpering. Sarah sat down on the bench, held the child's head in her arms, and stroked her sunny hair. She gazed out at the soft late-afternoon light streaming through the open doorway across the room, and her eyes were glistening.

"Oh God," she whispered. "Did I sin so awful, awful *bad*—that I should be punished so?"

The child cradled her head on her mother's bosom and cooed contentedly, "Nah, nah, nah . . ."

2

CYRUS THACKER had experienced a period of secret panic when his employer, George Gilpin, had abruptly sold his land and moved away, leaving Cyrus with nothing but the little cabin in the woods where he lived. Cyrus was only twenty-two years old when that happened, but he felt as if his life were ruined. He no longer had a means of earning a living. He supposed he could go back to Corydon and work for Robert Morrow, but he had been brought up in the out-of-doors, and the thought of being cooped up in a store sickened him. He looked around, saw nothing, and became desperate. He took to chopping firewood and selling it in small amounts in the village for a few pennies, or sometimes a bite to eat.

One day when he was working near the river, a small steamboat hove to, and the ship's captain hailed him and inquired if firewood might be obtainable in the vicinity.

"How much you want?" Cyrus called.

As much as I can get," the captain said. "We're damn near out."

"How much you pay?"

"Two dollars a cord."

Cyrus nodded. "I'll have two cords ready for you in half an hour."

The captain swore, and declared he couldn't wait half an hour. Was there a regular woodyard anywhere near, he wanted to know.

Cyrus studied the young officer's face. "You new on this part o' the river?" he asked.

It was his first voyage below Louisville, the captain confessed.

"Ain't a woodyard for fifty miles," Cyrus lied.

The captain swore again, and said he'd wait.

Cyrus went to work, and had been hard at work ever since. Within six months he had acquired his property at the foot of River Street, and formally established his business. A few years later he was one of the wealthiest men in South Bar. Nobody knew that, because he kept to himself, buried his money, dressed in dirty clothes, and continued to live in his primitive hovel in the woods. Most shocking of all to the pious villagers, he had stopped going to church.

The day after he had hired Isaac Hargrave, Cyrus greeted his new employee with a big smile.

"Well, how are you this morning, Isaac lad? Sore?"

Isaac grinned. "A mite, sir."

"Yes, I reckon you pulled on some muscles yesterday that you ain't pulled on in years. Now today I want you to slow down a bit, and move into it kinda easy-like. It takes a little while to git used to this kind o' work."

"Yes, sir."

"And, lad, you mustn't go 'round callin' me 'sir' all the time. You do that, an' first thing you know, I'll be takin' on airs, thinkin' I'm a gentleman."

Cyrus chuckled and clapped the boy on the shoulder.

"Now, then," he went on, "for today we're splittin' poplar. That oak over there, that ought to be loaded on carts and moved down to the river. After that, the green hick'ry ought to be stored in the shed to age."

139

"I'll take care of it," Isaac said smartly, and started away.

"Oh, Isaac—"

The boy paused. Cyrus came up to him again.

"What did your mama say? About your workin' here?"

Isaac tried to think of a diplomatic way to answer. "Well, she uh . . . she has some doubts about it."

"She don't think I'm a proper person for you to associate with." Cyrus offered the statement experimentally.

"Oh no, it's not that. She thinks I'm not strong enough to work at a hard job like woodcutting." Isaac smiled indulgently. "You know how mothers are."

Cyrus pointed across the yard. "Y'see them fellers over there, Isaac?" He was pointing to his other employees, a pair of big barrel-chested men who were working a long saw between them, demolishing a huge log.

"Them's my muscles. And they're all the muscles I need. Oh, sure, I'll make some use o' your muscles too, but I didn't hire you for that. I hired you mainly for *this*." Cyrus tapped his forehead.

"A business needs muscles, and it needs brains. You stay with it and learn the tricks, and pretty soon you'll be workin' in th' office, 'stead of in the yard. That's how I figger. You kin tell your mama that."

Isaac was impressed. He nodded eagerly. "I sure *will*."

"And another reason I hired you is . . . I thought maybe it might gi' me a chance to, uh . . . git acquainted with your mama agin."

Cyrus watched Isaac's face for a reaction. Isaac smiled.

"You think it might work, boy?" Cyrus asked eagerly.

"I don't see why not," Isaac said.

"Of course, *that's* somethin' you must *not* tell her."

"Oh, I won't. You can trust me, Cyrus."

Cyrus nodded. "I know I can. Now git busy, lad. And remember, slow an' easy the first few days."

Cyrus gave his new employee another clap on the shoulder and beamed with satisfaction as he watched him go to work.

In the afternoon Lucius came to the woodyard. He climbed up on the board fence and took a turn observing Isaac at work.

"Aren't you watchin' Martha today?" Isaac asked him.

140

Lucius shook his head. "I'm watchin' *you*," he said teasingly.

In a few minutes Isaac said, "You want to help?"

"Will you pay me?"

"Sure. If you do a good job."

Lucius came down off the fence. "What you want me to do?"

"Take these pieces and stack 'em over there on that cart. Stack 'em neatly, so they won't fall off."

Lucius tackled the task with energy. After a while Isaac came to look, and frowned in disapproval.

"No, Lucius! I said *neatly*. That's a mess. Straighten it up, now."

Lucius grimaced. "What difference does it make?"

"A whole lot o' difference! Cyrus wants the work done neatly, and he's the boss."

Lucius walked away. "Ain't gonna work in no dumb woodyard," he muttered.

"You'll be sorry," Isaac said. "If you did a good job, Cyrus might hire you when you're older."

"And I ain't gonna work for Cyrus!" Lucius snapped back. He went out of the woodyard and started down toward the river.

"Stop sayin' 'ain't,'" Isaac called after him. "Grandpa says we shouldn't say that."

"I don't keer!" Lucius yelled.

He went down to the river, sat down at the edge of the board wharf, and stared out across the water. A few minutes later Isaac came, leading little Martha by the hand. In her other hand Martha clutched a bouquet of clover blossoms. She brushed the tiny flowers against her nose, sniffed at them, and smiled up at Isaac.

"Nah, nah, nah," she said.

"Yes, Martha," he said. "Pretty."

When Martha saw Lucius, she ran toward him, held her treasure up for him to see, and babbled excitedly, "Nah, nah, nah, nah!"

Lucius nodded to her and looked away. Isaac walked up and glared at him.

"I thought you said you weren't watching Martha," he said accusingly.

Lucius grinned. "I wasn't."

141

"Lucius! You're gonna get in trouble, leavin' Martha alone!"

"She wanted to stay in Mrs. Jemison's pasture awhile. She loves to pick them dumb clover flowers. I knew she'd come along after she got tired of it."

"That field is full o' bees, Lucius. She'll get stung."

"Naw, she won't. Nothin' won't ever hurt the idiot. Jesus loves her. Mama says so, and Reverend Daniels says so. Everybody says so."

Isaac frowned darkly. "Lucius, you just better stop that smarty talk. You watch Martha now, and don't you let her out o' your sight, you hear?"

Isaac went back to the mill. After a while he came back again, straining at a creaking cart heavily loaded with wood. Martha was playing quietly near the water's edge. Lucius was still sitting on the wharf, his back against a piling. Isaac sat down beside Lucius, and wiped his brow on his sleeve.

"Whew! Hot work."

Lucius had his eyes fixed on some distant point across the river.

"Isaac?"

"What?"

"You think Papa will ever come back?"

Isaac didn't answer immediately. "No," he said finally. "He won't ever come back."

"I think he will," Lucius said.

"He won't. He ran away from us because he didn't love us. He won't ever change his mind, so you might as well forget about it."

"Maybe he didn't love *you*," Lucius said. "Maybe he didn't love Mama. But he didn't not love *me*, 'cause he didn't *know* me. I was too little."

Isaac gave his brother an angry scowl. "You're crazy!" he blurted. "You're jes' plumb crazy. He didn't love *any* of us, and he's not ever goin' to."

Abruptly he got up and walked rapidly away, back to the woodyard.

Lucius continued to gaze out over the bright sunlit sheet of water.

"He loves *me*," he said under his breath.

142

3

CYRUS THACKER stepped up onto the stoop at Sarah Hargrave's house, took off his crumpled old hat, nervously ran his fingers through his thinning hair, and knocked on the door. In a moment, Sarah appeared. She drew back when she saw who it was.

Cyrus smiled brightly. "How do, Mrs. Hargrave, ma'am. Good day to you." He clutched his hat by the brim, and rotated it in his hands.

"What is it, Mr. Thacker?" Sarah's voice was cold, her face hard and forbidding.

"Oh, I was, uh . . . jes' passin' by, ma'am. An' all of a sudden the thought struck me that I ought to stop an' say good day to you. Thought maybe you might like to hear 'bout how Isaac's progressin' in his work."

Sarah's expression remained stony. "I'm not particularly interested in it, Mr. Thacker."

Cyrus's smile turned sickly. He went on twisting his hat, and began to stammer. "Oh, I uh . . . well, I thought maybe, uh . . ."

Sarah relented a little. "Well, all right. How is he doing?"

The smile brightened again instantly. "Oh, jes' fine, ma'am. Jes' jim-dandy. I'm downright astonished by that boy, Miss Sarah. I hired 'im on mainly out o' kindness, on account o' he seemed to want it so bad. But, Lord 'a' mercy, in less'n a month he's done got to be such a big help, an' I done got in the habit o' dependin' on 'im so much—now it seems like I can't figger how I ever managed without 'im, and that's a fact. Jes' thought you might like to know that."

Sarah was unmoved. "Well, that's very nice. But I also know he's neglecting his duties here at home. He's got no business fooling around that sawmill. He ought to be here helping me, and helping his grandfather—"

"Oh, but Miss Sarah, that boy's got such a good head on his shoulders, he deserves to make use of it. You wouldn't want to stand in the way of his development, would you? Why, you ought to be proud o' that boy, he's such a fine—"

"Why should I be?" Sarah snapped. "He's no son of *mine*."

Cyrus gaped at her. Sarah closed her eyes and put a hand over them. When she looked at Cyrus again, she revealed a different mood.

"But you're right, Mr. Thacker. He's a fine boy, I know he is. And I *am* proud of him."

"Why, of course you are! Maybe you ain't his mother, but he sure is your boy, I kin tell you that. Don't know where *else* he could o' learned his sweet an' gentle ways."

Sarah lowered her eyes and withdrew a little into the shadows. "Was there anything else, Mr. Thacker?"

"Uh, no, ma'am." Cyrus backed away. "Jes' wanted to tell you 'bout Isaac."

"I'm glad to hear it. Thank you for letting me know."

"Oh yes, ma'am. It's a real pleasure t' converse with you. An', uh . . . well, good day to you, ma'am." Cyrus gave her a bow, with a flourish of his hat.

"Good day, Mr. Thacker."

Sarah closed the door, and Cyrus pushed his hat down on his head and walked away rapidly. There was a spring in his step, and he was humming to himself.

4

ONE GOLDEN DAY in July, little Martha Hargrave lay on her back in a bed of clover and stared at the sky. Puffs of cotton-ball clouds drifted slowly above her, floating in blue space. Martha reached up, trying to touch them, stretching her fingers as far as they would go. Having no success, she got up and stood on tiptoe and reached, but felt only the warmth of the sun and the soft air of summer. She lowered her arms to a horizontal position, extended on either side. She twirled. Round and round she went until she became dizzy, then flopped laughing to the ground and lay still, with her face buried in the cool clover.

Then she opened her eyes and gazed wonderingly through the labyrinthine passages of a shadowy green world, a vast miniature forest of clover trees, under which microscopic, multi-legged creatures prowled like beasts of the jungle. A tiny monster with a shell-like back appeared, peeping out from some subterranean cavern, inches from Martha's eyes. She reached for it; instantly it vanished. She scratched at the ground, looking for it, and destroyed the world it had lived in. It was gone and forgotten. Martha rolled on her back and gazed into the sky again.

Suddenly something bright fluttered over her head, very close, so close that she could almost hear the feathery beats of little wings. She raised herself on an elbow and looked around quickly, and saw a butterfly come to rest in the clover a few feet away. It was quite large, and resplendently colored in a fantastic pattern of black and yellow. The broad wings quivered, and moved slowly up and down.

Martha's eyes opened wide with excitement. On her hands and knees she crept toward the beautiful creature. When she got close, the butterfly rose from the ground, hovered for a moment, then flew away down the length of the field.

"Nah, nah, nah!" Martha cried in protest. She scrambled to her feet and ran after it.

The butterfly came to rest soon, but flew again when the child came near, and stopped and flew again, and still again, until at last it fluttered out over a rocky ledge and rose like a blowing leaf on a breeze that ruffled the surface of the river.

Martha followed, her face upturned, her eager eyes fixed on the elusive thing she longed to touch. She reached for it, standing tiptoe on the ledge of rock with arms outstretched, and pleaded with it to come back.

"Nah, nah, nah . . ."

She gasped suddenly and clutched at the air. The shining sheet of water below her tilted crazily before her eyes, and as she twisted, she caught a glimpse of the deep summer sky and the puffy clouds. She opened her mouth to cry out, but no sound came.

The butterfly floated on the breeze, high and away, drifting mindlessly out above the broad stream toward the shore of Kentucky, soft blue in the distance.

Isaac looked up from his work at the woodyard, and saw Lucius coming toward him. The look on the boy's face made Isaac stop in his tracks and stare.

"What's the matter, Lucius?"

"Isaac, you got to help me."

"What is it? What's wrong?"

Lucius swallowed hard and struggled to get his message out. "I can't find Martha. She's run off."

"Lucius! You left her alone again!"

Lucius's face twisted in panic. "I didn't, I didn't! I was jes' layin' under a tree while she ran around pickin' her clover blossoms, and when I looked up she was gone. I

146

looked everywhere I can think of, but I can't find her no-place!"

The boy's lips quivered. His voice broke, and rose again in a piteous whine. "I didn't mean to let her run off, Isaac. I didn't do nothin' wrong, I didn't mean to——"

"Well, don't cry, Lucius." Isaac patted his little brother on the shoulder. "I'll ask Cyrus if I can take some time off and help you find her. And you don't need to worry, I promise I won't tell."

After an hour of fruitless searching, Isaac knew he had to break his promise.

A searching party was organized, and grew rapidly as the alarm spread. By late afternoon most of the able-bodied men in the village were out, combing the woods and fields, beating down the grass along the riverbanks, and peering fearfully into the dark green water.

It was Cyrus Thacker who found her. He saw the blond tresses trailing like spun gold in the shallows a quarter of a mile downstream from the woodyard. With a great bellowing cry of anguish, he plunged into the waist-deep water, brought the lifeless body out, and carried it in his arms to Sarah's house. By the time he got there he was trailed by a throng of other searchers, grim-faced and weeping, and Cyrus was weeping more than any other. He laid his burden down on a grassy knoll before the house, and Sarah ran out wild-eyed, rushing toward him.

"Get away, get away!" she screamed at Cyrus. "Take your filthy hands off my child!"

She gave the man a push that made him stagger, went down on her knees and cradled the stiff little body in her arms, and wailed.

Samuel was hurrying toward the house from a nearby field where he had been searching. When he saw Sarah huddled on the ground, and the thing she held, he stopped and leaned heavily against a fencepost and put his hand over his eyes. From somewhere Isaac appeared, and came toward Samuel. His slender frame shook with deep, gulping, uncontrollable sobs. Samuel tried to speak, but could find no words, nor voice. He put his arm around the boy, and they stood close together, holding onto each other.

People had formed a circle of silent grief around Sarah

147

and her dead child. In the midst of the group Cyrus stood, dripping wet and trembling. Tears rolled down his cheeks.

Someone took the news to Matilda, lying sick in her bed. She received it calmly. She clawed feverishly at her covers, but her face was as blank as stone.

"It is better," she whispered. "I always knew the Lord would take her soon."

After a while some of the men gently removed the child's body from Sarah's grasp. Samuel helped his daughter to her feet and led her into the house. She sat down and stared into the fireplace for a long time. People milled about, leaning over her, offering clumsy words of comfort as best they could. Sarah took no notice. Gradually the people drifted away, and the house became quiet. Sarah looked up finally, and saw her father and Isaac standing there as if patiently waiting for her to return from some distant place.

"Where's Lucius?" she said.

"He's not here," Isaac said.

"I can see that, Isaac. Where *is* he?"

Isaac squirmed. "I can't tell you."

"What do you mean, you can't tell us?" Samuel demanded.

"He wants to be left alone, Grandpa. He feels bad."

Samuel glowered. "Why, the little—"

Isaac appealed to Sarah. "He feels bad, Mama Sarah. He didn't mean to do anything wrong."

Between clenched teeth, Samuel growled, "When I get my hands on that little devil, I'll—"

"You'll leave him alone, Papa," Sarah said quietly.

"He needs a thrashing!" Samuel barked. "Will *you* do it? *Can* you do it?"

"You just leave him alone," Sarah said. "I'll handle it my own way."

She got up and went unsteadily to her bedroom, and closed the door behind her.

Hours later, after nightfall, Sarah walked alone across the fields under misty starlight. She carried a lantern, and its light made a round little island of soft yellow, moving through blackness. Sarah went to an old seldom-used barn on her father's land, opened the creaking door, stepped inside, and lifted the lantern high above her head. She saw

148

the reflection of light from the boy's eyes, peering down from a dark corner of the loft.

"Come down, Lucius," she said. Her voice echoed hollowly under the time-darkened roofbeams.

Lucius remained silent and motionless, and stared at her.

"Everybody's had supper but you," Sarah said. "Aren't you hungry?"

There was no response.

"Lucius? I want you to know that I don't hold you to blame. Do you hear me, Lucius? You are not to blame. Come down now, please?"

"How'd you know I was here?" he asked sullenly.

"Isaac told me."

"He promised he wouldn't. He promised he wouldn't tell about Martha, and he promised he wouldn't tell where I was. He always breaks his promises. He's a dirty, no-good—"

"Lucius, those were promises that no kind and loving brother could possibly keep."

Sarah set the lantern down and stepped to the bottom of the ladder leading to the loft. "Come on, Lucius. What's done is done, and can't be helped. We just have to make the best of it. So come down, won't you?"

"I like it up here," Lucius said.

"You can't spend the rest of your life in a dirty old hayloft."

Lucius was silent for a moment. "If I come down, will Grandpa gi' me a lickin'?"

"No, of course not."

"Yes he will."

"No he won't. This is just between you and me. And I told you I don't hold you to blame."

Sarah held her arms up toward him. "Come on, Lucius."

Lucius gazed at his mother a few seconds longer. Then he crawled to the edge of the hayloft and climbed down the ladder into her arms. When he was on the ground, he looked earnestly up at her.

"Mama?"

"Yes?"

"I couldn't help it. Martha just ran away from me before I could see where she went."

Sarah knelt beside him and looked deeply into his eyes, and saw that they were red and swollen.

149

"What happened, Lucius? Tell me what happened, and I will never tell anybody, ever. It will be our secret, all our lives."

Lucius stared at the lantern on the ground near his feet.

"Tell me, Lucius," Sarah whispered.

Lucius went on staring at the lantern. "I lay down under a tree," he said. "And I went to sleep."

Sarah closed her eyes. She put her arms around the boy and hugged him. For a few moments she was unable to speak.

"We must pray to God, and ask Him to forgive us both," she said finally, in a whisper.

"Both who, Mama?"

"You and me. And especially me. It was more my fault than yours."

"No, Mama. I guess it was more my fault."

"Well . . . maybe God will forgive us. Somehow I think He will. And I think Martha will, too."

Lucius was thoughtful for a moment. "Mama?"

"Yes, Lucius?"

"Do you think Papa will, when he comes back?"

She gave him no answer to this. She got to her feet and smiled down at him.

"Come along now. Life goes on, after all. We have to get you some supper."

She picked up the lantern and took her little boy's hand and led him home.

5

IN WINTER the work at the woodyard was brutal. Isaac labored mightily, dragged himself home exhausted in late afternoon, and cheerfully set to work again, helping Sarah with chores in the house and around the grounds. In the evening he would sit by the fire soaking his icy feet in a pan of warm water, and speak enthusiastically of the sawmill work and of his friendly relationship with Cyrus Thacker, while Sarah massaged the aching muscles in his arms and shoulders.

"I thought you said Cyrus wanted you for your brains, not your muscles," she would say tartly.

"That comes later," Isaac would explain. "First I have to learn the business."

Once Lucius, lolling on the hearth, looked at his brother with open contempt, and snorted.

"Ain't nothin' to learn about *that* dumb business," he said. "All you do is chop wood and haul it down to the river, and then go back and chop more wood and haul *it* down to the river. Anybody can do *that*."

"There is too lots to learn," Isaac said. "You have to know which kinds of wood make good fenceposts, and which kinds make good building lumber, and which make good firewood, and all that."

"Maybe Cyrus has to know it. All *you* have to know is how to chop and tote, chop and tote, chop and tote."

151

"You ought to want to learn things, Lucius," Isaac said solemnly. "You know what Grandpa says—if you don't learn things you'll never amount to anything."

"That's all right," Lucius said. "Long as I don't amount to bein' a dumb woodchopper for Cyrus Thacker."

"Cyrus is a good man, and I don't know why you always say bad things about him."

"Because I hate him."

"But why? What did he ever do to you?"

There was a pause. "He chased my Papa away," Lucius said.

"He did *not!*" Isaac said hotly. "Papa went away because he didn't want to live with us anymore."

Lucius sprang to his feet, livid. "That's a lie!"

"All right, that's enough of that, now," Sarah said with authority. "Stop it, both of you." She settled herself in a chair by the table and spread the contents of her sewing basket before her.

Isaac watched her. "You've never told us what *you* think, Mama Sarah," he said. "About why Papa went away."

Sarah pursed her lips and squinted at her needlework. "I can't tell you what I think, because I don't know what I think. Nobody knows why your father went away, or why he never came back. Least of all you two; you were both babies. So I think you ought to leave the subject alone."

Lucius had sat down on the hearth again, and was hugging his knees and staring sullenly into the fireplace.

"I won't ever leave it alone," he muttered.

Sarah's needle paused. Her brooding eyes lay on Lucius for a moment before she resumed working.

The seasons turned; it was spring again, and the withered earth was reborn in warmth and bursting greenery. And Cyrus Thacker came again, clutching his hat nervously, and knocked on Sarah's door.

She greeted him casually. "Hello, Mr. Thacker." She did not seem surprised to see him.

Cyrus beamed. "Afternoon, Miss Sarah, ma'am. Mighty pretty spring weather, ain't it?"

"It is, isn't it?"

"Yes, ma'am, it sure is. Kind o' weather makes the old

folks feel young, and the young folks feel downright wicked!"

Cyrus chuckled, and twisted and twisted his hat.

Sarah waited. "What was it you wanted, Mr. Thacker?"

Cyrus waved his hat toward the road. "Got myself a brand-new buggy," he said proudly. "Wanted to show it to you."

Sarah leaned out of the doorway and looked. "Oh yes. It's very pretty."

"Got it yesterday. Delivered off the steamboat from Cincinnati."

"That's nice."

"It was made in Cincinnati, y'see. I ordered it special."

"I see."

"Steamboat took on ten cords o' wood on one end, and unloaded my new buggy at th' other. I says, 'Even exchange, eh, Cap'n?' Cap'n says, 'No, Cyrus, I reckon you owe me a few dollars on the deal.'"

Cyrus chuckled again. Sarah smiled faintly.

"I took Isaac for a ride in it this mornin'," Cyrus said. "He liked it a lot."

"I should think he would," Sarah said.

Cyrus stared at her. His hat was reduced to a shapeless pulp from twisting. "I was wonderin', Miss Sarah, uh . . . I was wonderin' if you'd care to . . . uh . . . go for a little ride."

Sarah didn't answer immediately.

"Old Red, he's a gentle horse," Cyrus added. "He goes nice an' easy."

"I wonder how you have time for such idle pleasures, Mr. Thacker," Sarah said.

"Didn't used to. But now that I got Isaac at the mill . . . I tell you, Miss Sarah, that boy's a jewel. I kin leave 'im in charge, an' not worry a lick."

"It must be nice to have hired help." Sarah said acidly.

Cyrus looked crushed. Sarah softened a bit.

"But . . . it's nice of you to ask me. Thank you, anyway. Maybe some other time."

Cyrus recovered instantly. "Fine! What other time?"

"Well . . . I don't know. Maybe Sunday afternoon."

"Good, good!" Cyrus quivered with eagerness. "I'll pick you up about two o'clock, how'll that be?"

153

Sarah began to hedge. "Well, I don't know, Mr. Thacker, I'll have to see . . ."

Cyrus wasn't listening. "That's fine, ma'am. Be seein' you on Sunday, then. Two o'clock. Sure hope it's a nice day, jes' like this 'un." What remained of his hat swept the air in a gallant flourish. "Afternoon, Miss Sarah."

He was bounding away toward his horse and buggy before Sarah could say anything more.

Cyrus's wish was realized; Sunday was a beautiful day. And in the afternoon the citizens of South Bar gaped at the sight of Cyrus Thacker's shiny black new buggy moving along the village roads with the stately grace of a royal carriage, Cyrus sitting tall and proud in the driver's seat, and beside him, primly pretty in a new bonnet, Sarah Hargrave. A new morsel of gossip had been deposited in their midst, and the people pounced upon it with relish.

The next Sunday Cyrus and Sarah went riding again, this time taking a long, rambling excursion into the countryside. When they returned to Sarah's house, Isaac came down to the road to meet them. Cyrus got out of the buggy, clapped Isaac on the back in genial greeting, and helped Sarah down. Sarah looked at her escort, and seemed to hesitate for a moment.

"Will you stay for supper, Cyrus?"

Cyrus's eyebrows went up in surprise. "Why, thank you, ma'am. I'd be proud to."

And Isaac beamed his approval with a broad grin.

For a man reputed to be a recluse, Cyrus was an energetic talker. He told anecdotes about his boyhood in Pennsylvania, praised the food, remarked on the cozy and charming house, and engaged Isaac in a lengthy discussion of plans for expanding the sawmill. Sarah listened, and noted Isaac's responses, while pretending to a demure disinterest. She noticed that Cyrus spoke to Isaac as if to an equal, and the boy replied knowledgeably and seemed to grow in maturity before her eyes. Sarah glanced secretly at Cyrus, and felt an odd glow of warmth.

The meal was nearly done before Cyrus looked around in sudden curiosity. "Say, where's the young'un, Lucius?"

Sarah sighed. "I *never* know where that boy is. I declare,

154

he's a trial to me. Just nine years old, and already unmanageable."

"Don't he know when suppertime is?"

"Yes, but you know how little boys are."

Cyrus shook his head. "No. Reckon I don't."

"Oh, it's nothing," Sarah said. "I'll fix him something to eat when he comes home."

"Reckon he ought to go to bed without supper once or twice," Cyrus said.

Sarah smiled apologetically. "I suppose I spoil him a little. Isaac thinks I do, don't you, Isaac?"

Isaac shrugged. "It's all right, Mama Sarah. He's the only one around you *can* spoil. I'm too old for it, and Martha's not around anym—"

Isaac choked off his words and stared at his plate, red-faced.

"That's true," Sarah said gently. "Martha's not around anymore."

After a moment Cyrus said, "Reckon Lucius needs a man in the house. Somebody to be a father to 'im."

Then, as Isaac had done, he lowered his eyes and blushed at what he had said.

A little while later, Samuel came to visit. He was taken aback to see Cyrus there, but recovered quickly, and extended his hand.

"How do, Cyrus. Pleased to see you."

Cyrus was on his feet, stiffly respectful. "Mighty pleased to see *you*, Mr. Gilpin, sir. And how's Mrs. Gilpin these days?"

"Ailin'," Samuel said glumly. "Always ailin'."

"I'm sorry to hear it."

"I have a nice pot of stew for you to take home, Papa," Sarah said. "I think you'll enjoy it."

"*I* will, certain," Samuel said, and sighed. "Matilda enjoys nothing anymore. Just lies in her bed and stares out the window. She talks of George a great deal now. Longs for him."

A brooding silence enveloped the room. Samuel made an effort to shake off the mood; he turned to Cyrus and inquired after the state of his business. Cyrus spoke at some length about the sawmill, and of the great asset that Isaac was proving to be. Samuel gazed absently at Cyrus

155

and paid little attention. After a few minutes he took the food that Sarah had prepared, and departed.

Cyrus fell to pondering, his eyes resting on Sarah. "That's a shame about yer mama," he said.

"Yes."

"And about George. Don't anybody know where he is?"

"Oh yes, we're in touch. Indirectly, through Robert Morrow. He's somewhere up in northern Illinois, running a small farm and trying to get back into politics."

"Well, why don't you get word to 'im that his mama's sick, and he ought to come home?"

"He knows. Mr. Morrow keeps him informed of everything. But he doesn't respond." A wistfulness came into Sarah's eyes. "I don't understand it. He just seems determined to keep himself distant from us. In permanent exile. As if he wants to punish us forever. And punish himself, too." Sarah's voice trailed off.

Cyrus was frowning. "But what's he want t' punish you folks for? What'd *you* ever do against 'im?"

Sarah picked vaguely at a loose end of the tablecloth. "We loved Oliver," she said softly.

After taking his leave, Cyrus walked down to the road where his horse and buggy were tied, and found Lucius there, examining the vehicle.

Cyrus beamed a hearty smile at the boy. "Well, hello there, Lucius! We were all wonderin' where you might be. You missed your supper."

Lucius's face was blank. "Did you eat supper at our house?"

"Sure did. Your mama invited me. An' a mighty fine cook she is, yes sirree. You an' Isaac are lucky fellows."

Lucius said nothing. His hand moved lightly around the wide curve of the buggy wheel.

"How d'you like my new buggy?" Cyrus said. "Pretty fancy, eh? Would you like to take a ride?"

Lucius took his hand off the buggy wheel and looked away. "Are you goin' to be hangin' around my mama all the time?"

Cyrus considered the question gravely. "I expect I am, Lucius. If she'll let me."

Lucius picked up several pebbles and began to throw

156

them, one after another, into the bushes at the far side of the road.

"You better watch out," he said. "If my papa comes back and finds you hangin' around my mama, you'll be in trouble."

Cyrus stepped closer to the boy and looked solemnly down at him. "Lucius, I think mighty highly of your mama. I place great value in her friendship, an' I place great value in Isaac's. An' I'd value your friendship jes' as highly, if I could have it. I'd sure be much obliged if you'd consider the matter."

Lucius sent the last of his pebbles spinning violently into the brush.

"You jes' better watch out," he said fiercely, and walked away from Cyrus, going toward the house.

Cyrus's face was grim as he got into his buggy and drove away.

6

BY SUMMER the buggy rides of Cyrus Thacker and Sarah Hargrave had become a regular and routine feature of Sunday afternoons in South Bar, and though the new association was still being carefully watched by a hundred curious eyes, it had ceased to attract special attention.

During one of these excursions, on a hot day in July, Sarah put her hand on Cyrus's arm and asked him to turn right at the next crossroads. Cyrus frowned at her.

"What you want to go on the old Willow Creek Road for, Sarah? That's a rough road."

"I'd like to go to the cemetery, please, Cyrus."

Cyrus's frown deepened. "Don't know what you want to do *that* for," he grumbled. It was a lie; he knew very well.

At a certain place along the wooded road, Cyrus parked his buggy, helped Sarah down, and followed her up the path to the quiet old cemetery. There he stopped and watched as she made her way to a far corner of the burial ground and knelt beside a small grave. After a moment he followed, took off his hat, and stood beside her.

"It's one year today, Cyrus," Sarah said.

"Yes, ma'am. I know." Cyrus bent forward and gazed at the oak-plank marker on which an inscription was cut in deep-chiseled letters:

Martha
Beloved daughter of Oliver and Sarah Hargrave
Born April 28, 1817
Died July 10, 1824
One of God's gentlest creatures,
She will make heaven a happier place.

"I remember the day Isaac came down to the woodyard and picked out that plank," Cyrus said. "I helped 'im. We spent pert' near an hour lookin' for the very best piece we could find. Then he took it to your father for the words to be carved on it."

Cyrus studied the inscription, his lips moving silently as his eyes scanned the letters. Then he turned and looked around the deserted graveyard. Songbirds twittered in nearby trees, and occasionally darted out into the sunlight, making playful splashes of color and movement, and disappeared again. Cyrus turned back and looked down at Sarah. He was twisting his hat again, something he hadn't done in several weeks.

"Miss Sarah?"

"Yes, Cyrus?"

"I ain't never had the gumption to talk to you about it. But I'd like t' talk to you about it now. I feel like there's

158

a burden o' guilt in my heart. Maybe I was to blame for little Martha not bein' born right."

Sarah's eyes remained on the grave marker. "You are not to blame, Cyrus."

"I feel like I was, some way."

"You're not. For a long time I tried to tell myself you were. But it's not true. You are not to blame."

Cyrus hung his head. "I felt so bad," he mumbled. "You jes' don' know how bad I felt. I wanted t' come an talk to you, an' try t' tell you, but I knew you was powerful mad at me, an' I jes' . . . I jes' didn't dare . . ."

Sarah looked up at him. She held out her hand, and he took it and helped her to her feet.

"But you *have* come, Cyrus. You've come and talked to me, and now everything's all right."

She smiled. Cyrus gulped.

"Thank you, Miss Sarah," he said in a hoarse whisper.

Sarah walked a few steps farther, knelt at the side of another, much smaller grave, and read aloud the inscription on its marker.

"Infant son of George and Emily Gilpin. Born October nineteenth, died October twenty-first, 1816."

She pulled some weeds away from the side of the tiny grave. "We have to watch after this one too," she said. "It's too sad for a dead child to lie in a cemetery and be forgotten."

In the fall Matilda died. Toward the end of summer she had seemed to get stronger, and was up and about, working the garden. One sultry day she became overheated, and fell down in a faint. Samuel got her to her bed and summoned Sarah, who found her in a cold sweat and mumbling vacantly.

There was by then a man in South Bar who called himself a doctor, and practiced a blend of theatrics and quackery that he referred to as medicine. Dr. Reece was past middle-age, but vain about good looks that had not yet entirely deserted him. He wore natty clothes and oiled his hair heavily, and it was charitably said of him that his treatments of the sick had not noticeably increased the community's mortality rate.

Samuel distrusted him utterly, but Sarah now insisted he be called. He examined Matilda at length, pronounced her afflicted with the "ague fever," and prescribed a foul-smelling concoction that reduced the patient to wretchedness and weeping. Samuel cursed the physician and sent him packing.

Matilda was bedridden again for six weeks, becoming increasingly remote from reality and lucid communication. In early October, she passed her sixtieth birthday without knowing it, and a week later died peacefully in her sleep. She was buried in the little cemetery in the woods, not far from her two grandchildren, Martha Hargrave and the unnamed Gilpin infant, on a raw day when the wind scattered the fallen leaves in all directions over the dry and crackling ground. Reverend Jonathan Daniels presided. He spoke mellifluously of the dear departed, repeatedly citing her distinguished role as the loving wife of the founder of South Bar. Sarah stood at her father's side, and on the other side of Sarah, alert with solicitous attention to her, stood Cyrus Thacker.

7

FROM THE JOURNAL of Lucius Hargrave:

As I look back to my childhood and that simple rustic life on the banks of the Ohio River, I find that my memory of those early days is strangely spotty. I recall isolated scenes and events, but the day-to-day progression of that monotonous existence is faded and blurred, like the remnants of a long night's dreaming that fled with the morning sun. It was a mostly tranquil period. But there were times of grief, moments of stark tragedy, and a secret suffering that

160

oppressed my heart for years. One of the worst of these was an event of such overwhelming horror that to this day, many years later, I cannot contemplate it without a stab of excruciating pain. That was the death of my little sister Martha.

There is hardly a word that describes Martha—wayward she certainly was, and unruly. But perhaps these terms are too strong. I am convinced that her nature was basically angelic, and that she never meant to cause trouble. She always seemed to me—and I still remember her this way —as an airy little sprite of the forest, no more capable of accepting the constraints of human society than (if I may be permitted a touch of whimsicality) a butterfly would be, fluttering upon a summer breeze.

Despite her innocence, Martha was a trial. She delighted in running away and hiding, often deliberately placing herself in some hazardous position, such as in the topmost branches of a tree, just for the mischievous pleasure of seeing the worried looks in the faces of those who came searching for her. In vain would our mother scold and lecture. Martha's merry young eyes perceived no danger, only innocent fun.

Once, on a hot summer afternoon, we discovered her gone. As silently as a shadow, she had disappeared. Isaac and I went to look for her, as we always did. But, alas, she had grown too skillful in her mischief, too cunning. We were unable to find her. We called for help, and a searching party was formed. Just before dark her body was found floating in the river. She had evidently attempted to hide on the steep banks that bordered the stream, and had fallen in. She departed this world at the age of seven years and two months, having lived and died in perfect innocence.

I always think of clover blossoms when I think of my little sister, for they were her favorite things. She loved to pick bouquets of them and, in the kindness of her child's heart, offer them to people as if they were a priceless treasure. I like to picture her romping through some heavenly clover field, adorned with tiny blossoms, reveling in such happiness as an ordinary mortal can never know.

But the cloud that most persistently darkened the days of my childhood was the continued absence of my father. As

161

I have related, he left South Bar under the most trying circumstances, accompanied only by his faithful black manservant, Camus, to go downriver and seek some more peaceful homesite for his little family. He never returned.

Need I mention that the mystery of Reverend Hargrave's disappearance was forever afterward the subject of the most spiteful speculation among the bloodthirsty gossips of South Bar? Many vivid theories were advanced, savored, and squeezed dry of every possible drop of titillation they would yield. The favorite was that the Reverend had deliberately and willfully deserted his family. This malicious tale appealed most strongly to base instincts, and therefore quickly gained ascendancy. Without a trace of credible evidence to support it (indeed, it flew in the face of all that was known about the good and pious Reverend), it quickly came to be accepted as incontrovertible truth.

I never believed it. Not for one moment, not even in the privacy of my innermost thoughts, did I ever entertain the idea that such an outrageous accusation could contain a shred of validity. The real truth was beyond easy knowing, and certainly beyond the reach of the gossipy tale-tellers of South Bar; they were as chattering monkeys, invading a temple and trying to improvise theology. No. What happened to my father was not so simple, not so sordid, not so *ordinary* as that. He was overwhelmed and ground under at last by the cruel torments of this world, or he was caught up in some higher calling that transcended all earthly connections; in any case, his fate was as far above the feeble comprehension of common folk as is saintliness itself.

But someday, I was certain, it would be revealed to me. I knew that I would find my father, and the truth about him would shine upon me like a resplendent holy light, and my faith would be vindicated.

One other thing troubled me deeply as a child, particularly in the later years as I grew toward manhood. It was a matter that may seem trifling compared to the grievous things I have already mentioned, yet it caused me profound distress. My beloved mother, overworked, reduced to poverty, and nearly bereft of her senses from loneliness, took up with that most contemptible of ignorant clods—and one of her adored husband's enemies!—Cyrus Thacker.

162

8

THE WINTER of 1825–26 was a hard one in South Bar, and the work at the woodyard was reduced to a near standstill. But when the spring thaw came and the sap flowed in the trees again, the mill hummed with renewed life and a greater prosperity than it had ever known before.

One day Isaac came home from work brimming with inner excitement, and sought out Sarah, who was working in the vegetable garden.

"Mama Sarah, Cyrus says to tell you he won't be around for a few days. He has to go to Corydon on business."

"But what about the mill, Isaac? Who'll be in charge?"

It was the question Isaac was waiting for. He swelled with pride. "I will."

Sarah's face displayed both amazement and amusement. "You? In charge?!"

"Well, why not? Cyrus says I know as much about the business as he does, now. He just hired two new men to do the heavy work, and he says they're to take their instructions from me while he's away."

Sarah smiled and ran her fingers through the boy's hair. "My goodness, Isaac! Managing a business at seventeen! I'm so proud of you!"

"Don't say that unless you mean it, Mama Sarah," Isaac said gravely.

163

"Oh, I *do* mean it, Isaac, truly I do!" She gave him a quick hug, and her eyes shone.

On the Sunday after Cyrus returned from Corydon, he came and took Sarah on the first buggy ride of the new spring season. He drove straight to the top of a little rise overlooking the woodyard, and pulled his horse to a halt. Sarah looked at him curiously.

"Wanted to show you somethin', Miss Sarah." Cyrus waved his hand at his enterprise below. "Look at that. It's growin'. Gittin' bigger every day."

"Yes. It's very impressive."

"Next thing, we're goin' to put us up an office building. Nice and comfortable. I'm going to have my office in there, an' Isaac's goin' to have his, right across the hall. No more wood choppin' for that boy, no sirree. He's too good for that."

"Nobody's too good for honest labor, Cyrus."

"Goin' to put up a new sign too, Miss Sarah. An' you know what it's goin' to say?"

"What?"

"It's goin' to say 'Thacker and Hargrave, Associates, Wood Products.'"

Sarah was momentarily struck speechless. "Why . . . *Cyrus!*" she managed at last.

"Y'see, Miss Sarah, I think it's time I made Isaac a partner. He already is, for all practical purposes."

"Well, I'm . . . I'm happy to hear it, Cyrus. If you're absolutely sure—"

"Oh, I'm sure, all right. An', Miss Sarah . . ." Cyrus took off his hat and began to twist it, examing the tattered edges. "There's somethin' else I'm sure about. Well, you know . . . I mean t' say . . . We been keepin' company quite a spell now."

"Yes, we have."

"And, uh . . . well, what I'm thinkin' is, I'd, uh . . . I'd kinda like to make *you* a partner, too. I mean t' say, in a different way, of course."

"Is this a proposal, Cyrus?" Sarah asked.

Cyrus slapped at his knee, as if Sarah had just solved a baffling puzzle. "By golly, that's it! That's what it is, exactly. A proposal."

"But Cyrus—I'm already married."

164

Cyrus edged a little closer and dropped his voice. "Miss Sarah . . . the reason I went to Corydon last week was to talk to a lawyer. Friend o' Robert's—very smart fella. I wanted to find out what can be done when a lady's been deserted by her husband an' maybe wants to think about gittin' married agin—"

"Cyrus!" Sarah had colored. A hand went to her cheek. "Cyrus, you had no right—"

" 'Scuse me, Miss Sarah, please. I jes' felt like I had to know, before I talked to you about it."

"Well, I just don't understand—"

"Wait, listen to what I found out. This lawyer says to me, he says, 'Deserted for how long?' I says, 'Pert near ten years now.' He says, 'No contact at all?' I says, 'None.' He says, 'In that case, the matter is easily settled. The man can be declared legally dead, and—' "

Sarah went rigid and looked away. Cyrus edged closer still.

"Miss Sarah? It hurts me to see you livin' such a hard life, tryin' to manage on nothin' when all the while I got more money'n I know what to do with, and jes' long to share it with you."

"I manage very well, Cyrus, thank you."

Cyrus picked up her hand and held it. "But I *love* you, Miss Sarah. If I had all the money in the world, I still wouldn't be happy, unless you'd consent t' be my wife. That's how much I think of you."

Sarah wavered a little. "Well, I appreciate it, Cyrus. And I'm deeply honored."

"Will you think it over, then, Miss Sarah? You don't have t' give me your answer right away. Jes' take as long as you want.I ain't a-goin' t' rush you, not one little bit."

Sarah was quietly thoughtful for a moment. "Yes, I will, Cyrus. I'll think it over."

"Thank you, ma'am, thank you. That's all I ask." He slapped the horse's rump sharply with the reins and yelled. "Giddyap, ye ol' devil!" and laughed as the horse pulled them away in a bound.

Several weeks went by, and as many buggy rides, and the subject was not mentioned again. Then, one fragrant Sunday afternoon in May, Cyrus helped Sarah into the

165

buggy as usual, climbed in beside her, and started Old Red off on a typically aimless jaunt.

After a minute or two, Sarah gave the driver a cunning sideways look and said, "Cyrus?"

"Yes, ma'am?"

"Do you know that I've never seen your house?"

"My house?"

"Yes. Where you live."

Cyrus laughed. "Why, my goodness, it ain't hardly a house, ma'am. It's jes' a little cabin."

"Well, I'd like to see it. Can we go there?"

Cyrus was appalled. "Why, Miss Sarah, ma'am, you don't want t' see a dirty ol' shack way out in the country. Why, it ain't fittin' for a lady—"

"Are you afraid somebody might gossip about us, Cyrus?"

"Lord, no! Let 'em gossip! I'm afraid you'd be . . . well, you'd be depressed by such a shabby ol' place."

Sarah folded her hands in her lap and looked straight ahead. "You know, Cyrus, I've been thinking a lot about what you asked me, not long ago. And I realize I've grown quite fond of you."

Cyrus licked his lips nervously. *"Have* you, ma'am?"

"But I also realize I don't know you very well."

Cyrus looked hurt. "Why, Miss Sarah! It's been ten years since I came here—"

"Yes. Marching Oliver along with your rifle cocked." Sarah giggled.

"Never mind that," Cyrus said gruffly. "I don't want t' talk about Oliver. I jes' want t' say that the very first day I saw you I loved you, and I've loved you every single day o' them whole ten years."

Sarah was serious again. "Still, I'd like to know you a little better before making a decision about *marrying* you. And to know a person well, you have to know his dwelling. You can look around somebody's house and learn a lot about him, the kind of person he really is."

Cyrus stared glumly at his horse's rump. "Yes." He sighed. "That's what I'm afraid of."

Sarah laughed. "Don't worry, I won't go there expecting to find everything neat and clean, as if a woman were in charge. I'll expect to find a bachelor's quarters."

166

"Well . . . all right," Cyrus mumbled. "If you insist." There was a worried look on his face.

When Sarah was ushered into the house she paused briefly, surprised by its smallness. There was only one room, with the sleeping area at one end and cooking facilities at the other. The furniture consisted of two or three straight-backed chairs, a small table, and a bed—that was all. The floor and the walls were bare. There was no clutter, and no bachelor's disorderliness.

Sarah walked around the little house and looked at everything, while Cyrus stood in the doorway and watched her. In the kitchen area, Sarah looked into the several cupboards, inspecting. Cyrus twisted his hat and waited. Sarah looked in all the corners, behind the stove, everywhere. Cyrus shifted from one foot to the other, and grew restless.

Finally Sarah came back to the doorway where Cyrus was standing, and fastened on him a long, penetrating look.

"It's nice, Cyrus. Very nice. I'm surprised."

"Oh, well . . . thank you, ma'am." Cyrus's tense facial muscles relaxed and formed a grin. Instantly he was the genial host, taking Sarah's arm and guiding her to a chair.

"Won't you sit down a bit?"

"Thank you."

Sarah took a seat, and Cyrus pulled another chair close to hers, and sat down.

"Could I fix you a cup o' coffee or somethin'?" he offered.

"No, nothing, thank you."

Cyrus leaned back and looked pleased. "Well! Now that we're here, it seems real nice and cozy. I'm glad I brought you."

"So am I, Cyrus."

"Do you figger you know me better, now you've seen my dwellin'?"

"Oh yes. Much better. I've found out something about you that throws a whole new light on things."

"Have you now?" A trace of uneasiness had crept back into Cyrus's face. "What was that, ma'am?"

"There's a woman who comes here."

The color drained from Cyrus's face. "A woman?"

"Yes. A woman."

167

"Wh—what makes you think—is it because it's so neat? A man can keep a neat house too, y'know. It ain't only a woman who—"

"There's a pair of women's shoes in the kitchen. Inside the tall cupboard."

"Is there now?"

"Yes. Very small ones. She must be a light, delicate thing."

Cyrus frowned in thought. Suddenly he smiled brightly.

"Oh, *them*! Why, them's the housekeeper's shoes, ma'am. Oh no, *that* don't mean nothin'—"

"You've never mentioned having a housekeeper, Cyrus."

"Why, no, I haven't, because it ain't interesting. It ain't a bit interesting—"

"I disagree, I think it's very interesting. Who is she?"

"Oh, uh . . . jes' a woman from the village. She comes in twice a week, does the washin' and a little cookin'—"

"What's her name?"

"Her name?" Cyrus seemed to have difficulty with the question. "Uh . . . Nell, I b'lieve."

"Nell *who*, Cyrus?"

"Uh, lemme see now . . . uh . . ." Cyrus pondered over this one in vain.

"Is it Nell Parker?"

Cyrus snapped his fingers. "That's it! Nell Parker. Caleb Parker's oldest daughter. She's a plain little thing, but she does good work—"

"I know her. Mr. Parker once bought a piece of land from Papa."

"Did he now?"

"Nell isn't plain at all. She's very pretty."

Cyrus's eyebrows went up in surprise. "You think so?"

"What else does she do for you, Cyrus? Besides housework."

Cyrus was seized with a fit of stammering. "Wh—uh—wh—what can you mean, Miss Sarah?"

"I'm sure Nell's looking for a husband, isn't she? I think I know how she'd go about setting her traps for a wily old bachelor like you."

"Oh, Miss Sarah, you got the wrong idea! Nell's a respectable young woman!"

"Of course she is. Intelligent too, as well as pretty. That's why I'm impressed."

"You're . . . impressed?"

"I certainly am. I've got high-class competition, and that impresses me." A hint of a smile played around Sarah's lips—a sly, teasing, seductive smile, something that Cyrus had never before seen on her face. "Suddenly I realize what a very attractive man you are, Cyrus."

He stared at her, struck dumb by a new kind of fascination.

Sarah got up and began to stroll around the room. She stopped beside Cyrus's bed, and gazed down at it. It was neatly made up, covered by a patchwork quilt that was ancient and frayed, but clean.

"Yes," Sarah spoke softly, as if to herself. "I have an entirely new attitude."

She sat down on the edge of the bed. Cyrus was watching her, entranced. She looked at him gravely, and patted the space beside her.

"Come here, Cyrus."

He went to her and sat down.

"Has Nell been in this bed?" Sarah asked.

Cyrus was pained. "Aw, Miss Sarah, don't ask a question like that—"

"Tell me, Cyrus. It's very important for me to know. Has she?"

Cyrus squirmed. His face was twisted in misery. "I *knew* I shouldn't 'a' brought you here—"

"I won't be angry, Cyrus," Sarah said gently. "I promise. Tell me."

Cyrus nodded, staring at the floor. "Yes, ma'am. She has."

"Is she . . . is she nice?"

Cyrus looked away. "I can't talk to you about such as that, Miss Sarah. It ain't fittin'."

"Just tell me one more thing. That's all I'll ask. Are you *deceiving* her?"

Cyrus looked his questioner squarely in the eyes. "No, ma'am! I'd never do that! She wants to marry me, but I've told her flat out, I ain't willin'. She knows it very well."

"But she offers her personal services anyway. And you take what's offered."

Cyrus hung his head and looked sheepish. "I never said I was a saint, Miss Sarah."

169

"And I'm not trying to act superior, Cyrus. After all, *I'm* not a saint, either. That's perfectly well known, isn't it?"

Cyrus raised his eyes to Sarah's. "You are to *me*, Miss Sarah. To me you're the finest lady in the whole world."

A soft smile stole over Sarah's face. "All right, then. I'm satisfied." Her hands were at work, unbuttoning her dress.

Cyrus went slack-jawed. "Miss Sarah—"

"Would you close the door please, Cyrus? And lock it?"

Cyrus rose slowly. "Miss *Sarah!*" he croaked.

"And close the curtains too."

Cyrus was trembling. "Miss Sarah, I never meant . . . I mean . . . what are you *doin'*, Miss Sarah?"

Sarah stood up and slipped out of her dress. Her ample breasts, inadequately covered by a thin cotton petticoat, stood out as full and golden as an autumn harvest.

"What am I doing?" she said. "I'm fighting the competition, that's what I'm doing."

Cyrus stood helplessly gripped in paralysis. Sarah waited.

"Well, Cyrus? Are you going to lock the door and close the curtains and come to bed, or are you going to humiliate me?"

Humiliation was out of the question; hastily Cyrus moved toward the windows. By the time he had secured the house and turned again toward Sarah, she was lying nude in the center of his bed. The golden harvest lay displayed, bountiful beyond measure. With an explosive grunt, Cyrus was galvanized into action. He flung off his clothes and stood over Sarah, tall, lean, rock-hard and muscular, and breathing heavily.

Sarah's eyes drifted up and down his body. "Oh, Cyrus," she breathed. Her voice was low and husky. "You're beautiful . . ."

She opened her arms to him, and he lowered himself into them with a great rumbling sigh of contentment.

Afterward they lay inert and limp, entwined in each other's arms and legs. Cyrus's head lay on Sarah's bosom. Her fingers played idlly in his thick black hair.

"Cyrus?" she whispered.

"Hmm?"

"Do you still want me to marry you?"

170

He raised his head and smiled at her. "Oh, more than ever, Miss Sarah. More than ever."

"All right. I will."

He gazed down into her eyes for a long, blissful moment. "Thank you, ma'am. And I promise I'll spend th' rest o' my life jes' tryin' to make you happy." He kissed her lightly and laid his head down again.

"You must promise me something else, besides, Cyrus. And swear to it."

"What's that?"

"No more Nell Parker."

Cyrus chuckled. "I done swore that to myself, already."

In a little while Sarah said, "It's getting awful late. I've got to get home."

"Mmmm, not yet," Cyrus mumbled. He kissed a breast and snuggled closer.

9

LUCIUS HARGRAVE, ten years old, sat on a log at South Bar's outermost point of land, around which his grandfather, Samuel Gilpin, had brought his family over a quarter of a century before. The reflection of the summer sky gave the surface of the river a soft blue-gray sheen. Lucius could not contemplate a body of water without an irresistible urge to assault it with stones. He had gathered a mass of ammunition and piled it at his feet, and was flailing away, spinning the pebbles expertly off the glistening surface and counting the number of skips. Five skips was his record.

Just then a steamboat slid into view from upstream. Lucius forgot about his game and sat with hands locked around his knees, to watch the ship. When it was opposite the point, Lucius stood on the log, went up on tiptoe, and waved his arms vigorously. Sometimes people on board the passing vessels would notice him and wave back, and the boy would feel a strange exhilaration, and see himself as a grown-up man involved in the affairs of the world.

Today no one noticed him. The steamboat slipped downstream, and showed its stern to the point. Lucius looked glumly down at the muddy shallows, and felt like a small boy again. He picked up a pebble, drew back his arm to throw, and was suddenly aware of his mother standing a short distance away, watching him.

She came toward him, smiling. "Hello, Lucius."

"Where'd *you* come from?" he demanded.

"I just had a few minutes to spare," Sarah said cheerfully. "So I thought I would come and see what you were doing."

Lucius started throwing stones again. Sarah sat down on the log and watched.

"What kind of a game is that you're playing?" she asked.

"You have to see how many times you can make the rock skip."

"How many times can you do it?"

"Seven or eight," Lucius lied. "When I can find the right kind of rock."

"Could I try?"

"All right." Lucius picked out a choice pebble, smooth and flat, and handed it to his mother.

Sarah got up and went to the edge of the river and flung the stone with an awkward motion that twisted her entire body. The missile careened crazily, spun down like a wounded duck, plopped into the water a few yards away, and disappeared.

Lucius's expression was one of patience under travail. "That was my best rock," he said wanly.

"I'm sorry," Sarah said.

Lucius shrugged. "I didn't wanna say anything, but girls can't do things like that."

Sarah smiled apologetically. "I guess you're right. Maybe

172

I just ought to watch instead." She sat down on the log again.

Lucius threw two or three more stones. None of them performed very well.

"Hard to find good ones," he explained.

"Shall I look for some for you?" Sarah offered.

"Naw." Lucius came and sat down next to Sarah. He picked up several of his remaining stones and juggled them idly in his hand. After a moment he glanced at his mother and said, "Did you wanna talk about sump'm?"

Sarah blinked in mild surprise. "Well . . . yes, I did, Lucius. I wanted to ask you something."

"What?"

Sarah smoothed her skirt and cleared her throat and thought about what she wanted to say. "Lucius—why don't you like Cyrus?"

Lucius stopped shaking the rocks. " 'Cause he chased my papa away."

"That's not true, Lucius."

"Yes it is."

"No it isn't. You don't know anything about it. You were just a baby."

"I've heard what people say, Mama."

"All you've heard is what other *boys* say. They don't know anything about it, either."

"They tell me what their fathers and mothers say. They say, 'Look at ol' Cyrus, ain't he the sly one? Chased ol' Oliver away, and now he's movin' into Oliver's house and takin' Oliver's wife.' "

"Well, that's just what I mean, Lucius. You've heard nothing but nonsensical gossip. Cyrus didn't have anything to do with your father running away, and he's never been anything but a perfect gentleman toward me."

Lucius was rattling the rocks again, so loudly that Sarah had to raise her voice to be heard. She put a hand on the boy's arm.

"Lucius, listen to me. Cyrus has asked me to marry him."

Lucius flung the stones as a salvo into the water, and sat staring stolidly after them. "Are you goin' to do it?"

"Only if you'll promise not to spoil it for me."

"I ain't gonna promise nothin'," Lucius muttered.

173

"Lucius?" Sarah's voice was gentle and pleading. "Lucius, look at me."

Lucius looked, but his face was set in stone.

"I haven't had very much in the way of happiness, Lucius. Don't you think I deserve whatever chance I can get?"

"You're already married," Lucius blurted. "My papa's your husband."

"No, Lucius. Your father deserted me nine years ago. We don't know why he did it, and we don't know where he went. We don't even know if he's dead or alive."

"He's alive!" Lucius cried. "He's alive, and he's gonna come back someday, and when he does, he's gonna—"

Sarah stopped him with a firm shake of her head. "I don't believe it, Lucius. Nine years is a long time. And anyway, after everything that happened, even if he did—" She glanced up at the sky, changing the tone of her voice and the direction of her speech. "I have to take what's left of my life and make the best of it, while I can. And I need you to help me. Please?"

"He's your husband, anyway," Lucius said stubbornly. "How come an old woman like you has to have *another* husband?"

"Do I look like an old woman?"

Lucius snorted and looked away.

"I'm twenty-eight, Lucius. I'm still young; I have many good years yet. Must I live them alone?"

"You got me and Isaac."

"You and Isaac will grow up and leave, and have families of your own. I'll be lonely, Lucius. I'm lonely now. Are you too young to understand about loneliness?"

Lucius thought about it. "No, Mama."

"Well, then, please. Let me have this chance."

Lucius stared at his feet. He was grinding them relentlessly into the dirt.

"Do you love Cyrus, Mama?"

"I'm very fond of him."

"That ain't enough."

"Yes it is, Lucius. It's enough."

Lucius went on grinding his feet. Sarah waited.

"Will you do this for me, Lucius? Will you be kind, and make friends with Cyrus, and give me this chance?"

Lucius got up and walked along the river's edge, eyes

174

down. He picked up a pebble, examined it, found it suitable, and sent it spinning over the surface of the water. It skipped four times before sinking.

He looked at Sarah. She smiled at him.

"All right, Mama," he said. "I'll do it."

"You'll be friends with Cyrus?"

"I won't make trouble, Mama. That's what I promise."

"Thank you, Lucius. I knew you wouldn't let me down." She came to where he was standing, and hugged him.

He accepted her embrace without protest and without response, and when she released him, he went on looking for stones.

10

SAMUEL GILPIN and his grandson, Lucius Hargrave, sat at the big table in Samuel's house, having supper together in the long twilight of a summer evening. Lucius toyed with the food on his plate without much interest.

"I like Mama's cookin' better'n yours," he told his grandfather.

"So do I," said Samuel.

A few minutes later, Lucius said, "When's Mama comin' home?"

"In about a week."

"What'd she have to go to Cincinnati for?" Lucius muttered.

"Don't play the fool, boy," Samuel snapped. "Cyrus and your mother are on their honeymoon trip, you know that."

175

"Honeymoon!" Lucius almost spat in contempt.

Samuel glared at him. "Your opinion of it is entirely irrelevant. So's mine. The right thing for us to do is hope and pray she's having a good time, and that she'll be happy. She deserves it."

There was a short silence, then Samuel glanced at the boy.

"Hurry up, lad, finish your supper," he said. "We've got a lot of work to do in your books tonight."

Lucius pushed his plate aside. "Don't wanna work in no books," he said.

"You've got to want to, Lucius. Otherwise you'll just go on forever being an ignoramus."

"I don't keer."

"Of course you care! Do you want to be an ignoramus all your li—"

"I don't keer!" Lucius shouted.

Samuel leaned forward and matched the boy's belligerent look with one of his own. "You *do* care."

"Why?" Lucius demanded.

"Because if you don't grow up to be a man of education and literate speech, nobody of any consequence will ever listen to anything you have to say."

"Don't wanna be no man of education," Lucius grumbled.

"What *do* you want to be, then?"

"I'm gonna be a steamboat man," Lucius announced.

"Oh, is that so? That's mighty interesting. What kind of a steamboat man, Lucius?"

Lucius frowned. He did not understand the question. "Just a regular steamboat man, on the river."

"Well, you know, there are lots of different kinds of men on the steamboats. There's the captain, the first mate, the pilot, the engineer, the clerk, the steward, and the deckhand. Which kind of man are you going to be, Lucius?"

"I'm gonna be the captain," Lucius said without hesitation.

Samuel snorted, "No, you're not. You're not going to be the captain. The captain has to understand the workings of the entire ship, from top to bottom, and entertain the passengers with witty conversation. You're not going to be the mate, either. The mate has to know how to run

176

the ship while the captain's busy entertaining the passengers. And the pilot has to navigate the river, and know every twist and turn of it for hundreds of miles. The engineer has to know how to repair the machinery when it's broken. The clerk has to keep accounts and records, and the steward has to look after the ship's supplies. Every one of those jobs requires education. No, I'll tell you what you'll be, my boy. You'll be a deckhand. You'll work stripped to the waist and sweating, in hot weather and cold, loading the firewood that Cyrus and Isaac sell, and throwing it into the furnace, and getting your face and chest burned to a crisp in the process, and eating scraps from the table, and sleeping on sacks of potatoes on the cargo deck—"

Lucius slapped his hands on the table top and pushed his chair back. "I won't! I'm gonna be the captain!"

"Fine," Samuel said mildly. "In that case, let's get on with your lesson for today. Have you read the chapter I assigned in the English reader?"

Lucius sat hunched in his chair with his eyes fixed on the floor. "I forgot which chapter it was," he mumbled.

"Chapter nine. The chapter on Didactic Discourse. Did you read it?"

"I read part of it."

"Why didn't you read all of it?"

"I don't understand it."

"Do you understand what 'didactic' means?"

"No."

"What do we do when we don't know the meaning of a word, Lucius?"

"Look it up in the dictionary."

"But you didn't do that, did you?"

"No."

Samuel sighed. " 'Didactic' means that which is intended primarily to instruct, to teach a lesson. The conversation we're having now is essentially didactic in nature."

Lucius flung himself out of his chair and lurched to the doorway, and stood there staring out into the dusk.

"Come back here, Lucius," Samuel said. "Come back and sit down."

Lucius turned and glared at his grandfather. "How come I have to learn so many big words?"

"You have to know words because words represent

177

ideas. When you learn a new word, you've discovered another little corner of human thought." After a moment Samuel added, "Now come on back here."

Lucius returned to his chair and sat down. The hard defiance on his face had softened into an expression of piteous misery.

"I can't learn all them things, Grandpa," he whined.

"All *those* things."

"I can't. I don't want to, and I won't."

"You can," Samuel said in a low, hard voice. "You *do* want to. And you will."

Lucius sniffed. "You never made Isaac learn all that stuff. How come you pick on me so much?"

"There was never any reason to 'pick on' Isaac, as you put it. He always did his lessons like a good and dutiful boy."

"He never learned much."

"He learned his arithmetic fine. As for the rest . . . well, he did the best he could."

"How come I have to learn so much more'n him?"

"Because, Lucius, you are Oliver's son."

"Why, so's Isaac!"

"Biologically, yes, I suppose he is." Samuel pulled his chair closer to the boy's.

"Lucius, listen to me. Try to understand what I say, and never repeat it to anybody. Isaac is a good fellow— honest, hard-working, loyal, trustworthy. But in the little office of Thacker and Hargrave, Associates, Isaac has reached the highest place of his life. That's as far as he can ever go. You, on the other hand, Lucius, you . . ." Samuel placed a hand on the boy's shoulder, and his eyes were aglow with a strange light. "You are Oliver's *true son.*"

Lucius stared at his grandfather in astonishment. "What's that mean, Grandpa?"

"You have his intellect, my boy. His keen mind, his sharp eye, his imagination, wit, resourcefulness . . . his *capacity*. You are made of the same stuff he was made of. You can do anything, you can go—" Samuel's arm arched through the air, describing the round world. "*Anywhere.*"

Lucius gulped hard, and sat transfixed before Samuel's ferocious manner.

178

"I jes' wanna go home, Grandpa."

Samuel set about clearing the dirty dishes from the table. "You are to stay here until your mother and Cyrus return from their trip. And we're going to use the time to good advantage, I can tell you that. You've been neglecting your studies. You're supposed to come here every day, and lately you've been coming twice a week, at the most. Now we're going to make up for lost time."

While Samuel cleared the table, Lucius sat motionless, gazing absently out through the open doorway across the room. The shadows of evening were deepening; the line of forest on the far side of the fields was turning a dark blue.

"Grandpa?" Lucius said.

"Yes?"

"You really think I'm like my papa?"

"Very much like him."

Lucius was lost in thought for a few minutes. "Grandpa?"

"What is it, boy?"

"Do you think he'll ever come back?"

Samuel stood over the boy and looked down at him. The old man's face was granite.

"Maybe," he said brusquely. "Maybe not. Either way, you don't have time to wait around. You've got your life to live, and you'd better get started."

Lucius stared pleadingly up at his grandfather.

"Fetch your reader, boy," Samuel snapped. "Open it to chapter nine. We will now learn about Didactic Discourse."

11

IN THE EARLY SUMMER of 1829, Sarah observed her thirty-first birthday, celebrated the third aniversary of her marriage to Cyrus, and announced that she was at last pregnant. Cyrus, who had long since begun to fret over the continuing lack of offspring, was overjoyed, and spent every spare moment mulling over a long list of names, masculine and feminine, and planning every detail of the growth and development of the unborn child.

In October he took a steamboat to Pittsburgh, to buy additional equipment for the woodyard, which was rapidly becoming a complete sawmill. When he returned home he brought with him, in addition to the new machinery, a trunk filled with toys and infants' clothing.

He found Sarah abed with a raging fever. Young Lucius was sent to fetch Dr. Reece, still the only physician in the community, though his reputation for professional competence had declined steadily over the years. Dr. Reece examined the patient at length and pronounced her to be suffering from "swamp fever."

"Swamp fever?" snorted Cyrus. "Ain't a swamp within a hunnerd miles o'here!"

Dr. Reece bristled. "Mr. Thacker, I know swamp fever when I see it," he said stiffly. He prescribed a syrupy, foul-smelling medicine of his own invention, labeled Dr. Reece's Herbaceous Liver Tonic.

In the middle of the night Sarah began to twist and

turn in her bed, became wild-eyed, and cried out in pain. While Cyrus tried to comfort her, Isaac saddled a horse and rode through the night to bring Dr. Reece back again. The doctor shut himself in with his patient while Cyrus and Isaac sat in the front room and debated whether or not to summon Samuel. They decided against it. Once Sarah screamed, and Cyrus leaped to his feet and would have burst into the sickroom, had not Isaac grasped his arm and pulled him back to his seat. Lucius, sleeping the healthy sleep of a thirteen-year-old, was oblivious to it all.

After almost an hour, Dr. Reece came out. His hands were bloody, and he was wiping them on a rag.

"She has lost the child," he announced casually.

Cyrus was on his feet again, staring. "Wh—what?"

"It was no more than six months along, I'd estimate," Dr. Reece said. "At that stage, of course, there was no chance of survival."

The doctor glanced at Isaac. "Would you bring me some fresh water, please?"

Isaac went to get water.

"It would have been a boy," Dr. Reece said to Cyrus. "Too bad." His manner remained casual.

Cyrus's fists were opening and closing as he stared at the doctor. "You mean you . . . you *killed* my *son*?"

Dr. Reece grimaced. "I didn't kill your son, Mr. Thacker. I saved your wife."

Isaac brought a pail of water and a wash basin.

"Thank you," the doctor said, and went to work washing himself.

"Where is the baby?" Cyrus said.

"I'll take the remains away with me," the doctor said over his shoulder. "You don't need to worry about—"

"Where is he?" Cyrus said. "I want to see my son."

Dr. Reece turned toward Cyrus as he wiped his hands again. "Don't torture yourself, man. At that age they don't hardly even look human. Concern yourself with your missus instead. The fever's going down, that's a good sign. I've given her a strong sedative, so she ought to sleep now for eight or ten hours."

The physician paused, noticing for the first time the look of despair on Cyrus's face.

"Look here, Mr. Thacker, it's just one of those things— happens all the time. Don't fret about it. Your missus is

181

a fine, healthy woman. Give her about six weeks to regain her strength, and—" He slapped Cyrus on the arm and winked. "Get busy making another baby."

Cyrus said nothing. His eyes were fiery coals as he glared at the doctor.

In the gray stillness of dawn, Sarah became restless again, and clutched at her bedcovers feverishly, whimpering in her sleep. Cyrus crept into the room, knelt at the bedside, and stroked her brow.

"Water . . ." she murmured.

Cyrus brought a cup of water, lifted Sarah's head, and put the cup to her lips. She sipped a little, then turned away and seemed to sink back into a deep sleep. Cyrus sat down on the side of the bed and contemplated his wife's face. Though her brow was creased by a faint frown, she was quiet. After a minute or two, the man's eyes drifted away from the sleeping woman and wandered across the room to the window. Beyond the yard, the trees of the orchard were barely visible, rising like dark specters from a ground-hugging layer of early-morning mist.

"I thought we might 'a' named 'im Samuel, after your pa," Cyrus said softly. "We could 'a' called 'im Sammy."

Sarah didn't stir. All the world was still.

"Little Sammy," Cyrus whispered. "Poor little Sammy."

Sarah turned her head from side to side and began to whimper again. The frown on her face had deepened.

Cyrus laid his hand against her cheek and said, "There, there, sweetheart. Jes' rest easy now."

She mumbled something unintelligible, in a weak voice. Cyrus leaned down close to her.

"What's that you say, sweetheart?"

"My darling . . ." she whispered.

Cyrus put his face down next to hers and kissed her on the cheek. Her eyes came open wide, staring up and beyond Cyrus's neck.

"Don't leave me. Please . . ." Her voice was stronger, but trembling.

Cyrus planted light kisses on her forehead. " 'Course I won't, sweetheart. You're my own dear wife."

Her arms tightened around his neck. Her eyes roamed without focus, fixing on nothing.

"Take me with you," she pleaded. "Oh, Oliver . . .

182

Oliver, my darling, I'll go with you. Anywhere . . ." She closed her eyes again, and became still.

Cyrus held her for a moment longer, then gently pulled her arms down off his shoulders and lowered her head back onto the pillow. She appeared to be sleeping again. Cyrus got to his feet, tucked the covers around her with great tenderness and tiptoed out of the room.

12

FROM THE JOURNAL of Lucius Hargrave:

My mother kept a home and raised my brother Isaac and me without assistance from anyone, and to us she seemed an angel of virtue, quite above ordinary human frailties. But there came a time when Mama's constancy failed. With secret anger I watched as Cyrus Thacker, who had played such an ignoble role in besmirching my father's good name, came to compound his sins by paying court to the wronged man's wife. And with dismay I watched her slowly weaken and finally succumb to his villainous attention. By some cunning maneuver of doubtful legality, the sacred marital vows of my parents were cast aside as if they had never existed, and my mother became another man's bride. I was as desolate as Isaac was delighted (for he too had long since fallen victim to Cyrus's wiles), but I was determined never to let my true feelings show, lest I injure my poor mother, who, misguided though she was, had surely suffered enough. So I kept silent, and did my best to put on a cheerful face.

Meanwhile, my early years were weighted with a burden that must fall in one form or another on every child: education. My tutor was my grandfather, Samuel Gilpin, and he attacked his duty with a ferocity that kept me constantly cowed and trembling. I will never forget with what shuddering horror I viewed the books he heaped upon me—the endless reading assignments, the pages of dense printing, like an impenetrable jungle through which I was expected to claw my way with my bare hands.

There was an ancient arithmetic book that had been used by a number of pupils before me, and with each successive user, the sums had been written in and later rubbed out, so that by the time I inherited the book, its pages were nearly worn through.

There was a huge geography book, containing maps of all the states of the Union—twenty-four at that time. Beyond the youngest and westernmost one, Missouri, a broad white patch of emptiness spread across the page, labeled: Indian Territory—Uncharted. How could a boy of ten or twelve look at such words without feeling a quickening of the pulse and a shiver of fear?

The standard work for all-purpose education was Noah Webster's *Elementary Spelling Book*, which, despite its modest title, concerned itself with a good deal more than spelling. It also contained proverbs, fables, and moral lessons, many of which I was forced to commit to memory.

But my grandfather's favorite text, and surely the most diabolical creation ever put on paper since the invention of the printing press, was Lindley Murray's *English Reader*. The official title deserves to be rendered in its awesome entirety, and I think I can do it: *The English Reader, or Pieces in Prose and Verse from the Best Writers, Designed to Assist Young Persons to Read with Propriety and Effect; Improve Their Language and Sentiments; and to Inculcate the Most Important Principles of Piety and Virtue, with a Few Preliminary Observations on the Principle of Good Reading.* Was there ever devised a more effective instrument for striking terror in the heart of a small boy?

Old Samuel Gilpin was a harsh taskmaster, it is true, but looking back, I see that I was wrong in thinking him

184

cruel; he acted with my own best interests at heart. During the time when I was growing up, there were no public schools in rural Indiana. If my gruff old grandfather had not hammered some smattering of education into my stubborn head, it would never have been done at all. Years afterward I recognized the priceless service he had rendered me, and yearned to go back, clasp his hand, and say thank you. But by then it was too late.

My educational development progressed in other ways as well, along lines of which my grandfather would hardly have approved. I very early picked up from older boys in the village a vocabulary of smut—a glossary of terms by which one could affect an easy familiarity with the details of carnal coupling. I learned that the first duty of a bride is to take off her clothes and submit her body to her husband's pleasure, which activity immediately results in the birth of a baby.

And now, in my worldly wisdom, I observed Cyrus Thacker and my mother exulting in their roles of husband and wife, and detested what I saw. When Cyrus looked at my mother, there was on his face an expression I took to be pure animal lust. Into my mind's eye came a horrid picture of that hateful man ravaging her poor body like a fiend unleashed. I felt sick. *Why* had that foolish woman fallen into this depraved condition, wantonly abandoning all the quiet and sensible virtues I had so treasured in her?

Time passed. A year went by, and another, and my mother showed no signs of producing new offspring. I became hopeful. Had I judged her wrongly? Maybe she was not permitting Cyrus to use her body in that disgusting way, after all. But the day came when she was at last swollen with child, and she coyly asked me if I would not like to have a new little brother or sister. I assured her I would be delighted, but inside I was numb with grief. There could no longer be any doubt. She was doing *that* with Cyrus. She was my father's wife, but she was living in sin with a contemptible interloper! My poor child's heart sank into bleak despair.

What was supposed to have been a happy day turned out a tragic one; the infant did not survive a difficult birth, and once again our family was plunged into mourning over the death of a child. My own sadness was tem-

185

pered, I am forced to admit. I had seen the death of Martha as a cruel blow delivered by a heartless Providence, but this event seemed to me a stroke of stern justice—divine punishment for the most sordid sinfulness.

But for me the worst was yet to come. When I was fifteen years old, the thing I dreaded most happened: I was put to work in the woodyard.

For many years, while Cyrus and Isaac went off together in the morning and came home together at night, I remained at home with my mother to help with household chores, and to trudge off every afternoon to grandfather's house for my daily schooling. But Cyrus watched my physical development closely (he cared not a rap for mental development), noted my robust physique, and eventually decided it was time I was set to doing "real work."

I knew it would be unendurable to me. I had seen those two businessmen at their occupations—Cyrus dozing all day in a room marked "Office of the President," Isaac across the hall in a little cubicle labeled "Vice-President," poring over lumber orders—both of them putting on preposterous airs and addressing each other as "Mr. Thacker" and "Mr. Hargrave." Outside in the yard, a half-dozen burly primitives labored year-round through the freezing desolation of winter and the scorching hell of summer, chopping, sawing, and hauling lumber. And now I was to be one of them. Very well. I uttered not a word of protest, but resolved to accept my fate with the calm patience that I had inherited from my father.

Sometimes people would look at me and remark how like him I was. And often there would be a strange look in their eyes, and I know they had meant to deliver a sly and devious insult. I had nothing but contempt for their ignorance; I could take such a comment in only one way—as the highest possible compliment.

So I toiled for Cyrus in the woodyard, and I did it with all the outward appearance of good spirits and sunny disposition. Though I could never in a thousand years hope to elicit a word of praise from the surly man, I was determined never to give him the slightest cause for complaint. I tried hard, and I did my work well. But secretly I brooded. I knew there was a great wide exciting world

186

out there beyond the confines of sleepy little South Bar, Indiana, and I was itching to get at it.

Carefully, deliberately, breathing not a hint to anyone, I laid my private plans. Meanwhile, I remained pleasant and submissive for my mother's sake. I knew very well what I had to do: bide my time, wait until the slow progression of nature had given me the maturity I needed to stand on my own two feet—then go.

13

IN THE SPRING of 1832, a wealthy Philadelphia banker named Edgar Whitcomb took his young wife on a steamboat tour of inland America. Mrs. Whitcomb was an amateur writer, and made copious records of her observations in a luxurious leatherbound diary.

On Board the *Cincinnati Queen*
Saturday, April 21st, 1832.

Dear Diary:

The early French explorers dubbed it *la belle rivière*. It was a lovely name for the loveliest of rivers, the beautiful Ohio.

Our ship, the *Cincinnati Queen*, is quite typical of the current river steamers. It is really nothing more than an oblong wooden box measuring some 165 by 35 feet, the enclosed area on the lower deck of which is occupied by a giant woodburning furnace and a huge boiler. This hor-

187

rendous machinery is somehow connected to a pair of enormous sidewheels, which transform quantities of river water into spray and toss it high in the air as they thrust the vessel forward at the breathtaking pace of ten or twelve miles per hour. It is said that the ship's boiler develops a pressure capable of blowing everybody on board to kingdom come at any moment, which dreadful event does occasionally occur. It frightens me a bit to think of it, though Edgar assures me we are perfectly safe, and of course I trust my dear Edgar completely—he is most impressively knowledgeable. (I must confess, however, I have been saying my prayers with uncommon fervor every night before I go to sleep.)

The passengers are divided into two distinct groups— cabin class, on the upper deck, and steerage, on the lower. This is a sensible arrangement, in that it affords folk of genteel background, such as Edgar and myself, a merciful degree of isolation from the common people on the deck below. (Our fellow passengers in cabin class are common enough, heaven knows!)

Most of the deck is taken up by a large central area known as the Main Cabin. Here meals are served, socializing (such as it is) takes place, and endless card games are forever in progress. Surrounding the Main Cabin are the staterooms—really just tiny cubicles enclosed by flimsy partitions, removable during the daytime hours.

The captain of this vessel is a genial, talkative man by the name of Jochum. His bleary eyes are screwed into a perpetual squint. His hair and beard are curly, close-cropped, and unwashed. He exists in what appears to be a state of constant confusion, which Edgar says is drunkenness. We understand he is part-owner of the *Cincinnati Queen.* That, according to Edgar, must be the sole reason he is captain. Edgar says if his station were commensurate with his level of competence, he would be the lowliest of the deckhands. (Edgar can be rather tart-tongued at times.)

I must mention one among our fellow travelers who seems of unusual interest. (Goodness knows I am not given to casting my eye boldly upon men other than my husband, but I cannot help but notice this man, so splendid is his appearance.) He is in his early thirties, I would guess, tall and handsome, with thick wavy hair of a pleasing light brown color. He is very well dressed, and has the speech,

188

manners, and general deportment of a gentleman. His name is Albert Pettingill. Despite his obvious good breeding, Mr. Pettingill moves with an easy conviviality among his less polished traveling companions. He spends much time playing cards with them, and laughs indulgently at their vulgar jests—though, I have noticed, he never descends to that level himself. I think he is a most charming man, and wish we could see him socially, but Edgar will not listen to such an idea. He says he has chatted with Mr. Pettingill once or twice, and has been strangely unable to ascertain the man's profession. He would never trust such a person, says Edgar, and I'm sure he's right. A pity. My, my, traveling certainly does expose one to a welter of curiosities!

So our journey progresses. After several days of steaming from St. Louis, on the Mississippi, we are now within a few hours of the city of Louisville, on the Ohio. It is a lovely spring day, and Edgar and I have been on deck since early morning, enjoying the fresh air. A little while ago we observed an amusing scene, which I may later compose into a piece under the heading: "Folkways of Rural America."

We came upon a little village on the Indiana shore called South Bar, which Captain Jochum tells us is one of his regular refueling points. There the ship stopped and the deckhands poured ashore and fell to work loading on board huge quantities of firewood. While this operation was in progress, a village youth came rowing around the ship in a small skiff. I had thought he was a full-grown man at first, judging from the size of the fellow, but upon looking closer, I saw that he was a lad in his teens, though of fine manly physique, a most engaging smile on his broad young face. As soon as he was alongside, he stowed his oars and stood up, balancing himself skillfully in his shaky little craft with his bare feet planted wide apart on the seat, and in a loud and confident voice hailed the captain.

"Ho, there, Cap'n Jochum, sir!"

Captain Jochum, who was standing near Edgar and me at the railing, waved his hand at the boy and returned the hail, greeting him as Lucius.

"You ready for me to come aboard yet, Cap'n?" the boy inquired.

189

"What d'ya think you'd do if you did come aboard, hah? What d'ya think you're good for?"

"Anything you want done, Cap'n," the youth shouted back. "Polish your shoes, wait on tables, peel potatoes, sweep the floors. Or keep the ladies company, if you please."

To my astonishment and chagrin, the impudent boy looked directly at me, and winked. The captain roared with laughter, as did the passengers who were standing near.

Obviously stimulated by his audience, the boy in the skiff began to perform daring acrobatic maneuvers, making his little boat twirl in a circle by some skillful twisting motion of his body. He was rewarded by laughter and applause, which inspired him to even more daring efforts. The passengers were enjoying his good looks and boyish antics, and he was plainly enjoying the attention.

At that moment the Mr. Pettingill I mentioned earlier made his way through the crowd and took a place next to Captain Jochum, and I heard him say to the captain in an undertone, "Let the boy come aboard for a few minutes, Elisha."

Captain Jochum appeared surprised at this. "What the dickens for? I can't use 'im."

"Maybe *I* can," Mr. Pettingill said. "I have a feeling he's exactly what I've been looking for."

A lively game was going on now. Several of the passengers had taken to tossing coins at the boy in the skiff, and he was reaching for them at great peril to his balance. One of the coins sailed over his head. The boy leaped for it—and came down with a mighty splash in the river. A howl of hilarity arose from the spectators, and when the boy's head surfaced with his bright grin still in place, and he held aloft the coin he had caught, a great cheer went up.

Captain Jochum leaned over the rail again and called, "Lucius! Come on board for a minute. Gen'l'man here wants to talk to you."

Lucius was in the act of climbing back into his skiff. "About what?" he yelled.

Mr. Pettingill leaned forward and called to the boy, "About possible employment."

Young Lucius emitted a whoop of excitement that set off another ripple of laughter among the spectators, and

190

swam furiously for the ship, towing his skiff behind him. As we watched, Mr. Pettingill descended to the lower deck and helped the boy aboard, then escorted him up the stairs, past the rest of us, on up the second flight of stairs to the top level, and out of our sight.

The crowd began to drift away, and Edgar and I did likewise. Something in my mind was turning over and over, puzzling me. As always when I am puzzled, I sought Edgar's opinion. (But of course, I employed the utmost circumspection.)

"Dear me," I remarked. "That Mr. Pettingill does seem to be a very cultivated gentleman, don't you think, Edgar?"

"Hmph!" Edgar snorted. "*Too* cultivated, if you ask me. I told you, I don't trust his kind."

After a carefully calculated pause, I went on, "What interest could a man like him possibly have in a young bumpkin, do you suppose?"

Edgar gave me a long look. "Well, my dear, there are certain unsavory possibilities that come to mind," he said. "But I would be disrespectful of my pure, sweet wife, if I allowed myself to discuss such vile things with her."

My ears burned. I must have blushed terribly. "Thank you, Edgar," I said quickly, and looked away.

Goodness me! I really must try not to be so curious. It's terribly unladylike.

191

14

MR. ALBERT PETTINGILL fished some keys out of his pocket, unlocked a narrow door just aft of the pilot house, and ushered the boy into a dark, secluded room. It contained a bunk, a table, two straight chairs. A small Oriental rug occupied a patch of floor in the center. Mr. Pettingill glanced at the rug, and then at the boy.

"You're dripping," he observed accusingly.

"Oh—" Lucius brushed uselessly at his wet clothes. "Sorry, sir."

Mr. Pettingill rummaged in a corner, found a towel, and handed it to Lucius. "Get off my rug, please," he said. "You're getting it wet."

Lucius jumped back. " 'Scuse me, sir." He stood in a corner, on the bare floor, rubbed himself dry with the towel, then wrapped it around his shoulders. Mr. Pettingill watched. He appeared to be pondering something, and his face seemed to reflect indecision.

"Look here," he said, "we only have a few minutes, so let's not waste time. My name is Pettingill. Albert Pettingill." He extended his hand, and waited patiently while the boy extricated his own hand from the folds of the towel.

"Pleased to meet you, sir," Lucius said finally, smiling and nodding.

Mr. Pettingill crossed the room and sat down in one of the chairs. "You neglected to tell me *your* name," he said.

"Oh . . . it's Lucius, sir. Pleased to meet you, sir."

Mr. Pettingill sighed. "You have a last name too, I hope."

Lucius grimaced with embarrassment. "Oh yes, sir. It's Lucius Hargrave, sir. Pleased to meet y—"

"All right, all right!" Mr. Pettingill said wearily.

There were a bottle of whiskey and two glasses on the table. Mr. Pettingill poured a small amount of whiskey in one of the glasses, and sipped it.

"So you're interested in employment, are you, Lucius?"

"Oh yes, sir, I'll say!" Lucius bounced up and down with eagerness. "I've jes' *got* to have employment, sir! I can't stand that woodyard no longer. If I don't git away from there pretty soon, I'll go crazy. My stepfather, he's about the meanest man that ever—"

Mr. Pettingill closed his eyes and waved his hand for silence. "Now listen, Lucius. I will ask you a question or two, if I may."

"Yes, sir."

"And I would like brief, concise answers, please. No elaborations."

"Yes, sir."

"All right. First—how old are you?"

Lucius took a deep breath. "I'm eighteen, sir."

Mr. Pettingill drained his whiskey, and poured himself another measure. "I'm a businessman, Lucius," he said.

"Yes, sir. I figgered you were. The minute I saw you, I figgered—"

"Now, business can be brutally competitive. Sometimes it's necessary to—shall we say—stretch the truth here and there, to gain a slight advantage over a competitor. In fact, I think that's true not only of business, but of life in general."

Lucius nodded in ready agreement. "Yes, sir, I reckon you're right, sir. I reckon once in a while you jes' got to—"

"But!" Mr. Pettingill said explosively, and Lucius jumped in alarm. "There is one person to whom one never lies. A man may lie, if necessary, to his wife, his children, his parents, his friends, his enemies, naturally—but *never*, under any conceivable circumstances, to a business partner. And that includes . . . a prospective employer."

Lucius gulped. "Yes, sir," he said in a small voice.

193

"Now then, Lucius—how old are you?"

"Sixteen, sir."

Mr. Pettingill smiled. "Fine. Now we can proceed. Are you willing to work hard?"

"Oh yes, sir! I've always been a good worker, you can ask my mama, or my brother Isaa—"

"Can you think clearly under stress?"

"Uh . . . sir?"

"Never mind. Can you stand late hours?"

"Oh, I love to stay up late. When I was a kid I used to sneak out of bed—"

"What about your parents? Are they likely to object to your going on board a steamboat?"

"Oh, I can handle my mama easy, sir. She'll agree to whatever I tell her."

"What about your father?"

"It's my stepfather, sir. He don't count."

"What do you mean, he don't—he doesn't count? If he comes at me with a gun, claiming I've led you astray, he'll count. What about him?"

Lucius hung his head and looked forlorn. "Aw, no danger o' that, sir. None a-tall. He hates me, always has. He'll be glad to be rid o' me, 'cause I'm jest another mouth to feed, he figgers."

"Very sad," Mr. Pettingill said dryly. He finished his whiskey and got to his feet.

"Look here, Lucius, I'll be perfectly frank with you. What I'm looking for is a young man about your age who is smart, energetic, alert, speaks when he's spoken to, listens carefully when he's told something and doesn't have to be told it again, and is willing to work hard at learning a difficult and demanding profession in which the rewards can be great, but are always uncertain. Do you imagine you might be such a person?"

Lucius hesitated momentarily. "Uh, Mr. Pettingill, sir, what kind o' profession are you—"

"I forgot to mention that he must also be willing to forego asking a lot of eager questions, right off, considering that he will learn everything he needs to know in proper order and at the appropriate time."

"Uh . . . yes sir."

"I can't offer you a regular salary. If you prove to be satisfactory, you'll start off getting twenty percent of what

194

I make. Sometimes that's a good amount, sometimes not so good. But I think you can look at me, Lucius, and see that, generally speaking, I'm accustomed to traveling first class."

Lucius let his eyes drift over Mr. Pettingill's beautifully tailored suit. He drew himself up to his full height, still several inches less than Mr. Pettingill's, and said firmly, "I'm your man, sir."

The employer looked his employee up and down. "I wonder," he murmured.

"Oh, you won't regret it, sir. I promise you, I'll—"

"As for your parents—they can't be expected not to ask questions, so you can say you've been hired by a special representative of the steamboat company, someone who travels up and down the river seeing to it that the vessels are properly operated, and the paying guests properly looked after. It's an important job, and one that has tremendous potential for a bright young man."

Lucius beamed. "Oh yes, sir. It sure sounds great—"

There came a loud clanging of the ship's bell, from far below.

"Wood loading's done," Mr. Pettingill said crisply. He retrieved his towel from Lucius's shoulders. "You get ashore now, and be ready to come aboard when we return downriver. That should be exactly one week from today. All right?"

"Yes, sir, I'll be ready and waitin', sir. You can depend on—"

"Fine." Mr. Pettingill gave the boy a pat on the shoulder, and turned away from him.

The ship's bell was still clanging. Lucius stared with earnest eyes at the back of Mr. Pettingill's head.

"Mr. Pettingill, sir? I'll make good, I swear I will."

Mr. Pettingill was pouring himself another drink. Without looking around, he snapped, "Get off the ship, damn it! We're pulling out!"

"Yes, sir!"

195

15

IN LATE AFTERNOON a flatboat lay low and quiet in a shallow cove half a mile downstream from the South Bar landing. It was a secluded place, protected by dense foliage and reachable from the village only by a narrow footpath. And in a clearing on the grassy bank, a man sat with his back against a small tree, puffing absently on a pipe, eyes half-closed and fixed in dreamy inattention on a lofty thunderhead far off in the sky over Kentucky to the south.

The man's name was Nate Collins; he was perhaps thirty-five years old, but his grizzled, grimy, weatherbeaten face admitted to neither age nor youthfulness. He was a small man, in all dimensions—short, thin, pinched-faced, with beady eyes set close together. He wore a buckskin jacket, and in his belt on one side a pistol, on the other side a knife. Nate inhabited a violent world, but because of his delicate build he had a distaste for physical combat. He preferred more sophisticated methods of settling disputes.

Nate was drowsy on this peaceful springtime afternoon. Soon his pipe was out, and he allowed it to droop neglected from his lips. But when someone came down the path along the riverbank and entered the clearing, he reverted, catlike, to instant alertness, ready for friend or enemy.

Then he relaxed again. "Oh, it's you, Luke. Didn't hear you comin'."

"Can I talk to you for a minute, Nate?" Without waiting for an invitation, young Lucius Hargrave sprawled down on the grass beside the older man.

Nate unhurriedly knocked the cold ashes out of his pipe and put it away. "I reckon. What's on your mind?"

"You know how I been helpin' you build your boat, and brought you lumber from the woodyard and all, and you said you'd take me in as a partner this year? Well—"

"Naw, naw, that ain't what I said. I said you could come along this year as a learner. A *learner*, Luke—there's a hell of a difference 'tween that and a partner."

"All right, a learner. Anyway, I can't come, Nate. I've had a change of plans. Hope it don't leave you short-handed."

Nate shrugged it off. "Naw, it don't matter. I got Josh and Otto, that's all the crew I need. Fact is, another body on board mighta made it a bit crowded."

"Well, good. You know, I wouldn't want to put you out or anything. It's just that something's come up all of a sudden, and I think it'd be better for me."

Lucius waited to be asked for an explanation, eager to provide it. But Nate was blissfully free of curiosity. He leaned his head against the tree and gazed dully at his flatboat rocking almost imperceptibly in the placid water of the cove.

"Tell you the honest truth, Luke, I don't figger you'd be worth a damn on a flatboat, anyway. You ain't the type. Not tough enough. You got to be tough to ride a flatboat, Luke. Got to be tough to live with the likes o' Josh Everett and Otto Grieshaber. They're animals. Nothin' but animals."

"Then how come you hire 'em as crew?"

" 'Cause they're damn good flatboatmen. Best on the river, and that's a fact. And I get along with 'em fine, no problem a-tall. Only trouble is, neither one of 'em talk English worth a good goddamn. That's mainly why I said you could come along, Luke—so I'd have somebody to talk to."

"Yeah, I know." Lucius chuckled, and shook his head in sympathy. "Josh and that Kentucky backwoods drawl of his, and Otto spoutin' his crazy mixture of English and

197

German—can't hardly understand a word they say, can you? Listen, I'm really sorry to let you down like this, Nate. But this other thing that came up, it's just too good to miss."

"Yeah, yeah, that's all right. It don't matter, Luke. Maybe next year." Nate's eyelids were drooping again.

Lucius squirmed with impatience. "Hey, Nate, don't you want to know what I'm gonna do?"

"Hmm? Oh, sure. I'm listenin'."

"I'm goin' to work on a steamboat."

Nate's eyes opened wide. "You're what?" For the first time he displayed a modicum of interest—distinctly disapproving.

"I met this fella by the name of Mr. Pettingill. He's a big man in a steamboat company, maybe the owner or somethin' like that—rides up and down the river on the *Cincinnati Queen*. He wants me to come to work for him. Ain't that great? Hundreds o' people along the river to choose from, and he picks me? Now, you know I couldn't turn down a chance like that, could I?"

Nate was scowling. "You're crazier'n hell, Luke boy."

"What d'ya mean?"

"Them steamboatmen can't be trusted. Crooked as the river, every dang one of 'em. Son o' bitches, dressed up in fancy clothes. Naw, you don't want to go to work for one o' them."

"Oh, no, Mr. Pettingill ain't like that at all. He's a real high-class gentleman. He's—"

"Ha!" Nate spat, signifying contempt.

"The *Queen*'ll be back downriver next Saturday," Lucius said firmly. "And I'm goin' on board."

Nate shrugged. "Well, lots o' luck to you." He was losing interest again.

"The thing is, though, Nate, uh . . . you said I could go with you for the work I did on the boat, and the lumber and all. But since I can't go, I thought maybe you could, uh . . . you could pay me instead."

Nate blinked, frowned, looked hard at the boy. "Pay you?" He seemed unsure of what he had heard. *"Pay you?"*

"Well, I mean . . . it must be worth *somethin'*, ain't it?"

"Sure. Worth a ride to New Awleens. But you don't want that, so—"

198

"I need money, Nate. Need it bad."

"I ain't got no money. When I get back in the fall, maybe I'll have some. Talk to me then."

"I won't *be* here then."

Nate smiled, revealing gaping holes once occupied by teeth. "Well, there you are." He was clearly unperturbed by the problem.

Lucius was growing agitated. "Listen, Nate, you got to help me. It's a whole week till next Saturday. How'm I goin' to get through it?"

Now Nate was puzzled. "I don't get you."

"I can't go back to that damned woodyard. I came ashore from talkin' to Mr. Pettingill on the *Queen,* and I stopped and looked at those men workin' in there—you talkin' about animals, Nate, there you got *animals.* Saw a log and drag it away, saw another log and drag it away, saw and drag, saw and drag, sweatin' and groanin' and strainin' every day of their miserable lives, rain or shine. I tell you, Nate, I can't go back there. Not for a week, not for a day, not even for an hour."

Gravely Nate considered the problem. "Well, you can come stay here with us, I reckon. Till Wednesday, that is. We're shovin' off Wednesday mornin'."

"All right. Thanks. I'll stay here with you till Wednesday, and after that, I don't know. Maybe I'll just stay here by myself till Saturday comes." Shoulders hunched despondently and looking like an abandoned orphan, Lucius stared at the ground.

Nate smiled again; his heart was touched. "Lemme tell you somethin', Luke. You don't want to go on one o' them ugly smoke-belchin' steamboats. Them things ain't safe. Sooner or later, every dang one of 'em blows up and scatters human bodies all over the river and the countryside around. Why, they tell me the average life of a steamboat is five years. How old's the *Cincinnati Queen,* Luke?"

"Umm . . ." Lucius seemed reluctant to answer. "She was launched in 'twenty-eight, I think."

Nate slapped his thigh, greatly pleased. "Well, now, looka there—she's gettin' on toward five years old. She won't last much longer. And when she goes, and you're flyin' through the air in two or three different directions, you'll wish you'd never set foot on the damn thing. You'll wish you'd 'a' went with me."

Lucius was listening intently, a look of painful uncertainty on his face. Nate thought he saw an advantage, and pressed on.

"Now a flatboat, Luke, it ain't only safe, it's a dang sight more fun. On a flatboat you ride smooth and quiet, right next to the river. You can *feel* the river, Luke, just like it was your mother, an' you was a little baby. You can feel it movin' an' murmurin' under you, so sweet an' peaceful it lulls you right to sleep. But on a steamboat you're ridin' on a two- or three-story building that creaks an' groans an' rocks like it was about to collapse an' fall down any minute, an' all the time down in its innards the boiler's spittin' an' sputterin' an' gettin' ready to blow the whole mess to kingdom come."

Nate leaned his head back against the tree and laughed. "Christ, Luke, you couldn't get me on board one o' them damn floatin' coffins for nothin'."

Lucius sat still for a while, rubbing his hands together and thinking about what he had heard. Then, with a sigh, he got to his feet.

"Well, thanks, Nate. I appreciate your advice."

"Come on back this evenin' if you want to," Nate said genially. "Josh an' Otto'll be here by then. We'll break out a jug o' whiskey from the cargo an' have a little party."

Lucius remained thoughtful. "I could still come with you if I wanted to, huh, Nate?"

"I made a deal with you, didn't I? I don't go back on a deal. It's you that's goin' back on it."

Lucius's boyish face brightened with a sudden happy thought. "Y'know, I'm in a pretty good spot right now, ain't I? I could go one way or the other. I could make a choice."

Nate grinned up at him. "See you later, Luke boy."

Lucius gave the man a jaunty wave and turned away, and as he walked back up the path toward town, his step was springy with youthful confidence.

16

AT THE END of the day, when Cyrus and Isaac came home from work, Sarah was busy in the kitchen.

"Hello!" she called out cheerily.

"Where's Lucius?" Cyrus growled. His face was grim.

Sarah looked at him in surprise. "What do you mean? Wasn't he at work?"

"Not since early this afternoon. You mean he ain't been here?"

"Why, no . . ." Sarah searched the faces of both men. "What's the matter? Did something happen?"

"Oh, nothin' unusual," Cyrus said. "Lucius jes' walked off the job, that's all. Nothin' unusual 'bout *that*."

"He didn't just walk off the job," Isaac said. "He was actin' real strange, so I told him he could go home early—"

"See? That's what I mean about special privileges!" Cyrus stomped about the room, fuming. "An' I'm tellin' you for the last time, Isaac, I won't put up with it. Lucius is supposed to follow the same rules the other men do. If he gits special treatment, the others think it's unfair, an' they're right, by God—"

Sarah was standing before Isaac, ignoring Cyrus's tirade. "What was he acting strange about?"

Isaac began to fidget. "Well . . . I don't exactly know what about. He rowed out to a steamboat this afternoon, and—"

201

"Jes' what he's got no dang business doin'!" Cyrus grumbled. "If I've told him once, I've told him a thousand—"

"Cyrus, be quiet!" Sarah snapped. "Go on, Isaac."

"When he came back in, he was actin' funny."

"In what way funny?"

"Like maybe somethin' had happened. His clothes were damp—he said he'd fallen in the river. I told him he could go home and change. Maybe he just went for a walk instead. I reckon he'll be home soon."

"He better be," Cyrus muttered.

Sarah gave her husband a cold look and went back to the kitchen. Cyrus followed her.

"I'm goin' to have it out with that boy, Sarah, once an' for all. I've had about all I can take. He ain't worth a hill o' beans—I swear I'd be better off without 'im."

"Then why don't you apprentice him somewhere else? I always thought it was a mistake for Lucius to work for you."

Cyrus snorted. "Hell, I wouldn't wish that lazy, smart-alecky young jackanapes on anybody else. That'd be an insult!"

Sarah's eyes flashed anger. "Lucius hates that woodyard, always has, and you know it. You can't expect a boy to be good at work he hates."

" 'Course, I knew you'd take his side," Cyrus said, and glared at her. "You always do. That's his main trouble, bein' coddled all his life by—"

"Excuse me," Sarah said. She brushed Cyrus aside as she bustled about the kitchen.

Cyrus continued to follow her. "It ain't fair, damn it. All my life I've wanted to have a family business. To have sons, an' have my sons in my business with me. All my life I've dreamed about it."

"Well, you can't arrange people's lives just to suit what *you* want, without a thought to what *they* might want. That's selfish."

"What the devil's selfish about wantin' to fix your sons up with a ready-made business? And what son wouldn't be grateful for a chance like what I'm offerin' that good-for-nothin'—"

Sarah whirled on him. "Lucius is not your son!" She spat the words at him like snake's venom.

In the silence that followed, she became flustered, wiped

202

her hands nervously on her apron, and turned back to her work.

" 'Scuse me," Isaac mumbled from across the room. "Guess I'll go wash up." He went out toward the back of the house.

Cyrus still stood in the kitchen. His eyes were fixed on Sarah's back.

After a moment she spoke again, very softly, without looking at him. "I'm sorry, Cyrus. I didn't mean it to sound like that."

Cyrus sighed. "Guess I'll go wash up too," he said, and went out.

They ate supper in a strained silence. Sarah kept one ear cocked toward the door, listening for Lucius's footfall. They had finished their meal and Sarah was clearing the table when Lucius came whistling up the front walkway out of the twilight and strode in, flashing a smile in all directions.

"How do, folks!" He went into the kitchen, pinched his mother's ribs, and kissed her on the cheek.

"Sorry I'm late, Mama. Got any leftovers?"

She was frowning at him. "Lucius, you ought to be ashamed! Where have you been?"

"Talkin' to some people," he said flippantly. "Talkin' business."

"Well, you're naughty!" Sarah said.

He chuckled at her feeble scolding, and pinched her again.

"Stop that! Go and wash your hands, and I'll bring you a plate."

"Much obliged, sweetheart." He went to the table and sat down, and beamed his amiable grin at first Isaac and then Cyrus.

"Your mother said for you to wash your hands," Cyrus said in a low, hard voice.

"They're clean." Lucius held his hands up for inspection. "I didn't do much work today, so they didn't get dirty." He giggled.

Sarah brought a plate of food and set it in front of him, and he attacked it with relish. From the other side of the table, Cyrus watched him.

"Seems to me like I recollect the first time I ever came

203

here for a meal," Cyrus said. "You were late, an' your mama had to save you somethin' to eat. Here 'tis seven or eight years later, an' you still ain't learned when suppertime is."

Lucius looked vacantly around the room while he chewed a huge mouthful. Cyrus went on, "The rules around here are very simple, Lucius. Everybody does his share o' the work. Your mama works here at the house, an' me an' Isaac, we work at the sawmill. An' most of us show proper respect an' consideration for the others, like not shirkin' our duties, an' bein' on time for meals, and such as that. But seems to me like you ain't had much respect for rules, Lucius. You jes' do as you please, an' to hell with everybody else. Now I think it's time you learned better'n that."

Lucius ate heartily, and while he ate, his eyes roamed idly around the room.

"I'm talkin' to you, Lucius," Cyrus said sharply.

Lucius's wandering gaze came around to rest on Cyrus, and his lifted eyebrows registered mild surprise.

"Oh, 'scuse me. What did you say?"

Cyrus's face darkened. His voice took on a hard rasp of anger. "I *said* . . . it's time you learned a little respect. An' it's time you learned to start carryin' your share o' the load around here."

Lucius nodded. "Oh." He turned his attention back to his plate.

Cyrus leaned over the table toward the boy. "What did you do today, Lucius?"

Lucius was in no hurry to answer. He smiled. "What did *you* do today, Cyrus?"

"*What?!*"

"What do you do down at the sawmill all day *every* day? Except sit on your ass and prop your feet on the desk?"

The color drained from Cyrus's face.

"Lucius!" Sarah was standing over the boy, her eyes wide with shock.

"I've seen him," Lucius said. "He don't do nothin' all day but sleep. Isaac does all the work. If it wasn't for Isaac, the place would've gone to hell a long time—"

"Shut your mouth!" Cyrus shouted. "I'm the owner! The *owner*, you understand that? I built it with my own hands, on land I bought an' paid for an' cleared myself. I

204

brought Isaac into the business with me, an' he made the most of it, an' was grateful. Now I'm givin' you the same opportunity, an' what do *you* do? You jes' thumb your nose at me. You're nothin' but a—a . . ."

Cyrus stopped. His jaw dropped open. Lucius was grinning and thumbing his nose.

Cyrus's mouth worked soundlessly for several seconds. "By God!" He got up slowly and began to unfasten the heavy leather belt he wore, and as he fumbled with it, he came around the table toward Lucius. "By God, boy, I'm goin' to teach you some manners right now!"

Lucius was on his feet with a force that sent his chair toppling. "If you're thinkin' of layin' that belt on me, lemme give you a little advice. Don't try it."

Cyrus was pulling the belt free. "Why the hell not? Should 'a' done it a long time ago!"

"I'll tell you why not," Lucius said evenly, and took a small step forward.

Cyrus swung his belt loose and gripped it hard, ready for use. Lucius took another step toward him.

"The last time anybody hit me was when Grandpa used to rap me on the shoulder with a cane whenever he thought I wasn't doin' my lessons good enough. One day I jes' got sick of it. I said, 'Grandpa, the next time you hit me with that cane, I'm goin' to take it away from you and hit you back.'"

There was a soft gasp from Sarah. "Lucius—you didn't!"

Lucius kept his eyes fixed on Cyrus. "I did. And you know what happened? Grandpa put that cane away, and I never saw it again. I was thirteen years old then. I'm sixteen now." He had moved forward until he was eye-to-eye with Cyrus. His voice went down to a husky whisper.

"And I'm tellin' you straight and plain—just try to hit me with that belt, and I'll take it out o' your hands and lick . . . your . . . ass."

Cyrus stood rigid. Nothing moved except the quivering muscles of his jaw.

Sarah tried to come between them. "Stop this, now. Please?"

Cyrus brushed her roughly aside. "By God, I ain't goin' to stand for this!" His voice was choking with fury, and the dangling belt twitched in his hands like a captive rep-

205

tile. "I won't have no damn sassy young'un stand here in my house an' talk to me like I'm dirt—"

"*Your* house?!" Lucius bellowed. "Your house be damned! This is my *father's* house!"

Sarah was clinging to him. "Lucius, stop it, stop it!"

Lucius was unaware of her. "My father built this house for his wife and his children. He didn't build it for *you*—"

"He never built it a-tall!" Cyrus roared. "Everybody else in South Bar built it for 'im. Oliver Hargrave never in his life dirtied his hands with *honest* work—"

Lucius sprang at him.

And Isaac, who had been sitting tensely watching, came to life. He leaped between the antagonists, thrusting them apart, and the blow that Lucius was in the act of delivering to Cyrus caught Isaac on the side of the head. He went down with a stifled moan.

Instantly Sarah was kneeling over him. "Oh, Isaac! Isaac, are you hurt?" She cradled his head in her arms, stroked his brow, and turned an anguished face upward.

"You stop it this instant, both of you, do you hear me?! You're acting like animals!"

The eruption had subsided as quickly as it had begun. Lucius picked up the chair he had knocked over, and sat down. Cyrus stood crushed, the belt in his hand dangling lifelessly.

Sarah helped Isaac to his feet. "Isaac, dear, are you all right?"

"I'm all right," Isaac mumbled. He pulled away from her and went back to his chair and sat down heavily. He glanced briefly at Lucius, then looked away, and gingerly rubbed the side of his head.

Sarah turned to Lucius. She pulled herself up to a great height, and looked down on him with tremendous anger.

"I will be a long time forgiving you for this, Lucius."

He turned his eyes meekly up to her, but said nothing.

"You owe us all an apology. But most of all you owe it to Cyrus."

Lucius remained silent.

"Well?" Sarah said. "I'm waiting."

Lucius got slowly to his feet. He stood before his mother and put his hands gently on her shoulders.

"I had somethin' to tell you when I came in, Mama. Somethin' important. I never had a chance to tell you."

206

"What is it, Lucius?"

Lucius glanced past Sarah at Cyrus, and shook his head quickly. "I'm goin' now. I'll come back later and talk to you. In private."

Sarah reached out to him. "Going where?"

"I'll come and talk to you on Monday morning, and tell you everything."

"But I don't understand, Lucius . . ."

He had turned away from her, and was going to the door. She followed.

"Lucius, wait . . ."

"G'night, Mama," he called over his shoulder.

Then he was gone, striding rapidly down to the front road and disappearing in the gathering darkness, and Sarah stood in the doorway and gazed forlornly after him. After a long time, she turned and looked at Cyrus and at Isaac. Neither had moved. Sarah went to the table and picked up Lucius's plate and took it to the kitchen.

Without a word Cyrus shuffled out of the room, the tip of his belt trailing on the floor.

17

ON MONDAY MORNING, Sarah went about her household chores with a determined effort at concentration, and tried hard not to look toward the front road. Nevertheless, she saw Lucius as soon as he was close enough to be seen, coming from the direction of the village. She was hanging out washing on the line behind the house, and she quickly applied her attention to the work and appeared unconcerned when Lucius entered the yard and came toward her.

"H'lo, Mama." He leaned on the clothesline post and smiled at her.

"Good morning, Lucius," she said stiffly, and gave him a brief glance. "Where have you been since Saturday night?"

"Stayin' with some friends o' mine."

"In the village?"

"At the river. On a flatboat."

Sarah made a face. "That's no place for a boy from a good family."

Lucius chuckled.

"I was worried about you," Sarah said peevishly.

"Was dear ol' Cyrus worried about me too?"

Sarah ignored his teasing mood. "Everybody missed you at church yesterday."

"Aw, c'mon, Mama, that's a joke, and you know it. I ain't been to church three times in the last three years, and neither have you."

Sarah ignored this too. "Why aren't you at work?"

"I ain't goin' back to the woodyard, Mama. Never ag'in."

"Oh? What are you going to do, then?" Sarah kept herself busy, not looking in his direction.

"I'm leavin', Mama. Goin' away."

She stopped short, and turned her eyes on him.

"Lucius?" She went to him and put a hand against his cheek. "Have you had anything to eat today?"

He shrugged. "A little."

"Come inside. I'll fix you some breakfast, and we can talk."

While she bustled about the kitchen, he sat at the table and watched her. Neither spoke. In a few minutes she set before him a plate of steaming buckwheat cakes, dripping with butter and maple syrup. She sat down opposite him, and tried not to notice as he attacked the food like a ravenous wolf. When he was nearly done, she spoke to him.

"Cyrus said I should tell you he'd be willing to forget all about Saturday, if you want to come on back to work."

"I ain't gonna forget about it, and I ain't goin' back there."

208

"It seems so silly. Just because of a little spat . . ."

Lucius finished his last bite and pushed his plate away. "Aw, that didn't have nothin' to do with it, Mama. My mind was made up a long time ago. It jes' happened that Saturday was the day my big chance finally came, so I decided I wasn't goin' to take no more off o' Cyrus. That's all."

"Well . . . do you want to tell me about it? Your big chance, and all that?"

"Sure do. That's why I'm here. Y'see, I rowed out to a steamboat called the *Cincinnati Queen* Saturday, when she stopped to take on wood. I do that quite a bit, y'know, to drum up trade for the woodyard. Cyrus thinks I'm jes' foolin' around. He's too dumb to realize that half the business he gets is because I've made friends with the steamboat captains. Well, anyway, I went out to the *Cincinnati Queen* to pass the time o' day with Cap'n Jochum, 'cause I been trying' to get him to hire me on."

"Hire you on! As what?"

"Anything. I jes' want to get on board. So Saturday, Cap'n Jochum invites me to come on the ship for a few minutes, 'cause there's a man who wants to talk to me. It was a real fine-lookin' gentleman by the name o' Mr. Pettingill. Mama, you know how Grandpa's always tellin' me I should try to associate with intelligent, educated people, so I can better myself? Well, this Mr. Pettingill's about the most high-class educated gentleman you ever did see. And Mama, he offered me a job!"

"What kind of a job?"

"He's a big man in the steamboat company, and I'm gonna be his assistant. Ain't that great?"

Lucius watched his mother's reaction, and grimaced with annoyance when he saw her face register dismay rather than joy. "Well, it's very respectable, Mama. Ain't that what you want me to do, go into some respectable business? It's a lot better'n a dirty ol' woodyard, that's certain."

"Lucius, you can't just . . ." Sarah's hands fluttered toward him in a kind of futile protest. "Why, you don't even *know* this Mr. Pettingill!"

"Oh, sure I do. We went to his private stateroom and had a nice long talk, and got to be real good friends. He asked me all about myself, 'cause he wanted to be sure I came from a good family and all. He's a very serious man,

209

Mama. He said if I wanted to work for him I'd have to be very sober and industrious. Why, he's jes' the kind o' man you'd like, Mama. If you ever met him, you'd—"

Sarah closed her eyes and stopped listening. "Lucius . . ." She gripped her temples, covering her face with her hand. When she looked at him again, her expression was hard. "You can't do this, Lucius. It's idiotic. It's absolutely out of the question."

He gazed at her for a moment in silence. "I'm goin' to, Mama," he said quietly. "When the *Cincinnati Queen* comes back down the river next week, it's gonna stop for me. And I'm goin' on board."

Sarah stiffened. "I won't allow it," she snapped. "Neither will Cyrus. We'll send after you, and bring you back, by force if neces—"

He had risen, and stood towering over his mother, looking down at her with burning eyes. "You better not try it, Mama. You do, and I'll make you wish you'd 'a' let me die in my cradle."

Sarah stared at him, and heard in his firm young voice a tremendous force of will that she knew was stronger by far than her own and Cyrus's and Isaac's all put together. Her lips quivered slightly. She looked away.

"There's an old leather satchel somewhere," she said after a moment. "Used to belong to your father. You might as well have it, to carry some of your things in."

Very slowly, as if under a fearsome weight, she got to her feet. "Let me see if I can . . . if I can find it."

"Thank you, Mama." Lucius leaned forward and kissed her moist cheek. "I knew I could count on you. You'll always be my friend."

She turned away from him unsteadily, her eyes vague and wandering, and went out of the room.

210

18

LATE IN THE AFTERNOON Isaac was at the lower end of the woodyard issuing instructions to several workmen when he heard his name called. Lucius was standing at the yard gate, beckoning to him. Isaac dismissed the men and hastened forward.

"Lucius, where have you been?"

"Don't start that, brother, I ain't got time for it."

Isaac stopped abruptly and stared at the leather satchel at Lucius's feet. "Where did you get that?!"

"Mama gave it to me."

"That belongs to Papa! Mama Sarah never lets anybody touch Papa's old things!"

"She does if it's a special occasion."

Isaac frowned. "Lucius, what's goin' on? What are you up to?"

Lucius slapped Isaac playfully on the arm. "This is where I part company with you for a while, brother. And with Thacker and Hargrave, Associates, forever."

"What? What are you talkin' about?"

"I jes' came to say goodbye and collect my back wages. I figger the company owes me eight dollars."

"Jes' where do you think you're goin'?"

"Down the river, brother. Either I'll sign on with Nate Collins, or go to work for a certain Mr. Pettingill, when the *Cincinnati Queen* comes back next Saturday. Either way, it's goodbye, South Bar!" Lucius grinned.

Isaac was shaking his head in disbelief. "Lucius, you must be out of your mind! You can't go off on a steamboat with some total stranger—and even *you* couldn't be crazy enough to join up with that thug, Nate Collins!"

Lucius groaned. "Oh Lord, you sound jes' like Mama!"

"You know what kind o' man Nate Collins is? He's wanted in Kentucky for attempted murder!"

"That's a damn lie!"

"Everybody *knows* it's true!"

"Who's everybody? I'll tell you who—the same gossipin' sons o' bitches who made up dirty stories about Papa years ago—"

"Shhh!" Isaac put a hand on Lucius's shoulder and looked around apprehensively. "Don't talk so, Lucius!"

"Sorry, brother." Instantly Lucius became meek. "I don't want to bother you, I know you're busy. I jes' want to collect my wages, and I thought maybe, if you could spare a few extra dollars . . ."

Isaac's face reflected an intense inner struggle. After a moment he pulled forth his wallet and opened it.

"How much you need?"

"Whatever you can spare."

Isaac emptied his wallet and handed the bills to Lucius. "Here's twenty-four dollars. It's all I got on me."

Lucius took the money and quickly stuffed it into his pocket. "Much obliged, brother. That's eight dollars wages, plus a sixteen-dollar loan. That'll help a lot."

"No. That's a twenty-four-dollar going-away present. Now go on in the office and ask Cyrus for your wages."

Lucius shook his head. "Oh no you don't, brother! You don't talk me into goin' in there and givin' him a chance to start in on me agin'!"

"If you're goin' to up and quit like this, Lucius, the least you can do is have the decency to go and tell him so, and be honest about it. If you jes' walk away without tellin' him, you don't deserve your wages."

"I'm tellin' *you*. Ain't that good enough?"

"No, he's the boss."

Lucius glowered. "Well, forget it, then. It ain't worth eight dollars to me." He picked up the satchel.

"Well, all right, if you're scared o' Cyrus, why—"

"*Scared* of 'im?! By Christ, if you hadn't got in the way the other night, I would 'a' killed the son of a—"

212

"Lucius!"

"All right, brother. You want everything done all polite and proper? So be it. Now you watch and see if Cyrus is polite and proper to *me!*" Lucius strode rapidly toward the little office building at the opposite end of the yard.

"You jes' watch your temper, Lucius," Isaac called anxiously after him.

And Cyrus, standing at a window, quickly turned away when he saw Lucius coming.

Lucius knocked on the door to the Office of the President. When he heard Cyrus say, "Come in," he opened the door, stepped up to Cyrus's desk, and stood very stiffly.

"Good afternoon, Mr. Thacker."

Cyrus was sitting at the desk, absorbed in a sheaf of papers. He glanced up in mild surprise.

"Afternoon, Lucius."

With immense dignity, Lucius delivered a little speech: "Mr. Thacker, as an employee of Thacker and Hargrave, Associates, I wish to inform you that I am resigning my position, effective now. It has been a very pleasant and worthwhile experience working here, Mr. Thacker, but after careful consideration, I believe my true place in the world is elsewhere. Therefore I'll be leaving South Bar very shortly. I have come to bid you a most respectful farewell, and to request the wages due me, which are in the amount of eight dollars."

Cyrus's eyes were fixed on Lucius, and dark with melancholy. "Sit down, Lucius," he said quietly.

"I don't have time, Mr. Thacker."

"Sit down."

Lucius sighed, set his satchel on the floor, pulled up a chair, and sat down. Cyrus gazed thoughtfully across the desk at him.

"You've always hated me, Lucius."

"I can't deny that, Mr. Thacker."

"Why?"

Lucius's answer was slow, and icily deliberate.

"Because you were my father's enemy."

"No. That ain't true."

"It *is* true."

Cyrus leaned across the desk and looked at Lucius as if he hoped to convey a message directly from his eyes to the

213

eyes of the boy—a message more forceful than his limited command of language could deliver.

"Lucius—lemme try an' explain how it was with me. I was employed by your uncle, George Gilpin—"

"I know all that, Mr. Thacker."

"Listen to me, Lucius. Listen. Your Uncle George was a fine man, one o' the finest men who ever lived in Indiana. It's your misfortune you didn't know 'im. But he was an unhappy man, Lucius, a tormented man. He wanted real bad to have a career in politics, to play a part in the development o' this state, an' he worked at it with all his might. But while he was doin' that, his life was bein' destroyed from within his own family. Two of the people he loved most, his wife an' his sister, were bein' used an' abused an' dishonored by his brother-in-law, Oliver Har—"

Lucius was on his feet. "I'm in a hurry, Mr. Thacker," he snapped. "I ain't got time to listen to a long, boring rigmarole about dear Uncle George."

"But if you'd jes' try to see this thing from my point of view, Lucius, an' not be so—"

"I got to go, Mr. Thacker. Can I have my wages now?"

"Mr. Thacker." Cyrus echoed the boy, and mimicked his false formality. "Lucius, I've tried my damnedest to be your friend. I knew I couldn't take the place o' your father, and I never tried to, but I did try to be your—"

Lucius was leaning on the desk, thrusting himself toward Cyrus. "Can I have my wages now?"

Cyrus picked up the sheaf of papers on his desk and waved them in Lucius's face.

"Look a' here. You know what these are? They're back orders for lumber. Our customers are complainin' they can't git fast enough service here. South Bar is growin', boy, and the business would grow too, if I could keep enough good men on the job. I counted on you, Lucius. I counted on you, and you let me down."

"Eight dollars, Mister Thacker. For eight dollars you can buy yourself the pleasure o' bein' rid o' the worst employee you ever had. Ain't that worth eight dollars to you?"

Cyrus slapped the papers down on the desk and pushed his chair back. "All right. You want to be on a strictly

214

business basis, *Mister* Hargrave? Fine. How do you figger I owe you eight dollars?"

"Two weeks' wages. This week and last. Four dollars a week. Very simple."

"Oh, I see. This week and last. Very interestin'. Today's Monday, *Mister* Hargrave. You ain't done a lick this week. An' as for last week, I'd say you were in the yard a third o' the time, if that much. The rest o' the time, you were either frolickin' on the river in your skiff, or down at Nate Collins's flatboat. Maybe you ought to ask Nate for last week's wages, 'stead o' me."

Lucius opened his mouth to speak, but Cyrus cut him off.

"Jes' a minute, I ain't done yet, *Mister* Hargrave. Suppose I say, all right, two weeks' wages. When's the last time you paid your mama the dollar a week you're supposed to pay for room an' board?"

Lucius huffed with anger. *"I* don't know, ask *her!* I can't remember things like that!"

"I did ask her. She didn't want to tell me, tried to change the subject. Finally she admitted you ain't paid in over two months. So I reckon that jes' about wipes out your back pay, don't it?"

"Why, you goddamn cheap—"

"Hold on, *Mister* Hargrave, I still ain't done." Cyrus was on his feet. "One more little item to figger in."

Lucius stood staring, his chest heaving. "What else, damn you, what else?"

"The lumber you been takin' out o' the yard all winter long, for Nate Collins to build his flatboat with."

Lucius went slack-jawed. "Wh—what are you talkin' abou—"

"Don't bother denyin' it. The men have seen you, an' they've been keepin' me informed."

Lucius's face was beet red. The veins stood out on his temples. And as his rage grew, Cyrus became calmer.

"So, considerin' everything, *Mister* Hargrave, I'm real glad you came in to settle our account. 'Cause the way I figger it, *you* owe *me* about twenty dollars."

The muscles in Lucius's jaw worked furiously as he groped for sound, but no words came. Suddenly Cyrus smiled. He pulled out his wallet.

"But that's all right. I'm willin' to forget all that, and

215

pay you the eight dollars you think I owe you. 'Cause a minute ago you said somethin' that made sense to me. You said it ought to be worth eight dollars to be rid o' you. Now, that's about the most sensible thing I ever heard you say."

Cyrus was taking money out of his wallet. "So here's eight dollars—no, damn it, make it *ten* dollars, it'll *still* be a bargain—"

"Keep your filthy money!" Lucius spat the words.

"I'm tryin' to perform a community service, *Mister* Hargrave. South's Bar's a place where *decent* people live, you don't want to stay here." Cyrus thrust a handful of bills into Lucius's midriff. "So take it. Take it and go."

"I said—" Lucius slapped at Cyrus's hand, and the money fluttered to the floor. "—keep your goddamn filthy money!"

He slapped again, and Cyrus's wallet flew out of his hands. Cyrus scrambled for it, pulled out more money and tossed it wildly into the air, and it drifted down around them.

"Here's some more filthy money, *Mister* Hargrave!" Cyrus was fairly shouting. "Take it, take all you want! It'll be a bargain to be rid o' you, at *any* price!"

Lucius's eyes were narrowed slits of burning hatred. "You son of a bitch," he growled. "You goddamn rotten son of a—"

"All right, *Mister* Hargrave." Cyrus began to pull his belt loose. "Now I'm gonna give you what I meant to give you Saturday night, an' should 'a' given you years ago."

Slowly and deliberately, Lucius moved forward. "Go ahead." His voice had become a husky whisper. "Hit me with that belt. Jes' . . . *once.*"

Cyrus had the heavy belt off, and spun it in a circle. The leather whistled viciously.

"There ain't but one way to git the poison of Oliver Hargrave out o' your blood, boy, and that's to beat it out!"

Lucius stood still. "Go ahead, you yellow bastard," he whispered between clenched teeth. "I'm waiting."

In a lightning-like arc, Cyrus swung the belt, and Lucius leaped to meet it.

Isaac was at the far end of the woodyard when he heard the sounds of violence. He ran toward the office at top

216

speed. The several yard workmen dropped their tools and followed him. Isaac burst into the building and ran down the short hallway to the door of Cyrus's office, where he met Lucius coming out.

"Lucius, what hap—"

He was nearly knocked off his feet as Lucius barged past him, and past the other men who had come in after Isaac, and who now stood in the hallway staring dumbly at Lucius, at Isaac, and at each other.

At the front door, Lucius stopped and looked back. In one hand he held his leather satchel. The other hand grasped a crumpled wad of money. Hastily he thrust the money into his pocket.

"Better look to Cyrus, brother," he said to Isaac. His voice was calm and steady, and betrayed no stress. "The clumsy bastard had a little accident."

Isaac ran into the office and found Cyrus lying on the floor, flat on his back. Blood trickled from the corner of his mouth and rolled across his cheek into his ear. The injured man moved his head slowly from side to side, and stared at the ceiling. His lips moved soundlessly. He did not seem to be aware of Isaac lifting his head and wiping his face with a cloth, or of the circle of mute, staring faces that had gathered around.

"Are you all right, Cyrus?" Isaac asked in a trembling voice. "Are you hurt bad? Speak to me, Cyrus!" He turned desperate eyes up at the other men. "Somebody run for Dr. Reece! Quick!"

One of the men rushed out.

"Lucius?" Isaac called. "Where's Lucius!" His voice was rising in hysteria.

"He done gone, Mr. Hargrave," one of the men said.

"Well, go after him!" Isaac screeched. "After him, all of you, and bring him ba—"

"No!"

Cyrus had found his voice. He struggled to rise, but couldn't, and fell back panting. Isaac cradled his head, and wiped his bloody, perspiring face with the cloth.

"Shouldn't we get him, Cyrus?" Isaac pleaded. "Shouldn't we bring him back?"

The workmen stood silently poised, waiting for instructions.

Cyrus swallowed hard and fought to regain control. He

217

stared past the men around him toward some point in space.

"Let 'im go," he mumbled. "He's gonna follow his father straight to hell, an' no power on earth can stop 'im. So let 'im go."

19

AT DUSK Nate Collins's flatboat was lashed to the bank in the little cove, and Nate and his two crewmen sat cross-legged on the rough deck planking, playing cards.

Nate's companions were a study in contrasts: Josh Everett, tall and lanky, barefoot, black-eyed, and black-bearded, dressed in patched and faded cotton duck pants that were several inches too short for his long legs—a young backwoodsman from the remote mountains of eastern Kentucky who had never in his twenty-odd years of life owned a pair of store-bought shoes; and Otto Grieshaber, a sturdy blond pink-cheeked German of about thirty, whose baggy trousers were held up by a pair of enormous leather suspenders over a too-tight undershirt, beneath which huge muscles bulged and rippled. Otto smiled constantly and laughed readily. Josh's swarthy face rarely displayed expression of any kind, other than a permanent dour immobility.

Lucius Hargrave came walking rapidly down the path along the river. The three men glanced up briefly as he entered the clearing by the cove, then returned their attention to the card game. Lucius flung the leather satchel he was carrying into the boat and leaped in after it, causing the craft to rock wildly.

"Mein Gott!" Otto bellowed. "Go careful dere, *Kindchen!"*

Lucius was panting heavily and crouching, as if trying to keep out of sight. "We got to shove off, Nate." There was a compelling urgency in his voice. "I been thinkin' about what you said, and I decided I'd come with you this year, after all. And we got to shove off right now."

The three men stared at him.

"What the hell you talkin' 'bout?" Nate demanded. "You the cap'n o' this here boat?"

"I'm not foolin', Nate. Every minute counts."

"Thought you said you was goin' on a goddamn steamboat. Gonna be a servin' boy for some dandy dressed-up *gentleman.*" The mincing sarcasm with which Nate delivered the word "gentleman" brought a sneer and a snicker from Josh.

Lucius kept peering anxiously over the edge of the gunwale, watching the path from the village. "Listen, Nate, I ain't got time to explain it now, but I got to come with you, and we *got* to shove off, right this minute."

"Vas der madder vid you, *Kindchen?"* Otto said. "You gone in der head, hah?" He laughed.

"Tell 'im to shut up, an' let's play cards," Josh growled.

Nate was studying Lucius's face. "What's goin' on, Luke?"

"They found out about the lumber. That damned Cyrus has spies out all over the place. He knows, and he's mad as hell about it."

With no change of expression, Nate went back to examining the cards in his hand. "So what's goin' to happen next?"

"He's goin' to get the sheriff, and they're comin' down here to arrest us all, that's what's gonna happen. Unless we shove off. Come on, Nate, let's *go!"*

Nate glanced at his crewmen. He saw that Otto's broad face was completely placid, and that Josh was scowling. "Well, what d'ye think, boys?"

Josh rendered a succinct opinion. "Shee-it."

"I mean besides that," Nate said. "What else d'ye think?"

"I say let 'em come," Josh muttered. "We'll lick the lot of 'em."

Lucius pleaded his case with the ship's master. "Aw, come on, Nate. I don't want to fight my own relatives!"

Josh objected, "Hell, we cain't git nowhar' now, it's pert' near sundown."

"We can cover three or four miles," Lucius countered. "That's enough."

Nate looked at Otto. "What d'ye think, Greasy?"

The big German gave a shrug and fingered his cards. "Vell, ve ain't never run from a fight before. But den, maybe ve shouldn't fight vid *Kindchen*'s people. Dat ain't nice." He nodded. "*Ja*, ve go, I t'ink."

"Shee-it," Josh said again.

"All right, we go," Nate said. He threw down his cards and shot a frown at the new crew member. "But understand, Luke, it don't mean I'm cuttin' you in on a share. Can't afford it. I'm jes' lettin' you ride with us, an' givin' you a chance to learn somethin'."

"That's fine, Nate. I'll work for nothin' but board, and I'll be a big help, you'll see."

Josh emitted a snicker of acid scorn.

"Want me to cast off, Nate?" Lucius asked. He was on his feet, itching with eagerness.

Nate chuckled. "All right, go ahead. Might's well start makin' yo'self useful."

Lucius leaped over the side, splashing heedlessly in the muddy shallows, and untied the mooring line. Otto and Josh manned a pair of long poles and pushed off, and Lucius had to scramble into waist-deep water to get back on board. In two minutes the ungainly craft was out in the channel and moving with the current.

"All right, Luke, you can stow yo' gear in there," Nate said, and jerked his head toward the squat, flat-topped cabin that occupied the center of the boat deck. "Take the far left-hand corner. Then come out and get a fire goin' in the stove, so Greasy can start supper."

Lucius took his satchel, went into the cabin, and felt his way through the damp, smelly, windowless chamber to his assigned corner. There he sat down and waited for his eyes to become accustomed to the gloom. Then he opened the satchel and peered inside. In addition to the few articles of clothing that he had hastily stuffed into it were three

220

items his mother had added. One was a cake of her special homemade soap, wrapped in a piece of cloth. Then there was a second piece of cloth, rolled up tight and tied with a string. Lucius opened it and found five crumpled dollar bills.

"Good ol' Mama," he murmured, and stuffed the money into his pocket and reached into the satchel for the last item. It was the Gilpin family's copy of the *English Reader*.

Lucius squinted in the dim light as he read the endless title that rambled over the cover of the worn old volume. A slow smile spread across his face. He opened the book at random, scanned a few lines, and chuckled softly.

From outside, the shrill voice of Nate Collins reached him. "Hey, Luke! Haul yo' ass out here an' git that fire started!"

Lucius scrambled up, rushed to the cabin door and out on deck, and flung the book as far as he could across the darkening waters of the Ohio River. As it spun off into oblivion, he stood with feet planted wide apart, eyes shining, and shrieked with the wild joy of an unchained fiend.

"What the hell's the matter with you, you crazy fool kid?" Nate barked at him.

Lucius's reply was shouted at the top of his voice and hurled in the same direction in which the *English Reader* had gone, toward the silent and somber forest of the Indiana shoreline a hundred yards away.

"I did it, by God, I did it! I got away! I'm free, I'm free. I'm *free!*"

He clutched his midriff and howled with exultant laughter while the three flatboatmen stared at him, dumbfounded.

20

FROM THE JOURNAL of Lucius Hargrave:

From the first day I went to work at Thacker and Hargrave, Associates, all my thoughts were directed toward one goal: escape. It was the dream that sustained me and gave me the fortitude to endure all the crude jokes played upon me by the dull, oafish louts in the woodyard, and all the hardships my merciless taskmaster Cyrus Thacker could devise for my benefit. Devise he did, with a vengeance—yet I accepted it all in stoic silence, and plotted my eventual flight.

The path it would take was perfectly obvious: the river. Every spare moment I could find I spent at the wharf, observing the traffic. No steamboat passed South Bar without being subjected to my scrutiny. Wistfully I gazed upon the handsomely dressed gentlemen who strolled those lofty decks, and longed to be one of them. At length I selected a favorite ship, a trim beauty called the *Cincinnati Queen,* whose master was a man named Elisha Jochum. I made friends with Captain Jochum, and began to importune him for employment. At first he refused to take me seriously, but I persisted, knowing that in most human endeavors, persistence is as important a talent as any other. Reward came at last. One day Captain Jochum invited me aboard. There was a passenger, he said, who would speak to me about a possible position.

I remember the scene most vividly; it was a fine spring day, a few weeks after my sixteenth birthday, and I stood on the deck of the *Cincinnati Queen* and shook hands with the man who had asked for me. Albert Pettingill was his name, and I thought him quite the finest gentleman my eyes had ever beheld. Mr. Pettingill entertained me lavishly in his private suite of rooms on the top deck. He explained that he was an executive in the steamboat company that owned the *Queen,* that he traveled constantly, overseeing the company's extensive operations, and that he was looking for a young man to travel with him—someone vigorous, intelligent, and of high moral character, who would be willing to work hard, learn the business, and perhaps carve out for himself a fine career. The *Cincinnati Queen* would be coming back downriver in a week, he added. Would I be willing to come on board?

He was a long time in getting around to this, the point of our interview, and I was long time in convincing myself that I had heard correctly—that after an exhaustive search, he was choosing *me* as his assistant—yet that was the truth of it. I hesitated not an instant. With a calm dignity that I believe Mr. Pettingill found surprising in one so young, I expressed my thanks, and accepted.

By the time I reached home that afternoon, I felt ten feet tall. My head was spinning with joy. The world and all it contained were mine at last, I was certain. I was so bursting with excitement that I could hardly wait to rush in and hug my mother and pour out to her the news of my incredible good fortune. But when I saw Cyrus hunched over the table and glaring at me, I knew that instead I faced an ordeal. Clearly he planned to engage in his favorite pastime—to challenge me over some triviality and generate a quarrel. I resolved to avoid it. I would not stoop to his level. After all, in a week I would be permanently free from that sadistic man; he could no longer harm me.

Cyrus began his attack in a low key. First he noted that I was late for supper, went on to complain about my table manners (which were far superior to his), and proceeded then to trot out one of his most overworked subjects: I spent too little time in the woodyard, too much rowing out to greet passing steamboats.

I started to point out that half the river trade he profited so nicely by was the direct result of *my* efforts—but what

223

is the use, I thought. We had been over it all so many times. I simply nodded, and offered humble apologies.

Cyrus' anger grew. He was infuriated by his inability to start a fight with me. With a snarl on his lips, he attacked me with the most despicable weapon in his arsenal: he began to insult the noble name of my father.

This I could not stomach. Though my supper was barely touched, I arose from the table and bade my mother good night, promising to return later to speak with her in private. Then, without another glance at the blustering Cyrus, I took my leave.

But where to go? It would be a week before the *Cincinnati Queen* returned. Suddenly I felt like a homeless waif. Fortunately, there was one friend to whom I could turn for help—Nate Collins, a man of considerable ingenuity and practical wisdom—and to him I hastened.

Nate was a colorful river character, a practitioner of what was already in those days a rapidly disappearing profession. He was a flatboatman. Every spring he built a boat, loaded it with local farm produce, and with two or three companions as crew, floated down the Ohio and the Mississippi to New Orleans. There he disposed of his cargo at a fine profit, realized an additional bonus from the sale of his flatboat for its lumber (once downriver it was forever useless as a boat, since no power on earth could propel the ungainly thing upstream again), and made his way home on foot, soon to start the annual process over again.

There was no room for charity in Nate's flinty heart, but it happened that he was indebted to me, since I had helped him build his boat that year, and through my position at the woodyard had procured lumber for him at an attractive price. He listened to my troubles, and not only gave me leave to take shelter at his mooring site, but urged me to come with him to New Orleans. He already had two stalwart men, but felt I would be a valuable addition to his crew. His first offer I accepted with heartfelt thanks, and declined the second.

A day or two later I returned home to disclose my plans to my mother, and to say goodbye. Bless her soul, she accepted the news bravely, and gave me a wondrous gift: an old leather traveling bag that had belonged to my father. I clutched it in my hands, and tears came to my eyes as I realized that I held the object that would be the most

224

precious material possession of my life. We spent a tender hour alone together, Mama and I. We talked of many things, and felt closer to each other than we had ever felt before. Then I kissed her and departed quickly, for we were both making a valiant effort to contain our emotions, and could not carry it on much longer.

Passing through the village on the way back to Nate's mooring site, I heard talk that chilled my blood. That villain, Cyrus Thacker, had trumped up the most absurdly false charges against me, claiming I had stolen lumber for Nate Collins' use. He had enlisted the aid of the sheriff, and was planning to have us all cast in jail like common thieves!

I ran to Nate at top speed, to warn him. Fortunately, his crewmen were all present and the cargo loading completed, so a simple solution to the difficulty presented itself: they would depart immediately, and I should come with them. I agreed. My heart broke as I thought of my new friend Mr. Pettingill, and the splendid oportunity he had offered me, now possibly lost—but I had to agree, there was no other way.

It was late in the day when the flatboat glided forth on the powerful current of the Ohio. The sun was low in the west, and cast a golden glow on the sky, the earth below, and the majestic river. And just as certain large birds that are ugly and awkward on the ground are transformed in flight into poetic miracles of grace and soaring beauty, thus did the cumbersome homemade barge become a splendid ship, proud mistress of the great waterway, its natural home. A rhapsodic scene—enough to bring a lump to the throat of the most stone-hearted of men—and in my distraught condition, too much to be borne. I watched the place of my birth recede across a widening stretch of water and slip from my view—forever, for aught I knew—and I pressed my brow against the side of the cabin and cried like a baby.

Part Three

1

NATE COLLINS, a small king of a tiny kingdom, sat easily on his throne and surveyed the world in its April greenery. April was Nate's favorite time of year, for that was when he was usually doing what he liked best: floating down the Ohio-Mississippi water highway on his flatboat, bound for New Orleans. Nate's throne was a wicker chair, the only article of furniture on board. It was fixed in place near the rear edge of the top deck—the flat roof of the cabin—from which point Nate could rest his hand on the end of a long tiller and guide his little ship with almost no expenditure of energy.

On the scale by which his peers measured wealth, Nate Collins was a rich man, though his entire worldly goods at the moment consisted of the flatboat and its cargo. The 1832 model was a typical craft of its kind: a squat, ugly, rectangular monstrosity, forty feet long and eighteen feet wide. The central twenty feet of its deck area were occupied by a cabin barely four feet high; wooden steps led up onto the roof, while other steps led down into the cabin, the floor of which was about two feet below the outer deck level. Ordinary cargo—such as bales of hemp, stacks of hides, barrels of salt pork, dried apples, cider, corn, and lard—was piled high fore and aft on the decks, while the dank, airless interior of the cabin provided a more secure hold for particularly attractive types of freight, such as kegs of whiskey. Whatever odd corners remained were utilized as sleeping space by the men. The sole function of the craft was the transportation of cargo; not the slightest thought had been given in its design to such frivolous considerations as human comfort. Nate had done the designing himself, and Nate was a practical man.

So on the long afternoon of the second day of his 1832 voyage, Captain Nate guided his little ship with ease down the broad, shining Ohio, and as darkness fell, he chose a small wooded cove on the Kentucky shore for the night's mooring. He barked orders to Otto and Josh, who picked up their poles and expertly maneuvered the boat to shore and secured it with heavy ropes. A great mass of silent, brooding forest stood around them on three sides in the cove, a mass that became a solid wall of blackness as the last trace of daylight faded. Soon, by the orange light in a little black iron stove, the men sat crosslegged on the deck and ate from tin plates their supper of potatoes and salt pork and dried apples stewed in river water.

"Hey, Greasy," Nate said. "How many potatoes you cook? We get enough here fer a goddamn army."

Otto laughed. "Ve got anudder mout' to feed, *Kapitän*." He grinned at Lucius. "*Kindchen* likes to eat *gut, ja?*"

Lucius smiled weakly.

"Don't gimme that," Nate spat. "It's *yore* goddamn belly you're thinkin' about. We eat light from now on, y'hear?"

"*Ach*, never!" said Otto, laughing. "Otto never eat light!"

"Fat kraut," Josh muttered.

It sounded like an insult. Lucius looked in quick alarm from Josh to Otto. Otto laughed loudly, leaned over, and poked Josh playfully in the ribs.

"Keep yo' hands off me, kraut," Josh growled.

Otto laughed again.

"Tomorrow you turn the cookin' over to Luke," Nate said to Otto.

"I don't know how to cook," Lucius said hastily. "At home, my mother always did the cookin'."

Josh stared at him. "Christ Almighty!"

"I teach you cookin', *Kindchen*," Otto said. "Everybody got to know how to cook."

"Don' work 'im too hard," Josh said caustically. "He ain't used to work."

230

"Why, sure, I'm used to work," Lucius protested. "I work like a son of a bitch at the woodyard."

There was a general eruption of laughter. Lucius blushed.

"Everybody ought to know how to cook," Otto said. "Two t'ings everybody ought to know. How to cook, and how to fuck."

Josh snickered.

Otto turned twinkling eyes on Lucius. "You ever fuck a voman, *Kindchen?*"

Lucius squirmed. "Why . . . sure I have. Sure, lots o' times."

"You ever fuck a pig?"

Lucius shrugged and made no answer. Otto clapped him on the shoulder.

"You vant to learn dat, you ask Josh. He's der big expert on pig fuckin'."

"Shut yo' mouth, kraut," Josh mumbled.

"Someday I teach you how to fuck a voman, pig-fucker," Otto said to Josh. "But maybe you too big *Dummkopf* to learn, eh?" He poked Josh in the ribs again.

"Git away from me, you bastard!" Josh snarled. He slapped at Otto's hand, and the big German laughed.

Nate spoke. "One thing you got to unnerstand about Greasy here, Luke. He talks a goddamn blue streak, mornin', noon, an' night, but there ain't but two English words he knows the meanin' of. That's 'eat' and 'fuck.'"

Josh cackled. Lucius chuckled, and Otto's great, booming laugh sounded above all.

After supper, Otto brought forth a battered old flute, seated himself on deck, and began to play a lively jig tune. Nate clapped his hands in time to the music while Lucius watched and listened with fascinated attention. Then Josh was moved to dance. He whirled wildly about the deck, his long arms extended like a scarecrow's, flailing the air, his huge bare feet pounding the deckboards until the boat shuddered and rocked in the water.

Nate grinned, stomped his feet, and shouted to the dancer, "Go it, Josh, you goddamned ol' pig-fuckin' bastard, go it!"

Josh danced with greater abandon, and over his usually dour face spread a look of glassy-eyed bewitchment. His thin lips were drawn back in something that was half-grin

231

and half-grimace. At length he grew dizzy from his gyrations, staggered against Otto, and knocked the flute out of the player's hands.

"Vatch out, you damn clumsy oaf!" Otto bellowed, not laughing for once.

Josh swayed drunkenly and fell on top of Otto, and the two went rolling in a tangle of arms and legs. It was Nate who provided the laughter now, in a shrill cascade of giggles.

"Go it, you bastards! Let 'im have it!" he shrieked.

As if following orders, Josh disentangled himself from Otto, scrambled to his feet, and delivered a vicious kick to Otto's middle. Otto grunted and lunged at Josh's groin. Josh leaped backward, bellowing with rage. Otto was up and charging, enveloping Josh in a bear hug. Josh bellowed again, and arched his torso backward, his face contorting hideously. His hands groped for Otto's thick neck, closed around it, and squeezed.

Lucius shrank back against the side of the cabin, his eyes wide with fright. Nate danced around the fighters and screeched his encouragements to both.

"Give it to 'im, Greasy! Give it to 'im, pig-fucker! Go it, go it!"

The gladiators crashed to the deck, locked in their deadly embrace, and rolled. Otto wound up on top. He pressed his great bulk down on his opponent, released his bear hug, and clawed at Josh's face. Josh closed his eyes tight, and held his death grip on Otto's throat.

"Stop 'em, Nate! Stop 'em!" Lucius yelled.

Nate paid no attention. He scampered around the prostrate men, giggling in delight.

Otto's broad face was livid, his mouth agape, searching for breath. He tried to press his thumbs into Josh's eyes. Frantically, Josh twisted his head from side to side. Otto's hands followed, and held Josh's face still between their palms. The thumbs found the eye sockets, and gouged.

Josh's body quivered and went rigid. He released his grip on Otto, clawed at the German's hands, and screamed, "Nuff! Nuff!"

As instantly as it had begun, the combat ceased. Grunting and gasping, the German struggled to his feet, staggered across the deck, and with a heavy thud, sat down with his back against the gunwale at the front of the boat.

232

Sweat poured from his head, and his chest heaved mightily. Over his face spread a contented smile.

"Mein Gott! Dat vas *gut!"*

Josh lay flat on his back, panting, his eyes tightly closed. Nate bent over him, grinning.

"Hey, pig-fucker! Git up!"

Josh sat up, rubbed his eyes, blinked several times, and squinted at Otto. "I'll git you next time, you goddamn fat-ass kraut." He spoke in a calm, flat voice, devoid of anger.

Otto laughed. *"Gott im Himmel!* I kill you vid vun hand, you know dat."

Josh got up and moved on unsteady legs toward the door of the cabin, and went inside. A deep quiet suddenly prevailed. Nate gazed for a moment into the blackness of the forest that lined the shore, then yawned and stretched.

"Time to turn in," he said. "If we log a couple o' good days, we can be in Paducah by Sunday night." He followed Josh into the cabin.

Lucius had picked up Otto's flute. He came across the deck to where Otto was sitting, and handed it to him. Otto smiled up at him.

"Danke." With loving care he wiped the instrument, put it to his lips, and began to play very softly. After a few moments he glanced up again at Lucius. "Sit down, *Kindchen."*

Lucius quickly accepted the invitation. Otto went on playing, a long, lyrical melody that was starkly simple, yet touched with a quiet nobility. When he had finished, he lowered his flute to his lap and gazed off into space. Lucius studied the man's face, now soft in serenity, containing no trace of brutishness.

"What was that tune you were jes' playin', Otto?"

"Dat vas der slow movement from der Ninth Symphony of Beethoven."

Lucius frowned. "The *what?"*

"De great Choral Symphony. Vunce I heard it played by a great orchestra." Otto smiled. "Ah, *Kindchen.* If any man could hear dat and not haff tears in his eyes— he vould be not man, he vould be animal." Otto gave Lucius a quizzical look. "You never heard of Beethoven, *Kindchen?"*

233

"No."

Otto chuckled. "You see? Dat's vy I call you *Kindchen*."

"What's that 'kinkin' mean?"

"Baby."

"What?! I ain't no baby! I left home, didn't I? When you leave home, you got to be a man, no matter how young you are."

Amusement shone in Otto's eyes. He slapped Lucius on the knee and started to play again. Lucius watched him.

"I don't understand somethin', Otto."

"Vat's dat, *Kindchen?*"

"You and Josh started fightin', jes' like you were goin' to kill each other. Then all of a sudden you stopped, and you weren't even mad or anything—"

Otto was softly laughing. "Ah, no, *Kindchen*, ve don't fight. Ve play. Just for fun."

"Fun? That was *fun?*"

"Fun, *ja*. American fun. Dat's vat de flatboatmen like best—fight, fight, fight, all der time. A choke, a gouge, a kick in der groin. Fun." Otto laughed. "You see vat happens to me, *Kindchen*. I come to America, and I learn bad habits."

Otto's face went serious. He leaned closer to Lucius and lowered his voice.

"You know vat kind o' people ve got here, *Kindchen?*" He jerked his thumb toward the cabin.

"What kind?"

"Peasants. Common peasants. In Europe, men like Nate and Josh vould liff in a hut and vork de fields of a duke or a baron. Dey vouldn't be floatin' down a river on a boat, t'inkin' dey vas merchants."

Lucius pondered this. "You're right, Otto. You and me, we're different from them, ain't we? We got somethin' better in our blood. I come from a good family, and you come for a good family too, I can tell."

Otto nodded. "Dat's right. You got *gut* blood, *Kindchen*. Jes' like me. Now, dis riverboat t'ing, dat's only a beginning for me. For you too. Dere's better t'ings for people like us. Someday, *Kindchen*, I vill haff a big store, and people like Nate Collins vill take off dere hats ven dey talk to me, and call me 'mister.' "

Lucius's eyes gleamed. "That sounds great, Otto. You s'pose maybe, uh . . . you and me could be partners?"

234

Otto shrugged. "Vy not?" He glanced at Lucius, and chuckled at the look of eagerness on the boy's face. "You stick vid me, *Kindchen.* I teach you everyt'ing you need to know, *ja?*"

"Sure, Otto. I'm stickin' with you, that's sure."

Otto put his flute to his lips and began to play again, and from inside the boat cabin came a screech from Nate Collins.

"Hey, Greasy! You an' Luke git yo' asses t' bed, and shut up that goddamn noise, y'hear?"

Otto stopped playing, and sighed. He and Lucius exchanged a look full of patience and common understanding.

Otto tapped the boy on the knee. "Tomorrow I teach you der first t'ing," he whispered. "How to make flapjacks."

2

THERE WAS LITTLE WORK to be done aboard the flatboat; there were few resources of any sort by which to combat idleness and boredom. The river took care of the locomotion, and the rest was insignificant. Meal preparation was the principal daily chore, and this Otto had taken as his responsibility, out of a conviction that no one else was capable of preparing food fit to eat. Lucius was supposed to learn this job, but Otto's idea of teaching was simply to do it, while Lucius watched and admired. After a number of days, Otto was still doing it, while Lucius continued to watch and admire. It was an arrangement that suited them both.

Josh was the fisherman. He had a small barrel filled with dirt, in which dwelt a multitude of earthworms. Using these as bait, Josh trailed several lines off the back of the boat each morning, and spent most of the daylight hours slumbering in whatever patch of shade he could find on the rear deck, occasionally getting up to check his lines. He caught a number of fish, most of which he threw away, keeping only his favorite varieties.

Navigating was Nate's specialty. It consisted of sitting in his private wicker chair in the shade of a small canvas awning on the roof deck, smoking his pipe, surveying the river through squinting eyes, and from time to time making slight adjustments on the long tiller pole at his elbow.

Lucius spent the long days alternately sleeping and swimming in the river. Sometimes Otto would join him in the water, stripping naked and flopping his huge bulk over the side and striking the water with a great howl, creating a splash that drenched the deck and sent Nate and Josh scurrying for cover, cursing. Nate and Josh were agreed that bathing was harmful to the body, and should be avoided. They glared at Otto and Lucius cavorting in the water, and rumbled with disapproval.

On an afternoon of soft, balmy air and blue skies, a mood of deep quiet pervaded the boat. Otto was napping in the cabin. Josh was draped over the rear gunwale, watching a deep-trawling line, and dozing. Nate was sitting in his wicker chair smoking his pipe, and Lucius was in the water, idly back-floating.

Nate took his pipe out of his mouth and called to the boy, "Come aboard, Luke. I wanna talk to ya."

Leisurely Lucius climbed aboard, dried himself, and pulled on his pants. He vaulted up onto the edge of the roof deck, and sat with his feet dangling.

"How d'ya like bein' with us, Luke?" Nate said after a moment.

Lucius shrugged. "It's all right." He brushed his fingers vigorously through his wet hair. "I'd like it a lot better if I was on the payroll."

"Well, now, I never said you couldn't *git* on th' payroll, if you turned out to be a good boatman."

236

"Like, uh, how much, Nate?"

"Maybe I could cut you in on ten percent o' the cargo, when we sell it in New Awleens."

"How much do Josh and Otto get?"

"Twenty percent apiece."

"How come *I* don't get twenty?"

Nate spat. " 'Cause they're experienced men, goddamn it. You're jest a learner."

Lucius made a face. Nate frowned at him.

"An' since you're a learner, I think it's high time you started doin' a little learnin'."

"What the hell is there to learn?" Lucius demanded. "The damn boat runs itself."

"The hell it does! You leave it alone and it'll run itself aground inside o' twenty minutes. The river's dangerous, Luke. You got to study it, watch how the currents shift, and how the banks change from one place to the next."

Lucius snorted. "Aw, the dumb ol' river looks the same here as it did at South Bar. It don't change none."

Nate spat again. "Hell, you're blind as a goddamn bat, Luke. You can't be a boatman if you don't know how to navigate, an' you ain't never gonna learn how to navigate with a rotten attitude like that."

"What is there to know about navigatin'?"

"Plenty." Nate swept an arm toward the vast space around them. "Y'see that water out there, Luke? Five or six hunnerd yards of it, from one side to th' other. Most of it dead, like a pond. Useless to a flatboat. You got to know how to keep to the channel, where the flow is, so you'll go downstream, 'stead o' stagnatin' in one place all day. At the same time you got to hold to one side o' th' channel, so you can keep—"

Nate stopped short and eyed Lucius fiercely. The boy was stretched out flat on his back on the deck, gazing up into the blue sky.

"Goddamn it, Luke! I'm tryin' to teach you somethin'. Why the hell don't you pay attention?"

Without altering his position, Lucius said, "I'm listenin', Nate."

"Yeah, but you ain't lookin'. You gonna have to start makin' a little effort, boy, 'less'n you want to be a crewman all your life, like Josh an' Otto. You want to be an owner like me, you got to git educated."

237

Lucius sat up. His manner was suddenly respectful. "You think I could own a boat someday, Nate?"

Nate's pipe was cold. He leaned over and knocked the dead ashes out on the deckboards.

"That's what I wanted to talk to ya about, Luke boy. I thought maybe next year we might think about goin' in partners."

"Y'mean . . . you and me? Fifty-fifty?"

"Shore."

Lucius's eyes were wide. "Gosh, Nate . . . *could* we?"

"I wanna build me a *big* boat, Luke. Twicet as big as this 'un. Carry maybe ten, fifteen ton. But I cain't do it all by myself; I need a partner."

Lucius edged closer. "How come you wouldn't choose Otto or Josh to be your partner, Nate?"

"I'm lookin' fo' brains, Luke. Otto—he's a big dumb kraut with nothin' in his skull but bacon fat. An' Josh—he cain't even read his own name, let alone write it. But you, Luke, you got the brains. I been watchin' you, an' I kin see you got 'em. You wanna come in partners with me, Luke, I guarantee you we kin be rich men in five years."

Lucius was paying rapt attention. "You mean that, Nate?"

"Goddamn right I mean it."

"Well, then, I'm with you. Count me in."

"But you got to start workin' at it, goddamn it. You got to start studyin' and learnin'—"

"Oh, I will, Nate, I swear. I'm gonna start right this minute—"

"Shhh!"

Otto had stepped out of the cabin. He looked around sleepily, stretched, and produced a mighty yawn.

"Don't say nothin' about it," Nate whispered to Luke.

Lucius gave a quick, secretive nod. He leaped to his feet, stripped off his pants, and with a high, yodeling yell, dove off the roof deck.

Josh scrambled up and rushed to the side, and glared murderously at the boy splashing in the water. "Goddamn, you crazy bastard!" he yelled. "Scarin' all the fish away!"

Otto, observing, shook with laughter.

238

3

TOWARD SUNDOWN of the sixth day, they came to the mouth of the Tennessee, flowing in from the south and thrusting its cool Appalachian waters against the placid Ohio current. And a little while later, the yellow flicker of campfires became visible on the Kentucky shore downstream.

"There's Paducah," Nate announced.

They moored near a cluster of other flatboats. In a clearing on the bank a huge bonfire was crackling, throwing a glare over a wide circle. On the edges of this circle blazed a number of individual campfires, around which boatmen were gathered in groups, while others wandered from one group to the next. A hubbub of shouts, raucous laughter, singing, and the chatter of good fellowship rose over the entire area.

"*Gott im Himmel!*" Otto said. "Every boat on der river's here!"

"Lots o' Tennessee boys," Nate said, grinning. "Ain't nobody makes as much fuss as Tennessee boys."

Josh quivered with excitement. "Goddamn! We gonna have us some fun tonight!"

"Jes' a damn minute," Captain Nate snapped at him. "You on watch tonight. Greasy goes ashore, an' the kid, if he wants. You git your turn at New Madrid."

Josh bellowed in anguish and outrage, but Nate ignored

him, turning to issue brief instructions to Otto and Lucius.

"Now, we kin break out a keg o' whiskey from the cargo, but I want no gittin' drunk, y'hear? An' no fightin'. Half the flatboats on the river go to ruin 'cause their crews do too much drinkin' an' too much fightin'."

Otto laughed. *"Mein Gott, Kapitän!* You take all der fun avay!"

In a few minutes Nate and Otto and Lucius went off toward the central bonfire, Otto with a whiskey keg on his broad shoulder. Josh perched on the boat's gunwale, glumly watching them go.

Less than an hour later Nate and Lucius were back, Nate supporting the boy, who moved along with drooping head and stumbling feet and no idea of direction. Josh was sitting on the deck with his back against the cabin wall, and he cackled in high glee.

"The kid got drunk!" he jeered.

With Nate's help, Lucius climbed aboard, and stood swaying dangerously and glaring in Josh's general direction. "Tha's a lie," he mumbled, and collapsed heavily, flat on his back.

Josh shrieked with mirth.

"Th' stupid bastard!" Nate growled. He too was swaying, and his speech was thick. "I interduce 'im to some o' my friends. Perfessional men, some o' th' best in th' business. An' what does he do? Makes a goddamn fool o' himself."

He pointed a commanding finger at Josh. "I want you to keep an eye on 'im. Don't let 'im set foot off th' boat ag'in." He turned and walked away, tottering unsteadily as he went.

After a while Lucius struggled up to a sitting position. Beads of perspiration stood on his forehead, and on his face was a look of pure misery. Josh, still sitting with his back against the cabin wall, grinned at him.

"Ain't you never had a drink befo', kid?"

Lucius tried to look indignant. "Sure I have. At home I drink all the time. I can outdrink anybody in South Bar. But there's somethin' about Nate's whiskey . . ." He took a deep gulp of air, and very carefully lay back down again.

"You got better stuff at home, huh?" Josh asked.

"Oh, the best. My grandpa has it shipped in special."

"Yo' folks rich, huh, Luke?"

240

"Rich? I should say so. They own practically all of southern Indiana."

Josh came across the deck and flopped down beside Lucius, propping his head on an elbow and gazing at the boy with new interest. "I reckon when you're rich you kin git lots o' women, huh, Luke?"

Lucius was startled by the question, but recovered quickly. "Oh sure. I used to have practically any woman in town, whenever I wanted."

"Well, I be dawg! You lucky, Luke. You sho' had it good." Josh rolled onto his back and gazed up at the night sky. "You know somethin', Luke. I didn't never have a woman till I come on th' river, an' I was twenty-one years old then."

Lucius reacted with incredulous horror. "Good Lord, Josh!"

"There warn't no gals whar we lived, way out in th' middle o' th' woods. I was pert' near a grown man 'fo' I ever *saw* a woman, 'cept my granny an' my sister Carrie. There was us five boys, see, an' Carrie. She was th' onliest gal. Me an' my brothers, we used to chase th' damn pigs in th' woods. We'd ketch us a sow an' tie 'er up, some o' th' boys'd hold 'er while th' others'd fuck 'er. Tha's why th' kraut calls me 'pig-fucker.' I tell ya, Luke, pigs ain't half bad once you learn how to handle 'em. I've had a few women I didn't think was no better. 'Course, you got to git a big ol' fat sow. Young 'uns ain't no good. Too much muscle."

Josh giggled softly, falling into a reminiscent mood.

"One time my brother Wally got tarred o' pigs, an' 'cided he was gon' try it with Carrie. So he took 'er out in th' woods an' tole 'er he wanted to do it with 'er. She was 'bout twelve er thirteen, plenty old enough, but she ain't never done it befo', an' she was scairt to. Well, Wally, he had one o' them mouth organs he got off'n a peddler oncet, an' Carrie, she always hankered after that dang mouth organ. So Wally told 'er she could have it if she'd do it with 'im, an' she said all right. Well, it made 'er bleed, an' her an' Wally both got scairt 'cause they thought she was hurt. Carrie run home cryin' an' blabbed th' whole goddamn thang . . ."

Josh had to pause to recover from a fit of giggles before going on.

241

"Well, suh, Paw got out his squirrel rifle. When Wally started to come home, Paw walked out on th' porch and farred at 'im, point-blank. I reckon he missed, 'cause Wally lit out fo' th' woods, an' we didn't find no blood on th' ground. But ever' time Wally'd come near th' house, Paw would walk out an' raise 'is rifle, an' Wally'd light out ag'in. After 'bout three days o' that, Wally gave up an' stopped tryin'. He wandered off somewheres an', y'know, we ain't seen Wally from that day till this."

The humor of the situation overcame Josh completely. He slapped his leg and cackled.

"Funny," Lucius said.

A waning moon had risen, and threw a pale shimmer over the river. From a distance, the sounds of merrymaking around the community campfire continued unabated. Josh stretched, and slapped his belly.

"Well, I swar, Luke, I feel purty good now. Goddamn! Jes' wish we had us a woman, tha's all."

He was suddenly struck with an inspiring thought. "Hey, I jes' remembered. Thar's a woman in Paducah I used to visit. Name's Molly, lives on a barge a little ways downstream. Le's go see 'er, want to? She only charges a dollar. You got two dollars, Luke?"

Lucius was immediately uncomfortable. "Uh, well . . . yeah, but—"

"Loan me one, will ya? I'll pay you back later. Le's go."

"You're supposed to be on watch, Josh."

"It ain't far. We'll be back soon. Come on, Luke, Molly's th' best damn piece o' ass on th' river." He grinned. "An' I'll let you go first."

Lucius's discomfort became acute. "Aw, no, Josh, I . . . I don't think we better."

Josh's eyes narrowed shrewdly. "Wha's th' matter, Luke, you scairt? Maybe all that braggin' you did was a lot o' crap, huh? Maybe you ain't never had a woman befo'."

Lucius took another deep breath and, with a mighty effort, hauled himself to his feet. "Come on, goddamn it, I'll show you," he said with forced bravado. "Let's go get her."

The barge was moored in a secluded slough half a mile downstream from the boatmen's camping area. It was whitewashed, and shone brightly on the water in the moonlight. At Josh's soft knock the door opened, and a woman was silhouetted against a faint candleglow behind her.

"Hullo, Jake," she said. "Ain't seen you in a coon's age."

He grinned at her. "Josh," he said.

"Oh yeah, Josh. I see so many, I cain't hardly remember 'em all." The woman opened the door wider, and retreated.

"C'mon, Luke," Josh said, and went inside.

Lucius stepped inside and looked around, wide-eyed. It was a small, dingy room, dimly lit by one candle on a corner table. A large bed occupied half of the floor space. The woman stood at the far end of the room, gazing blankly at her visitors. She was not young, not old, with long, straight, dark hair that hung over her shoulders, and coal black eyes. She wore a full-length housecoat that was tattered and soiled and hung partially open in front, exposing heavy, low-hanging breasts.

Josh moved close to her. His eyes dropped down her body, and up again to her face. "You lookin' mighty purty this year, Molly," he purred in a honeyed voice. "An' now, if you don' mind, we'll jes' git right to it. I'm s'posed to be on duty at th' boat, an' I got to git back in a hurry."

"I won't hold you up," the woman said casually. She moved past Josh and went to the bed. With a quick movement she threw off her housecoat and lay down naked on the bed, flat on her back. She arranged her arms languidly above her head, spread her long legs in a V, and looked expectantly at the two males.

"Well, what are you waitin' for?"

Josh glanced at Lucius with a smirk. "After you, Luke."

Lucius stood transfixed, staring at the woman. His eyes roamed back and forth between the dark, bushy pubic region and the great flattened breasts that spread across her chest. He swallowed hard, moistened his lips with his tongue, and wiped at his perspiring brow with the back of his sleeve.

"Christ, it's hot in here," he mumbled.

The woman lifted her head and looked closely at him for the first time. "Oh my Gawd! Don' tell me I got a damn virgin on my hands!"

Josh cackled. "Come on, Luke, time's a-wastin'."

"You go first," Lucius said weakly.

243

"Goddamn it, you bastards want it or not?" the woman barked.

Josh was throwing off his clothes. "Git ready, Luke. It won't take me long."

He crawled into bed and lowered himself on the woman's body, squirmed to find his position, and went to work with a long sigh.

"Ooo-wee!" He glanced up at Lucius while he worked. "It's good, Luke. Mighty, mighty good . . ." He closed his eyes and concentrated, grunting and blowing, gradually increasing the tempo of his movements.

Lucius stood with his back against the door and watched, paralyzed in fascination. The woman's head was turned in his direction. Her dark, expressionless eyes were fixed on his face. She seemed unaware of the heaving body above her. Soon Josh's thrashings reached a peak of intensity, and the woman responded to the extent of raising her legs slightly and contributing a few small hip movements of her own. Josh uttered a low groan and quivered violently. Then he lay still, eyes closed, panting. A beatific smile lit his face.

The woman gave him a poke in the ribs. "Git up, you bastard, give the kid a chance. Le's git this over with."

Reluctantly, Josh permitted himself to be prodded to his feet. He reached for his pants. The woman took her housecoat, lying on the bed beside her, and used it to wipe the inside of her legs.

"Your turn, kid," she said to Lucius, and when he made no move, she gave him a hard look. "Well, c'mon, what you waitin' for?"

She and Josh were both observing him, she frowning, Josh grinning.

Lucius took a few timid steps forward. "Wait outside, huh, Josh?"

Josh was just buckling his belt. "Oh no you don't, Luke! I wanna larn some o' yo' high-class ways o' doin' it. That is, if you *got* any."

The woman was up and trying to pull Lucius's clothes off, muttering, "Looks like I'm gon' have to rape the li'l infant."

Lucius pushed her roughly away. "Get in the bed, damn it." With a burst of angry determination, he shucked off his clothes and advanced on her.

244

She sat at the edge of the bed watching him, and her eyes went wide with surprise. "Lawd 'a' mercy, jes' look a' that! You ain't even got a—"

"Shut up!" Lucius snapped. He pushed her down and came over her, clutching at her breasts.

Josh was laughing again. "Git it, Luke, git it!"

Lucius huffed and puffed and growled and grunted, and pushed himself against the woman with all his might, gyrating his lower torso fiercely. Josh stood at the side of the bed watching, and fairly yelling with delight.

"Attaboy, Luke! Give 'er a good 'un!"

Then the woman began to giggle. It began softly, then grew louder and more abandoned until it became raucous laughter. Abruptly, Lucius ceased his exertions and lay still, panting.

The woman rested her chin on his shoulder and gasped with merriment. "Lawd Jesus, I ain't never seen the like!"

She rolled her body, expertly depositing her young lover on his back, then got out of bed and stood beside Josh.

"Jes' look at that!" she squealed. "Th' po' bastard ain't even got a hard-on!"

Josh and the woman leaned against each other, rendered temporarily helpless by peals of ringing laughter.

Lucius raised himself slowly and sat on the side of the bed. Perspiration rolled off his face and dripped on his bare legs. He gripped the sides of the bed and stared in glassy-eyed stupefaction at the floor.

Josh stopped laughing. "Uh-oh." He rushed to the door and flung it open. "Out, Luke. Out!"

Lucius raised his misery-laden eyes to the doorway, gathered his strength, and bolted.

"Lawd 'a' mercy, wha's wrong with 'im?" the woman said in alarm.

Josh chuckled and picked up Lucius's clothes. "Nothin's wrong. I reckon you jes' didn't appeal to 'im."

He went to the door and peered out. "Hey, Luke. You all right, boy?"

From the .darkness at the side of the boat came the sounds of retching. Josh tossed Lucius's clothes on the deck.

"Here's yo' duds, Luke. Git dressed an' go on back. I'll be on d'rectly." He stepped back into the cabin and closed the door.

245

Lucius lay on his stomach, head and arms hanging limply over the side of the boat, fingers trailing in the dirty water. His eyes were glazed, and his breath came in short convulsive pants. He could hear Josh and the woman inside the cabin, laughing still. He gulped, uttered a low, piteous moan, and waited for death to release him from his unendurable shame.

But death declined to come. When Josh returned to the flatboat a little while later, he found Lucius reclining in Captain Nate's chair on the roof deck, watching the last-quarter moon climbing slowly toward the zenith.

"Hey, how you feel, Luke?" Josh was exuding good cheer.

"I'm all right," Lucius answered quietly.

Josh sprawled on the roof deck beside the chair, stretched his legs, and sighed contentedly. "Goddamn, that Molly's some piece, Luke. I had another go after you left. Too bad you didn't feel up to it." He watched Lucius out of the corner of his eye.

Lucius stirred slightly. "Yeah, well . . . not my type, y'see? I'm used to more, uh . . ."

"Yeah, more high-class women." Josh was chuckling. "Never mind, Luke, you don' need to explain." Then, turning serious: "Only thang is, you didn't pay 'er."

"Oh damn. I forgot."

"She was mad as hell. I told 'er we'd pay 'er next trip, an' she got even madder. She went off to git her boyfriend, said he'd bust my head for me. I said, 'Honey, tell yo' boyfriend to git his buddies together, an' me an' my buddy'll tie 'em all in knots an' throw 'em in th' river.'"

Lucius was pained. "Oh Lord, Josh, I wish you hadn't said that."

"Aw, hell, I didn't mean *you*, kid, I meant me an' Greasy. We kin whup any dozen o' them damn river rats without even workin' up a sweat."

Josh lay back and gazed up at the moon, and chuckled again as he thought over the night's adventures. "Lordee, Luke, that sho' was a funny sight, you tryin' to do it with Molly. Jes' wait'll I tell Nate an' Greasy 'bout it."

Lucius was horror-stricken. "Aw, Josh, no! You . . . you wouldn't do that, would you?"

246

"Why the hell not? It's funny."

"I thought we were friends, Josh."

"Why, sho' we are. Cain't we have a laugh amongst friends once in a while?"

Lucius took a grip on Josh's arm. "No, Josh. Don't tell." Josh grinned at him. "What'll you gimme?"

"I'll give you a dollar."

Josh made a sour face. "Don' want no dollar."

"Well, what *do* you want?"

Josh paused a moment for dramatic effect. "That leather satchel o' yours."

Lucius recoiled as if from a physical blow. "God, no! That belonged to my father, Josh. I'll never part with it, no matter what."

Josh sat up. "Listen, Luke. All my life I been pore, I ain't never had nothin' purty, never. An' that satchel's about th' purtiest thang I ever did see. I jes' want it so *bad.*"

It was a moving confession, and Josh looked up into Lucius's face, hoping to see pity. It was not there.

"No," Lucius snapped. "Goddamn it, *no!*"

"All right, then," Josh said amiably. "Me an' Greasy an' Nate'll have us plenty o' good laughs about what happened at Molly's this evenin'."

"You won't tell," Lucius said with a show of confidence. "If you did, you'd be in trouble. Nate'd know you didn't stay on watch."

Josh laughed. "Aw, hell, that don' matter. He'd jes' cuss me a little, then fo'git about it. It'd be worth it, Luke."

Lucius sighed and gripped his forehead, struggling with painful choices. Then he got up and went down to the cabin, and returned shortly with the satchel. After one last moment of agonizing indecision, he gritted his teeth and held the treasure out to Josh. Josh clutched it to his breast and looked up at Lucius with shining eyes.

"You know what this means, Luke? It means we're lifelong buddies now, you an' me. You always gonna stick up fo' me, and I'm always gonna stick up fo' you. Tha's the way it's gonna be. Ain't it, Luke?"

Lucius's voice was bleak. "Yeah, Josh. That's the way it's gonna be." Limp in defeat, he turned and went with dragging steps back down to the cabin.

247

4

THAT SAME DAY—Saturday—had been one of unseasonal chill and gusty winds at South Bar, Indiana, and also a day on which business reached one of its unpredictable peaks at Thacker and Hargrave, Associates, a condition that strained the company's modest capacities to the utmost. A number of steamboats tied up at the wharf during the afternoon, awaiting their turns to take on firewood, and from time to time a captain would express his impatience with the time-consuming process by firing off angry blasts on his ship's whistle. Isaac Hargrave, as foreman of the yard, pressed all available manpower into the task of servicing the ships. His men cursed as they bent to their labors, and sweated heavily in spite of the cool weather, but their curses and complaints were halfhearted, for they knew that only a steady flow of trade would keep their jobs secure and their families fed.

Late in the afternoon the rush had abated but little, and Isaac stuck his head into Cyrus Thacker's office and said, "'Scuse me, Mr. Thacker, could I see you outside a minute?"

Cyrus was in conference with a customer, and was visibly annoyed by the interruption. Outside in the hallway, he frowned his displeasure at Isaac. "Well, what is it?"

"We're down to forty-eight cords," Isaac said. "The ship out there now's takin' on twenty-eight. One more shows up, we'll run slap out."

248

Cyrus' annoyance grew. "Dammit, man! I'm trying to pacify Jim Graham in there, on account o' we ain't meetin' his order for lumber for his new warehouse. Don't pester me about firewood. When we run out, we run out." Cyrus had his hand on the doorknob, ready to go back into his office.

"And the ship out there's the *Cincinnati Queen*," Isaac said hurriedly.

Cyrus was stone-faced. "What about it?"

"I jes' thought maybe you'd want to, uh . . . make some inquiries, or somethin'—"

"Well, you thought wrong. I ain't interested." Cyrus went back into his office and closed the door behind him with a thud of finality.

A few minutes later his junior partner opened the door and looked in again. "Sorry to keep interruptin', Mr. Thacker. But there's a gen'lman here off the *Cincinnati Queen*, wants to see you."

"I'm busy, Isaac," Cyrus said in a hard voice.

Cyrus' visitor rose. "That's all right, Cyrus. I got to be goin', anyway."

Cyrus escorted his customer all the way to the outer door of the building with his hand on the man's shoulder. "Listen, Jim, I swear I'll have that lumber ready by the end o' next week, if I have to git out there an' cut it myself, y'hear?"

When he returned, he seemed almost surprised to find Isaac and a tall, well-dressed stranger waiting for him at the door of his office. He addressed Isaac, ignoring the stranger.

"First thing in the mornin', I want you to put all the men you can spare on Jim Graham's order. If we don't git crackin' on that, we're gonna lose a damn good customer."

Isaac was suffering some impatience of his own. "This gen'leman here's waitin' to see you, Mr. Thacker. He ain't got much time."

The stranger stepped up to Cyrus and extended his hand. "Albert Pettingill's the name," he said crisply. "I was looking for your boy Lucius."

Cyrus shook hands grudgingly and took his time looking the man over, letting his eyes drift down over the expen-

249

sive suit to the shiny shoes and back again, ending with a grim inspection of the immaculately groomed hair.

"Ain't no boy o' mine," he muttered, and went on into his office.

Pettingill glanced inquiringly at Isaac, who smiled apologetically and tried to explain. "Y'see, Lucius and Mr. Thacker never got along very well, Mr. Pettingill." He waved a hand toward the office. "But come on inside. You got a few minutes yet."

Inside the office, Cyrus stood behind his desk with his feet wide apart and scowled to see that he had been followed in. "Look here, Pattingale, I don't know what the hell you—"

"Pettingill, please."

"Whatever. I'm a busy man, so let's not waste time. What the hell did you want with Lucius?"

"All quite honorable and proper, Mr. Thacker, I assure you. It happened that I had a conversation with Lucius on my way upriver last week, and he seemed like a bright lad, pleasing personality and all that—I made him an offer of employment on the steamboat line."

"What kind of employment?"

"As administrative assistant to me. I'm an executive in the company, you see. It would be a fine opportunity for him."

"Is that so?" Cyrus said, plainly disbelieving.

"We agreed to meet again today, but since I didn't see him around, I thought I'd come in and—"

"Well, he ain't here," Cyrus said brusquely. "He's gone."

"So I am told. May I ask where he went?"

"You may ask, but you ain't likely to find out, 'cause we don't know. And I'll tell you somethin' else—we don't give a damn."

Isaac started to protest. "Aw, now Cyrus—"

"And furthermore, Pettingale," Cyrus went on, keeping his scowl fixed on the stranger, "I don't know what damn fool mischief you had in mind, takin' up with a young boy like Lucius, but I'll say this—I think you deserve each other. I think you're both cut out o' the same cloth. And that ain't meant as a compliment."

Albert Pettingill arched an eyebrow. "I beg your pardon?"

"He went downriver, that's all I can tell you. An' if you

250

happen to run across 'im anywhere, you can do 'im a big favor. You can tell 'im there's a warrant out for his arrest, an' if he ever sets foot in South Bar again, he'll be clapped in jail, where he belongs."

Pettingill's eyebrow climbed a little higher. "Indeed? On what charge?"

"He stole lumber from the yard an' gave it to his no 'count friends. For six months he robbed me, right under my nose."

"Really!" Amusement crinkled Pettingill's handsome face. "Well, perhaps the boy had promise, after all."

Cyrus's anger flared. "What's that you say, sir?!" he roared.

The visitor was already on his way out. In the doorway he paused long enough to nod and say, "Good day to you both." And then he was gone, closing the door softly behind him.

As he emerged through the woodyard's main gate and started down toward the river landing, he suddenly became aware of someone at his side. Isaac Hargrave had overtaken him, and now began to speak in breathless haste.

"'Scuse me, sir. I can give you some information about Lucius, if you want."

The older man glanced at him with little apparent interest. "Well?"

"Y'see, him and Mr. Thacker had a big row last week, and Lucius figgered he'd better get on out o' town right away, so as not to make matters worse. So he went down the river with some friends. They're headin' for New Orleans on a flatboat."

"A flatboat!" Pettingill closed his eyes and shuddered delicately. "Good God!"

"Well, that's jes' what I wanted to tell you, sir. Lucius didn't really want to do that. He'd 'a' much rather waited and gone with you. So I thought if you'd keep an eye out, you might spot him somewhere along the way."

"The river's full of flatboats, Mr. Hargrave. They all look alike."

"It'd be worth your while to look for 'im, though. Listen, you don't want to believe all them bad things Mr. Thacker was sayin' about Lucius—he was jes' mad, and bein' spiteful. No, the truth is, Lucius is a fine fella. Smart as a whip,

251

and a good worker. We never had no better worker at the woodyard, no sirree. And honest! I tell you, that boy's as honest as the day is long. Why, he'd no more think o' lyin' or stealin' than—"

They had reached the wharf. Pettingill stopped at the steamboat's gangplank, turned to Isaac, and waved him silent. "Never mind, please. I appreciate your trying to help, but never mind."

Isaac was insistent. "You ought to look for 'im, sir. It'd be an awful shame if you missed the chance to hire 'im."

Pettingill gave him a patient smile. "In me, Mr. Hargrave, you see a man in perfect balance between optimism and pessimism. I am a pessimist in that I believe that if something can go wrong, it will. But I am an optimist in that, when it does go wrong, I haven't the slightest trouble convincing myself that it was all for the best."

"Oh no, not in this case," Isaac said fervently. "Y'see, I can tell that Lucius was right, you're a fine gen'lman, and I agree with Mr. Thacker, I think you and him are cut out o' the same cloth, only I *do* mean it as a compliment. Lucius comes from a mighty good family, sir, as I can see you do too. Why, do you realize Lucius's grandfather, Mr. Samuel Gilpin, *founded* this town, back in 1800?"

Pettingill's response was subtly mocking. "Good heavens, no! I never knew that!"

The older man let his gaze roam over what he could see of the village: the ugly bulk of the woodyard, the almost empty little dirt road that led past it from the wharf and listlessly climbed a slight rise away from the river between a few forlorn houses half-hidden among trees, leading, as far as could be told, nowhere. No wonder Lucius had been so frantic to leave.

The whistle of the *Cincinnati Queen* suddenly cut the air with a piercing shriek that echoed off the sleepy hillsides back beyond the village. It was time for departure. Albert Pettingill smiled at Isaac.

"You've been very kind, Mr. Hargrave, and I sincerely thank you."

"Maybe next time you come upriver," Isaac said brightly, "you can plan to stop by and take supper with us. Goodness, we'd be so pleased, we'd . . ." He trailed off, noticing that the other man was firmly shaking his head.

"There will never be another time," Mr. Pettingill said,

252

and smiled again to see Isaac's jaw drop in surprise and consternation. Then, without another word, he turned away, striding with easy familiarity along the narrow gangplank to the ship.

Isaac shouted hastily after him, "Well, you keep an eye out for Lucius, now, y'hear? You'll be glad you did, sir, 'cause he's a fine young fella, jes' the finest fella you'd ever hope to——"

His words were obliterated by a second blast of the steamboat's whistle, as deckhands scurried to disengage the gangplank and throw off mooring lines. It was useless in any case; Albert Pettingill had already disappeared into the main cabin.

5

THE SUN was riding high and brilliant when Nate Collins came painfully back into the world of the living. He opened his eyes, winced, closed them tight again, and uttered a soft, misery-laden moan. Five minutes passed before he struggled to his feet and forced his bloodshot eyes to make an inspection of his surroundings. The only crewman in evidence was Lucius, who was sprawled in the captain's chair on the roof deck, his arm draped casually over the long pole that controlled the tiller.

"What day is it?" Nate croaked.

"Sunday," Lucius called out cheerily. "An' everything's all right, Nate, I been takin' good care."

An expression of deep disgust came over Nate's weather-

253

beaten face. Moving gingerly and grunting with every exertion, he climbed up onto the roof deck and grasped the tiller.

"Tha's great," he growled. "Tha's jes' great! You're headin' straight fo' that sandbar up ahead."

"What sandbar?" Lucius demanded.

"Git out o' my chair!" Nate bellowed, and cringed from the self-torture.

Lucius jumped up, looking injured. "I been navigatin' by myself all mornin' and I ain't run aground, have I? You might at least say thank you!"

Nate lowered himself into his chair, and sighed. "Yeah, you been doin' fine, Luke. A damn sight better'n them other two bastards, that's sure. I thank ya."

Lucius was satisfied. "Oh, that's all right, Nate. I knew somebody had to do it, so I did it. That's the kind o' fellow I am, y'know? I see somethin' needs to be done, I jes' do it."

"Yeah, yeah," Nate mumbled. He was busy with the tiller.

"I reckon by the time we go in partners next year, Nate, I'll be expert at navigatin'."

"I doubt it. But you're learnin' fast, I got to admit. An' I hope you larnt somethin' last night too, Luke boy."

Lucius hesitated. "Uh . . . how do you mean, Nate?"

"You an' Greasy both got blind stinkin' drunk, an' I bet you feel rotten now, don't ya? I kin excuse ya this once, but Greasy, he's old enough to know better. Disgustin' it was, jes' plain disgustin'."

Lucius was properly repentant. "Yeah, you're right, Nate. Believe me, I won't never let that happen to me again."

"Well, I hope not."

"Anyway, I got myself sobered up and spent the rest o' the evening helpin' Josh guard the boat. Fact, Josh wasn't payin' much attention, so I did it myself, mainly."

"Good boy, Luke, I'm much obliged. My Lord, seems like the youngest member o' the crew's turning out to be the best 'un."

"It'll be different next year, Nate. When we're partners, we'll hire us on a better crew than we got now, huh?"

"Damn right we will." Nate reached out and slapped Lucius on the leg. "Now you go down an' give them two

254

no 'count bastards a swift kick, an' tell 'em to git their asses out here and grab th' oars. I wanna cross to the right bank now. We'll be hittin' the Mississip' 'fo' evenin'."

Around noon, Nate hailed a steamboat as it plowed past, heading upstream. He yelled to a stevedore lolling on the cargo deck, "Ho, there! What's higher, th' O or th' M?"

The shouted reply was almost lost in the sound of the ship's thrashing wheels. "The M's runnin' high. You'll have to row for it."

"Goddamn!" Nate muttered.

Josh and Otto, lolling on the foredeck, groaned in unison.

"What's it mean?" Lucius asked.

"It means the Mississippi's up, an' we gonna have to row our asses off to git onto it," Josh grumbled.

Nate explained more fully. "Y'see, Luke, when th' Ohio's higher'n the Mississip', it'll shoot you pert' near 'cross to t'other side, an' all you got to do is hang on fo' dear life. But when the Mississip's higher, it backs up th' Ohio. It'll be like we fightin' our way upstream the last few miles."

"Bad luck, huh?" Lucius said.

"Not so bad," Otto said. "Ven ve git on der big river, ve go zippin' down to New Orleans lickity-split. High vater iss fast vater."

In the course of the day, a change came over the scenery. The land on either side flattened and fell away and the river broadened, as if in preparation for matching its dimensions to the great central stream ahead. The current became confused, the water more turbid. By late afternoon, progress had ceased. The flatboat drifted, going nowhere.

Nate shouted an order, "Stand to th' oars!"

Otto and Josh set the huge oars in their sockets and stood poised and ready.

"Stand by to relieve on fifty strokes!" Nate barked at Lucius. To the others he bellowed the first order for action. "Pull!"

The oars sliced into the water. Otto and Josh strained against the tall handles, their faces flushed and contorted with the effort.

"Set!"

255

The oars rose as one, and swept forward to a new position.

"Pull!"

Gradually the sluggish craft developed momentum. After ten minutes, Nate rasped out a new order.

"First relief!" He motioned for Lucius to take Josh's oar. Lucius leaped forward to obey.

"Set!" Nate yelled. Then: "Pull!"

Lucius tried to follow the example he had seen. He strained to his utmost, but soon fell behind the cadence.

"Set!" yelled Nate. "Keep up, Luke! Pull!"

Lucius began to pant. Sweat poured from his body. The muscles in his back tightened in pain.

"Keep up, Luke, goddamn it!" Nate shouted. "Set! Pull!"

After three minutes, Lucius gave up. He leaned against his oar and gasped, "I can't!"

"Goddamn it!" Nate snapped. "Relief!"

"He ain't done his fifty!" Josh complained.

"Relief, I said!"

Josh cursed vigorously and snatched the oar from Lucius, and the boy collapsed on the roof deck in helpless exhaustion.

Nate's cadence droned on: "Set! Pull! Set! Pull!"

After a while, Nate yelled, "Hold!"

The rowing ceased. The oar blades hung dripping in midair. The boat began a slow spin to the left.

"All right, stand down," Nate said.

Otto and Josh pulled the oars in, and stashed them. A deep, almost unnatural silence descended.

A few minutes later, Lucius lifted his head and looked around. The boat was silently revolving on a sheet of roiling water that stretched away in all directions. Lucius raised himself on an elbow and stared at the eerily quiet turbulence around him. The flatboat shuddered as it struck a new crosscurrent, rocked gently, and began to spin lazily in the opposite direction.

"My God!" Lucius croaked. "What's happening?"

"She's comin' 'round real nice," Nate said calmly.

"Real nice," Josh agreed.

"New Orleans, here ve come!" Otto said, chuckling.

"Where's the Mississippi?" Lucius asked.

The others laughed.

256

"Are we *on* it?" Lucius said shrilly.

Nate pointed to the west, where the sinking sun was turning the sky pink and yellow, and the earth below a shadowy blue. "Look over yonder, Luke."

Lucius looked, and was barely able to make out a dark shoreline of scraggly forest, a quarter of a mile away.

"See that land?" Nate said. "That there's Missoura."

"My God!" Lucius stared. "It don't look much different from Indiana!"

The others laughed again. Spirits were rising. Otto went to get his flute.

"Now dat ve be in New Orleans soon," he said with a wink, "I t'ink I practice some French tunes."

"When we gonna make New Orleans, Nate?" Lucius asked. "Tomorrow?"

Josh and Otto cackled in high glee.

"Not hardly," Nate said. "Tomorrow we make New Madrid." He grinned at his junior crewman. "They's a heap o' diff'unce."

Lucius was staring at the land to the west, lying low and mysterious across the darkening water.

"Missouri," he breathed. "Goddamn! I'm way out West now!"

6

THE WHARVES of New Madrid were aswarm with vessels of every size and shape, from yawls and skiffs to flatboats, keelboats, and barges—and among these, towering, multi-tiered steamers. Nate Collins grumbled at the

257

lack of choice docking space available, making it necessary to moor a quarter of a mile downstream from the main landing. It was late afternoon when they secured the boat and prepared to go ashore.

"First off, the duty," Nate announced then. "Greasy had shore leave at Paducah, so Josh gits it this time."

Otto winced. *"Ach!"*

Nate proceeded to deliver a stern lecture, aimed at Josh. "Now, goddamn it, I don' want a mess o' foolishness like we had at Paducah. 'Nother night like that an' I'll cut off shore leave fo' the rest o' the trip. You know the rules, now stick to 'em. No gittin' drunk, an' no fightin'. I was mighty 'shamed o' the way certain parties acted in Paducah—downright mortified." He glared accusingly at Otto and Lucius, who hung their heads like scolded schoolboys, while Josh snickered.

To Josh, Nate continued, "Now, back on board by midnight, y'unnerstan'? I don' want you stumblin' in at break o'day, tellin' me some story 'bout how you met this woman who was too good to leave."

Josh grinned delightedly, clearly proud of his reputation as a prodigious lover.

"An' don't go chasin' pigs in de streets, Josh, dat ain't nice," Otto added, and laughed heartily when Josh scowled at him.

Nate threw a leg over the gunwale, ready to leave the boat. "If you need me, I'll be at Kelly's Tavern." He glanced at Lucius. "Want to come along, kid? I'll buy you a drink. *One* drink."

Lucius hesitated. "I'll be along a little later," he said.

Nate climbed off the boat and strolled away toward town. Josh had already jumped ashore and was hurrying purposefully off in another direction, bent on a private plan of his own.

Otto rushed to the side and shouted after his fellow crewman, "Hey, you, Josh, you find nice clean voman, you bring her back here, *ja?*"

Josh paid him no attention.

As dusk came on, Lucius sat on the edge of the roof deck, studying the steamboats in the distance. Otto had become a mass of lethargic flesh in Nate's wicker chair. Lazily he fingered his flute, from time to time blew a few half-

258

hearted notes, and occasionally squinted curiously at Lucius.

"Hey, vat you lookin' at, *Kindchen?*"

"Jes' watchin' the steamboats."

"*Ach!* Ain't you never seen a steamboat before?"

Lucius was pondering something. "Le's see—this is Monday evenin'. If a steamboat passed South Bar last Saturday, would it be down this far by now?"

Otto frowned at him. "Ves de madder vid you, *Kindchen?* Vat you so damn interested in steamboats for, all of a sudden?"

"I like steamboats. I got lots o' friends on steamboats."

Otto found this irresistibly funny. "*Ach,* you don't say!" He shook with laughter.

With a grimace of annoyance, Lucius got up and scrambled off the roof deck, crossed quickly to the forward gunwale, and vaulted ashore.

"Hey, vere you goin'?" Otto called.

"For a walk," Lucius called back.

"You be careful now," Otto shouted. "New Madrid is some vicked town for little *Kindchen* like you."

Lucius strode rapidly away with Otto's merry laughter ringing in his ears.

Along the wharves he strolled, marveling at the density and diversity of river traffic and the bustle of activity attached to it. There were huge flatboats, three or four times the size of Nate Collins's craft, loaded with mountains of cargo in bales and barrels and hogsheads, and occasionally on the hoof. On one boat, hog slaughtering was in progress, and the shouts of the men at their bloody work, mixed with the squeals of the animals being dragged to sacrifice, made an earsplitting din. The water around the boat was a red brown stew of discarded entrails.

As twilight faded to darkness, Lucius turned away from the river and wandered along the main street of the town. It was teeming with humanity—mostly rivermen—transients who would be in port for an hour or a day, and who never rested in their quest for pleasure. Lucius came upon Kelly's Tavern, a dingy little saloon, remembered that Nate had mentioned it, and peered into its dim interior. It was packed with noisy patrons. Lucius stood in the doorway, indecisive. Several men brushed past him, going

259

in. Lucius followed them. He wandered aimlessly in the crowd and suddenly noticed Nate, sitting at a little table with a woman. There was a bottle of whiskey on the table in front of them, and a simpering smile on Nate's face as he talked in low tones to his companion.

Catching sight of Lucius, Nate raised his glass and said, "Hey, Luke, ready for that drink now?"

The woman looked up and gave Lucius an inviting smile.

"No, thanks," Lucius said, and moved quickly on.

At a doorway leading to a back room, he paused and looked in through dense clouds of tobacco smoke at several groups of men sitting silently around gaming tables. Every player was staring hypnotically at the cards in his hand, and on each face was the same look of almost painful concentration. Lucius went on, threading his way along the length of the bar that occupied one long wall of the room. At the far end, nearest the front entrance, there was a single unoccupied seat. Lucius took it.

Business was lively, and two bartenders were scurrying to keep up. While he waited, Lucius stared dully into a large mirror on the wall behind the bar, scanning without interest the reflections of the mass of humanity in the room behind him.

Soon a bartender stopped in front of him and said, "What'll you have, kid?"

And at the same moment, a tall man in a crumpled felt hat walked behind Lucius's seat, heading toward the street. Lucius glanced at the man's image in the mirror, and his mouth dropped open.

"I said what'll you have?" the bartender snapped.

Lucius sat as if paralyzed. Suddenly he whirled in his seat and stared toward the front doorway. The man in the crumpled felt hat was just disappearing into the darkness outside.

The bartender fumed. "I ain't got all night, goddamn it. For the last time, what'll—"

The boy was off his stool and bolting for the exit. For an instant he was framed in the doorway as he looked up the street, waved his arms wildly, and yelled, "Cap'n Jochum! Cap'n Jochum, sir! Wait!"

He was gone, and the bartender shook his head in befuddlement, and turned to the next customer.

260

7

MR. ALBERT PETTINGILL was dining at the Palace Hotel.

The Palace was in no way palatial; it was a squat, ugly, boxlike wooden frame building, and it sat at the upper end of the street facing a small square, half a mile from the river. The decor of its tiny lobby ran to the rococo, the brass-gilded, and the heavily brocaded, with numbers of oil lamps along the walls serving an ornamental purpose, but doing little to dispel the high-ceilinged gloom.

A good part of the ground floor was occupied by the dining room, which was humming with the conversations of diners at the peak of the evening's business hour. And in a rear corner, farthest removed from the paths of traffic, Pettingill sat at a small table and chewed placidly on a piece of roast beef. Having disposed of a mouthful, he reached for his wineglass, took a few careful sips, paused to reflect a moment, and prepared to begin again. Then he was approached by a waiter.

"'Scuse me, Mr. Pettingill, sir?"

Pettingill did not take kindly to being interrupted at dinner. He glared at the waiter and snapped, "What is it?"

"There's a young fellow at the door, sir, wants to see you. Says you know him."

Pettingill frowned across the dining room at a young man standing uncomfortably in the entranceway. "You mean that stevedore there?"

261

"Yes, sir, tha's him."

"Ridiculous!" Pettingill growled, and reached for a biscuit. "I know very few people in New Madrid, and I don't know anyone like *that*, anywhere."

"Yes, sir, tha's what I figgered," the waiter said. "Tha's why we didn't let him in, he's so dirty and all."

"Send him off," Pettingill said.

The waiter nodded and went away. Shortly he was back.

"Mr. Pettingill, sir? The young fellow says to tell you he's Lucius Hargrave, from South Bar, Indiana."

Pettingill put down his fork and stared intently across the room. "'Pon my word, I do believe it is." He nodded quickly. "Yes. Bring him over here."

The waiter's eyebrows went up in surprise and disapproval. "Yes, sir," he mumbled, and went off.

Pettingill placed another piece of roast beef in his mouth and began his careful chewing process. Then the dirty, unkempt boy was standing before him, shifting nervously from one foot to the other and grinning.

"H'lo, Mr. Pettingill. Sure is good to see you, sir. You remember me, don't you, sir?"

Pettingill chewed very slowly, and looked the boy up and down. He swallowed, reached for his wineglass again, and sipped.

"You look awful," he said finally. "What in God's name have you been into?"

"I been on a flatboat, sir. And I'm sure glad I ran into you, 'cause I want to explain what happened—"

"For God's sake, sit down!" Pettingill said irritably. "It's positively embarrassing to be seen with you."

Lucius pulled out the chair on the other side of the table and sat down. "Sorry about my appearance, Mr. Pettingill. I ain't had a chance to get a bath lately, and—"

"And the laundry facilities on flatboats are not first-class, either, I suppose."

"That's right, sir, they ain't. All our space is taken up by cargo. We got about six tons o' prime cargo, bound for New Orleans. Whiskey, salt pork, dried apples, tobacco—"

Pettingill waved him silent. "Never mind. When did you eat last?"

"Oh, we eat good on the flatboat, sir. Potatoes and salt pork and cornbread, and fish from the river—"

262

"I mean when did you last have a civilized meal, served on a tablecloth, with clean silverware?"

Lucius grinned again. "Not since I left home, sir."

Pettingill snapped his fingers for the waiter. "Bring this young man a roast beef dinner," he ordered. "Pile it on thick, he hasn't been eating very well lately."

The waiter sniffed disdainfully and went away.

Lucius rested his elbows on the table and leaned toward his benefactor, beaming. "I sure appreciate this, Mr. Pettingill. Golly, it's a lucky thing we came across each other like this. I jes' happened to meet up with Cap'n Jochum down the street a few minutes ago, and he kindly told me where I could find you. I been watchin' for the *Cincinnati Queen* every day, you can bet. I'll tell you the truth, I was beginnin' to get worried, 'fraid I'd missed you. Flatboats move a lot slower'n steamboats, y'know, and—"

Pettingill held up a hand, palm outward. "Lucius, my boy, desist. You do assail a person's eardrums unmercifully with that chatter of yours."

Lucius's grin grew wider. "'Scuse me, sir. I was jes' so excited 'bout runnin' into you—"

The waiter approached, bearing dishes.

"Here's your dinner," Mr. Pettingill said. "Give your vocal cords a rest now, and enjoy yourself."

Having finished his own meal, he leaned back in his chair, lit a cigar, and nursed a cup of coffee. Through narrowed eyes he watched his young guest attack a steaming plate of roast beef and potatoes. In a few minutes he leaned forward and spoke in an undertone.

"Lucius, your table manners would shock a penful of starving hogs. Stop that shoveling. Don't swallow your food whole. Take small mouthfuls and chew thoroughly. It is essential to good digestion, and good digestion is essential to good health."

Lucius's ready grin flashed again. "You sound jes' like my grandpa, Mr. Pettingill."

"Thank you," Mr. Pettingill said coldly.

"Oh, I wouldn't say that to jes' anybody. My grandpa's 'bout the smartest man in Indiana."

"Not only that, he founded South Bar back in 1800. Right?"

Lucius's eyes opened wide in astonishment. "That's right! How'd you know that?"

263

"My boy, you'd be amazed at the mountains of trivia I collect along the way."

"Yes, sir, I reckon," Lucius said uncomprehendingly, and turned his attention back to his food. Pettingill observed him a bit longer, then sighed and averted his eyes.

Soon Lucius pushed his clean plate away, leaned back in his chair, and gave his belly a resounding slap, causing his host to wince in pain.

"Mighty fine eatin', sir. I'm much obliged, an' I'm ready to start work now, anytime you say."

Pettingill carefully flicked the ashes off his cigar. "Well, now, Lucius . . . let's not be hasty here. I know I discussed the subject of employment with you, and as I recall, we agreed to discuss it further the next time we met. But when I came back through South Bar, you were nowhere to be seen. So naturally I assumed—"

"Well, that's what I wanted to explain, sir. Y'see, I was partners with a friend o' mine on this flatboat venture. But when I got the offer to go with you, I told my chum he could have my half free and clear, I had somethin' better lined up. Well, he jes' about broke down and cried. Said I was goin' back on my word, said I was ruinin' him, 'cause he jes' couldn' do it without me. So, rather than let him down, I agreed to go along partway, till he could find somebody to take my place. That's done now, so I'm free to go. And here I run into you! Ain't that lucky?" Lucius's voice exuded confidence, but his eyes were pleading. "Ain't that lucky, Mr. Pettingill?"

Pettingill was plainly unconvinced. "You see, the thing is, Lucius, I'm wondering if you're really the person I'm looking for. I had thought to take on someone as sort of . . . raw material, so to speak. But now that I see you again, I get the feeling you're perhaps just a bit . . . rawer than I realized."

Lucius's eyes were wide with panic. "Mr. Pettingill, you promised! Why, I could've . . . my stepfather wanted me to be manager of the woodyard, but I turned him down 'cause I wanted to go with you. Are you gonna go back on your word?"

Pettingill looked uncomfortable. "Well, I—"

"I been countin' on it, Mr. Pettingill. Here I am, a thousand miles from home, jes' waitin' for you to come along,

264

'cause I took you at your word . . ." Lucius's voice trembled, and broke off.

For once, Albert Pettingill was perplexed and uncertain. He sat gazing half in pity and half in distaste at the distraught youth across the table. Finally he spoke.

"Look here, Lucius, I wouldn't want you to think I'd betray a trust. Not my style at all, you know? So, since you've come all this way, let's give it a try, shall we?"

Immediately Lucius's face was lit with a broad smile. "Thank you, sir! I knew I could count on—"

"But I warn you, it won't be easy. You have a lot of grueling work ahead. Brain-crushing work. Weeks, months, even years of it, before you can hope to be a professional."

Lucius was listening eagerly. "A professional what, sir?"

Pettingill waved a vague hand in the air. "I speak of professionalism as a state of mind, Lucius. A state of grace, as it were. A style, a flair, a touch of elegance, which can be achieved only through hard work and single-minded determination. The question is, are you up to it?"

"I'm up to it, sir," Lucius said firmly. "I'm ready."

Pettingill sniffed. "We'll see." He took a pencil and a small notebook from his pocket and began to write. "Where are your things?" he asked.

"On the flatboat, sir. But I'm travelin' light."

"Yes, I can imagine." Pettingill ripped the sheet of paper from the notebook, folded it, and handed it to Lucius. "Give this to Jimmy Peal, the steward on the *Cincinnati Queen. You* call him Mr. Peal, mind. The *Queen's* leaving early in the morning, and *that,* my boy, is when we start to work."

"Yes, sir. Uh . . . when are *you* comin' aboard?"

"In time for departure." Pettingill was amused by the puzzled look on Lucius's face. "You see, there's a certain lovely lady here in the hotel who expects to enjoy my charming company until dawn's early light."

Lucius colored. "Oh."

Pettingill smiled, thinking of something pleasant. "Ruby's her name. Ruby James. Best thing available for five hundred miles below St. Louis. Not up to the quality of New Orleans, mind, or even Natchez. But in the hinterland, Ruby's the finest."

"Yes, sir." Lucius stuck the note in his pocket and got to his feet. Carefully he set his chair back under the table.

265

"Thanks for the dinner, Mr. Pettingill."

"You're entirely welcome, my boy."

"I'm goin' straight to the ship now, and get me a good night's sleep, so I can be ready to start work in the morning."

"Good."

"And Mr. Pettingill . . ." Lucius shifted from one foot to the other, and groped for words. "You won't regret this, sir. You said it takes hard work and determination. Well, I'm goin' to work harder'n anybody you ever saw, 'cause there ain't nobody on this here river's got more determination than me."

"That's fine, Lucius. And I think the first thing we'll do is work on your speech."

Lucius frowned. "What's the matter with it, sir? Don't I talk good?"

Pettingill sighed yet again. "Good night, lad."

"G'night, sir. And I'll be up early in the morning, rarin' to go. It'll be great to get . . ."

Pettingill was looking past him, not listening.

"Well . . . g'night, sir," Lucius mumbled, and turned to go.

As he started across the dining room, a tall black-haired woman in a blazing red dress brushed past him, moving toward Albert Pettingill, and Lucius had an impression of jewels and gleaming white teeth and a heavy perfume of enchanting sweetness.

He heard the woman exclaim in a shrill voice, "Albert! Darling!" and Pettingill's murmured response: "Ruby, love. How nice to see you."

Without looking back, Lucius hurried out of the room.

266

8

A HUNDRED CAMPFIRES flickered along the river landing, where as many small craft served as home for a teeming transient population. On Nate Collins's flatboat, Otto Grieshaber had a blaze going in his potbellied iron stove in one corner of the foredeck, and was squatting before it, stirring something in a pan. He glanced up and grinned as Lucius Hargrave clambered aboard and entered the circle of feeble light.

"Hey, *Kindchen!* You back just in time for some'ting to eat."

"Josh here yet?" Lucius asked warily.

Otto chuckled. "He vas here vid a voman, but she vas dirty, so I sent 'em away. I said, *'Dummkopf,* don' bring me no dirty fifty-cent voman, bring me *clean* voman. A clean voman's vort' a whole dollar,' I told him."

He was talking to thin air; Lucius had disappeared into the cabin without waiting to hear the details of Josh's visit. Otto stirred his stew with a long wooden spoon, tasted gingerly, made a face, and stirred more vigorously. Soon Lucius emerged from the cabin, carrying his satchel and huffing with indignation.

"Can you beat that? I couldn't find my satchel. Looked all over, finally found it hidden under Josh's blanket. The bastard was tryin' to *steal* it!"

Otto fixed Lucius with a bemused look. "Josh said

267

you giff it to him, *Kindchen*. You vat dey call Indian-giffer?"

"Hell, no," Lucius snapped. "Josh is what they call a damn liar." He moved toward the side of the boat.

Otto watched him, surprised. "Hey, vere you goin' *now?*"

Lucius paused, with one leg thrown over the gunwale. "To spend the night in the hotel. Ran into a friend o' mine up there—a friend off a *steamboat*. He's got a room at the hotel, and two beautiful women, one for him and one for me."

"Dat's nice." Otto smiled. "You got nice friends, *Kindchen*."

"Yeah," Lucius said grimly. "Wish I could say the same for you, Greasy."

He started to jump off the boat, but the sound of Otto's voice—usually so booming and boisterous, now so oddly soft—stopped him.

"Hey, vait a minute, *Kindchen*."

The big German hauled himself to his feet and came to stand beside Lucius, looking closely into the boy's eyes. "You leafing us now, *ja?* You got somet'ing bedder to do?"

Lucius gripped his satchel tightly and made no answer.

"You can tell me, *Kindchen*," Otto said coaxingly.

Lucius had been trying to avoid Otto's gaze, but now looked him squarely in the eye. "All right, Otto. I'll tell you exactly how it is."

The other man chuckled. "Oh, it's Otto now, eh? Vat happened to Greasy?"

"That ain't your name. And mine ain't Kinkin', either. It's Lucius."

The amusement disappeared from Otto's face. "All right. Tell me how it is."

"Well, first off, I had this bad thing happen to me in Paducah, and Josh was gonna blab it to everybody. That's how he got my satchel—it was the only way I could get him to promise not to tell."

Otto slapped his thigh and laughed. "*Ja*, dat's Josh, all right. Lemme see, dere's a vord for dat in English. Black-mail, I t'ink day call it." Then he grew serious again. "But dat's not'ing. No reason to go running avay."

"Naw, that ain't the main thing. Josh can tell you all

268

about it now, and make up a few extra lies to go with it—I don't care. The thing is, I never meant to come on no damn flatboat. It ain't for me, and I always knew it. I'm goin' on a steamboat, and I'm gonna learn good manners, and how to talk real polite, and how to dress up in nice clothes and be a gen'leman. A *gen'leman,* Otto. Just what a flatboatman loves to make fun of, 'cause he could never be one himself, not in a thousand years."

Otto nodded solemnly. "Vell, dat's *gut.* I t'ink you very smart lad."

Lucius was getting restless. "I got to say g'bye now, Otto. 'Cause you're right, I'm leavin', and I won't be back. And I'm sorry in a way, 'cause it might 'a' been fun to be partners with you sometime, like we talked about. I think we could 'a' been friends." He extended his hand. "G'bye, Otto. And good luck."

Otto clasped the boy's hand, and his eyes were sad and gentle. *"Auf Wiedersehen,* Lucius. I vish you *gut* fortune. You not a *Kindchen* no more."

That was all. With a quick movement, Lucius swung his other leg over the side and leaped ashore, and was immediately swallowed up in the darkness.

Otto went back to the little stove and looked down at the pan simmering on its iron top. The contents were burnt and smoking. With casual disinterest he lifted the pan off and laid it on a flat rock beside the stove. Then he went up onto the roof deck and lowered himself into the captain's chair, groped for his flute on the deck beneath him, and gazed absently off into a black, star-speckled sky.

"Poor *Kindchen,"* he murmured under his breath.

He raised the silvery instrument to his lips and began to play a sweetly sorrowful tune.

9

FROM THE JOURNAL of Lucius Hargrave:

That part of my life spent on Nate Collins's flatboat lasted less than two weeks, yet during that brief period, new experiences rushed at me with breathtaking speed, and left me stunned.

First came the geographical revelations. The river was wide and the river was long, longer than I had ever dreamed a river could be. It snaked leisurely around one broad bend after another, opening between curves into straight expanses of water, shining for miles. Sometimes the great bends ahead lay suspended in blue space for hours—perhaps half a day—and would seem like mighty gates guarding the entrance to some fabled world inhabited by giants, far in the western distance. Eventually, each would slip silently away behind us, only to yield to another vista very much like the one before. And no sooner had I grown accustomed to the vast dimensions of the Ohio than the stupendous immensity of the Mississippi loomed before me, and I was struck speechless with new awe. I knew about the Mississippi—or I thought I did; I had certainly read about it under the strict tutelage of my grandfather—but now at last I realized how feebly inadequate my childish conception of it had been. I began to develop a profound admiration for the explorers and pioneers of the past—those intrepid men who had first dared venture into this immeasurable wilderness—and for the first time, I comprehended the true meaning of the word courage.

But it was not merely the opening up of the panorama of the country that dazzled my senses. It was even more the astonishing multitude of people who dwelt therein. It soon occurred to me that the most nearly unique feature of humanity is its fantastic variety.

My companions aboard the flatboat were a study worthy of years, could I have spared the time for it. They were all simple unlettered men, but they possessed an innate knack for dealing with the world at their own limited level, which was quite sufficient for their purposes. I learned from them, and I believe they learned from me—though they took continual delight in jesting about my youthfulness, and pretended to vast worldly experience in their attempts to impress me. I quickly perceived that, despite their boasting and bravado, they suffered from secret feelings of inferiority, always acutely conscious of their humble origins. They looked upon me as a product of a family in which education and refinement and civility were primary values, and felt more than a tinge of envy, I am certain.

The first lesson I learned from my flatboat friends was that even among the lowly there exists a rigid social order. Nate Collins was the owner of the boat, and therefore captain, and therefore lord and master. He sat in his little wicker chair on the top deck and gazed out over what he considered his own personal domain, the river, and dreamed of the riches that he thought would someday be his.

Josh Everett was the peasantry. From a remote homestead in the hill country of Kentucky, Josh was like a wild beast running loose in the company of men. He had animal appetites, and pursued their gratification with animal-like directness. On the surface he seemed harmless enough, but underneath lurked a streak of viciousness. I took care to spend as little time in his company as possible.

Between these two extremes, Otto Grieshaber represented a kind of seedy middle class. He had been born in the city of Munich in Germany, and carried with him some remnants of Old World culture. He played charming old German melodies on the flute that was his most prized possession, spoke with nostalgic pride of his national heri-

271

tage, and like Nate, dreamed of acquiring wealth. He was possessed of an indestructibly cheerful disposition, for which I was thankful, for it made living in the cramped confines of the flatboat with such unsavory characters as Nate and Josh at least barely tolerable.

It was soon painfully clear to all of us that I did not fit anywhere in the social structure inhabited by these men, a fact that seemed to baffle them considerably. Each in his own time and way approached me, ostensibly to form some sort of alliance, but in reality, I was quick to see, probing for some means by which he could use me to his personal advantage. I listened to them with all possible courtesy, and assured each one that I would give his proposal the most respectful consideration. This I did, true to my word—though by then I knew very well that my worldly fortunes, whatever they might prove to be, surely lay elsewhere than with my fine friends, Nate, Otto, and Josh.

By the time we had reached New Madrid, Missouri, just beyond the confluence with the Mississippi, I had concluded upon the pressing necessity of parting company with my rustic companions immediately, the sooner the better. I had noticed to my horror that I was beginning to take on some of their uncouth ways.

But how was it to be done? Where could I go and what could I do, sixteen years old, not yet wise in the ways of the world, and five hundred miles from home? I wandered forlornly in the streets of New Madrid, rubbing shoulders with indifferent strangers and struggling with my perplexity, searching for the solution I had little hope of finding. Then it was that whimsical Fate chose to smile upon me.

As I walked along the crowded streets, I suddenly found myself gazing in stupefaction into a familiar face—that of Captain Elisha Jochum, master of the *Cincinnati Queen!* Of course the steamer had overtaken us on its downstream voyage, and had just that afternoon docked in New Madrid. Captain Jochum greeted me cordially, and volunteered the information that my good friend Albert Pettingill was at that moment taking refreshments at the Palace Hotel, a few steps up the street, and would surely be overjoyed to see me. My heart leapt at this sudden turn of luck. I hastened there and found Mr. Pettingill in the dining room. Cordiality is an inadequate word to describe his reaction on discovering me standing before him. He jumped to his feet and shook my hand with such effusive delight that I was almost embarrassed, and deeply touched. I apologized for not having kept our appointment in South Bar, and explained as best I could. He was sympathetic, forgave me instantly, insisted that I sit down and join him at dinner, and said of course I would come aboard the *Cincinnati Queen* that very night, and we would proceed with our original plan.

But my strict upbringing had imprinted upon me a sense of duty that will no doubt remain tenaciously with me till the day I die, and now it seized me in a torment of conflicting emotions. Here was the thing I had most wanted, restored to me—yet the thought of abandoning my flatboat companions in mid-voyage suddenly seemed unthinkable. I explained to Mr. Pettingill that I had a commitment to those men, and it would be dishonorable of me not to live up to it. Coolly he reminded me that I had a prior commitment to him. Furthermore, of the hundreds of young men he had interviewed in his years-long search for an assistant, only I displayed the combination of intelligence and good character he was seeking; on the other hand, there were hordes of well-qualified flatboatmen in New Madrid looking for work—my companions would have no difficulty at all filling a vacancy on their crew. His logic was irrefutable. I consented to come with him.

When I returned to the flatboat to collect my belongings and take my leave, I found no one there but Otto. I was pleased—relieved not to have to see the others, glad to have a parting moment with Otto—and saddened as well, for I had detected in him alone among the flatboatmen certain rough-hewn qualities that I could have learned to admire. He was not surprised to hear of my decision to leave. We shook hands and said goodbye quickly, then turned away from one another, each knowing we would never meet again.

Such are so many of the numberless encounters of life: briefly joined, empty of meaning, and fading away with scarcely a trace of memory.

10

At ten o'clock in the morning, two hours after the *Cincinnati Queen* had departed New Madrid, Jimmy Peal, the elderly steward, approached Mr. Albert Pettingill's private stateroom on the top deck and knocked softly. He was carrying a tray. Hearing no response, he repeated the knock, then opened the door a crack and peered in. The occupant of the bed was a motionless lump beneath jumbled bedcovers.

"Mr. Pettingill? It's ten o'clock, sir. You want your breakfast now?"

There was no sign of life from the lump on the bed. Jimmy came in and set the tray on a small table, and shook the sleeper.

"It's ten o'clock, I said. Your breakfast is—"

"All right, I heard you." The muffled growl from beneath the covers was accompanied by a sudden spasmodic movement of arms and legs.

"Come out o' there, Mr. Pettingill," Jimmy said. "I got to talk to you about somethin'."

Albert Pettingill's head appeared. He scowled up at the steward. "What is it?"

"That young feller you sent on board last night. Lucius somethin'-or-other."

Pettingill blinked several times, and frowned. "Oh . . . yes."

"What you want me to do with 'im? He's all over the

274

ship, gettin' in everybody's way, makin' a dang pest of 'imself."

Pettingill had negotiated himself into a sitting position. "What I want you to do, Jimmy, is fix a big tub of hot water and make him take a bath. And be sure it's thorough."

Jimmy stared, aghast. "What?!"

"And when he's clean, bring him here to me."

Jimmy turned away, muttering, "What am I s'posed to be, a dang nursemaid?" He went out and closed the door with a bang.

It was an hour before Jimmy returned, knocked on the door again, and opened it. Pettingill had finished his breakfast, and was groomed and dressed and sitting in a small armchair, reading a book.

"Here's your infant, all scrubbed," Jimmy said crossly.

Behind the steward, Lucius Hargrave's grinning face appeared. "Mornin', Mr. Pettingill."

Pettingill closed his book. "Thank you, Jimmy. That'll be all."

Jimmy picked up the breakfast tray and departed. Lucius stood stiffly in the center of the room, waiting expectantly. In one hand he held his leather satchel in a tight grip.

Pettingill looked his visitor up and down, and his face clouded. "Did you have a bath?"

"Yes, sir, sure did," Lucius said cheerfully.

"But, my God, boy, you're still wearing that same dirty shirt you were wearing last night!"

Lucius's cheerfulness was undimmed. "I only got two shirts, sir. And this is the cleanest one."

Pettingill sighed. "Did you have some breakfast?"

"I'll say I did!" Lucius's eyes gleamed. "I swear, I never saw so much good eats as they got on this here ship! Why, I had bacon and eggs, and johnnycakes, and—"

"All right, Lucius, that's fine," Pettingill said wearily.

Lucius babbled on. "Y'know somethin', sir? I never realized how nice it is on a steamboat. I used to watch the roustabouts loadin' the firewood, and I thought, my Lord, that's bad work. But, shucks, for the passengers, it's a mighty fine life, ain't it, sir? Nothin' but strollin' up and down the deck, eatin' and sleepin' and socializin' all day. Mighty fine."

Pettingill fidgeted. "Lucius—"

275

"And you know what else I discovered, sir? The river looks a lot different, way up here on top of a steamboat, from what it does on a flatboat. Down there all you see is muddy water, and scum floatin' on it. Up here you see that smooth surface stretchin' for miles, clean and shinin', and along the banks, all that green countryside jes' rollin' away in the distance. Why, it's downright beautiful!"

Pettingill was drumming his fingers on the tabletop. "Sit down, Lucius."

"Yes, sir." Lucius grabbed a straight-backed chair, pulled it close to Pettingill's chair, and sat down. He leaned forward, grinning.

"Oh, and how was your evening, sir? That Ruby was some pretty thing."

Pettingill was stony-faced. "Lucius?"

"Yes, sir?"

"You talk too much."

Lucius colored. "Oh . . . sorry, sir."

"Now I want you to listen to me for a few minutes, because I have some important information to impart to you."

"Yes, sir."

"New Orleans is a thousand miles away. It will take us a little more than three days to get there. Those three days, Lucius, are going to be the most grueling three days of your life. We are going to spend very little of that time eating or sleeping, and none at all strolling on the deck and admiring the beautiful scenery. We are going to spend it right here in this room, working. We are going to work, and work, and work, until you are ready to drop, and then we are going to work some more. We are going to work on your habits of personal cleanliness, we are going to work on your speech, we are going to work on your taste and on your manners, and most of all, we are going to work on the techniques of our profession. By the time we arrive in New Orleans, we will know whether we have begun a fruitful partnership, or merely expended a dreadful amount of energy for nothing. Whether or not we succeed will be entirely up to you. Are you ready?"

Lucius's face had gone pale and solemn. "I'm ready, sir."

"Very well. We will begin with the basic tools of the trade."

276

Pettingill pulled the small table at his elbow around to a position between himself and Lucius. Then he reached into an inside pocket. Lucius watched, barely breathing. With loving care, Albert Pettingill placed on the table a deck of playing cards.

Late in the afternoon, Jimmy Peal knocked again on Mr. Pettingill's door, and when he heard the call to come in, opened the door and stuck his head in the room.

"It's five o'clock, Mr. Pettingill. You want dinner now?"

Pettingill gave him a blank look.

"Well, you didn't stop for lunch," Jimmy said. "Thought maybe you'd want an early dinner."

Pettingill smiled across the table at his pupil. "Good heavens, how time flies when one is busy, eh, Lucius?"

Lucius was slumped wearily in his seat. "Yeah."

"Don't say 'yeah,' Lucius. Say, 'Yes, indeed.' Or, 'Assuredly so.' Or, 'Quite right.' "

Lucius sighed.

Pettingill glanced at the steward while he shuffled his deck of cards. "All right, Jimmy, bring dinner. Thank you."

Jimmy went out. Pettingill extracted a card from the deck and held it up, facing himself.

"What is it?"

Lucius studied the intricate design on the back of the card. "Uh . . . queen of clubs."

"Very good. But don't stare at the card, Lucius. You must only glance at it, in the most inconspicuous manner."

"But them little squiggles ain't that easy—"

Pettingill recoiled as if struck. "Oh God! Your language!"

"Those little squiggles are not that easy to see."

"There, that's better." Pettingill handed the deck of cards to the boy. "Now I want you to put these in your pocket, and whenever you have a spare minute, take them out and study them. Learn them. Learn them so well that you can identify them as easily from the back as from the front."

Lucius gazed glumly at the cards before putting them in his pocket. "You're not like my grandpa at all," he grumbled. "You're a lot worse."

277

The instructor smiled. He had taken out another pack of cards, and was shuffling them.

"Now, here we have something quite different, Lucius. This is what we call a trimmed pack." He selected two cards and held them up side by side. "Notice the difference."

Lucius inspected the cards. "I don't see no difference."

"What?"

"I don't see any difference."

"Not the design, Lucius. The shape."

Lucius looked again, and shook his head helplessly.

"You're not using your eyes, boy!" Pettingill snapped. "See this card? Its sides are straight. See this one? Notice the sides are curved slightly inward. Feel it. It's a tiny bit narrower in the middle than at the ends. Right?"

Lucius took the card and ran his fingertips along the sides. His face lit up.

"Yeah, that's—" Hurriedly he corrected himself. "Yes, that's right."

Pettingill shuffled the deck. "The trimmed cards are the aces and face cards. With this deck, I can deal all night and give myself nothing but choice hands and you nothing but trash."

He dealt a pair of poker hands. "What have you got?"

Lucius looked at his cards, and threw them on the table. "Trash."

Pettingill laid down his cards: two aces, two queens, and a jack. Lucius shook his head in dazzlement. The dealer scooped up the cards and shuffled again. Lucius hunched forward and fastened his eyes on the man's hands, trying to follow the flashing movement of the cards.

"I'll never learn to do that," he mumbled.

Jimmy Peal came in, bearing a large tray of food. Pettingill cleared the cards from the table, and smiled across at Lucius.

"You're doing fine, lad. Just fine. Now we'll take ten minutes for a bite to eat, and get right back at it."

Lucius slumped in his chair and sighed.

Late that night, Albert Pettingill took a stroll on deck. The weather was balmy, with a soft breeze stirring. After a turn around the ship, Pettingill stopped and leaned against the railing, turned his face toward the breeze, and took several deep breaths. In a few minutes, Captain Jochum came out of the pilothouse a short distance away, noticed the man at the railing, and approached him.

"Evenin', Albert," he said.

"Evening, Elisha."

"Nice breeze tonight."

"Yes, indeed."

"How you progressin' with young Hargrave?"

"Splendidly. I'm pleasantly surprised. I wouldn't want *him* to hear me say this, but . . . the boy's loaded with talent."

Captain Jochum gave a soft snort. "I think you're a darn fool, takin' a young'un like that. You ought to git yourself a grown-up partner."

"You run the boat, Elisha. I'll take care of my business, all right?"

"Why, sure, Albert. I *do* run the boat. An' I spend half my time tryin' to explain who *you* are, an' how come you have a fancy private apartment on the top deck."

"Too bad you can't just tell 'em the truth," Mr. Pettingill said. "Too bad you can't tell 'em I own the boat, and the captain as well."

Captain Jochum glowered. "You don't own the boat, Albert. You own fifty-one percent. An' you don't own *me,* just because I'm in debt to you."

"Oh well, no matter," Pettingill said, and looked away disinterestedly. "One day I'll sell out. Tell you the truth, I'm getting a little sick of this creaky old tub. The *Minerva*'s a lot nicer."

"*That* scow!" Captain Jochum growled his scorn.

Pettingill turned back to the captain with a new thought. "Any fresh pigeons on board?"

"One. A Mr. Blake. Big stout fella. Got a money belt on 'im that sticks out six inches all around. Says he's goin' to New Orleans on business, but he's lookin' for fun— that's easy to see."

"What's his occupation?"

"Owns a mercantile store in New Madrid."

"Perfect. Maybe I'll give the boy a shot at him."

The captain's mouth fell open. "You goin' to send a greenhorn kid into operation that quick? You must be out o' your mind!"

279

"Run the boat, Elisha," Pettingill said patiently, and walked away.

When the early morning sun streamed into the high windows along the port side of Albert Pettingill's apartment, he arose, wrapped himself in a silk dressing gown, and stepped to the corner of the room where Lucius was sprawled asleep on a mattress. He nudged the boy gently in the ribs with his toe. The sleeper snorted and turned over. Pettingill nudged him again.

"Lucius! Get up. Time to go to work."

Lucius opened his eyes and gazed frowning up into the man's face. He groaned.

"I just got to sleep a minute ago."

"Nonsense!" Pettingill said. "You've been buzzing like a sawmill, all night long." He went to the other side of the room, picked up a porcelain pitcher, and poured some water into a wash basin. Soon he glanced around at Lucius.

"Come alive, boy. Jimmy will be here with our breakfast in a few minutes."

Lucius sat up and locked his arms around his knees, and looked at the man with a thoughtful expression. "I was wonderin', Mr. Pettingill. How come you get all this fancy service, in a private room and all?"

Pettingill came back to the center of the room, rubbing himself with a towel. "Because I'm an important person. And now that you're with me, you're important too. So get up."

Lucius got to his feet, stretched and yawned, and went stumbling toward the washbasin. "Funny you should mention a sawmill, sir. I was thinkin' last night, while I was lyin' in bed—by all rights I ought to be choppin' wood at my stepfather's sawmill right now. 'Stead o' that, here I am learnin' to be a gambler on a steamboat. Sure is funny."

Pettingill sat down at the table, reached for a deck of cards, and laid out a game of solitaire. After a while, Lucius came and took his seat on the opposite side.

"I'm ready, sir," he said. "What'll we do today?"

Pettingill fixed the boy with a grim look. "There's a bit of confusion in your mind, Lucius. We must clear it up immediately."

"Yes, sir?"

280

"I am not a gambler. Neither will you be, I hope. If you should by some mischance develop into one, you will no longer be associated with me."

Lucius blinked. "I don't understand, sir."

Pettingill played his game of solitaire, and delivered a little lecture.

"A gambler, Lucius, is a man who is addicted to betting. He is not addicted to cards, or race horses, or dice—he is addicted to *betting*. He has a craving for excitement. He thinks that with no particular skills, training, or experience, he can somehow conjure up a magical spell and outwit a scientifically constructed system. He is a man who loves to take chances, and he believes in luck. In other words, he is a blithering idiot. Now, *I* do not bet on chance things, Lucius. I invest in a business venture that is carefully designed to produce a mathematical *certainty* in my favor. I have none of the instincts of a gambler, and it is a cross I have to bear that I must go through life being called one. Well, so be it. For those ignorant outsiders who flounder in this confusion, I care nothing. But for you, it won't do. It is absolutely essential that you comprehend the difference between fools who are gamblers, and clever people like us, who make our living off them."

Lucius nodded. Pettingill continued.

"But we mustn't deplore the existence of gamblers, my boy. That would be as foolish as an eagle deploring the existence of rabbits. For gamblers are our prey—the tender, fat pigeons on which we feed. And fortunately, the world is full of 'em. Flocks and flocks."

Pettingill chuckled. "They all have one thing in common, the thing that keeps our conscience at ease. They all have, deep down in their greedy hearts, a desire to take *our* money, by fair means or foul. If they didn't have that . . . why, they wouldn't be pigeons."

Lucius nodded again. "I think I'm beginning to understand, sir."

"Good." Pettingill suddenly swept the cards up off the table. "Now today we're going to put away the cards for a while, and consider another facet of our profession, quite as important as any other, I assure you. That's the art of acting."

"Acting, sir?"

"That's mainly what we are, lad. Actors. Our stage is the social hall on the main deck, downstairs. But we do not play for applause; we play for money."

Jimmy Peal knocked on the door, stuck his head in, and inquired if they were ready for breakfast.

"Jimmy!" Pettingill said. "Come in here a minute, will you?"

Jimmy came in, frowning suspiciously.

"Stand up, Lucius," Pettingill commanded. "Stand next to Jimmy here. Let's compare your sizes."

"What's all this?" Jimmy began to protest, as Lucius stood next to him.

"Um-hmm. Just as I thought," Pettingill said. "You're a pretty close match. Jimmy, I want you to sell us a suit of clothes."

"What?!"

"That gray suit of yours—that will do nicely."

"That's my best suit!"

"I know." Pettingill took a roll of money out of his pocket. "How much is it worth?"

"Why, it's worth—twenty-five dollars."

"I'd have thought about ten." Pettingill peeled off several bills. "We also need a couple of your best shirts, and some underwear, please."

Jimmy shook his head vigorously. "I can't do that, Mr. Pettingill. I ain't got it to spare."

"Here's forty dollars." Pettingill thrust the money into Jimmy's hands.

The steward gazed at it for a moment, then stuffed it in his pocket. "Which you want first, breakfast or the clothes?"

"Why, the clothes, naturally," Pettingill said. He smiled at Lucius. "Gentlemen always dress for their meals. Even breakfast."

Lucius smiled back. He sat down again, and carefully crossed his legs.

"Assuredly so," he said.

282

11

LATE IN THE AFTERNOON of the third day, as the *Cincinnati Queen* approached New Orleans, Lucius appeared in the social hall. There were a few passengers lolling in wicker chairs, a few strolling in and out, and a number of others sitting at the bar at the forward end of the room. Lucius wandered toward the bar. He was dressed in an ill-fitting gray broadcloth suit that was slightly worn in the seat and at the elbows, and he looked stiff and uncomfortable.

He stopped at an empty seat next to a heavyset middle-aged man, leaned forward, and said, " 'Scuse me, sir. This seat taken?"

The man turned and scrutinized him. "Sit down, son," he boomed.

Lucius sat down. The bartender approached him, and Lucius ordered a whiskey. The big man beside him turned beady black eyes in his direction.

"You old enough to drink, son?"

Lucius flashed a quick smile. "Oh yes, sir. My pa taught me to drink like a man and hold my whiskey like a gentleman. I been doin' that since I was twelve years old."

The man chuckled. "That so? Where you from?"

"Indiana, sir."

"You're a fur piece from home."

"Yes, sir."

Lucius's whiskey was set before him. He pulled a roll

of cash from his pocket, peeled off a bill, and handed it to the bartender. Then he picked up his drink and tested it with a careful sip. The stout man watched him. Lucius took a strong pull on the drink, and gulped it down.

The stout man chuckled. "Yep, you sure *do* drink like a man!"

"I'm goin' to New Orleans to look for work," Lucius announced. "I've never been there before."

"Me neither, son," the stout man said. He leaned closer to Lucius. "Don't tell nobody, but I'm fifty-two years old, and this is the first time I was ever more'n a hunnert miles from New Madrid." The man shook with a little wheezing laugh. "I told my wife Myrtle I had to go to New Orleans on business, but I got a wad saved up that Myrtle don't know about, and I aim to have me some good times." He nudged Lucius in the ribs with an elbow. "Know what I mean, son?" The wheezing laugh sounded again.

Lucius smiled. "Yes, sir. I know what you mean."

The man beamed at him, and extended his hand. "By the way, my name's Blake. What's yours?"

Lucius shook hands, and was seized with a brief attack of stuttering. "Uh, my name's, uh . . . Walker, sir. Tom Walker. Pleased to meet you."

Blake snapped his fingers at the man behind the counter. "Le's have two more whiskeys here, bartender."

"Thank you, sir," Lucius said.

Blake was suddenly frowning at him. "Funny, I ain't noticed you before, Tom. Where you been?"

"I been ridin' below, on deck passage," Lucius said. "But I got in a little card game with some o' the deck-hands yesterday and won a few dollars, so I thought I'd treat myself to cabin class, just for one day."

Blake's frown deepened. "Oh, you oughtn't to gamble, son. That's the worst thing you can do."

Lucius hung his head in shame. "Yes, sir, you're right, I know. I promised my mama I wouldn't do it, and I'm never gonna break my promise to her again."

"Good boy."

Lucius finished his first drink, and started on the second. "I'm sorry to hear you've never been to New Orleans, Mr. Blake. I was hopin' you could tell me about it."

"Well, it's a damn big place, I know that much."

284

"Pretty dangerous too, I hear," Lucius said. "Full o' thieves and gamblers, and I don't know what-all."

"Lots o' high-class whores too," Blake said. "That is, I *hope* so." He winked at Lucius. "I mean, Myrtle is all right, but she's about as excitin' as a pair of old shoes. Once in his life, a man deserves to slip on a pair o' jewelled slippers an' go dancin'. You know what I mean?" He nudged Lucius again, and wheezed with laughter.

Lucius grinned. "You're absolutely right, sir."

Blake turned abruptly serious. "A young fella like you, though, you got to be careful. Jes' don't talk to strangers, that's the main thing. Long as you don't do that, you'll be all right."

The boy shrugged. "Oh, I'm not worried. I can spot a crook a mile off."

The big man laughed again. "O ho, you can, can you? Well, you jes' watch your step, m'lad, 'cause you're jes' the kind o' sucker the crooks are lookin' for."

Lucius smiled, and sipped his drink. Then he leaned toward Blake and spoke in a low voice. "Now, f'rinstance, take a peek at that character on your right."

Albert Pettingill was sitting at the bar, two empty seats down from Blake, on the side opposite Lucius. He was sipping a glass of wine and gazing absently around the room. His eyes met Blake's, and he smiled faintly.

"Well, what about 'im?" Blake said out of the corner of his mouth to Lucius.

Lucius's voice dropped to a whisper. "I'd be willin' to bet he's a professional gambler."

"Now what makes you say that?"

"He jes' looks like one. So fancy-dressed, and all. And he popped up out o' nowhere. Have you seen him before?"

"No, but I hadn't seen you before, either."

"That's 'cause I was in deck passage. But that Fancy Dan hasn't been travelin' second class, you can bet. Where's he been hidin'?"

Blake considered the question. "Well, we'll jes' ask him." He turned toward the man on his right.

"Beg pardon, sir?"

Pettingill was instant attention. "Yes?"

"I don't recall seein' you before."

Pettingill coughed delicately and patted his upper chest.

285

"Bad luck. I've been confined to my stateroom, nursing a dreadful cold."

"Oh, too bad. Hope you're better."

"Much better, thank you. Kind of you to inquire." Pettingill slid across the intervening seats. "May I join you?"

"Why, certainly." Blake extended a hand. "My name's Oscar Blake."

"Alfred Welles at your service, sir," Albert Pettingill said. "That your son beside you?"

Blake laughed. "No, no, this here's young Tom Walker, from Indiana."

Lucius eyed the newcomer, unsmiling.

"You old enough to drink, Tom?" Pettingill said.

"'Course I am," Lucius snapped, and took a reckless gulp of his drink. Blake laughed again.

"Well!" Pettingill said cheerfully. "Sure is nice to have a little human company again, after several days in solitude. Will you gentlemen have a drink with me?"

"Why, certainly, thank you, sir," Blake said readily. Lucius said nothing.

Pettingill snapped his fingers at the bartender and ordered three whiskeys.

"Believe me," he said to Blake, "three days alone with nothing to do but fiddle with a deck of cards can drive a man out of his mind." He had brought forth an old, worn deck, and was idly shuffling. He smiled at Blake. "In a way, though, they're ideal traveling companions. They take up very little space, don't have to be fed, and are always available."

Lucius nudged Blake on the arm with his elbow, and shot him a significant look.

"So you play cards, Mr. Welles?" Blake inquired.

"Oh no, not really. Mostly I do tricks. Idle amusement, for friends."

He spread the deck in his hands and extended it toward Blake. "Pick a card."

Blake glanced at Lucius with a wink, and pulled a card from the deck.

"Look at it and put it back," Pettingill instructed. It was done.

Pettingill shuffled the deck thoroughly, sifted through it, extracted a card, and laid it face up on the bar.

Blake's eyes went wide. "Why, that's it, by George!"

He grinned in delight, and glanced at Lucius. "You see that, Tom? Amazing!"

Lucius was not impressed.

"Do another one," Blake demanded eagerly.

"Here's one that's always good for a chuckle," Pettingill said. He had taken three cards from the deck—two aces and a queen. He showed them to Blake, and laid them facedown in a row.

"It's called three-card monte, and it comes from Mexico. You notice I put the queen in the middle. Now the point is to keep your eyes on the cards while I move them around, then turn up the queen, if you can. Ready?"

Blake nodded and leaned forward, staring at the cards. Pettingill slid the cards around with dazzling speed. After a few seconds he stopped. Blake studied the cards, and hesitantly chose one. It was an ace.

Blake laughed. "Let's try it again," he said.

The process was repeated, with the same result.

"You see?" Pettingill smiled. "The old saying is true—the hand is quicker than the eye."

"Shit," said Lucius.

The two men turned shocked eyes on the boy.

"What's that?" Pettingill said.

"Your hand's not quicker than *my* eye," the boy said.

The card dealer bristled. "Would you care to lay a little wager, young man?"

Oscar Blake frowned at Lucius, and shook his head negatively. Lucius ignored him. He laid ten dollars on the counter. Pettingill took out a roll of bills and covered Lucius's money. He displayed the queen, and placed it facedown between the two aces.

"Ready?"

"Ready," Lucius said curtly.

Pettingill began to switch the cards. Lucius watched with icy concentration. When the cards were still, he reached out and turned up the queen.

Blake roared with laughter as Lucius picked up the money. "So, Mr. Welles. Looks like you met your match!"

Pettingill's smile was serene. "Luck," he said. "Once in a while, you're bound to guess right."

"Oh, is that so?" Lucius said belligerently. He counted out a hundred dollars on the bar.

287

Blake was aghast. "Oh no, son, you don't want to do that—"

"Cover that, and go to it," Lucius snapped at Pettingill. Pettingill covered the money, and arranged the cards.

"Ready?"

"Ready."

Pettingill's hands flew. Afterward, Lucius stared at the cards for a long time while Pettingill smirked, and Blake stroked his chin nervously. Then Lucius reached out and again turned up the queen.

A roar went up. The bartender and several other men had gathered around to form a fascinated audience. One of the spectators slapped Lucius on the back as he scooped up his winnings.

Pettingill's composure seemed to be shaken. He looked around.

"The trouble is," he said, "this bar counter is not the right height."

His comment brought forth an outburst of derisive laughter.

"No, really," Pettingill protested. "To work well, I need to be at tabletop level."

Lucius got up. "All right, let's move over to a table, then."

In a sudden noisy shuffle, the little company of players and observers dispersed and reconvened at a table at the far end of the room. Pettingill laid the cards on the table and was about to sit down, when the bartender called to him.

"Oh, sir? You didn't pay for them drinks you ordered."

With a grimace of annoyance, Pettingill went back to the bar.

Lucius sat down quickly and pulled Oscar Blake into the chair next to him. "Hey, Mr. Blake, want to have some fun?"

Blake frowned. "You better quit now, son. Quit while you're ahead."

Lucius glanced toward the bar. Albert Pettingill was involved in a minor altercation with the bartender. Lucius turned back to Blake, and winked.

"Watch this," he said. He took a small pencil from his pocket, found the queen, then hurriedly made a light mark

288

on one corner of its back. "*Now* do you think I ought to quit?"

Blake grinned, and winked back at Lucius. There were soft snickers among the several spectators as they gathered closer, eager to join in the conspiracy.

Mr. Pettingill returned to the table, fuming. "Stupid bartender," he muttered. "Trying to overcharge me." He sat down opposite Lucius and Mr. Blake, and glanced up at the men standing around the table.

"Feel free to join in, gentlemen." He motioned to the few empty chairs remaining. They were quickly filled.

"Now, then," the card dealer said. "Who cares to wager?"

Lucius was already counting money and stacking it in the center of the table. "There's two hundred," he said.

Attention shifted to the next man, Blake. He rubbed his chin thoughtfully for a moment before reaching for his wallet.

"I'll go two hundred," he said, and counted it out.

The next man put down a contribution. "There's a hundred for me."

"That's five hundred," Lucius said. Pettingill studied his fingernails, and looked disinterested.

The remaining three men pledged fifty dollars each, and added their money to the pile.

"There's six-fifty," Lucius said to Pettingill. "Let's see you cover *that*."

Pettingill went on studying his fingernails. "It's not enough," he said.

Lucius slapped several more bills on the table. "That's three hundred for me, and that's all I got."

One of the fifty-dollar bettors added another fifty.

"That makes eight hundred," Lucius said. He glared at Pettingill. "Cover it, and play the game."

Pettingill gave a disdainful little shrug. "I won't play for less than fifteen hundred," he announced.

"God *damn* you!" Lucius roared.

At that instant, a bell clanged at the forward end of the room, and the bartender bellowed, "Attention, please! The ship is now approachin' N'Orleans landin'. Bar closes in five minutes!"

Pettingill fidgeted. "We're about out of time, gentlemen. Anybody going to make up the seven hundred, or not?"

Lucius grabbed the arm of the man next to him and spoke between clenched teeth. "Come on, Mr. Blake. Call the yellow bastard's bluff. This is your main chance."

All eyes centered on Oscar Blake. He was rubbing his chin again, and staring at the card with the faint pencil mark.

"Well, I ain't never been a gamblin' man, but—" He took a deep breath, and reached for his wallet.

Pettingill smiled and reached for his own wallet.

A bustle of activity was growing along the outer passageways, as passengers prepared to disembark. Business had picked up sharply at the bar, where a number of customers had developed a last-minute thirst.

Pettingill arranged the three cards and looked at Lucius. "Ready?"

Everyone hunched forward.

"Ready," Lucius said.

Pettingill's hands became a whirling blur as the cards whipped around the tabletop. The activity lasted for thirty seconds, then abruptly ceased. The card with the pencil mark was in the center position.

Pettingill looked at Lucius. "Well? Pick the queen."

Lucius looked at the man beside him. "You're the top bettor, Mr. Blake. *You* pick it."

Blake looked around the table. The other players nodded their agreement. Blake forced a little smile. He reached out and turned over the center card. It was the ace of spades.

In an instant, Pettingill had scooped up the money from the table, and was on his feet. "Thank you, gentlemen, it's been fun. I hope we meet again someday, when there's more time. Now if you'll excuse me . . ."

He waved a hand, and strode rapidly out of the room. No one else at the table had yet moved or uttered a sound. Lucius sat with his mouth open, speechless.

The bartender clanged the bell again. "Bar closes in two minutes!" he shouted.

"We got skinned," one of the fifty-dollar bettors said bleakly.

One of the hundred-dollar bettors leaned acros the table and scowled at Lucius. "You goddamn stupid smart-aleck kid, you think you know so much—"

"I marked the *queen!*" Lucius whined. His face twisted

290

in misery. Frantically he grabbed the three cards and examined them, front and back. They were the ace of diamonds, the ace of clubs, and the ace of spades. On the back of the ace of spades was the tiny pencil mark.

"It was the queen I marked, I *know* I did! Now what became of it?" With pleading eyes, Lucius searched the faces of the other men. "You saw me mark the queen, you know I—"

"Aw, shut up!" one of the men said. He got up with an angry lurch that almost overturned his chair, and walked away. The other players got up and followed, muttering darkly. Only Lucius and Oscar Blake were left.

Lucius propped his elbows on the table and buried his face in his hands. "It was the queen, Mr. Blake," he whimpered. "I marked the queen, I swear!"

Once more the bell clanged. "Last chance!" the bartender yelled. "Bar closes in thirty seconds!"

Blake sat like a stone, staring at the three aces on the table. "It's all right," he said in a soft voice. "It wasn't your fault."

He reached out and patted Lucius gently on the shoulder. "You're a good boy, Tom."

12

AT DUSK, the miles-long levee at New Orleans continued to bustle with the same kind of activity that had gone on without respite since early morning. Young Lucius Hargrave clutched his old leather satchel and strolled up and down, listening to the boisterous shouts of black steve-dores and the chatter of steamboat passengers, and scan-ning the forest of masts rising from the thousand vessels moored in the river. Besides the familiar steamboats and lesser rivercraft, there were seagoing ships, lithe, lean, and towering, with an air of haughtiness about them, exotic names, and a look of foreign lands. Over the entire pan-orama hung the tireless hum and clatter of human com-merce. Soon Lucius tired of the show, returned to the mooring place of the *Cincinnati Queen*, sat down on a weatherbeaten packing crate, and waited. After a while, Albert Pettingill came off the ship, carrying a valise. He spotted Lucius and walked toward him, and the boy got to his feet.

"Sorry to keep you waiting, lad," Pettingill said. "Just had a row with Jochum. The son of a bitch was trying to give me false freight receipts." He grimaced with annoy-ance and started off across the landing at a brisk pace, motioning for Lucius to follow.

"My boy, let me give you a piece of advice. Don't *ever* accept part ownership of a steamboat as payment for gam-bling debts. Just call it a business loss and be done with it. Steamboat captains are by all odds the most unscrupu-lous villains alive!"

Lucius nodded gravely, and scampered to keep up. Pet-tingill suddenly smiled.

"But never mind that. Here we are in New Orleans, and it's time to enjoy ourselves. Hungry?"

"Yes, sir."

"Good. I know a little cafe on Bourbon Street where the chef is such an artist that it's almost sacrilegious to destroy his work by eating it. Follow me."

They came to the entrance to Canal Street, where Pettin-gill imperiously waved off swarms of outlandishly uni-formed carriage drivers, beseeching business. Lucius stared at the strange, grinning, jabbering, ebony-skinned men.

"So many Negroes in New Orleans," he whispered to the man at his side. "Are they all somebody's slaves?"

"By no means," Pettingill said. "I expect there are more free Negroes here than anywhere else in this country. If you're a black man in America, there's really no good place to be, but New Orleans is probably the least bad."

Darkness had fallen, and as they walked along Canal Street, Lucius gaped in openmouthed amazement at the incredibly broad boulevard, made more incredible by countless overhead lanterns stretching as far as the eye could see.

"My God!" Lucius breathed. "I never *saw* such a place! New Orleans is . . . why, it's . . . it's . . ."

Pettingill chuckled. "Yes, isn't it? But what you see here is nothing, merely American garishness. Wait'll you see the *real* New Orleans."

Lucius looked puzzled.

"You must realize, lad," Pettingill went on, "New Orleans is really two cities. The American one—young, raw, crude, and tasteless. And the French one—gentle, mature, atmospheric, and immensely charming." Pettingill smiled. "Perhaps you can guess which I prefer."

They came to Chartres Street, and Pettingill steered Lucius around the corner to the right. "Now we go into the French Quarter. *Now* you will see something."

Unthinkingly they slackened their pace as they walked along, and Lucius marveled at the intoxicating riches of sights and sounds: the soft yellow glow of lamplight everywhere, streaming from open doorways; the pastel walls of brick and stucco, making a canyon of the narrow street; the second-story balconies, hanging miraculously in the air; alluringly secluded courtyards, tiny paradises of greenery and stone pavement glimpsed through lacelike patterns of wrought iron; laughter floating up tiny side streets, and unseen music from somewhere—an ardent tenor voice quivering on the high notes of a love song above the ripple of some delicate stringed instrument; and the people themselves—lolling in their courtyards, strolling on the streets, perched on their ironwork bannisters overhead.

Pettingill watched his young companion's face, and chuckled at the look of speechless wonder he saw there.

They came to the Place d'Armes, where Lucius had to stop and stand for several minutes, admiring the spacious square and the great, dark, brooding bulk of St. Louis Cathedral dominating it—then up Orleans Street to Bourbon, and right again.

"We're almost there," Pettingill said. "Tired?"

293

Lucius shook his head vigorously. "I could walk around like this all night."

An hour later they were sitting, their gluttony gratified, at a little table in a dark corner of a tiny cafe, staring in numb contentment at the sleepy flame of a candle in the center of the table, and sipping away the last of their second bottle of wine.

"That was mighty fine, Mr. Pettingill," Lucius said. "I don't know what all I ate, but it was mighty fine."

Pettingill stirred. "Glad you enjoyed it, lad. And I think now's as good a time as any to talk about your performance this afternoon. Shall we?"

Lucius's face became tense. "Yes, sir. I was wonderin' when we would."

Pettingill reached into an inside pocket, brought forth a small notebook, and opened it. "I took the liberty of making a few notes," he said.

Lucius gulped. "Yes sir."

Pettingill consulted his notebook for a moment. "First. Observing you from a distance, I noticed you entered the room, spotted your pigeon, and moved in on him immediately. Too fast. Too aggressive. Put yourself in easy reach of the man, then wait for *him* to open the conversation. Initiate it yourself only as a last resort."

Lucius nodded solemnly.

"Second. Part of the bartender's job is to feed you colored water when he serves you whiskey, because we never drink while we work. Now—"

"What *was* that awful stuff?" Lucius blurted.

"Water tinted with burnt peaches, the only thing that gives the precise color and texture of whiskey. The point is, you don't just toss it off as if it *were* colored water, you drink it with respect, as if it were whiskey. The kind of veteran drinker you presented was a trifle odd for someone your age.

"Now, point number three has to do with marking the queen. Here accuracy is of paramount importance. You've seen the mark that's on the ace up my sleeve, you know what it looks like. Remember it, and make *exactly* the same mark on the queen, so that when I replace one with the other, it will look like the same card. All eyes are glued on that marked card, and the slightest variation in the

294

marks can blow the thing sky-high. Watch your pencil pressure too. The mark should be just plain enough for everybody to make out, but not so obvious that *I* would have to be a blind man not to notice it."

Pettingill studied his notebook further. "Oh, and one last thing. About false names: they're useful, but they can get you into more trouble than they're worth if you're not careful. Have your name ready on the tip of your tongue, so you don't have to go rummaging about looking for it when you need it."

Pettingill put his notebook away. "That about does it, I think." He picked up his wineglass and sipped, and studied Lucius across its rim. "Well, what are your reactions, lad?"

Lucius fingered his own wineglass and stared broodingly into the ruby liquid. He took a deep breath, sat up straight, and looked at the man opposite him.

"Mr. Pettingill, I want to thank you for all the trouble you went to with me. I did the best I could, but I guess I just don't have what it takes. I'm sorry it didn't work out. All I can say now is, I hope you'll advance me a small loan till I can find a job somewhere. I'll pay you back, I promise—"

Pettingill was laughing quietly. "Lucius, Lucius! The criticisms I gave you were all insignificant trifles, easily corrected—"

"That's not all of it, Mr. Pettingill. There's lots worse, that you don't know about."

"Really? Such as what?"

"It bothered me, the whole thing. I sort of felt bad about it."

Pettingill continued to be amused. "Is that all?"

"No, sir. You know that extra hundred you gave me to put away for emergency?"

"Yes?"

"I gave it to Mr. Blake." Lucius hung his head in abject humiliation.

Pettingill's smile had not wavered. "And what makes you think I don't know about it?"

Lucius gaped. "You . . . you *know?*"

"Well, of course I know. The bartender was there, watching. Don't forget, he's in my employ too. He reports everything."

295

Pettingill waved an impatient hand in the air. "Look here, Lucius, these sudden attacks of soft-heartedness are to be expected in beginners. It's nothing to be ashamed of. Fact is, I think it's a good thing in a way—shows you have good instincts, even if they are misguided."

Lucius frowned, and dared to show a trace of stubbornness. "Well . . . I felt sorry for him. I couldn't help it."

Pettingill's amusement bubbled forth in gentle laughter. "My boy, that old bastard Blake had a money belt on him that could have bought and sold both of us, three times over. If you had been an expert instead of a novice, we could have sucked him into a serious game, and lifted three or four thousand, instead of a piddling nine hundred."

He pointed a finger at Lucius. "And don't lose sight of one small point. Blake couldn't have been victimized by us unless he'd been willing to victimize somebody himself. If I'd been cheated out of my money by that marked card of yours, do you think he would've felt sorry for *me?*"

Lucius thought about it. "No, I guess not."

"You're damned right. So don't worry about your little lapse into sentimentality, lad." Pettingill took a dainty sip of wine. "Just don't let it happen again."

Lucius was shaking his head in perplexity. Pettingill reached across the table and slapped him playfully on the wrist.

"Cheer up. We've only finished the negatively critical part of your evaluation. Now comes the report on what was *right*. To begin with, you were honest with me about that extra hundred. I was waiting for that, and I want you to know I appreciate it."

A noble look came into Lucius's eyes. "That's one thing I've always tried to be, Mr. Pettingill," he said solemnly. "Honest."

"It's a splendid quality!" Mr. Pettingill said with enthusiasm, and added dryly, "If it's channeled in the right direction."

Lucius leaned forward with new interest. "What else did I do right, sir?"

"It's a good list. Your dramatic flair; your fine sense of timing; your cool, calm control; the skillful way you coaxed your pigeon into making a nice bet—all very impressive. In a word, my boy . . . you were superb."

Lucius looked at his mentor with a new light dawning. "You mean . . . you mean I was *good?*"

Pettingill gave Lucius his most charming smile. "Let me put it this way, Lucius. I'm delighted to offer you a partnership. Shake on it." He extended his hand.

Lucius shook hands in a daze. "Th—thank you, sir."

"Now!" Pettingill said with a burst of cheerfulness. "Our hotel is the Fontainebleau, just down the street here. Small, but elegant. Shall we go and freshen up a bit, and get on with the evening's entertainment?" Without waiting for an answer, he snapped his fingers for the waiter.

In half an hour they were out on the street again, with Mr. Pettingill hailing a carriage and saying to the driver, "The American Theater, please. Camp Street." He and Lucius climbed in and settled back on soft, well-worn leather.

"The theater is about the only reason I can think of for venturing into the American section of town," Mr. Pettingill said. "There's always a good play there. Very often Shakespeare. Nothing like a good Shakespearean performance to renew the spirit and enlarge one's view of life. You agree?"

"Oh, absolutely," Lucius readily agreed.

The play at the American was *As You Like It.*

"Wonderful!" Albert Pettingill pronounced. "I feel like a comedy tonight. The tragedies are more important works, of course, but they can be depressing at times, don't you think?"

Again Lucius was in complete agreement.

Pettingill slapped Lucius on the knee. "And depression is not what we're looking for tonight, eh, lad?"

"I'll say not!" Lucius replied emphatically. The expression on his face registered uneasiness as he studied the crowd milling about in front of the theater.

The boy sat through the performance in a trance, staring unbelievingly at the action on the stage, and openly gaping at the finery in the audience around him. Afterward, the street in front of the theater was a maelstrom of thronging patrons and fleets of carriages, their drivers swarming like locusts, each loudly proclaiming the superiority of his vehicle over all others. Pettingill secured a carriage and barked instructions to the driver. "La Fontainebleau, please. Bourbon Street."

As they drove away, Pettingill leaned back comfortably and glanced at Lucius. "Well, lad, how did you like the performance?"

Lucius frowned, and pondered. "I thought it was, uh . . . very interesting."

Pettingill nodded. "Not at all bad, on the whole. One of the best I've seen recently."

"One of the best I've seen too," Lucius said.

"Which of the performers did you like best?" Pettingill asked.

This question gave Lucius no difficulty. "I like the lady who played Rosalind. She was real pretty."

Pettingill chuckled. "I knew you'd say that. Her name is Amanda Whitehurst, and I'm sorry to have to inform you that she's the only amateur in that otherwise professional cast."

"But don't you think she was good?"

"Good? She was awful. Why should we have to endure a Rosalind who drawls like an indolent slave girl?"

Lucius's admiration was unshaken. "I liked her, though. She's pretty."

"Well, yes. Offstage, Amanda's quite a charmer."

"You *know* her?!"

"As a matter of fact, I've been having an on-and-off affair with her for years. A number of other men have, too. She's that kind of woman—absolutely unhampered by stuffy conventions."

Lucius stared, fascinated. "Good Lord!"

"She's the daughter of one of the richest men in Louisiana, the owner of a big sugar plantation up in St. Charles Parish. I've always thought that must have something to do with Amanda's being able to succeed as an actress without a sliver of talent. She wants to act? She'll get the parts she wants, if Daddy has to buy the theater."

"He could *buy* the theter?"

"Old Amos Whitehurst could probably buy the Mississippi River, if he felt like it."

Lucius's eyes sparkled with a kind of enchantment. "God! Just think of *knowing* people like that!"

Pettingill smiled indulgently. "Well, Lucius, if you work

298

very very hard, and manage to acquire some degree of poise and polish, someday I'll introduce you into the old Southern planter society. It's amusing, in its own languid way."

Lucius looked sad, and shook his head. "It wouldn't do me any good to meet somebody like that Amanda what's-her-name."

"Why not?"

"I wouldn't know what to say to her."

"My boy, all a gentleman ever has to say to Amanda is, 'Good evening, darling. Shall we do it in the bed, on the couch, or on the floor? Before dinner, or after?' "

Lucius blushed violently, and stared out the window. Mr. Pettingill chuckled again.

"But that's far in the future, lad. A woman like Amanda wouldn't look at you now. There's somebody at the Fontainebleau who will, though."

Lucius looked around in quick alarm. "Who?"

"One of the loveliest ladies your eyes have ever beheld."

Lucius stared at his benefactor. The color had drained from his face. He squirmed.

"Oh, uh . . . Mr. Pettingill, I uh . . . I don't think I want to, uh . . . you know, it's been a long day, and I'm, uh . . . I'm . . ."

"Lucius, do you remember Ruby, in New Madrid?"

"No, I don't."

"Of course you do! You told me you thought she was very attractive."

"Oh . . . yes, I guess so."

"Well, the lady I have in mind for you makes Ruby look like a wrinkled old crone."

"Oh, well, I don't think I, uh . . ."

"Her name is Genevieve."

"Yes, but—"

The carriage had threaded its way through the rough and narrow streets of the *Vieux Carré*, and now stopped with a screech at the sign of the Blue Fountain.

Albert Pettingill leaned close to the boy beside him. "Lucius . . . men have been known to fight duels over Genevieve."

Lucius leaned back, closed his eyes, and gripped his forehead in his hand.

13

THE ROOM WAS a chamber of lavish opulence. An oil lamp of gleaming crystal, suspended from the high ceiling, cast a subdued glow over heavy brocade draperies of purple and gold, a wallpaper scene depicting a classical courtyard of manicured lawn and marble columns, a Persian rug ablaze with serpentine symbols, and a huge four-poster bed, covered with sheer netting.

Lucius stood rigid and perspiring in the center of the room. A woman was at his side. Her hand was creeping up his arm to his shoulder, and along his neck. She tweaked his earlobe.

" 'Allo, Lucius," she murmured. Her voice was a feather-soft purr.

Lucius stared straight ahead. Out of the corner of his eye he could see the woman smiling up at him, her white teeth and liquid eyes sparkling. He breathed deeply, inhaled her opiate perfume, and remembered the woman Ruby, in New Madrid. Then he remembered the woman on the flatboat in Paducah, imagined the moldy stench of that floating hovel in his nostrils again, and was threatened by a sudden twinge of nausea.

Albert Pettingill was standing near the door, regarding Lucius with a mixture of amusement and perplexity. "What's the matter, Lucius boy? Can't you say hello to Genevieve?"

Lucius forced himself to turn his head and look at the

woman beside him, and was struck by the incredible violet eyes and the creamy white skin of her shoulders, bare above a floor-length gown of shimmering green. She was young, she was diminutive, and she was beautiful.

" 'Allo, Lucius," she said again.

"Hello, Genevieve," he mumbled, and breathed a sigh of relief to discover that his powers of speech were still intact.

"Ah!" said Genevieve, and turned her smile toward Pettingill. "He is nice boy. He talk to me." She leaned forward and kissed Lucius on the cheek, and her breasts pushed softly against him.

Lucius felt himself blushing, and heard Pettingill's laugh.

"Well, that's fine," the man said. "I can see you two are going to become great friends, so I'll leave you now. Viola and I are just across the hall, you know. Number twelve."

He opened the door and smiled back at the two people in the room. "Sweet dreams," he said impishly. The door closed, and Lucius and Genevieve were alone.

She stood before him, took his hands in hers, and smiled beguilingly. Lucius tried to smile back, but succeeded only in producing a sickly grimace.

"Lucius," Genevieve said. "That is nice name, Lucius."

Lucius swallowed hard. "Thanks."

Genevieve took a small step closer. "Do not be afraid of me, Lucius."

"What d'ya mean, afraid?!" Lucius scoffed. "I'm not afraid o' nobody!"

Genevieve's smile faded. Her moist red lips took on a little pout. "Then you don' like me. I weel go away eef you don' like me."

Lucius became distressed. "Oh no, it's not anything like that—"

"Then you *do* like me?" Genevieve was smiling again.

"Oh, sure, uh . . . sure I like you, but—"

"You t'ink I'm pretty?" Her smile had become coy.

He studied her with a thoughtful frown, as if the question required careful analysis. His gaze wandered over her hair, deep auburn in color and very thick and curly; over her face, with its small, delicate features framed between a pair of glittering earrings; down the milk-white neck and

301

shoulders to the voluptuous cleavage at the front of the low-cut dress—then quickly back to her face.

"Oh, yes, uh . . . you're pretty, all right. Very pretty."

"Merci," she said graciously.

"But you see, I, uh . . . I have this problem . . . I don't think you'd want, uh . . . I mean . . . you wouldn't like it."

She became alarmed. "Is some'ting the matter weeth you?"

"I don't know. I mean, I guess so . . . I don't know."

Her alarm grew. "You have disease? Here?" She reached for his genital area.

Lucius leaped backward away from her. "Oh, no, no . . . nothing like that . . ."

She followed him. She reached for his belt. "Take off your clothes. Let me see."

"Go away!" He fled from her, panic-stricken, taking refuge behind a small table. She went around the table in pursuit.

"Come here, Lucius." she commanded. "Let me see."

He put out his hands protectively. "Stop, damn it! Leave me alone."

Her hands were on his belt, unfastening. He tried to push her away. Then her arms were around his midriff, pulling him close to her. The little pout was on her face again as she looked into his eyes.

"Ah, *chéri,*" she murmured. "Why you fight me? I wan' to love you."

Lucius stood petrified. The woman's hands were under his shirt, stroking his back. Her lips brushed against his.

"Love me, Lucius," she whispered.

"I can't," he gasped.

"Why not?"

Lucius squirmed. "I don't . . . I don't know how."

Her eyes went wide. She giggled. *"Mon chéri!* You don' have to know anyt'ing. I teach you."

Her busy hands were unbuttoning his shirt. Lucius twisted out of her grasp and fled again, taking refuge in a far corner behind a large chair. Genevieve stood in the center of the room and gazed at him with a hurt look on her face.

"I was right. You don' like me." She whimpered a little.

Lucius watched her warily. Genevieve loosened the bodice of her dress and pushed the straps off her shoulders.

302

"I weel just go to bed now, and cry myself to sleep."

The bright green dress dropped to the floor. Genevieve stepped out of it, picked it up, and laid it neatly over a chair. She stood looking soberly at Lucius.

"I might as well go to sleep, if nobody weel love me."

A petticoat followed the dress onto the chair. Lucius's eyes widened as he watched, spellbound.

"Not'ing makes a lady so sad as when nobody loves her," Genevieve said in piteous tones.

Shoes and stockings were deposited on the floor. Then the final garments—dainty black silken things—were laid on the chair, and Genevieve stood radiantly nude. She spread her arms in a graceful pose, and smiled.

"Weel you come and kees me goodnight, Lucius?"

Lucius didn't move. "Wh—where are you gonna sleep?"

"In ze bed. Where else?"

"Well, then—where am *I* gonna sleep?"

Genevieve's laugh was a merry tinkling sound. "Why, in ze bed too, of course. It's beeg enough for two." She extended her arms to him invitingly. "Kees me goodnight, *chéri?*"

Lucius shook his head. "I don't feel like it."

The little pout returned. "You are cruel, Lucius. I don' know how you can be so cruel to me." She went to the canopied bed, drew back the sheer netting that covered it, and slid inside.

For several minutes, all was stillness. Lucius moved quietly out into the center of the room and peered toward the recesses of the bed, dim and shadowy behind the curtain of netting. He saw Genevieve's curvaceous body totally exposed on top of the bedcovers, her auburn hair spread over the pillow, her arms arranged seductively above her head. She lifted a gracefully tapered leg and pointed her toes at Lucius. When she spoke, her voice was both intimate and far away.

"Come, *chéri.* I'm lonely."

Lucius moved back a few steps and looked around the room in the grip of uncertainty. He glanced up at the lamp above his head, quickly reached up and turned it off, and stood still in the darkness for a moment, listening. There was no sound. He began to undress. Soon he crept to the side of the bed opposite Genevieve, lifted the curtain, and

303

moving very slowly and cautiously, he crawled in. He stretched out flat on his back and lay motionless, barely breathing.

Genevieve's soft, purring voice touched his ear like a caress. "Lucius?"

He started. "What?"

"Why are you so quiet?"

"I didn't want to disturb you. I thought you might be asleep."

She giggled. "Ah, *mon amoureux!* You are so nice!" She reached out and stroked his arm. Then her hand moved across to his belly, patted it gently, and rested there.

"Come here, Lucius," she whispered.

"I *am* here," he said.

"I mean come close to me. Take me in your arms."

"I better not."

"You are going to make me cry, Lucius."

"I'm sorry. I told you, I got a problem."

Suddenly her hand moved down his belly and found his penis. Lucius gasped and pushed her hand away.

"Hey, stop it, will you?"

She was up on an elbow, leaning over him. *"Pauvre enfant!* You 'ave no erection!"

He turned on his side away from her. "Leave me alone," he growled.

She clutched at him and pulled him toward her. "No, Lucius. I weel not leave you alone until you make love to me."

"I can't, damn it!"

"Yes you can."

"You don't know how it is—"

"Yes I do. I've had many lovers with your deeficulty."

Lucius turned partially back toward her. "You have?"

"Yes. Eet's not'ing, really. You just nervous."

"I am?"

"Of course." Her lips were moving on his cheek, and nibbling his ear. "Eet's because you have not had woman before."

"What d'ya mean?! You don't know what you're—"

"You must not lie to me, Lucius. I cannot love you if you lie. You must always be truthful to your lover. Always. That is why I am professional woman instead of married

304

woman. I do not have to pretend. Now be truthful, and tell me how many you have had."

"Well . . . I had one. A riverboat woman. She was dirty and she was drunk, and she laughed at me."

"Awww! *Mon pauvre petit enfant!*" Genevieve stroked his brow and ran her fingers through his hair. "You deserve better, and you shall have better. Come to me."

She pulled him gently, and this time he responded and turned to her.

"Take me in your arms, *chéri*," she murmured. She lay back and opened her arms to him, and he moved into them.

"Now, take me here . . ." She too his hand and placed it over her breast. "And caress me. Gently, *chéri*. Tenderly. Weeth love."

He did as he was told.

"Now kees me."

Their lips melded in a soft, liquid movement, with a sigh that seemed to come from both of them. After a moment her hand moved down the side of his body and found his genitals. Lucius quivered and sucked in his breath sharply. She stroked him with a feather-light touch, and in the darkness her white teeth gleamed.

"Ahhh! You see, *chéri*? Everyt'ing is fine now. *C'est magnifique.*"

Suddenly he emitted a low groan, moved over her, and wrapped his arms around her in a powerful, demanding embrace.

"Gently, Lucius, gently!" she whispered. "You are beeg and strong! Do not hurt your leetle Genevieve. She is only a delicate flower, at your mercy . . . "

Lucius groaned again, and the sound was laden with deep, welling desire, struggling for release.

"Oh, Genevieve . . . you're wonderful! I love you, I love you . . ." He was devouring her like a starving man, with his mouth and his hands, and thrusting the lower part of his body between her widespread legs.

Genevieve lay back and closed her eyes, sighed with deep contentment, and surrendered all initiative to her lover. After a little while she encircled him with her arms and clutched at his back, and smiled with her own private joy.

305

"Ah, *chéri, chéri* . . ." she breathed. "You are . . . *a man!*"

At nine o'clock in the morning a maid knocked on the door of room fourteen, on the second floor of the little hotel called La Fontainebleau. It was a long time before the door opened. Genevieve stood there with a sheet wrapped around her, clutching it to her bosom. She pushed her disheveled auburn hair out of her face and squinted sleepily at the maid.

"What is it?" she mumbled.

"Pardon, mademoiselle," said the maid. "Monsieur Pettingeel, he inquire, weel you and Monsieur Hargrave join heem and Mademoiselle Viola in ze dining room for breakfast?"

Genevieve blinked vaguely. "Mmmm."

Over her shoulder, Lucius's face appeared, his tousled, sandy hair falling into his eyes. He wrapped his arms around Genevieve's waist from behind, and put his cheek against hers. He smirked at the maid.

"Tell Mr. Pettingill they shouldn't wait for us. We won't be down for . . ." He planted a little kiss on Genevieve's bare shoulder. "At least an hour."

Genevieve placed one hand against Lucius's head and pressed his face against the curve of her neck. "What can I do?" she murmured to the maid. "I cannot deny my lover. He is *magnifique*. He weel *not* be denied." With a languid smile, she pushed the door shut.

The maid shrugged disinterestedly and walked away.

306

14

FROM THE JOURNAL of Lucius Hargrave:

Sometimes I am overcome with wonder as I think back over my perilous transition from youth to manhood. I am entranced to contemplate with what capriciousness Fate tossed and turned me on the turbulent current of the world, and with what agility I leapt from one bit of flotsam to another, keeping myself afloat and my optimism undampened.

Consider my friend and benefactor, Mr. Albert Pettingill. Any rational person would have taken an instant distrust to his overtures toward someone like me—as indeed, my family in South Bar emphatically did. Here was a polished, sophisticated, and worldly man, past thirty years of age. What honorable interest could he possibly have in an ignorant boy of sixteen from a backwoods village? Yet in my youthful naiveté, I severed the bonds that bound me to safe associations, and placed myself in the hands of this stranger, and I did it without the slightest tremor of hesitation or moment of doubt. All I really knew of my new master was the intuitive feeling I had for him, and that seemed quite enough. Fate might have served me well at this point by teaching me a bitter lesson on the folly of trusting to blind instinct. Instead it chose to leave my innocence intact—and thus, unfortunately, vulnerable to future abuse.

Mr. Pettingill turned out to be the chief shareholder in

a steamboat company with extensive and highly profitable operations throughout the Ohio and Mississippi Valleys. That this lofty man, with an enormous pool of human resources at his disposal, had chosen *me* as his personal assistant, was an honor with which my youthful mind was hardly equipped to cope—yet I managed to take it in stride, and maintain my natural modesty.

My employer had a number of steamers under his direct supervision, including the *Cincinnati Queen*, which served the lower Mississippi and the Ohio, and several others whose runs were chiefly on the Mississippi. He had a fine office in New Orleans but was seldom in it, spending most of his time traveling on the *Cincinnati Queen*, his favorite ship, seeing to it that operations were kept at maximum efficiency, and service at the highest level. The task was herculean. That is why Mr. Pettingill wanted a bright, energetic young assistant to take some of the burden of details from his shoulders. He was not heavily endowed with patience; he wanted the thing done immediately, and he set me to a schedule of training that was merciless. Sixteen hours a day for three days, while the *Queen* made its way from New Madrid down to New Orleans, we worked without respite, until I was ready to tear out my hair and leap screaming into the river. But somehow I persevered, and my labors were duly rewarded. For there at last, resplendent before us, lay New Orleans!—by all odds the most magnificent sight my impressionable young eyes had ever beheld. Founded by the French over a hundred years before, acquired successively by Spain, by France again, and finally by the United States with the Louisiana Purchase, its rich international flavor was one of the wonders of the world to a wide-eyed lad from rural Indiana. I was enthralled; I could have spent an age wandering about, staring in dumbstruck admiration at the teeming spectacle. In fact we spent a week there, and the hours of those days and nights tumbled over each other in my fevered mind with such tumultuous abandon that in the end I was not sure whether it had been a week, a month, or a year.

First, in accordance with Mr. Pettingill's strict policy—business. We went to a huge emporium of commerce, recently built, I was told, called the Merchant's Exchange, just off Canal Street. There Mr. Pettingill introduced me as his nephew—an example of his whimsical sense of humor—and conferred at some length with a number of hard-eyed men, magnates of the financial empire of the Mississippi River (and who owed their existence to the river as surely as did the fish that swam in its muddy depths). I sat quietly, as I was instructed to do, while a complex transaction was negotiated, the result of which was that we would not be going aboard the *Cincinnati Queen* anymore, but on another steamer operated by the company—the *Minerva.* I gathered that the *Minerva* was a newer and finer vessel, and that its run was between New Orleans and St. Louis. This meant that we would not be traveling on the Ohio, and thus I would not soon again lay eyes on the old familiar sights of South Bar, Indiana. For a few minutes I experienced a bleak and chilling sensation I could not clearly identify—was it homesickness?—as I contemplated this knowledge, and thought of my dear mother.

But there was no time for melancholy reflection. We progressed quickly from business to pleasure as we went off to explore the fashionable clothing shops along Chartres Street, where Mr. Pettingill bade me stand still while busy little tailors with pins in their mouths held yards of fine fabrics against my torso, and made calculations for coats and trousers. Gleefully we descended upon linen counters, where Mr. Pettingill chose for me stacks of snow white underwear and a dozen shirts of the finest quality (a dozen!), with fancy lace fronts and embroidered cuffs. It was sheer intoxication. If I should return to South Bar after this transformation, I thought, would my mother know me? I wondered if I would know myself.

Then—ah, then—did the fabled city open wide its bejeweled gates for me!

We went in quest of the arts, of culture, of things of the intellect—the theatre, the opera, art exhibits, concerts, lectures, museums—the treasures, Mr. Pettingill assured me, for which human civilization exists. I looked and listened, tasted, felt, experienced, and absorbed, always with my mentor Albert Pettingill, the sophisticate and connoisseur, at my side to guide me. I was astounded to consider, in retrospect, with what miraculous speed and ease it had all happened.

Those few days of professional training on board the

309

steamboat had strained my mind to the snapping point; that week of cultural education in New Orleans literally overwhelmed it, leaving me numb, exhausted, but rapturously happy.

This, then, was the first major turning point of my life. Here, I told myself, is where my boyhood ends, and my manhood begins.

15

ALBERT PETTINGILL went on board the *Minerva* one morning about ten o'clock, when the day's dock activity was at its frantic, earsplitting peak. He was followed by four burly stevedores, bent under the weight of baggage. As he stepped on deck, he was approached by a large man with a gaudily braided captain's cap on his head. The man extended his hand and beamed a hearty smile.

"Welcome aboard, Mr. Pettingill!"

Pettingill shook hands perfunctorily. "Are our staterooms ready, Captain Bates?"

"All ready, sir. Number eleven and number twelve. Aft end o' the ship. Plenty o' privacy fer you and yer partner, jes' like you asked fer."

"Fine." Mr. Pettingill turned to the stevedores, who waited patiently for instructions.

"You there, and you," he said to the first two men. "Put that baggage in number eleven. Those are Mr. Hargrave's things."

The men moved off.

"And take care with that old satchel," Pettingill called after them. "That's an antique. Mr. Hargrave's very particular about it."

He gave crisp instructions to the second pair of stevedores, then turned back to the captain. "Departure time firm for noon, Captain Bates?"

"Firm, sir. Everything's all set."

"Good."

"Uh . . . where's your partner, sir? Thought he was comin' aboard with you."

"He'll be along directly. He felt compelled to spend a romantic farewell hour with his ladyfriend."

The captain chuckled. "Well, sure can't blame 'im fer that."

"Lucius is young. At his age, one tends to fall in love at the drop of a hat. Or should I say . . . at the drop of a petticoat."

The captain's chuckle grew to a cackle. "By gum, sir, that's rich!"

Then the laughter was replaced by a thoughtful frown. "Just how young *is* this Lucius what's-his-name?"

"Very young. Very, very young. But Captain Bates . . ."

"Yes, sir?"

"To you, he is Mr. Hargrave."

The captain blinked. "Oh, uh . . . certainly, sir."

"Ask him to come to my room as soon as he's aboard, will you?" Pettingill said, and walked away without waiting for a reply.

Mr. Lucius Hargrave's carriage moved down Canal Street toward the river. Young Mr. Hargrave reclined on the seat with his legs crossed, and gazed moodily out at the passing street scene. He breathed deeply; he sighed. Genevieve's perfume lingered—on his hands, in his clothes, in his mind. The sweet dampness of her parting tears still lay on his collar. Without interest he surveyed the buildings and carriages and pedestrians that glided past his view through the carriage window. He turned away from the morning glare, leaned back, gripped his temples in his fingertips, and closed his weary eyes.

"Ah, Genevieve," he murmured. *"Ma petite chérie."*

The carriage pulled up at the end of Canal Street, and

311

the black driver climbed down and opened the door to the passenger compartment. "Heah you be, suh."

Lucius stepped out of the carriage and turned a cold look on his attendant.

"My good man, you drive like a raving lunatic."

The driver grinned. "Beg yo' pardon, suh, sho' 'nuff."

"It's all very well to shake the teeth out of the heads of ordinary citizens, but if your passenger is a gentleman, it would pay you to take a little extra care."

"Yas, suh. You right, sho' 'nuff."

Lucius produced a large roll of cash from his pocket, pulled off several bills, and handed them to the driver. The man examined the money, found it more than satisfactory, and grinned his approval.

"Thank you, suh, thank you. I sho' do—"

His customer had already walked away.

Lucius picked his way through the crates and bales and baggage that covered the wharf. He took great care not to rub against anything that might soil his fine new tailormade suit. He paused and looked up and down the landing, and spotted the tall twin stacks of the *Minerva*, two hundred yards away. As he was about to move in that direction, someone touched him on the arm. He drew back sharply, and turned to glare at the offender.

A black man stood there. He was tall, powerfully built, perhaps thirty-five years of age, with handsome, finely molded features. He was dressed in a hip-length, tunic-like garment of vivid purple, tightly belted at the waist. He smiled, and the well-shaped head bobbed rapidly at Lucius.

"You want nice woman, sar?" The voice was as soft and silky as the clothing.

"What was that?" Lucius snapped.

The man took a step closer, and the silky voice dropped almost to a whisper. "Woman, sar. Pretty woman, nice and clean. One dollar. You come wid me, sar, I take you dere."

Lucius stared, incredulous. Over his face came a smile that was half-sneer.

"One dollar?!"

"Yes, sar, one dollar." The man's head moved up and down. "Not too much, sar, you'll see. You like fine. Best on Girod Street. Famous place. Everybody like to go to—"

"Girod Street? The Swamp?"

312

"Yes, sar. Best place in town. Best woman in town."

"My good man!" Lucius said huffily. "Do you suppose someone in *my* social position would stoop so low as to set foot in the Swamp? Do you really think I'm so deprived of love that I'd be willing to touch your filthy one-dollar whore?"

"Oh, you be surprise, sar. Nice woman. You be surprise—"

"Black or white?" Lucius demanded.

"Egyptian, sar. Egyptian princess."

"Princess?!" The word triggered a fit of hilarity in Lucius. "You mean a real, live princess, right here in New Orleans?!" He threw back his head and laughed uproariously.

The black man smiled and nodded his head, and waited patiently. "You make fun, sar," he said finally. "But you make mistake. Princess nice, clean, pretty woman. Mos' pretty woman in N'Orleans. An' she sing, sar. Oh, she sing like a mockingbird. She play de lute an' she sing de pretty love song so yo' heart will nearly break fo' love."

The young gentleman's amusement had subsided into a disdainful smile. He extracted a fine linen handkerchief from his coat pocket, and delicately blew his nose.

"I'll be on my way, if you don't mind," he said. "It's been very entertaining, listening to your idiotic babble, but I'm a busy man. I can't waste time like this."

"You make mistake, sar—"

"Look here, you fool—" Lucius eyed the black man with a sudden show of belligerence. "You do *not* have the prettiest woman in New Orleans, because *I* have her. She lives at the Fontainebleau Hotel, in the most fashionable part of the *Vieux Carré*. I have just left her after spending a glorious week in her arms, and do you know how much money I gave her as a parting remembrance? Two hundred dollars, my good man. Two . . . hundred . . . dollars. So go on back to the Swamp, and peddle your one-dollar whore to the dirty, common flatboatmen, and stop pestering gentlemen."

Lucius turned on his heel and strode away.

"You make big mistake, sar," the black man called.

Lucius went on, paying no attention.

The black man stood with a placid, expressionless face, looking after the young gentleman. "You big fool, sar," he

313

muttered under his breath. "Fo' one dollar, Camus sell yo' soul to de debbil."

He chuckled, turned, and sauntered off in the opposite direction.

Lucius leaned against the guardrail on the top deck of the *Minerva*, and gazed out over the panorama before him: the river teeming with floating traffic; the levee dotted with freight and crawling with human bodies in an elongated anthill stretching as far as the eye could follow in either direction; and the city beyond. The entire scene lay shimmering in the bright springtime sun.

"Ah, me," Lucius sighed. "Ah, me."

He was still there fifteen minutes later when Albert Pettingill climbed the stairs to the top deck and came toward him.

"Captain Bates just told me you were aboard. I was waiting for you."

"Sorry. I had to look at something here first."

"Look at what?"

"That." Lucius waved a hand toward New Orleans. "If this ship sinks and I die, I want to die remembering this view, the place where I spent the happiest week of my life."

Pettingill sighed. "Come now, Lucius. Genevieve is nice, I know. But aren't you being a bit . . . soulful?"

Lucius squinted into the sunlight in the direction of the *Vieux Carré*. "She loves me," he said in a faraway voice.

"Correction," Mr. Pettingill said. "She *loved* you. And no doubt she will love you again soon. But she will love any number of other men in the meantime, don't forget."

"That's not necessarily true," Lucius said icily.

"Oh, isn't it? Why, I shouldn't be surprised if at this very moment she were lying naked in somebody's arms, writhing in ecstasy."

With a violent lurch, Lucius moved away. He stopped after a few steps, leaned over the railing again, and stared glumly down at the river. Mr. Pettingill followed him.

"Dear me," Pettingill said. "We still have a lot of growing up to do, haven't we?" He regarded his partner with sympathy and amusement. Then, briskly, he began again, on a new subject.

314

"But look here, Lucius, we've got work to do. We're horribly rusty after a week's layoff. And I've got a feeling we'll find a whole covey of pigeons aboard. Should be a profitable journey."

Lucius was still bent over the railing, watching the river traffic. Mr. Pettingill leaned down next to him.

"You know, lad, we've got to keep our skills polished if we want to afford little playthings like Genevieve and Viola. Luxuries like that don't come cheap. And there are so many playthings like them, up and down the river. Wait till you become acquainted with Natchez-Under-the-Hill. And you remember Ruby, in New Madrid. There are others like her. And St. Louis. Ah, St. Louis!"

He gave Lucius a playful little nudge with his shoulder. "So cheer up, lad."

"Will you introduce me to Ruby?" Lucius asked without looking up.

"Why, of course! Share and share alike between partners, I always say."

Something far below suddenly caught Lucius's attention. Around the stern of the *Minerva*, a flatboat had floated into view, making for an empty spot at the landing. Otto Grieshaber and Josh Everett were poling, and Nate Collins was at the tiller.

"What the devil do you see down there that's so all-fired fascinating?" Mr. Pettingill asked in a tone that contained a hint of impatience.

At that instant, Nate Collins looked up in idle curiosity and scanned the steamboat above him. Lucius straightened and quickly turned away from the railing.

"Not a damn thing, Albert," he said airily. He smiled at Pettingill. "Let's go below and get to work, shall we?"

Pettingill chuckled, clapped his partner on the shoulder, and led the way down the stairs.

315

Part Four

1

May 12, 1834

Mrs. Sarah Thacker
River Road Route
South Bar, Indiana

Dear Mama,

I humble myself before you on bended knee, to plead for your forgiveness. It has been so long that I have not been able to find the spare hour to sit down and write to you. I am truly ashamed. Where has the time gone? The days turn into months, the months into years, all in a twinkling of an eye.

At eighteen, I am now fully a man in all respects, and I can assure you, Mama, in all respects a gentleman. If you saw me, you would not recognize the awkward country boy who kissed you goodbye more than two years ago, for that boy no longer exists. Someday, when I can break away from my work long enough to come and see you, I will make you proud.

You can hardly imagine how fortunate I have been. Sometimes I have difficulty believing it myself. As you undoubtedly know, I chose to go downriver with Nate Collins on his flatboat rather than wait for the *Cincinnati Queen* to return, since your husband made it clear I was no longer welcome at home. But you may be sure I did not long remain a menial on Mr. Collins's crew. The *Cincinnati*

319

Queen overtook us in New Madrid, Missouri, and my good friend, Mr. Albert Pettingill, found me there and insisted that I come with him, as we had previously agreed. I did so, and my natural abilities and willingness to work hard so pleased Mr. Pettingill that in a short time I was offered a partnership in his enterprise, and have been prospering in that happy arrangement ever since. Unfortunately, it places heavy demands on my time, which is one reason I have been so delinquent in communicating with you.

New Orleans is a wonderful city, and I fell in love with it at first sight, but I'm sorry to say we spend very little time here, or, for that matter, anywhere ashore. Our business takes us up and down the river from New Orleans to St. Louis, and we are hardly ever in one place longer than is necessary to have a proper bath and a good night's sleep. Chiefly our duties require us to carry on a continual inspection of the steamboat line, to make sure the traveling public is served with courtesy and efficiency in all areas. It involves many different kinds of operations. But enough of that; I don't want to bore you with dreary business details.

There is another, more personal reason that I spend little time in New Orleans these days. It is full of sad memories for me. Mama, your son has already suffered the torments of a tragic love affair. I had hardly arrived in New Orleans when I met an angel of French blood named Genevieve. She was an enchantress beyond compare, but modest, demure, and ladylike in every way. I fell immediately and deeply in love with her, and she with me. We would surely have married and lived in perfect bliss forever after, but for the cruel intervention of Fate. Last year, New Orleans was seized by a horrible epidemic of yellow fever, which claimed the lives of some six thousand unfortunate souls. I was out of the city during most of this period, and thus escaped the danger, but Genevieve, my beloved, was one of the victims. I am told she whispered my name with her dying breath. I was desolate. I can hardly bear to think of it even now, it is so painful. May heaven keep her in perpetual beauty.

Yes, pain is as much a part of growing up as is pleasure, I have discovered, and of course, I know you could have told me that. I freely admit that one of the hardest things I have had to face these past two years has been the

320

absence of your kind looks, soothing voice, and gentle wisdom. Many a night have I lain awake in cold, impersonal rooms, alone and friendless, thinking of you.

But no pity for me, please. It has all been worth it, a thousand times over. I am a man now, and what's more a gentleman, and a prosperous one as well. One day I will come and fetch you, and take you on a lovely steamboat trip on the Mississippi. Life is exciting along the big river, much more so than on the sleepy old Ohio. When Grandpa settled in southern Indiana, it was the western frontier. Now it is the old country, and the frontier is Missouri and the Mexican province of Texas. Nothing remains unchanged, and in that lies the eternal fascination of life.

There! You didn't know I was a philosopher, did you? Well, enough of that. How is my good brother Isaac? Has he taken himself a wife yet, the rascal? And Grandpa—I trust he is vigorous still? I hope you will show this letter to him, because I think he will be pleased to see that I have not neglected my studies. I have applied myself diligently to reading and writing (at Mr. Pettingill's urging), and have greatly improved both my speech and writing skills. Grandpa would like Mr. Pettingill very much. Those two certainly see eye-to-eye on the importance of education.

Please give Isaac and Grandpa my love and warmest greetings. How I long to see the three of you! I will try to come soon, perhaps this summer, if all goes well. Until that happy day, whenever it may be, you are constantly in my thoughts.

> Your adoring son,
> Lucius
> c/o J. Knight & Company, Steamboat Lines
> Number Fifteen, Merchants' Exchange
> New Orleans, Louisiana

P.S. My respects to your husband.

321

2

May 30th, 1834

Mr. Lucius Hargrave
c/o J. Knight & Company, Steamboat Lines
Number Fifteen, Merchants' Exchange
New Orleans, Louisiana

My dearest Lucius,

What a joy to hear from you! And what a terrible burden of worry has been lifted from my mind at last, to know that you are safe and well. And prosperous, too. That is good news!

Of course I have been angry with you all this time. In fact, I had long ago mentally composed a letter in which I scold you most severely for your cruelty in remaining silent for so long. It has been lying in my head just waiting for an address, to be written and sent off. But now that I have your beautiful letter, all thoughts of scolding have deserted me. I am overflowing instead with happiness and good wishes and love for you, my dear son. All is forgiven. I am not able to sustain anger against someone I love.

Isaac is so excited! He is going around town telling everybody about your letter. He even told Reverend Daniels, which is a little embarrassing, because Reverend Daniels is strongly displeased with me for having lost my enthusiasm for churchgoing somewhere along the years. Dear Isaac thinks the world of you, always has. I wonder if you have realized how much more than a brother he is to you, how much of a loyal friend and defender as well. He will not listen to an unkind word directed toward you from anyone, no matter who.

And there have been a few such words, Lucius, I can't pretend otherwise. When the *Cincinnati Queen* came back upstream on its first round trip after you left, Isaac went aboard looking for your Mr. Pettingill, to learn if there was any news of you. The captain (Jochum I believe his name was) raged at poor Isaac, saying he had thrown Pettingill bodily off his boat when he discovered the man was a scoundrel. Yes, you had come aboard, Captain Jochum said, and had been thrown off along with Mr. Pettingill. The captain said it was too bad a young boy like you had fallen into such bad company. Then, several months later, Nate Collins came to South Bar and went around town telling everybody that you had deserted him in mid-voyage, and had stolen half his cargo!

Cyrus and I and your grandfather were all terribly upset by these things, but not Isaac. He steadfastly refused to believe a word of it. One day he went up to Nate Collins on the street and called him a liar to his face, and told him to get out of town, and Nate did as he was told! People couldn't believe that gentle, soft-spoken Isaac could do a thing like that, but he did.

He never had any doubts about you, and now that we have your letter telling of your success, I can't see how any of us ever could have. Isaac was right. He had faith in you, and his faith has shamed us all.

No, Isaac has not yet taken a wife. He is marvelously tall and graceful and good-looking, like your father, and you may be sure there are several pretty maids in town who are sending him signals furiously, but he doesn't seem to notice. To tell the truth, they are mostly frivolous girls, and you know what a serious young man Isaac is. He is off every morning at the crack of dawn, and seldom comes home until after dark. I tell Cyrus it is unfair to let Isaac take on such a lion's share of the burden. Cyrus says Isaac is a grown man and a full partner, and can do as he pleases. I suppose I should be thankful that Isaac is so devoted to the business, else I fear it would suffer. Prosperity seems to have had one undesirable effect on Cyrus. It has made him a tiny bit lazy.

Now, about your grandfather. He is well, in fact he is in amazingly good condition for a man his age. He has grown a bit cross and cantankerous, but I suppose that is to be expected with the passage of years. He insists on keeping his farm and his orchard in production, and he works night and day as if his very survival depended upon it. Cyrus and Isaac urge him to sell his place and come and live with us, but Papa will not hear of it. Cyrus and Isaac want me to go and try to persuade him. I refuse. I know what's good for Papa, even if they don't. It's working his own land and preserving his sense of independence that keeps him happy. Anything else would be pure misery for him. (Sometimes I wonder if my menfolk are as wise as they fancy themselves to be.)

Anyway, here is the exciting news about Papa, and another reason I am so happy about establishing contact with you at last. On the twenty-second of August this year, Papa will observe his seventieth birthday, and I will have you know that the town council of South Bar has officially designated Saturday, August twenty-third as Samuel Gilpin Day! There will be a parade with a band playing, a public gathering in the new town park (which you haven't seen), a picnic, and speeches. Papa will be presented with a scroll commemorating the fact that he was the founder of South Bar. And finally, fancy new signposts will be unveiled along Main Street, showing its new name—Gilpin Street! Isn't it wonderful?

It has all been arranged by Morton King, with the connivance of a lot of others, naturally. (You remember Morton, son of Papa's old friend Rufus King?) Morton has been elected South Bar's first mayor. The village is growing up into quite a town, Lucius.

Well, of course, Papa grumbles and growls and says it's all a pack of nonsense, but deep down inside he's pleased, I know he is. I know you will be too, Lucius, because Papa has always loved you very much, even though you used to make him furious. "That boy was a rascal," he says to me. "But he has Oliver's mettle in him. He will do great things, you watch." I can only smile at this. It is not much of a compliment to you, in my opinion, but Papa means it as one, and that's what counts.

324

Oh, I am rambling on so—but I must tell you one more wonderful bit of news. Well, maybe you won't think it's wonderful, considering the bitterness you have harbored in the past. But I have to let you know, it's much too good to keep, and I hope you'll just put all that old silliness out of your mind and rejoice with us.

George is coming! Can you believe it? Robert Morrow (you know, your Aunt Emily's brother in Corydon) was here a few weeks ago, and told us he has heard that George and Emily are selling their property in Illinois and intend to return to Indiana sometime this summer. When Robert learned of the plans for Samuel Gilpin Day in August, he promised he would personally see to it that George would be here for the occasion. We are not telling Papa, we want it to be a surprise. Won't it be thrilling for him?

You'll come too, won't you, Lucius? Robert Morrow says George is deeply remorseful about all those terrible things that tore our family apart so many years ago, and wants to come back and embrace us all again, to forgive and be forgiven. Please find some of that same feeling in your own heart, Lucius. Please. I will spend every waking moment from now until August wishing for it, and hoping that you will come, so we can all be together again, if only for a little while.

Cyrus and Isaac and Papa all join me in that hope, and want me to convey their most affectionate greetings to you in the meantime. (Cyrus too, Lucius, please note.) He wants so very much to shake your hand, forget all past misunderstandings, and be friends with you again.

May whatever powers there be watch over you, my dear son, and keep you safe from harm.

All my love,
Mama

P.S. I am sorry to hear you have already tasted the bitter fruit of a tragic love affair. I believe I am in a position to sympathize with you to some extent. But you are young, and a man, and you will recover soon and be as good as new, I promise you.

3

BY THE EVENING of Friday, the twenty-second of August, the town of South Bar was adorned with colorful decorations, and signs proclaiming Samuel Gilpin Day on Saturday.

Sarah started early in the morning and worked all day, preparing for a birthday dinner party to be held that evening. Isaac came home from the woodyard a little earlier than usual, to help her. When she heard his footfall on the front step, she flew to the door, wiping her hands on her apron. She seemed crestfallen when she saw that it was Isaac.

"Oh . . . I thought maybe it was Robert Morrow, with George and Emily."

"It's too early for them, Mama Sarah. They won't be here till five o'clock, at least."

"Or I thought it might be . . ." Sarah turned away and went back to the kitchen.

Isaac followed. "I'm here to help you, Mama Sarah. What you want me to do?"

She put him to work peeling potatoes.

"Did any steamboats from downriver stop today?" she asked.

"Sure. Two or three."

"Were there any letters? Any messages of any kind? Anything?"

Isaac sighed. "Now, Mama Sarah, if there was any news from Lucius, I'd tell you, wouldn't I?"

Sarah didn't answer. After a few minutes, Isaac got up and went to her. Sarah was kneading bread dough. She pushed it and pulled it, and turned it over and pushed and pulled some more, and as she worked, her face was grim.

Isaac put a soft hand on her shoulder. "Mama Sarah, he's not gonna come. You jes' ought to get used to the idea, and stop frettin' about it."

"But why? *Why* doesn't he come? He said he would."

"He said he'd come when he could. He didn't say he'd come for Samuel Gilpin Day. He didn't even know about that."

"I wrote him in plenty of time. He could have made arrangements."

"How do you know he even got your letter?"

"I wrote him three times, Isaac. Three times."

"Well . . . he's a busy man, Mama Sarah. He's got lots o' heavy responsibilties. He'll come when he can. So jes' don't fret about it."

"Papa would have been so happy . . ."

"Oh, listen!" Isaac said with a quick chuckle. "Grandpa's goin' to be so out of his mind with Uncle George here, he won't know or care who else is around."

Sarah pummeled the bread dough fiercely. "*I'll* know," she said under her breath. "And I'll care."

Isaac sighed and gave it up, and went back to peeling potatoes.

At five o'clock Cyrus left the woodyard, and by prearrangement, drove his carriage to his father-in-law's house, to bring the guest of honor to the dinner party. Samuel was ready and waiting, and grumbling that he thought it was a pack of foolishness for Sarah to go to all this trouble.

"Why, shucks, Mr. Gilpin," Cyrus said amiably, "Sarah don't do nothin' she don't want to do. She loves it." He helped Samuel into the carriage and drove toward home.

When he came within view of his house, he saw a large carriage at the front gate, and recognized it as Robert Morrow's. He smiled.

"Well, well, well! Mr. Gilpin, I do b'lieve there's a nice little surprise waitin' for you."

327

Samuel snorted. "Now look here, Cyrus, I don't want a big fuss, you understand? I think it's nonsense, and I won't have it."

"Tha's all right, Mr. Gilpin, this is one little bit o' fuss you'll—"

Isaac had come out of the house and down to the front road to meet them. Cyrus glanced at him, looked closer, and knew that something was wrong. Isaac reached up and took the reins from Cyrus's hands.

"You go on in, Cyrus. I'll put the carriage up, and bring Grandpa in."

Cyrus jumped down from the carriage and said under his breath, "What's the matter?"

"You go on in," Isaac said. He climbed into the driver's seat and smiled brightly at Samuel. "H'lo Grandpa. Happy birthday to you."

Cyrus found Robert Morrow standing in the front room, and Sarah seated, pale and tight-lipped. Robert Morrow came toward Cyrus and nodded, unsmiling, and extended his hand.

"Hello, Cyrus. Good to see you."

In his early fifties, Robert Morrow was a commanding figure. His thick black hair had turned an iron gray, but his close-cropped beard remained dark. His face was stern, but his manner gentle.

Cyrus looked around quickly. "Where is everybody? Where's George?"

"He didn't come, Cyrus." It was Sarah who answered, in a bleak voice.

Robert Morrow put a hand on Cyrus's arm. "George and Emily arrived in Corydon just a few days ago, Cyrus. Henry brought them, and turned right around and went back to Illinois, because he has a farm to attend to. Well, George is completely exhausted. He decided not to come on to South Bar just yet. And I agreed with him. This isn't exactly the right time, considering his condition."

"His condition?"

"He's a sick man, Cyrus. A very sick man."

Cyrus was frowning darkly. "Why, all the more reason he ought to be here, where Sarah can help look after 'im. She's a fine nurse, she'd—"

328

"Yes, I know, Cyrus. But not just yet. Later. George couldn't stand the public display he'd be subjected to tomorrow, with all those ceremonies for his father."

Isaac and Samuel could be heard, coming in through the back of the house. Robert Morrow looked quickly at Sarah.

"You haven't said anything to him about George?"

Sarah shook her head. "We wanted it to be a surprise."

"Well, that's good. At least the old man won't have to be disappointed."

Sarah took a deep breath and pulled herself up out of her chair. "Well . . . let's put on our cheerful faces now, shall we?" she said, and went smiling to greet her father.

As the long summer twilight deepened, the guests began to arrive, and soon the house was teeming with people. Samuel's oldest and dearest friend Rufus King and his wife arrived first, then came Reverend and Mrs. Daniels. After that came the King's son Morton—Mayor Morton he was called—a big, jovial man, trailed by a quiet, wispy wife. Several other prominent men of the community came with their wives, and finally the gathering was complete.

Sarah was a radiant hostess, and beamed with pleasure as one guest after another heaped honor and homage on her father. At the dinner table, Mayor Morton King arose and read a copy of a resolution recently entered in the state general assembly by the local representative, Nelson Hall. In a long string of "whereases," the document cited Samuel Gilpin's distinguished history as one of the founding fathers of southern Indiana, and concluded with a resounding "now therefore," urging the proclamation of Samuel Gilpin Day statewide. This was received with a show of acute discomfort by Samuel, and with enthusiastic applause by everybody else. Mayor Morton then read a personal note of congratulations to Samuel from Assemblyman Hall, and sat down amid more applause. He neglected to mention that the Samuel Gilpin Day resolution had not been approved by the state assembly.

Samuel tried hard to maintain his pretense at disdain, but failed utterly, and was visibly pleased by all the attention. Rufus King, seated beside him, patted him on the arm and said, "This is nothin', Sam. Wait till you hear all the pretty words they got in store for you tomorrow."

Samuel put his hand over his brow and pretended to be appalled.

After dinner, the guests dispersed into smaller groups and the conversation became more general. Elizabeth Daniels asked Sarah about Lucius. Sarah immediately became tense.

"Oh, the poor boy. He wrote us a long letter to say how disappointed he was that he couldn't be here for Papa's celebration. He tried his best to arrange it, but it just wasn't possible. He's *so* busy. He has a very important job with one of the biggest steamboat lines on the Mississippi, you know. I think it's amazing, for one so young."

The several ladies listening gazed thoughtfully at Sarah, and murmured agreement.

"I'm just so *proud* of him," Sarah said emphatically, and quickly guided the conversation into other subjects.

Robert Morrow had been invited to stay overnight at the Thackers' house. After the dinner guests had departed, Sarah and Isaac began the cleanup work, while Cyrus prepared to take Samuel home. Robert went along, saying he would enjoy a breath of air.

The night was clear and balmy, and after saying good night to Samuel, Cyrus and Robert drove around the quiet streets of South Bar. They went down Main Street, which, as of the following day, would forever be known as Gilpin Street, and looked at the handsome new signposts, already in place. They drove past the domain of the Reverend Jonathan Daniels, the proud new Methodist Church, occupying the exact spot where Samuel Gilpin had once engineered the erection of a tabernacle in a forest clearing for the use of the Reverend Oliver Hargrave. They drove on down to the end of the street, at the river, and stopped to survey the grounds and buildings that comprised Thacker and Hargrave, Associates, Wood Products. Robert Morrow marveled at how the business had grown.

"The whole town's grown," Cyrus mused. "Things sure seem to move fast nowadays. Don't know what the world's comin' to. Seems like a hundred years ago I came to a tiny little village here, to work for George Gilpin."

"It *has* been a long time," Robert said. "That was the

330

year of the constitutional convention, as I recall. Eighteen years ago."

"Eighteen years," Cyrus repeated. He frowned in thought. "Let's see . . . George would be about fifty now."

"He's forty-nine," Robert said. "And he's older than Samuel."

Cyrus looked quickly at the other man. "Is it bad?"

"It's bad. It's . . . well, you'll have to see for yourself."

Cyrus was silent for a moment. "And Emily. How is she?"

"Emily is . . . distant. She sits and crochets and stares past you, and says nothing all day long."

Cyrus shook his head. "It's a damn shame. One little bit o' foolishness, so long ago, an' people's lives are ruined, ever after."

Robert replied with careful deliberation, "It wasn't the bit of foolishness that did the damage. It was the way George handled it."

"How d'you mean? What could he have done?"

"Oh, I don't mean to excuse Emily's conduct, just because she's my sister. But if George never intended to forgive her, he should have left her."

"Left her where? To do what? A decent man don't throw his wife out in the cold, Robert. No matter what she's done."

"No. Neither does he lock her in a tight cell of bitterness, until her soul is shriveled."

Cyrus pondered. "Well, you bring him here. Sarah'll nurse him back to health if it's humanly possible, an' maybe we kin talk him out o' bein' so stone-hearted, after all this time."

"I'll bring him here, Cyrus, because this is where he wants to be. But it's too late for anybody to help matters between George and Emily, with talk or anything else. And Sarah won't nurse him back to health, either."

"No?"

"No. He's coming home to die."

It was very late. The town lay in a tomblike stillness. Crickets sang a far-off summer's-night song, and down near the river, a sonorous bullfrog voice pulsed in mindless monotony.

After a moment, Cyrus drew a long breath, gave his horse a little slap with the reins, and drove home in silence.

331

4

IN LATE SEPTEMBER there came a gray blustery day, with dark, low-hanging clouds moving fast over the land and dripping a chill, intermittent rain. Summer was abruptly over.

Samuel Gilpin was stacking hay in his barn, and didn't hear someone approaching on the muddy lane outside. He looked around in surprise when the barn door creaked open, and Isaac came in.

"H'lo, Grandpa," Isaac said. He pulled off his hat and shook the rainwater off. "Looks like we're in for a bit o' weather this week."

"What brings you out in it?" Samuel said. He swung another pitchfork load of hay.

Isaac was hesitant. "He's here, Grandpa," he said finally.

Samuel put his pitchfork down and came toward Isaac. "George?"

"Yes, sir."

Samuel started for the door. Isaac caught him by the arm.

"You want to prepare yourself, Grandpa. He don't look good."

As Samuel aproached the house, he saw Robert Morrow's big carriage in front. He hurried inside.

Cyrus and Robert were hovering over Sarah as she knelt

beside Samuel's one big upholstered chair. George was seated, and Sarah was tucking a blanket around his legs.

"There!" Sarah was saying. "Now we'll get a fire going in here, and you'll be nice and warm in a few minutes."

Cyrus and Robert had moved back. Sarah felt a hand on her shoulder, and looked up at her father. He was bending over her, his eyes fixed on George. He was trying to smile. His lips twisted and twitched, but the smile refused to take hold.

"George," he said hoarsely. "George, my boy . . ."

George peered up, squinting as if the light were dim. His skin was wrinkled and sallow, his eyes sunken. He extended a trembling hand toward Samuel.

"Hello, Father. It's good to see you." The voice was empty, without force.

Samuel grasped George's hand in both of his own, and pressed it. Laboriously he knelt, his old bones protesting, and with a deep, half-stifled sob, clasped his son in his arms and held him in a long embrace.

Sarah rose and turned away, wiping at the corners of her eyes. Isaac was just coming in, and Sarah moved quickly toward him. She spoke in a whisper, as if not trusting her voice.

"Bring in some firewood, Isaac, please. Let's get a fire started for George. He's cold."

Isaac nodded and went out again. By the time he returned with an armload of firewood, the others had drawn up chairs and were seated in a tight semicircle around George.

Samuel was putting on a great show of cheerfulness. "Well, now, George, I can see they haven't been feeding you too well. But we'll fix that pretty quick, won't we, Sarah?"

Sarah forced a little laugh, and said, "Oh, I'll say we will! I haven't forgotten your favorite dishes, George, and I'm going to be cooking all of them. Roast pork with baked apples, and boiled cabbage, and . . ."

She broke off, and reached out and patted her brother's arm. "Oh, it's wonderful to have you home, George!"

And George looked from Sarah to Samuel and back again, and smiled a wan smile. He spoke haltingly.

"It's good of you . . . all of you . . . to welcome me like this, after . . . everything."

333

"Nonsense!" Samuel scoffed. "The past is forgotten, George. It's the present we're concerned with. And the future."

There was a strained silence. Isaac had gotten the fire blazing, and now came and stood over George's chair.

"Would you like to move a little closer to the fire, Uncle George?"

"No, thank you, Isaac. This is fine."

"Well, I'll bring in some more wood," Isaac said, and went out again.

"That's Isaac," George said musingly. "I can't believe that's little Isaac."

"He's so *good*, George," Sarah said. "Never still, always up and around, looking for ways to be helpful."

"He'd be—how old now?" George wondered.

"He's twenty-five."

"Quite a fine-looking fellow," George said. "And still unmarried. I'm surprised."

"Oh, he's just a homebody," Sarah said, smiling. "He seems sort of uncomfortable around young ladies."

A tiny glint of amusement appeared in George's watery eyes. "Not much like his father in *that* respect, eh, Sarah?" While the faces around him remained stony, George's wasted frame shook with a wheezing laugh.

Some residual store of good humor in the sick man had been tapped. As Isaac came in again and deposited another load of firewood on the hearth, George called to him, "Isaac! Come, pull up a chair. I haven't had a chance to talk with you."

Sarah had brought foodstuffs, and now gave Isaac her chair and went into the kitchen to prepare a meal.

"So, Isaac," George said. "You and Cyrus have a good business going, I hear."

Isaac shrugged. "Cyrus has, Uncle George. He's letting me benefit from it."

"Not so, George," Cyrus said. "Isaac's the brains of the outfit. It never would 'a' grown like it has without him."

Isaac looked uncomfortable. "Aw, I haven't done anything."

George continued to study Isaac's face. "And your brother Lucius. He's gone off to seek his fortune elsewhere, has he?"

334

Isaac brightened immediately. "Oh yes, sir. He's got a big important job with a steamboat company."

"He'd be about eighteen now, that right?"

"Yes, sir, that's right."

"That's mighty young to have a big important job, as you say."

"Oh no, sir, not for Lucius. He's so smart, he's bound to go right to the top at anything he does. It'll always be that way for Lucius, I know it will."

"Listen to him, George!" Sarah called from the kitchen. "The soul of modesty about himself, but when it comes to Lucius, he brags without shame!"

"But he's right," Samuel said. "Success will always come easy for Lucius. It's born in him."

"I'm sorry he's gone," George said. "I'd have liked to meet him."

"He'll come soon, Uncle George," Isaac said. "He's just so busy, it's hard for him to get away."

"No he won't," Cyrus said to George. "He won't come, and it's jes' as well he don't."

"How so?" George asked.

"Sarah's had one letter from 'im in two years. To hear him tell it, him and some crook he's in cahoots with are practically runnin' a steamboat company, jes' the two of 'em. Sure, he's too busy to come visit his mother. But don't feel sorry about not seein' him, George, 'cause he don't like you, and you wouldn't like him."

Samuel slapped his knee. "Cyrus!" he barked. "I must say I resent that kind of talk in my house!" The old man rose to his feet, quivering with anger.

Sarah had come out of the kitchen, and was at his side. "It's all right, Papa," she said soothingly. "Don't pay any attention to Cyrus. Sit down."

Obediently, Samuel sat down again, glaring at Cyrus.

"Beg your pardon, Mr. Gilpin," Cyrus said mildly. "Didn't mean to offend you, sir."

Later, when Sarah called everyone to supper, there was a general movement in George's direction. He allowed himself to be assisted to his feet, but then waved away the helping hands.

"I can manage, thank you," he said. "I'm not helpless yet."

335

He praised the food Sarah served him, but only picked at it, eating little. The others watched him secretly.

Samuel, too, ate without interest. Soon he pushed his plate away, turned a frown on the others around the table, and demanded, "Where's Emily? I don't understand why nobody's so much as mentioned her. Why isn't she here?"

For a moment there was no answer.

"She didn't come, Papa," Sarah said finally. "And don't ask anymore, because George doesn't want to talk about it." Her face was grim.

Robert Morrow attempted an explanation, searching carefully for words. "Emily is very tired, Mr. Gilpin. More than that, she is suffering from . . . well, depression, I think we should call it. We thought it best that she stay in Corydon for a while, where Cordelia can look after her."

"*I* could look after her," Sarah said plaintively.

Robert became uncomfortable. "Oh, of course you could, Sarah, but . . . I think you have quite enough here to—"

"Why don't you just tell them the truth, Robert?" George said.

"I only tell what I know, George. It's not my place to conjecture."

"It's no secret," George said, addressing Sarah. "One reason Emily didn't come is because she's still too mortified to face you."

"Oh, that shouldn't be, George!" Sarah turned to Robert. "Please, bring her here. Tell her I'll welcome her with open arms, and all my love. Life is worthless unless people can find it in their hearts to forgive—"

"She won't come, Sarah," George said quietly. "There's yet another reason. A much better one."

"You'll tire yourself with all this talking, George," Robert said. "Why don't you rest a bit?"

George paid no attention. His eyes remained fixed on Sarah. "Emily hates me, you see? She's glad to be rid of me. Her only hope—"

Robert tried to interrupt. "That's absolutely untrue, George, and most unfair—"

George pressed on, "Her only hope is that the separation will prove to be nice and permanent." Something resembling a smile twisted George's thin lips as he looked around the table. "And if you've all taken a good look at me, you know she has an excellent chance of seeing her hope fulfilled."

In the heavy silence that followed, Isaac said, "It's gettin' chilly again. I'll go put some more wood on the fire." He got up and moved away toward the fireplace.

Pale and tight-lipped, Sarah began to clear the dishes. Samuel sat very still, with his brooding eyes resting on the wasted face of his son.

Soon after supper, the visitors prepared to leave.

"You're coming home with us, aren't you, George?" Sarah asked.

"Certainly not," Samuel said. "He'll stay right here, where I can take care of him."

"But I could do it so much easier, Papa—"

"Nonsense!" Samuel barked. "I can do it just as well as you can."

"I think I'd like to stay with Father a few days, Sarah," George said. "If he's willing to have me."

Samuel beamed. "Of course I am! It'll do us both a world of good!"

"Well . . . all right," Sarah said wistfully.

"I'll bring your things in from the carriage, Uncle George," Isaac said, and went out.

When darkness fell and the night air grew sharp, George began to shiver. Samuel moved his son's chair nearer to the fire, and fed the blaze with a fresh log.

"It's the worst symptom of my illness," George said. "I am everlastingly *cold*."

"Well, we'll just take care of that," Samuel said cheerily, and tossed several more pieces of wood on the fire.

"You'll use up all your firewood in a few days, on my account," George said.

Samuel chuckled. "No cause to worry about that, with Isaac around. He comes here every other day, replenishes my wood, and sees to whatever else I might be needing."

"He's a fine young man, it seems."

"A perfect wonder." Samuel settled back and began to pack his ancient pipe. "He's so kind, so considerate, modest, unselfish—as Sarah says, so *good*—it's almost unbelievable. Yet I can't help worrying a little about him.

337

Evidently he's content to go on forever just being Sarah's boy. Something seems to be missing there."

"Strange," George mused. "If I didn't know he was Oliver Hargrave's son, I'd never suspect it."

Samuel was silent for a moment, as he sucked on his pipe and squinted into the fire.

"You know, George, I'm considered something of a bad-tempered old crank around South Bar. Oh sure, they can go around declaring Samuel Gilpin Days and naming streets after me. But nine out o' ten people around here will walk half a mile out of their way to avoid meeting me on the road. Why? Because for eighteen years they've been addicted to a certain pleasure that they know I can't abide. It's their favorite game by far. It's called Making Snide Remarks About Oliver Hargrave."

"I'm sorry, Father," George said meekly. "For what little time we have to be together, I'm going to try very hard not to offend you any further."

"Well, boy, if you feel that way, you'll stop talking that damned melancholy nonsense, and work up a little optimism. We've got years yet, both of us. You'll see."

George's face remained somber. "You've had many bitter disappointments, Father. And I was one of the bitterest, I know that."

"Now, George—"

"So many things have happened. So many times I should have been here, when I could have been of some help or comfort . . . Sarah being left alone the way she was . . . her little girl dying in that horrible way . . . Mother's death . . . I was going to come when I heard Mother was sinking, but by the time I had made the arrangements, I heard through Robert that it was too late. Not much of an excuse, eh, Father?" George gazed distantly into the fire as his thoughts wandered.

"And the good things. Sarah and Cyrus getting married —I was glad to hear about that. And the great success of the business, and what a fine fellow Isaac turned out to be. And the honors they finally bestowed on you. Sure took 'em long enough to get around to it."

"Pack o' foolishness," Samuel said. "I never did a damned thing here except build a house and raise my family. They should have honored *you*, George, you were one of the founders of the state."

338

"And while I was forming a state, I was losing my wife."

"Oh, George, there's no connection between those two things."

"I've made a complete mess of my life, Father. All the times I should have been here and wasn't—and now, when my usefulness is at an end, I've come back to be a burden on you."

"Damn it, George!" the old man growled. "I will not listen to any more of these morbid goings-on about the dead past. I told you, I'm interested in the future, and the future starts first thing in the morning. I'm going to have Dr. James over here to take a good look at you—"

"No Father. No more doctors."

"I don't mean that drunken old fool, Reece. I wouldn't let him set foot in the house. No, Dr. James is a fine young doctor, a graduate of Western Reserve—"

"You don't need a doctor to find out what's wrong with me, Father. I can tell you myself. There's a big stone lying deep down in my belly, and it's eating away my insides, little by little. I can see it very clearly in my mind's eye. It's shiny black, and it has a rough, jagged shape. It's heavy, and it's getting bigger and heavier every day. And it's cold. Cold, like ice. That's why I can never get warm."

"Are you in pain?"

"No. Just cold . . ."

Samuel was leaning forward, grasping his son by the arm. "George, I want you to set your sights on a simple goal. Fix it firmly in your mind, and don't let go. You're going to hang on until spring. That's all, just hang on until spring. Once the weather turns warm again and we can get you outside in the sunshine, you'll start to regain your strength. Then we can go on from there."

George's eyes were roaming toward the ceiling. Outside, a soft rain had begun to fall, and an occasional gust of wind moaned around the eaves.

"Father, do you remember when we built this house?"

"Of course I do."

"I did most of the roof work, you remember? I was fifteen years old, and I could climb like a monkey."

"Yes, and you did a fine job on that roof. It's still good and sturdy. after thirty-four years."

339

George nodded. "Yes. It's the one thing in my life I ever did right."

Samuel helped his son to bed, and tucked him in as if he were a small child, piling extra blankets on the bed.

"Good night, George. I hope you sleep well."

"Good night, Father."

From the door, Samuel looked back. "Remember what I told you," he said. "Think about springtime."

Before he returned to his chair by the fire, Samuel went to his bookshelf and took down his old worn copy of the *Encyclopedia of Medical Art*. He settled himself with the big book open in his lap and bent over it, frowning intently and mumbling to himself. After a long time he closed the book and laid it aside. It was very late, and the fire was nearly out. Samuel gazed somberly at the last flickering flames.

"Think about springtime," he whispered. He leaned forward and covered his face with his hands.

5

FROM THE JOURNAL of Lucius Hargrave:

LET IT NOT be imagined that, in the exhilaration of my newfound maturity, I callously turned my back on my humble Indiana origins. Far from it. I longed for my dear mother constantly, dreamed at night of the soft touch of her hand and the sound of her gentle voice. Almost as painful was the separation from Isaac, who had always been not only a brother, but much more—a friend. I wrote to them often, and promised to come and visit just as soon as circumstances would permit. But letters are dry and lifeless scraps of paper, poor substitutes for personal presence. As for my promises—alas, Fate wove an incredible web of conspiracy to prevent me from keeping them.

When I left home, I vowed never to show my face there again until I was so prosperous that no one, no matter how much ill will he bore me, could imagine that I had returned only because I was needy and looking for a few free meals. Perhaps it was an unreasonable attitude, but the bitter memory of Cyrus Thacker's hostility toward me stung me still for years afterward, and kept my determination strong.

Soon after I began my new career with Mr. Albert Pettingill, however, I discovered that despite a handsome income, our financial condition perversely refused to progress to the point where we could enjoy a feeling of comfort and security. We were basking in wealth one week, and groveling in poverty the next. At first I was baffled by this. But soon I came to realize that the fault lay mainly with my genial partner. Albert Pettingill, one of the most splendid people I have ever known, had one serious character flaw: he was an incurable spendthrift. Those first wonderful days in New Orleans were an orgy of extravagance staged partly for my benefit, and partly because it was simply Albert's way—when he had money, he could not rest until it was spent.

I was a different sort. I resolved to save my money as best I could until I had accumulated enough to provide me with a measure of independence. At long last (after two years, to be exact), I had achieved this goal, and felt confident enough to write to my mother that I would be coming soon to visit her.

The letter she wrote me in reply was a seemingly innocent trifle that contained a dagger thrust. She began by giving me the happy news that my dear old grandfather, Samuel Gilpin, was to be honored by the townspeople of South Bar in August. Of course I would want to be there, she thought, and of course she was right. Then, as casually as if she were discussing the weather, she dropped the

341

information that the ceremonies would also be graced by the presence of that unspeakable villain, her brother George.

I was shattered. I was physically ill. Never before in my life had I felt so desolate, so betrayed. To think that my sweet, gentle mother would be capable of welcoming back to her hearth and home the very devil who had destroyed her husband and wrecked her life and the lives of her children—it was almost more than sanity could bear.

May heaven be merciful in its judgment of me, for truthfulness compels me to confess that for a brief time I fell into a life of debauchery. I drank. I even sought forgetfulness in the arms of lewd women. Thank God, my better nature prevailed eventually. I regained my senses and returned to normal, decent living. Eventually, too, I talked myself into a more understanding attitude toward my mother. Poor woman, she meant naught but kindness.

But the nightmare of anguish I had lived through remains to this day an ugly stain on my life, and a dull ache in my memory.

6

April 5th, 1835

Mr. Lucius Hargrave
c/o J. Knight & Company, Steamboat Lines
Number Fifteen, Merchants' Exchange
New Orleans, Louisiana

Dear Brother,
I supose you will be serprized to get a letter from me as I am not much of one for writing as I have seen you

are not either. Grandpa Gilpin always scolded me about my writing and said Isaac you were not ment for a carear in literture and I am sure he was right. That is my excuse for never writing it is because I dont like to show off my ignorence but I wonder what your excuse could be since you are so good at it.

First of all I want to say that we all hope you had a happy birthday last Tuesday you are nineteen now and I can hardly believe it. Im sorry our greetings are late like this but we have been sorly distressed as you will here in just a minute.

Lucius I take my pen in hand with a heavy heart. I do it because Mama Sarah did not have the strength to do it and she asked me to so I will but I hate to. It is my sad duty to inform you that our Uncle George died last Monday. The malankoly details are like this.

Uncle George came back last fall and took up residents at Grandpa Gilpins house. You know Grandpa is very old now he is past seventy and doesnt get around to well but he insisted on taking the whole burden on himself and wouldnt let anybody else do anything hardly. Well Uncle George was bad off sick anybody could look at him and tell that. But Grandpa wouldnt admit it he just kept saying theres nothing wrong with George that a good rest wont cure. All we have to do Grandpa said was get him through the winter if we can only make it to spring everything will be fine. He called in Dr. James thats the new docter here in South Bar and a very good docter he is to everybody says. But right away Grandpa had a falling out with him and told him he is a quack and such insulting things as that and said get away from here and dont come back. Mama Sarah had a long talk with Grandpa and persuaded him to let Dr. James come back but after a while Dr. James came to our house to see Mama Sarah and he said Mrs. Thacker I have done all I can for your brother but there is nothing more to be done it is only a matter of time now maybe just a few weeks. He explained about this big thing called a tumer or something like that growing in Uncle Georges stomack and it was eating his insides away. Poor Mama Sarah she was just so broken up I tell you Lucius it is sad to see our poor mother greeve like that it just tore my heart out.

Well after that Grandpa wouldnt hardly let anybody in

343

to see Uncle George anymore. Reverend Daniels would go there and Grandpa wouldnt let him in. It got so he wouldnt even let his own family in except Mama Sarah once in a while when she stood outside the door and begged. Pretty soon then we heard that Grandpa was having crazy drunken old Dr. Reece in to treat George. Mama Sarah went to Grandpa and said please Papa you know Dr. Reece will only make things worse and Grandpa said thats not so Dr. Reece is a very good docter people around here just dont apreciate him. Mama Sarah said he is a fool and so are you why dont you leave George alone and let him die in peace. Well Grandpa got furious and said he was the only who ever cared about George and he told Mama Sarah to get out and stay out. Oh Lucius it was terible you better be glad you were not here to see it.

This was about three weeks ago about the middle of March and the weather was still cold and rainy. It was a hard winter and that made it worse for poor Uncle George because he was always cold no matter how much wood Grandpa threw on the fire. But by then it didnt matter anymore. Mama Sarah got in to see Uncle George one last time and she said he was just lying there all wasted away and not speaking to anybody not even Grandpa. Mama Sarah wrote to Aunt Emily in Corydon and told her the end was near and asked her please to come but she wouldnt. She sent a message to Uncle George saying that she loves him very much and wants to be with him again someday in heaven where all things can be forgiven. But she wont come to South Bar she must think everybody here hates her. Lucius have you ever heard of anything so sad?

Well so last weekend the weather turned warm all of a sudden. It seemed like spring arrived overnight in full bloom. Grandpa came over to our house Sunday morning and he was grinning from ear to ear and he said well we did it we made it to spring. What did I tell you he said everythings going to be all right now. Mama Sarah said oh Papa you are just fooling yourself but Grandpa wouldnt listen. It was good to see Grandpa in a cheerful mood again but it was heartbreaking at the same time.

Then at the crack of dawn Monday morning somebody comes knocking at our door. It was Charlie Dawson you remember the Dawsons. No I guess you dont the Dawsons

344

came here after you left. Well the Dawsons live in that little house out on Pine Road that belongs to Mr. Ellis. Charlie works for Mr. Ellis at the blacksmith shop. So I went to the door when I heard the knock and Charlie took off his hat and said excuse me Mr. Hargrave but Mr. George Gilpin is at my house and I thought I better tell you. I said what? What are you talking about man? Cyrus and Mama Sarah came to the door then and Charlie seemed like he was downright embaresed to be bothering us. You see its like this Charlie said I get up early and when I got up this morning I saw a man lying in the road. At first I couldnt hardly make out who it was then I saw it was Mr. George Gilpin. Me and Sadie we carried him into the house and put him in bed and Sadie fixed him a nice bowl of hot mush on account of he kept saying he was cold.

Well we told Charlie to go on back home and Cyrus went off to Grandpas house while I sadled a horse and lit out to get Dr. James. When I got to Charlies house with Dr. James Cyrus and Grandpa had got there before us. As we started in we met them coming out and tears were rolling down Grandpas cheeks. He had just got the news and the news was that George was dead. Dr. James went in to see for himself and came out saying yes its true George is gone. I didnt have the heart to go in and look for myself.

Poor Grandpa he was shaking his head and looking miserble and saying how could he have left the house without me hearing him. Grandpa had a piece of paper in his hand and he handed it to me. It was a note George had left. It said Dear Father I am going to leave you now because I cannot bear to be a burden on you any longer. Kiss Sarah for me it said I love you both and I am sorry for everything. I am just taking too long to die. Goodbye. George.

Charlie Dawson came to Grandpa and said your son seemed to be greatful to us he let Sadie feed him some of that hot mush and then he lay back and went to sleep for a few minites. Then he opened his eyes and smiled at us very sweet like and he said you are good people God bless you. And then he died those were his last words Charlie said.

The funeral was yesterday and Lucius I have never seen such a big crowd I guess everybody for miles around was there. Uncle Georges children Henry and Susan were there

345

they had come all the way from Illinois and got there one day to late to see there father alive. Everybody was there but Aunt Emily. We had one little bit of unplesentness because Mama Sarah and Grandpa had asked Charlie Dawson to be a polbearer and Reverend Daniels told them he didnt think it would be apropriate. Well Mama Sarah and Grandpa had there way you can bet but it seemed like there was a lot of talk people thought it was peculyar. I didnt I thought it was fine and I think Uncle George would have thought so to.

Lucius you never knew Uncle George and neither did I really but I know he always had this bad feeling in his heart about Nigro people so dont you think it is amazing he ended up like that. Well there I go again forgetting that you dont know the Dawsons they are Nigro people Lucius. Charlie is a freed slave who came here from Kentucky.

Well I am going to stop this now I am all worn out. Please excuse my terible writing Lucius. I would like to ask Grandpa to corect this for me but I wont he is in such a state of greef now and anyway why should I pretend to you you are my brother and you know me for what I am bad writing and all.

Oh Lucius why dont you come and see your poor mother she is so sad why dont you write at least. Try to have a little feeling for the people who love you.

Your friend and brother
Isaac

346

7

July 11th, 1835

Mr. Isaac Hargrave
Thacker and Hargrave, Associates
Number One Gilpin Street
South Bar, Indiana

Dear Isaac,

It was a pleasure to hear from you, even though the tale you had to tell was thoroughly depressing. What a waste of energy, to go on and on about the morbid details of that miserable George Gilpin and his long, drawn-out demise. Frankly, I'd have much preferred hearing about *you*, old chum. What are you up to these days? I find it hard to believe that you are still living under the same roof with Mama and Cyrus. At twenty-five or twenty-six or whatever you are, it is time you took steps to establish a separate abode and a life of your own, I should think.

What, for instance, do you do about sex? I know Mama is the soul of broadmindedness, but I can't imagine she allows you to bring lady friends home with you at night. Certainly Cyrus wouldn't. (There is no more strict moralist in the world than a reformed lecher.) When I think of your oppressed existence there, old chum, my heart bleeds for you.

In fact, my dear brother, I must tell you, you are missing the best of what life has to offer. The great cities of

347

the West, such as St. Louis and New Orleans, are throbbing with vitality and excitement. Luxurious hotels, elegant restaurants, dazzling palaces of theatrical entertainment—these are regular features of my daily routine. And the women, Isaac—ah, the women! Here are some of my favorites.

Marianne, in St. Louis—laughing blue eyes and golden ringlets. Ruby, in New Madrid—black hair and black eyes, and skin like polished marble. (Ruby used to be my partner Albert Pettingill's plaything until I supplanted him in her favor.) Ella, in Vicksburg—an undisputed queen, tall and aristocratic, with flaming red hair. Alice, in Natchez-under-the-Hill—a muscular, hard-drinking blonde who can crack your ribs with her embrace, and make you love it. Grace, in Baton Rouge—a dusky-skinned beauty who must have Negro blood. (Five seconds in her arms and you don't care.) Of course my all-time favorite was my darling Genevieve, in New Orleans. She is gone now, and I will mourn her forever. Meanwhile there are all the others.

Well, enough, before I begin to sound boastful. I only want to give you an inkling of what a dull and empty existence you are leading by comparison. I'd be proud to see you tell Cyrus to go to hell, pack up your things, and depart. A clean break—that's the only way. However, I should advise you strongly not to come to New Orleans. This is an extremely sinful place, and while I am perfectly accustomed to it, for one who has lived such a sheltered life as you, it would be a shattering experience. I think perhaps Louisville would be a big enough step for you.

I enclose with this letter another one, for my mother, which I will appreciate your handing to her. (*Don't* show her this one, please!) I do apologize for being so negligent in correspondence, but I have tremendous responsibilities in my work, and am kept busier than you can imagine. Nevertheless, I continue to nurse hopes of seeing you before too long.

Your most affectionate brother,
Lucius

P.S. Isaac, I strongly urge you to work on your writing skills. Go and see Grandpa, tell him you want more training. That old man may be cantankerous and tiresome, but

348

he knows the value of literacy, and he is a born teacher. You should have listened to him more respectfully when you were a boy, as I did.

Dear Mama,

I have received Isaac's letter acquainting me with the dreadful ordeal you have recently gone through. Mama, my heart aches when I consider all the anguish and suffering some people have caused you and me. Your brother George was prominent among those people, in my judgment. And to think that he could find a way of causing you still more pain, even down to his last breath! It is all too bizarre to contemplate. It may sound heartless of me to say it, but I truly believe it would be best for you to put all memory of that man out of your mind forever, as much as you can.

I deeply regret that circumstances quite beyond my control prevented me from coming last summer, and basking with you in the reflected glory of all those honors that were heaped on Grandpa. They were more than deserved, no one can deny it. Belatedly I convey to him my warmest congratulations, which I earnestly hope to repeat personally in the not-too-distant future. I continue to seek an opportunity to break away from my onerous duties and come to see you. But the minute I make even the most tentative plan, some emergency arises in our steamboat operations, and I must turn all my attention to it. I wish I could give you more detailed information about my work, but unfortunately, the confidential nature of it prevents me. Among other things, it has to do with surveillance against thieves, gamblers, and other undesirables.

But don't give up on me, Mama; sooner or later I will come, I promise. I have not passed a day in the last three years without suffering from that gnawing sense of loneliness that this continued absence from you brings. A more affectionate and loyal son a mother could not have!

As always, your most devoted
Lucius

P.S. Regards to your husband.

349

8

THE PARLOR of the Morrows' house in Corydon was cluttered with bric-a-brac and massive furniture, heavily draped, relatively cool, and faintly musty-smelling.

On a July afternoon Emily Gilpin sat there alone and seemed aware of none of those things. She stared absently at the floor in front of her for a long time. Occasionally she raised a long, bony hand, pushed the window drapery aside a few inches, and looked out, then let her hand fall back in her lap and her eyes drift back to the floor. She was dressed in a severe black dress. Her hair, which was pulled back tightly around her head, had lost its lustrous brown but had not turned gray; rather, it had paled to an ashen lifelessness that matched the thin, drawn face and sunken eyes.

Emily started when she heard a footfall behind her. Her brother Robert Morrow had come into the room.

"I'm sorry, Emily. Did I startle you?"

"Oh no, not at all. For a moment I thought they'd come . . ."

Robert sat down. "Well, it won't be long, I expect. If they left home at seven o'clock as Sarah intended, they should be here by now."

A kind of faint hopefulness lit Emily's eyes. "Maybe she won't come, after all. Maybe she changed her mind."

"Emily . . ." Robert grimaced with gentle impatience. "I wish you'd get over this foolish attitude of yours. Sarah loves you, and wants badly for all injuries, real or imagined, to be forgiven. Can't you be equal to her?"

Emily's eyes wandered restlessly. "It seems so useless now ..."

"It is not useless. It is entirely—" Robert stopped abruptly, and cocked his head to listen. There was the soft clopping of a horse's hooves on the road outside, and the grinding of wheels on loose gravel.

"They're here," Robert said, and got up.

Emily's hand went to her throat, and panic rose in her eyes. "Robert, you won't leave me alone with her, will you?"

Her brother's impatience reached the point of exasperation. "Good Lord, Emily, don't be ridiculous! Sarah's come all this way to see you. The least you can do is try to be civil!"

"All right," Emily murmured. She lowered her eyes. "If it must be, it must be."

Robert and Cordelia Morrow escorted their guests into the house amid a babble of multiple conversations.

"We would've been here sooner," Isaac was saying, "but we hit some hard rain, and that slowed us down."

Sarah was saying to her hostess, "I hope this isn't too much trouble for you, Cordelia—"

Cordelia Morrow cut the remark off with a trilling little laugh and said, "Oh dear, no! Robert and I love to have company, and it's been just *ages* since you were here!"

Cordelia was a petite and vivacious woman, with dark eyes that sparkled constantly, and speech that gushed like a fountain. She glanced toward Emily, who was sitting motionless in her chair at the far end of the room.

"Emily, love, look who's here!"

Sarah moved across the room and stood before Emily's chair. Emily looked up at her with expressionless eyes.

"Hello, Emily," Sarah said.

Emily's hands fluttered like injured birds. "I do declare," she said in a tone of casual surprise. "I believe it's Sarah Hargrave."

Robert came forward, frowning. "Now, Emily, let's not be vague. You know very well it's Sarah, and you know very well it's Thacker, not Hargrave."

"Sarah Thacker. Of course." Emily nodded. "I'd almost forgotten about Cyrus."

351

"He was sorry he couldn't come with us," Sarah said. "He sends you his very warmest regards."

Cordelia had taken Isaac's arm and brought him before Emily. "And this is Isaac, dear. Of course, we couldn't expect you to recognize *him* right off."

Isaac bowed stiffly. "H'lo, Aunt Emily."

Emily gazed thoughtfully at the tall young man. "Isaac. You were no more than seven or eight when we—"

"Yes, ma'am. Same age as Henry."

"Yes. You and Henry were such good friends, I remember."

"Yes, ma'am. And Susan too."

"Susan too. The three of you. They're both doing well. Henry has a farm in Illinois, and Susan's husband is in business in Chicago, you know."

"Yes, ma'am. We all had a nice visit together when they came to Uncle George's fu—" Isaac stopped short and gulped in sudden discomfort.

"Yes," Emily said. "George's funeral. I understand it was very beautiful."

"Uh, yes, ma'am, I guess you could say that. There was an awful big crowd. And lots and lots of flowers and all."

Emily nodded. "That's good. You know, George always did set great store by outward appearances. I'm sure he would have considered it extremely important to have an impressive funeral."

There was a strained silence.

"Excuse us, ladies," Robert said. He had taken Isaac by the arm. "I want to show Isaac my workshop. We'll join you a little later." He led Isaac out.

Cordelia turned a hostess-smile on Sarah. "Well, I expect you'd like to freshen up before supper, dear?"

"First I think I'll just sit and rest a bit, if you don't mind," Sarah said.

"Fine. I'll just go and see to a few things in the kitchen, then." Cordelia left the room, and the sound of her lilting voice trailed away after her. "I'm sure you and Emily have a thousand things to talk about . . ."

Sarah remained standing for a moment, gazing down at Emily. The other woman's eyes were again fixed on the floor. Sarah sat down and waited. Emily would not look at her.

"It's good to see you again, Emily," Sarah said finally.

352

Emily raised her eyes briefly, and lowered them again. "Thank you. It's good to see you."

"You're looking well."

Emily sniffed. "Nonsense. I look like walking death. I'm forty-seven, and I look sixty."

Sarah tried to protest. "Oh no—"

"Don't dispute me," Emily said sharply. She looked closely at Sarah for the first time.

"You're about thirty-seven, aren't you? As I recall, you're ten years younger than I."

"That's right."

"You look barely thirty. I wonder how you do it."

"I've always thought it must have a lot to do with a person's state of mind," Sarah said.

Emily sniffed again. "You're probably right. *Your* state of mind was always one of perfect serenity, wasn't it? I suppose that comes from a sort of . . . native innocence."

Sarah's smile was strained. "Well, anyway . . . I *am* glad to see you."

Emily studied her visitor's face in silence for a moment. "Why are you here?" she demanded suddenly.

Sarah was ready for the question. "To ask you to forgive me, Emily, for whatever wrongs I've done to you in the past, and to forgive you for any you may have done me."

"My goodness, that's a bit general, isn't it? Shouldn't we be a little more specific?"

"I don't want to be specific, Emily. I want to forget all of it. Wipe the slate clean, and start over again."

"Well, I'm afraid I have to disagree. If you insist on having this discussion, then I think we should discuss everything, bit by bit, in chronological order."

Sarah's lips compressed. "Don't be cruel, Emily."

"I'm sorry you think I'm being cruel. I think I'm just being methodical. Now, to start at the beginning, that summer when Oliver first came to South Bar—"

"Emily, please! That doesn't matter now!"

"Oh, I think it does, Sarah, it matters a great deal. Everybody has the wrong idea about all that, and I think the record ought to be set straight. They see you as the poor, innocent, suffering victim, and me as the evil, scheming female who got her just deserts. But that's not the way

353

it was at all. The real truth is, I'm the one who was originally sinned against."

Distress twisted Sarah's face. "I don't understand this, Emily. I wish you'd just stop . . ."

Emily was leaning forward. Her eyes were burning, and her words came in a fierce whisper.

"Oliver was mine before he was yours, Sarah. You took him away from me."

Sarah gasped and shrank back as if she had been struck. Emily went on, "Oh, not mine in the physical sense. You beat me to *that*, all right, by about two years. But that lovely summer night when you walked into his room and offered yourself to him in a way no gentleman could politely refuse—at that moment, my dear Sarah, Oliver was about to come to me."

Sarah stared. Her mouth worked for an anguished moment, but no words came. Her shoulders slumped; she clasped her hands tightly in her lap, and closed her eyes.

Emily watched her hungrily. "Did I hurt you, Sarah? Does it hurt to know that?"

Sarah nodded. Her lips moved soundlessly, forming the word: "Yes."

"I'm glad," Emily murmured. "For eighteen years I've dreamed of the sweet comfort this moment would bring me, if it ever came. Oh, I would never have gone to seek you out for it, Sarah. But since you're here, and the stage is so perfectly set . . ."

Emily leaned back in her chair and heaved a long, weary sigh of bitterness spent. "So there it is. It's done, and now you know."

Sarah's eyes remained closed. Her face was bent low on her chest. Emily watched her, and waited.

"Well, Sarah, aren't you going to point out that you were single at the time, and I was a married woman? Quite a difference, wasn't there? Aren't you going to accuse me of having been a bad wife to George?"

Sarah wiped her glistening eyes with a handkerchief, and made a determined effort to compose herself. "No, I'm not. I don't want to talk about it."

"That's too bad. Because then I could have told you about how George had long since stopped being faithful to me."

Sarah was shaking her head. "I don't want to hear—"

354

"Oh, I don't mean he took up with another woman; my noble George was much too refined for that. No, my rival was something much harder to deal with. My rival was George's career."

"Never mind, Emily," Sarah pleaded. "It doesn't matter now."

Emily went on as if she hadn't heard. "We loved each other deeply when we were first married, and it lasted for several years. But after George began to develop his political ambition, it was all ruined. Suddenly I was nothing more than part of his baggage—a nice, well-behaved, socially acceptable wife, and devoted mother to our children. There was nothing real between us anymore. I was just playing a role for the sake of George's public image."

A humorless smile played on Emily's thin lips. "Sarah, I wonder if you have ever paused to consider how very *clever* it was of Oliver to detect the exact nature of George's vulnerability? Cruel, yes, but wonderfully clever, you have to admit. He found the weak spot, and gave poor George a fatal thrust, just there . . ."

Sarah was squirming. "Oh, stop, Emily, I can't listen to all this!"

"What a pity. You came all this way to discuss something, then you refuse to discuss it."

"I didn't come here to *discuss* anything. I came to forgive, and to beg forgiveness. I just want to forget all those dreadful things, and be friends again. That's all."

"You want that, Sarah? You want that *still?*"

"Yes, I do. With all my heart."

Emily sighed again, and was silent for a moment. "Well, I must say, you're absolutely invincible. You've gotten the better of me again, as you always have. It seemed to me you came here just begging to be hurt, so I thought, all right, if that's what she wants. So I fired away at you with all I had, point-blank. When I saw I had hit you, I waited for you to lash back at me, and destroy your beautiful angelic pose in the process. But you didn't do it. Well, at least I'll have the pleasure of seeing her suffer, I thought. But I didn't. I couldn't. There is no pleasure in it, Sarah. No pleasure at all."

Emily lowered her face and gripped her forehead with a trembling hand.

355

Instantly, Sarah was kneeling at her side. "Emily, my dear, don't go on with this. You're only torturing yourself."

"All these years I've thought that sweet disposition of yours was just a pose," Emily said. "But it's not. You really *are* a saint."

"No, no, we are none of us saints." Sarah's arms were around Emily, pulling her into an embrace. "We are just poor, sinning mortals who need each other."

Emily raised her eyes to the other woman, reached out and touched her face. "Forgive me, Sarah," she whispered. "Forgive me, forgive me . . ."

9

December 14th, 1835

Mr. Lucius Hargrave
c/o J. Knight & Company, Steamboat Lines
Number Fifteen, Merchants' Exchange
New Orleans, Louisiana

My dearest son,

As we approach the end of another year, my heart is alternately buoyed with optimism and weighted down with depression. Optimism prevails most of the time, I'm glad to say.

Life is pleasanter here now than it has been for a long time. We are all in good health, including your grandfather, who continues to keep himself vigorous and active, working his place. Cyrus and Isaac are busy with plans

356

for expanding the woodyard again (for the thousandth time). And as for me, something I have yearned for these many long years has at last been realized. Your Aunt Emily and I have become reconciled, and are now the best of friends! I'm sure you can't imagine how much joy I find in this, because you can't know how deeply I was hurt by Emily's strange coldness toward me, which began way back in the time when your father was here. It was all a tragic misunderstanding, doubly tragic because it was so needless. Well, it is all cleared up now, thank heaven, and Emily is here to spend the Christmas season with us.

Meanwhile, Cyrus is all excited about an idea he has of building a big, fancy new house for us to live in. He has the site all picked out and the plans are being drawn. The property is what used to be the big walnut grove that was part of old Widow Jemison's land. It is now the northwest corner of Gilpin and Jemison Street, about a quarter of a mile up Gilpin from the woodyard. Cyrus says that since I am the only living child of Samuel Gilpin, it is only fitting that I should have a proper residence on Gilpin Street.

I am carrying on a mild argument with Cyrus on this subject. I argued a little about buying more property to expand the woodyard, too, but both Cyrus and Isaac kept hinting that I was only a woman, after all, and I ought not to stick my nose into business matters. All right, I told them, I'll keep my nose out of the business, but I do think I ought to have something to say about where I live, and I like my old house.

It's too small, Cyrus says. There's just the three of us, I say, and one day Isaac will marry and move out, and then there will only be two. We might still have children, Cyrus says. I laugh at him. You never can tell, he says, very solemnly. Poor Cyrus. He won't give up hope for children, even after all these years. Anyway, he says, you're the finest lady in South Bar, and I want you to have the finest house. Well, I think he's foolish, but what woman could find fault with that kind of attitude in her husband?

Now let me tell you about Isaac. That young man is finally showing an interest in members of the opposite sex. He is twenty-six now, not so *very* young, after all, and such a fine, handsome fellow that all the girls in South Bar have been trying for years to catch his eye, without suc-

357

cess. Well, at last he is taking some notice of them, and, oh, the fuss and flutter it is causing! There is Penelope, daughter of Mayor and Mrs. Morton King, and there is Reverend and Mrs. Daniels' daughter Anne, and several others.

Cyrus is singing the praises of Penelope King. He claims to think she and Isaac would be a match made in heaven, but secretly I suspect he is thinking only about Penelope's father being mayor of the village, and the Kings being altogether very influential people. Penelope *is* a lovely girl, though I think just a tiny bit too loud. Anne Daniels is also very nice, but rather empty-headed, I'm afraid.

Maybe these are unfair judgments, but frankly I'm a little apprehensive, for Isaac's sake. So many of the girls these days seem awfully scheming and grasping and ruthless. They act so sweet, but I think there is not one who would hesitate to claw the others' eyes out if it would win her a prize like Isaac. I do hope he keeps his wits about him. I am going to turn this letter over to Isaac for mailing, so will let him tell you more about all this, which I'm sure he will.

So all in all, things are going well with us, Lucius. My only cause for grieving is you. Your extended absence I am reconciled to—I always knew you would not stay here with us. But the long silences disturb me most painfully. Are you sick? Are you well? Are you dead or alive? I feel so hopeless, writing this letter, as if I could do no better than seal it in a bottle and set it afloat, trusting that it will drift down down the river a thousand miles, and somehow find its way to you.

May good fortune shine on you, my dear son. Meanwhile, I cling to the hope that one day soon I will have the joy of clasping you to my heart.

All my love, always,
Mama

Dear Lucius,

I had better add a little note and straiten things out because I see Mama Sarah is exaggerating something terible with all that talk about how the girls are chasing after me. To here her tell it Penelope King and Anne Daniels are having a big compitition to see which one will have the honer to marry the great Isaac Hargrave. I dont know where Mama Sarah gets that crazy idea Lucius. The fact is that Penelope King is just about the pretiest girl that ever lived in South Bar with the exseption of Mama Sarah herself and she has many admirers not just around here but from other towns even. She has very little time to waste on a plane fellow like me. Anne Daniels is a very nice person but there is no romanse there she would not dream of being interested in me in that way. Mama Sarah likes to pretend I am so hansome but you know better than that dont you Lucius. Besides when I am around girls I get nervus and start to stutter and stamer and say real dumm things that I cant believe I said. Especialy around a pretty girl like Penelope King I get so tungue tied I dont know what to do it is awful I tell you.

I am just amazed at what you wrote in your last letter about all the beautiful wemen you know and a little shocked to. There are no wemen like that in South Bar Indiana I can tell you how I wish I could meet even one like that. But Lucius do you tell each and every one you love her? If so I must conclude you are lying quite a bit because you cant love all that many diffrent wemen you rascal you. But maybe I don't understand maybe you mean you pay them money is that what you mean Lucius? I hope not I would hate to think that my brother would have anything to do with that kind of woman. It was a terible thing that you lost the Girl of Your Dreams your beloved Genevieve. Maybe you will find another Girl of Your Dreams I hope so. I would like to keep myself pure for the Girl of My Dreams when and if I ever meet her but meanwhile it is so hard being alone oh how I envy you even tho I am shocked at what you tell me.

It is so lonely here Lucius. Come soon so we can talk at least.

Your loving brother
Isaac.

P.S. I cant go to Grandpa about my writing Lucius he is so old now he just goes around shaking his head and mutering to himself and wont listen to what anybody says. Someday if we are together again maybe you will teach me. I have always known you are smarter than me and I don't mind a bit in fact I am proud of you.

359

10

FROM THE JOURNAL of Lucius Hargrave:

I have noticed that as I grow older I become more aware of time. I watch it flow past me, count off the increments of hours, days, and years, and fret sometimes over the irresistible progression. But when I was nineteen, I took no notice of such things. I was young, which is to say, immortal. Being alive was a permanent condition, and time was limitless.

At nineteen I had attained my full physical stature— one inch under six feet in height, and weighing between one hundred eighty and one hundred ninety pounds, depending on how well my partner Albert Pettingill and I were eating at the time. I'm happy to say that mostly we ate (and lived) well.

In the summer of 1834, I had made plans to go back to South Bar to visit my mother, but had been prevented from doing so by the appalling news that if I did so, I would come face to face with George Gilpin. So, despite a deep longing to see my mother, I put all travel plans temporarily out of my mind. In a twinkling it was spring again, and I received a letter from my brother Isaac, informing me that George Gilpin had died. Dear Lord, I thought, do not let an unchristian feeling of *satisfaction* creep into my heart over this news. My wish was granted; I can truthfully say I felt only sadness. Had George Gilpin been a bigger man, he would have been a tragic figure. As it was, he was merely pathetic. Heaven be merciful to him, I prayed, and I meant it.

I had every intention then of reviving my plans to go and visit my mother, but time played its usual tricks on me. Our work became more demanding than ever. Summer came and went, autumn turned to winter, and one frosty morning, I realized with a shock that another year had passed. Enough of this procrastination, I thought. I *will* go, and soon. I told Albert as much. Poor fellow—having been orphaned at an early age and raised by an unaffectionate grandmother, he found my desire to go home for a visit totally incomprehensible. He was willing enough to cooperate—the trouble was that after several years of working in close partnership with me, he was no longer able to function effectively in my absence. He had come to depend on me—so much so that I was beginning to feel a trifle burdened by it. At last, however, my plans were made and firmly set. I would go to South Bar in the spring of 1836.

But before the winter was out, Fate, waiting in the wings for her cue, swept onto the stage of my life and rearranged it with dramatic suddenness. I was about to turn twenty when I found myself involved in something so large, so sweeping, and so important, that all things else had to be put aside and forgotten.

For the first time in my life, I became dedicated to a Noble Cause.

Part Five

1

MR. STANLEY FIELDING, a wealthy English gentleman and writer of popular travel books, toured the Mississippi River Valley in the winter of 1835–36, and recorded his observations in his notebook.

Aboard the steamboat *Beacon of Liberty*
Friday, January 29th, 1836

We departed the city of St. Louis, in the inland state of Missouri, early Tuesday evening, and are about halfway down the majestic Mississippi to New Orleans.

I am told there is some uncertainty concerning the exact origin of the name Mississippi, though I can't think why—a careful examination of American Indian dialects reveals a clear line of descent. In the Chippewa language we have *Mee-zee* (Great) *See-bee* (River); the Sauk, Fox, and Potawatomi all render it roughly *Mee-chaw-see-poo* (Big River). Plain enough, it seems to me. But it is ingrained in human nature to love a mystery, and where one does not exist, people often feel obliged to manufacture one.

Great River it certainly is, immense and silent and brooding, and taking no notice of the human insects that infest its surface. To be sure, the infestation is not terribly severe. Americans like to say that the spread of civilisation along the river has been astounding. From the deck of this vessel, I look out over endless miles of virgin wilderness and wonder what they can be thinking of. The occasional places of habitation consist mainly of hovels clustered in forest clearings—hardly what one could describe as civilisation. Then one remembers that the natives here are also fond of proclaiming that someday the United States will reach to the shores of the Pacific Ocean, and one is reminded that boastful exaggeration is a national disease in America.

Another national disease is politics—or rather the lively discussion thereof. Currently, the political talk centers around the agitation going on in the Mexican state of Texas, where it seems that a motley collection of American adventurers are carrying on a thinly disguised manoeuvre to tear Texas loose from Mexico so that it can be ingested promptly by the United States. I pay little attention to all this. I learned very early in my tour that there are four pastimes to which American gentlemen are hopelessly addicted: drinking, gambling, wenching, and political debate. All are comparatively harmless unless carried to excess, which unfortunately all are.

I am fascinated by other distinctively American phenomena, one of the most distinctive of which is the river steamboat. They are sometimes referred to as waterborne barracks, sometimes as floating bathhouses. Another apt description might be floating pigsty—if one can imagine a pigsty done in rococo finery and gilt. My present conveyance, the *Beacon of Liberty,* is typical in its mixture of elegance and shabbiness, luxury and discomfort, good taste and bad.

As to my fellow passengers, I can only say that the ship is a perfect microcosm. Finely dressed gentlemen rub shoulders with rustics in tattered homespun, and think nothing of it. There are planters, merchants, vagabonds, drunkards, even a few women and children. Meanwhile, the lower deck is laden to the brim with bales of cotton, and chickens, horses, cattle, Negro slaves, and slave dealers. It is enough to dazzle the mind and benumb the senses.

I spend most of my time sitting in the cavernous Main Cabin and observing the activity around me. At the forward end of the Cabin is the bar, and at the aft end a cluster of tables that are constantly occupied by gamblers. What an inexplicable oddity, these gambling men! There

366

are those who by their appearances would seem to be in the last desperate stages of poverty, yet who can pull forth rolls of money, eager to be relieved of it. There is one young gambler—he can't be more than twenty years of age—who entertains his fellow players with clever tricks and lively chatter while he wins all their money. He is a big, strapping, handsome fellow with bright red hair and a beard to match. He virtually took charge of the gaming tables when he came on board at New Madrid, Missouri, on Wednesday, and has been at it ever since. Today I inquired of the ship's steward if in his opinion the young man is a professional gambler. The steward assured me he is not, only a Missouri River roughneck. The steward's inflection left no doubt that a Missouri River roughneck is the very worst sort.

At the other extreme on the social scale is another young man, whom I had the pleasure of being seated beside at breakfast this morning. His name is Bradford Kenyon, and he is apparently an authentic member of the Southern aristocracy. His clothes are stylish and obviously expensive, his manners flawless, and his speech the same —unless one counts the long, slow Southern drawl a flaw, which I do not. We began to converse, and I learned that Mr. Kenyon is on his way home to his family plantation not far from Natchez, in Mississippi. He is returning from New York and other Eastern cities, he said, where he and a number of companions have been working for several months at raising money for support of the movement for Texas independence. He told me that sympathy for the Texas rebellion is at a fever pitch in the lower Mississippi region, so much so that men are taking up arms, forming companies of volunteers, and marching off to join in the heroic struggle.

But for all his gracious Southern charm, I have the feeling that young Mr. Kenyon is just a bit foolish, for this evening at supper he joined me again, and brought along a new friend he wanted me to meet—none other than the redheaded card player! His name is Tom Walker, and I must say he is well-spoken and extremely amiable, not a roughneck at all. I took a liking to him—much to my surprise—but not sufficiently to accept the two young men's invitation to join them at cards after supper. I may appear to be a wealthy man, I told them, but appearances

367

can be deceiving. The truth is, I travel on a strict budget, and must avoid frivolous extravagances. They laughed and went off, arm in arm, to the gaming table.

I watched them go, and felt rather like a schoolmaster watching the antics of unruly boys. They are thoroughly likeable young chaps, both of them. Perhaps I am being a touch old-fashioned. Perhaps I should loosen up a bit, and . . .

Mr. Stanley Fielding was suddenly aware of someone standing over him. He looked up from his notebook, mildly startled. The man before him was tall, handsome, and well-dressed, with a neatly trimmed beard and thick, wavy hair that was streaked with gray.

"Mr. Fielding?" the man said.

"Yes?"

"I'm sorry to interrupt you, sir, but I'm impelled by desperation. I came aboard at Memphis yesterday afternoon, and after thoroughly inspecting my traveling companions, I have concluded that you are the only gentleman of quality on board, besides myself. I took the liberty of ascertaining your name from the ship's clerk."

Mr. Fielding's eyebrows registered surprise. *"Did you?"*

"Forgive my being so forward. My name is Alfred Welles. May I invite you to have a drink with me?"

Mr. Fielding closed his notebook and arose.

"Why, of course," he said. "Delighted."

368

2

ALBERT PETTINGILL snapped his fingers at the bartender and ordered two whiskeys.

"You're English, of course," he said to Stanley Fielding. "I knew it even before you spoke."

Fielding smiled. "Oh, is it so obvious?" Fielding was middle-aged, a trifle stout, and impeccably attired in Scotch tweed.

"Class shows," Pettingill said. "You Englishmen have it. We Americans don't."

Fielding was visibly pleased. "Kind of you, sir. Actually, for a moment, I thought *you* might be English too."

"Only from a distance, I regret to say. My grandfather emigrated to New York State from Hampshire in the seventeen-eighties."

"Ah! I have relatives in Hampshire myself."

They were well into their second round of drinks and a lively discussion of family origins, when young Bradford Kenyon came to the bar and leaned over the Englishman's shoulder.

"Beg pahdon, Mistuh Fieldin'. Tom Walker and I shuahly do wish you and youh friend heah would join us for a little game. Tom says we'll be glad to play for nothin', if you have a moral objection to gamblin'."

"Ah, Bradford, my dear fellow," Fielding said. "Have you met Mr. Welles?"

"No, suh, I don't believe I've had the honuh."

"Mr. Alfred Welles, of New York State, may I present Mr. Bradford Kenyon, of Natchez, Mississippi?"

Greetings were exchanged.

"I was just in youh paht o' the country, Mistuh Welles," Bradford Kenyon said.

"Oh? Business or pleasure?"

"The most serious business, suh. Workin' to raise money for the cause of Texas independence."

Pettingill chuckled softly.

Bradford Kenyon's eyes flashed. "You find that amusin', suh?"

Pettingill tried to look respectful, but a small smile continued to lurk on his face. "Not at all. It just seems to me all I hear from Southern gentlemen these days is talk about Texas independence. Why are you folks so fired up over that little exercise? It couldn't be because you're eager to extend the domain of slavery, could it?"

Bradford Kenyon's slight frame seemed to grow several inches. "That 'little exercise,' as you call it, suh, is a valiant attempt by brave men to throw off the yoke of despotism. It is very much on the same orduh as our own American Revolution—" Here Kenyon gave Stanley Fielding a hasty nod of deference. "That is, if our English friend will pahdon the comparison."

Fielding smiled his pardon, while Pettingill moved quickly to smooth ruffled feelings.

"Well, I certainly admire your spirit, sir. I trust my fellow New Yorkers were properly responsive?"

The Southerner immediately regained his pleasant demeanor. "I have no complaints about them, suh. No complaints at all."

"Good."

"Then may I tell Tom that you gentlemen will join us? Strictly on a friendly basis, of course. Tom says he'd like to quit the big game, and form a small select group at a cornuh table."

Fielding shrugged, and deferred to "Mr. Welles" for a reply. Pettingill was observing Kenyon with a bemused expression. Suddenly he leaned forward and spoke in a low, confidential tone.

"Look here, my young friend, let me be very frank with you for a moment. That fellow Walker is a professional gambler, are you aware of that?"

370

Both Kenyon and Fielding reacted with astonishment, to which Kenyon added a touch of indignation.

"Why, that's impossible, suh! You're mistaken, I'm shuah!"

"I am something of an expert," Pettingill said coolly. "I know one when I see one, and in young Walker I see one."

"I half suspected it," Fielding said. "But he seems so young."

"Strangely enough, the best ones often reach their peak at a very early age," Pettingill said. "A few years ago there was a young fellow who was such a demon that even other gamblers were afraid of him. Charles Cora was his name. An absolute genius. They finally ran him off the river. At the height of his fame, he was only about eighteen years old."

"Extraordinary!" Fielding breathed.

Bradford Kenyon shook his head in protest. "But I've been playin' cards with Tom for two days now, and I've won a little and lost a little. Why, he's no bettuh playuh than I am."

"Oh, he's not playing *now*," Pettingill said. "What he's doing now is waiting. Waiting for the suckers with the big money. The pigeons, as they are called."

His two listeners stared at Pettingill.

"Pigeons?" Fielding echoed, sounding apprehensive. "Who are they, might I ask?"

Pettingill smiled and sipped his drink. "You are, sir. And Mr. Kenyon here. And myself. We are the gentlemen of means on board this vessel, and young Walker knows it. His expert eyes spotted us in an instant. What he would dearly love to do is catch us all together in a nice, cozy, friendly little game."

"Well . . . I just cain't believe all this," Kenyon said forlornly.

"I can prove it if you like," said Pettingill in an offhand manner. "I can prove it, and I can ruin the young rascal before your very eyes."

"How so?" Kenyon demanded.

"I'd need the assistance of both of you. Would you be willing to join me in exposing a scoundrel?"

Fielding and Kenyon exchanged a look. Pettingill sipped his drink and waited.

371

"If what you say is true, suh," Kenyon said, "I'd be willin' to participate."

Fielding pondered, frowning. "Well, I suppose one could consider it a sort of . . . public service—"

"Good!" Pettingill tossed off the remainder of his drink, and beckoned his collaborators closer, to receive their instructions.

They took seats at a small table in a far corner of the room, and Bradford Kenyon went to inform "Tom Walker" that he would be welcome to join them. Lucius responded immediately, excusing himself from the main gaming table. He came walking ahead of Kenyon, smiling brightly, and flipping a deck of cards from one hand to the other in a flashing cascade.

"Look at him," Pettingill murmured under his breath to Fielding. "The compulsive show-off."

"Gentlemen!" Lucius boomed. He bowed, and extended his hand to the Englishman. "Mr. Fielding I've met. How are you, sir?" Then he turned his attention to Pettingill. "And you, sir, I have not."

"Mr. Walker, Mr. Welles," Fielding said, and before the names were out, Tom Walker had grasped Pettingill's hand and was vigorously pumping it.

"How do you do, Mr. Welles. Pleased to meet you, I'm sure. My, my, you look very much like somebody I used to know."

"Really?" Pettingill said archly, and raised an eyebrow.

"Yes. Fellow by the name of Pettingill. Ought not to mention it, though. Pettingill was a notorious gambler." Lucius laughed, and slapped his partner on the arm.

"Really!" Pettingill said again. He was not amused.

When everyone was seated, "Tom Walker" laid his deck of cards on the table and swept his bright smile over the company.

"Well, this is a pleasure, gentlemen, a great pleasure. I'm only sorry we don't have much time. We'll be getting into Vicksburg in a little while, and that's where I get off."

He picked up his cards and began to shuffle them. "So, what'll it be? Poker, euchre, seven-up? Three-card monte?"

"I thought three-card monte was pretty well discredited by now, Mr. Walker," Pettingill said dryly.

372

Lucius smiled. "Yes, the cardsharps have pretty well run that one into the ground, haven't they, Mr. Petting—er, Mr. Welles? So how about a little seven-up? A dollar a hand. All right?"

"You must excuse my ignorance, gentlemen," Mr. Fielding said. "I'm afraid I'm not really familiar with these popular American games."

"They weren't invented in America, Mr. Fielding," Lucius said. "Imported from Europe or Mexico, every damn one." He gave his cards a playful spin in the air. "Anyway, my friend Brad here likes tricks better than games. Don't you, Brad?"

Bradford Kenyon grinned, faintly embarrassed. "I admit it. Why don't you do that good one, Tom? The one you call 'four aces'?"

Lucius chuckled. He spread the cards face-up on the table in front of the Englishman.

"Will you examine them, sir? See that there are four aces in the deck—no more, no less?"

Fielding obliged. "Right you are. Four aces."

Lucius swept up the cards and shuffled them rapidly. "Gentlemen, I propose to lay this deck on the table and draw the four aces off the top, one after the other. Do I have a small bet that I can't?"

Pettingill immediately drew forth his wallet, extracted a ten-dollar bill, and laid it on the table. Fielding and Kenyon did the same.

As his hands flew, Lucius winked at Bradford Kenyon. "You pay attention now, Brad, and pretty soon you'll be able to do this yourself."

Bradford Kenyon giggled like a small boy.

Lucius suddenly slapped the deck of cards on the table and, with a flourish, turned up the first four cards. The four aces were displayed. Casually he picked up the money and stuffed it into a pocket.

At that moment the ship's steward, standing at the far end of the room, cupped his hands over his mouth and bellowed an announcement. "Attention, please. Docking at Vicksburg in five minutes. All continuing passengers be advised, the ship departs again at eleven o'clock."

"Too bad," Lucius said. He picked up his cards. "Sorry we didn't have time for a game after all, gentlemen. Maybe some other time—"

373

"We'll be docked at Vicksburg for two hours," Pettingill said. "You don't have to rush away immediately."

"I have friends meeting me," Lucius said. "Wouldn't want to keep them waiting."

"Come now, Mr. Walker. We deserve to see that little trick once more, don't you think? It only takes a minute."

Lucius hesitated. "For how much?"

Pettingill pulled out his wallet. "How about a hundred apiece?"

Lucius shrugged. "Why not make it *five* hundred?"

Pettingill glanced inquiringly at Fielding and Kenyon. Each gave a solemn nod.

"You're on," Pettingill said to Lucius.

"Fine." Lucius began to shuffle the cards.

Pettingill put a hand lightly on his arm and stopped him. "On one condition."

Lucius's eyes narrowed warily. "What's that?"

Pettingill twisted in his seat and snapped his fingers at one of the table boys. He handed the boy a dollar.

"Here, lad. Fetch us a brand-new package of cards from the bartender, will you?"

Lucius's face went dark. "What are you about, sir?" he said in a tight voice.

"The condition, Mr. Walker. You don't mind using a new deck, do you?"

"You think there's something wrong with my cards?" Lucius demanded. He held them out to Pettingill. "Here, look 'em over for yourself."

Pettingill put up a hand. "Not at all, my dear fellow, no offense intended. Merely a formality."

Then the table boy was standing at Pettingill's elbow with the new cards.

"Thank you, lad." Pettingill opened the package, spread the cards face-up on the table, and located the four aces.

"There we are." He gathered up the cards and handed them to Lucius. "You may proceed, sir. That is, if you can *cover* fifteen hundred dollars."

Lucius shuffled the cards and glared at Pettingill while fifteen hundred dollars was deposited on the table.

"I ought to take offense, sir," he muttered. "I ought to get up and leave this table without another word."

Pettingill looked distressed. "Believe me, Mr. Walker, I only—"

374

"But I won't," Lucius said with a sudden smile. "Because I can't wait to see the look on your face when I make a fool of you in front of your friends."

He handed Pettingill the cards. "Care to shuffle?"

Pettingill took them and shuffled, looking suddenly grim. Lucius produced his wallet, counted out fifteen hundred dollars, and laid the money on the table. He took the cards back from Pettingill and shuffled them again, and smiled at each of the three men, who were intently watching his movements.

"Well, now, who will do the honors this time?" he said cheerfully.

No one spoke.

Lucius put the cards down in front of Pettingill. "Will you turn' em up, sir?"

Pettingill turned up the top four cards—the four aces.

Bradford Kenyon expelled his breath explosively.

"By God, sir!" Fielding rumbled. "What have we here, eh?" He was staring accusingly at Pettingill.

Lucius had gathered up the money and placed the new deck of cards, neatly stacked, in the center of the table. "It's been fun, gentlemen. Sorry I have to run off like this—"

"Uh, Mr. Walker . . ." Pettingill said hastily. He had picked up the cards and was idly shuffling them. "Why don't you step outside and see if your friends are there? They may be late. Maybe you can stay a bit longer."

Lucius considered it. "All right. Why not? I'll go take a look."

He got up and started away. Pettingill called after him. "And Mr. Walker . . ."

Lucius turned back.

Pettingill held the deck of cards out to him. "Would you like to take these along with you? Just for safety's sake?"

Lucius took the cards, gave Pettingill a smile and a wink, and left the room, joining a milling throng of disembarking passengers on the outer passageway.

Mr. Fielding immediately turned an angry frown on Pettingill. "Now look here, I thought you said—"

"Yes, yes, I know." Pettingill waved him silent. "There's more to Walker's trickery than I thought. Apparently he's

375

being supplied with trimmed cards from the bartender. I should have thought of that."

"Excuse me, suh," Bradford Kenyon said. "I cain't help thinkin' Mistuh Fieldin' and I have a right to be a little bit ill-tempered right now. It has just cost each of us five hundred dolluhs to find out that Tom Walker is smartuh than you are."

A cunning look came over Pettingill's face. "Not quite." He held up a card—the ace of clubs.

"When I gave our young friend the cards a moment ago, I neglected to include all of them. So when he returns, we'll persuade him to play one more time, for *really* big stakes. Then we'll see who's smarter."

Indignation welled up in Mr. Fielding. "Look here, really . . . I refuse to be a party to this—"

"Don't be a fool," Pettingill snapped. "It's a crooked game, and Walker's a thief. Why not give him some of his own medicine?"

"He may be a thief, sir, but I am not. Neither is Mr. Kenyon, in my opinion."

"Thank you, suh," Mr. Kenyon said. "I appreciate youh—"

"Gentlemen!" Pettingill was making a visible effort to contain his impatience. "You have a golden opportunity to administer some richly deserved punishment to a scoundrel who's getting rich by victimizing innocent people like yourselves. Are you too cowardly to do it?"

The other men were silent.

Pettingill handed the ace of clubs to Bradford Kenyon. "Here," he said. "Put this in your pocket. Let's catch a thief, and have some fun in the bargain."

Kenyon hesitated a few seconds, gazing at the card. Then he looked up at Pettingill, and a sly smile crept over his face.

Lucius returned, flipping the cards from one hand to the other. "That was a good idea, Mr. Welles. My friends are not in sight, so I *can* stay awhile, after all."

He sat down and put the cards on the table. "Shall we have a little game, then, or do you gentlemen still want to fool around with that silly trick?"

"Oh, the trick, by all means," said Pettingill. "We're fascinated by it."

Lucius shrugged. *"I'm* a bit bored with it, frankly. How much is it worth to you?"

Pettingill meditated a moment. "Well, for my part, I'm willing to go a thousand."

"I'll go a thousand too," Bradford Kenyon said.

Fielding cleared his throat, and squirmed with some inner discomfort. "Gentlemen, if you'll excuse me, I believe I'll withdraw at this point. I'm really not a gambler at heart, to be truthful."

Pettingill gave Fielding a blistering look. "Why, neither am I, sir. But, having come this far, we should not give up prematurely. Don't you agree?"

"Yes, well . . . if you'll excuse me," Fielding mumbled.

Pettingill looked disgusted. "Very well, Mr. Walker, there's two thousand dollars on the table. Will you cover it?"

"Make it six thousand," Lucius said brusquely.

Pettingill slammed his palm on the tabletop. "Oh, come now, sir! What do you take us for, millionaires?"

"No, I take you for fools. You want to go on betting that I can't do a simple trick you've seen me do twice. Very well, make it worth my while. Put in six thousand."

Pettingill was becoming exasperated. "But that's impossible. A thousand is all I can spare, and Mr. Fielding's dropped out. Unless Mr. Kenyon . . ."

All eyes turned to the young Southerner. Kenyon gazed steadily at Lucius. His left hand, hanging limply at his side, moved inconspicuously to his coat pocket and patted it lightly. His soft, boyish smile appeared again, as he reached for his wallet.

"I'll put in another four thousand," he said.

"Good sport!" said Pettingill enthusiastically.

With icy calm, Lucius watched while the six thousand dollars was stacked neatly on the table, then counted out a matching sum of his own. Then he picked up the cards.

Fielding leaned back in his chair and thoughtfully rubbed his chin. Kenyon took a deep breath, leaned forward, and fixed his eyes on the cards.

Lucius shuffled with dazzling speed. His eyes were narrowed to slits, and his face had become an expressionless mask. He worked for a full minute, then slapped the cards down in front of the Englishman.

"Mr. Fielding, will you turn up the top four cards?"

377

Fielding was taken aback. "Really, I—"

"Please. As a disinterested party."

Fielding leaned forward and hesitantly turned up the first card. It was the ace of diamonds. Quickly he turned up the second and third, and the ace of spades and the ace of hearts were revealed. Fielding licked his lips. With trembling fingers, he turned up the fourth card. His hand recoiled as if from a hot stove, as he dropped the ace of clubs on the table.

"Good Lord!" he whispered hoarsely.

Lucius was on his feet, scooping up the money and thrusting it into a pocket. "Thank you, gentlemen. As I said before, it's been fun. Now I really must be going."

Pettingill pushed his chair back. "You villain!" he snarled. His facial muscles rippled, straining against fury. "You will *not*, by God! You've got some accounting to do—"

"Accounting, sir?!" Lucius boomed. "Why, certainly. With pleasure. You see, gentlemen, Mr. Kenyon here made a minor error early on, and was thereafter doomed. He had suggested we play four aces. A childish game, thoroughly suited to his tastes. Trouble is, he got the name wrong."

He smiled down upon the head of Bradford Kenyon, who stared fixedly at the tabletop, showing no signs of hearing. Lucius beamed his smile across the table at the other men.

"The name of the game, gentlemen, is *five* aces. You'll find the fifth ace in Mr. Kenyon's pocket."

With a jaunty salute, Lucius strode away, and Pettingill held out a useless hand, as if to hold him back by force of will.

"Good Lord!" Fielding said again.

Bradford Kenyon had not moved. He sat as if in a trance, slack-jawed and ashen, gripping the sides of his chair.

378

3

MR. ALBERT PETTINGILL lay on the bed in room 205 of the Riverview Hotel in Vicksburg, collar open, shoes off, deep in a state of dreamlike serenity. On a small table beside the bed were a bottle of whiskey and several glasses. Pettingill cradled a glass in his hands. He swirled an ounce of whiskey, sipped, and smacked his lips delicately. Suddenly he cocked his head, listening. Footfalls sounded along the hallway outside, and stopped at his door. There was a knock.

"Come in," he called.

The door opened and a shock of flaming red hair and a matching beard appeared. The visitor winked. "Thomas Algernon Walker at your service, sir."

Pettingill scowled. "Lucius, where the hell have you been?"

Lucius came in and closed the door. "Out looking for a certain lady." He crossed the room and poured himself a drink. "Goddamn these flighty bitches. You meet a sweet one, have a good time, come back a month later, and she's not to be found. It's hunt and chase, hunt and chase, all the time."

Pettingill sat up and swung his legs off the bed. "My dear boy, you know very well that's unnecessary. Rose and Lily are right here. They'll be knocking on the door any minute."

"Rose and Lily!" Lucius simpered. "Exquisite flowers

from the garden of love!" He snorted with contempt, and slumped into a chair.

"Well, this *is* Vicksburg, you know, not New Orleans. When you're on the road, you have to—"

"Oh God!" Lucius groaned. "What the hell do we have to stop here for, anyway. They hang gamblers in Vicksburg, you know."

"Really?"

"They strung up six of them a couple of months ago. You haven't forgotten that, have you?"

Pettingill smiled as he poured himself more whiskey. "Not being a gambler, I don't pay much attention to things like that."

Lucius glowered. "I see you're in one of your silly moods, Albert."

"Oh, come now, Lucius! It's time to relax. Drink up."

"Do you mind if we take a few minutes to discuss the little job we pulled tonight?"

"Oh, by all means, let's do that," Pettingill said with sudden briskness. "And I'd like to begin by remarking on that red chalk you've put in your hair."

"What's wrong with it?"

"It's ugly, smelly, messy, and thoroughly disgusting."

"There are quite a few angry people up and down the river looking for us, Albert. I need a disguise, and so do you."

"Well, *that* doesn't do the job."

Lucius finished his drink and set the glass down on the table with a thud. "Let's confine the discussion to important things, shall we? I'd like to know what the hell prompted you to pick up the Englishman. You call that a pigeon?"

In broad tones, he rendered a recognizable imitation of Fielding's voice: " 'Gentlemen, if you'll excuse me, I believe I'll withdraw at this point. I'm really not a gambler at heart.' Good God, he almost killed the whole thing!"

"We touched him for five hundred, just the same," Pettingill said. "It wasn't a total loss."

"Five hundred! That's not a fat pigeon, that's a starving sparrow."

"Young Kenyon was a fat pigeon. We took in six thousand for the evening, so what are you complaining about?"

"May I point out that Kenyon was *my* pigeon?"

380

Simmering anger began to show in Pettingill's face. "Any other complaints, Mr. Hargrave?"

"As a matter of fact, yes. How long should it take you to plant the ace?"

"My dear boy, that depends entirely on how cooperative the pigeons are. You know that."

"It shouldn't require more than two minutes, at the outside. I came back and had to stop and adjust my cravat, for God's sake, because you were giving a long-winded lecture, and still holding the ace in your hand!"

"Well, well. Look who's lecturing now."

"Well, goddamn it, you *need* a lecture once in a while. You've got so blasted much confidence in your own skills, you get lackadaisical."

Pettingill's face was grim. "My turn now?"

"Go ahead."

"What do you mean by blabbing my name in public, saying I remind you of a gambler named Pettingill? How dare you?"

Lucius chuckled. "Just a joke."

"A rotten joke. Arrogant, careless, and stupid."

Lucius shrugged, and poured himself another drink. "That's unimportant, Albert. What's important is technique."

"Oh, I see. The pupil has suddenly become the master."

"The pupil has no choice, since the master has suddenly become sloppy."

"Really?" Pettingill got up and began pacing the room. "Since you're so interested in technique, young man, let me point out something to you. Do you realize that I *invented* the concealed partnership technique?"

Lucius looked baffled. "The what?"

"The method we use, whereby one partner allies himself with the pigeon in an attempt to fleece the other partner. The approach that, for the first time, takes full advantage of your typical pigeon's weakness—his willingness to cheat somebody else. It's the most widely used technique on the river nowadays, and *I* originated it."

Lucius sat bolt-upright in his chair and bowed low. "All praises to the master of masters, the paragon of creative geniuses, Albert Pettingill!"

The master stood in the center of the room with feet planted wide apart, and glared at the insolent pupil.

381

"And another thing: for a year now, I've been letting you do the easy part of the work, while I—"

"The *easy* part?!"

"Yes, damn it, the easy part. All you have to do is manipulate the cards. Oh, you're good at it, I'll admit that, damned good. But the cards are predictable; they'll do what you tell 'em, every time. I, however, *I* have to struggle with that most perverse of all living things—human beings. I have to pick them out, approach them, overcome their natural suspicions, gain their trust, and nurse them along by slow and subtle degrees until they're ready to be led to the table. Then you do a trick or two with the cards, pick up their money, and go, leaving me with the anger, the threats, the accusations, the gnashing of teeth and the pulling of hair—"

Lucius yawned noisily. "What time is it getting to be?" he wondered aloud.

"By *God*, Lucius, pay attention. Do you have the slightest idea what I had to go through after you left the ship tonight?"

"Not the slightest, Albert. Tell me."

"I *will* tell you. Mr. Fielding marched himself straight to the captain, complaining that he and I and Kenyon had been robbed with the connivance of the bartender. Threatened to sue the steamboat company. Wanted to call the Vicksburg police and have them launch an all-out search for you. We had a devil of a time calming him down. And Kenyon! Good God, I've never seen such carryings-on! It was ten minutes before he moved from his chair or uttered a word. Then he stood up and announced that his life was ruined, and there was nothing left for him but an honorable suicide. I tried to comfort the boy, but he would not be comforted. 'It's only money you lost,' I say. 'That money was not mine to lose,' says he. 'It was entrusted to me by my friends working in New York, to be conveyed to the Sons of the South Society for Texas Independence.' "

Lucius was paying rapt attention, his face deadly serious. "Texas independence," he murmured. "My God, I had no idea . . ."

"I should *say* you had no idea!" Pettingill said indignantly. "Why, the miserable wretch was practically in tears. It was all I could do to refrain from stroking his brow and saying, 'There, there, now, don't cry, little one.' "

"Texas independence," Lucius said again, in a distant voice.

Pettingill snorted. "Texas independence, hell! Young Kenyon ought never to have been let out of the sight of his mother. What does an infant of such virginal innocence know of Texas, independent or otherwise?"

"It's a big thing, I suppose," Lucius said.

"Ha! A big land steal, yes. One of the biggest in history. I tell you, Lucius, if I weren't too lazy to take up a new profession, I'd chuck the cards away and become a land dealer. *There's* where the riches of the future lie."

Lucius was leaning back staring at the ceiling, hands clasped behind his back. "Hmm. The riches of the future . . ."

"Not for the likes of Bradford Kenyon, though. He's the most helpless, the most vulnerable of all human creatures —the idealist. Because the agitators in Texas are going to have to make do with five thousands dollars less, life is suddenly not worth living. Would you believe it, Lucius, the young fool actually made a move to throw himself overboard! Such ghastly melodrama these hot-blooded Southerners are capable of! It took the captain and the steward and Mr. Fielding and myself to subdue the poor fellow, and take him to his stateroom and persuade him to go to bed. For all I know, he may have shot himself by now. Disgusting behavior!"

Pettingill paused for breath, sat down on the bed, and refilled his glass. "Lucius, sometimes I think you don't fully appreciate what I have to put up with."

Lucius held out his glass for more whiskey. "You have my apologies, Albert. I will not forget myself like that again, I promise you."

Pettingill's geniality returned, and bubbled like a spring. "Nonsense, lad, think no more about it. It's time for fun and frolic now, and—" He paused with a sudden thought. "By the way, would you mind if we split up the night's take now, before the ladies arrive? I'm a little short of cash, and—"

Lucius groaned softly. "No arithmetic now, please. I'm too tired for that." He brought forth a large roll of money, counted off a number of bills, and handed them to his

383

partner. "Here's a couple hundred. That'll tide you over till tomorrow."

"But I don't like you to carry so much on you. You're a little careless, you know."

Lucius smiled as he put away the money. "Not anymore. I've suddenly become extremely careful. After all, I carry in my wallet the entire future of the Sons of the South Society for Texas Independence."

Pettingill threw back his head and laughed heartily. "Ah, Lucius, my boy, you have a delightful wit!"

Lucius was on his feet, frowning at a gold watch he had taken out of his pocket. "What's keeping Rose and Lily, I wonder. I think I'll go look for 'em." He started for the door.

"Oh, come now, Lucius, that's not cricket!" Pettingill protested. "They'll be along in a few minutes. Sit down and relax."

Lucius stood in the open doorway and grinned back at his partner. "You know me, Albert. When I want something, I want it *now*."

As Lucius reached the head of the stairway, he heard a tittering of female voices and the soft rustle of skirts, floating up from below. He darted into a shadowy corner and pressed his body against the wall.

Two buxom, heavily powdered, extravagantly coiffured women came up the stairs. On the second-floor landing they turned their backs to the corner where Lucius stood, and walked down the hall, whispering to each other and giggling behind their hands. They stopped in front of room 205, and knocked.

By the time Albert Pettingill opened the door for them, Lucius Hargrave was striding rapidly through the lobby downstairs, heading for the street.

384

4

BRADFORD KENYON of Natchez, Mississippi, aged twenty-one years, intelligent, cultivated, delicately handsome, of soft smiles and gentle ways that made him the darling of Natchez society—with everything in the world of man and nature to live for—stared down into the roaring darkness where the great starboard wheel thrashed the river, and again contemplated suicide. Fortunately for Bradford and the people who loved him, his inclination to consider rash solutions to problems rarely led to overt action.

The setting would have been fitting enough—it was past midnight, and the *Beacon of Liberty* was steaming downstream in the middle of the channel under a cold, clear sky. The ship had departed Vicksburg at eleven, in the midst of a clamor of grinding paddlewheels, shouting stevedores, clanging bells, and the massive churning of dark water. Now only the monotonous rumble of the wheels remained; all else was quiet. The decks were deserted, except for the melancholy young man leaning on the guardrail amidships, staring down into longed-for oblivion. He shook his head, he groaned, he gripped the rail intensely and, from time to time, heaved a deep sigh, his boyish face contorted with suffering. He did not hear the soft footfall behind him, and he was violently startled when someone spoke.

"Good evening, Brad."

He whirled as if struck. "What?! You're on board still?!"

"I'm on board *again*," Lucius Hargrave said. "A last-minute change in plans."

Bradford turned back to face the river. "I thought you had run away like a cowardly cur."

"Well, I must be something more than a cowardly cur, because I'm here, you see?"

Lucius leaned on the rail next to Kenyon. The Southerner kept his gaze fixed on the darkness before him, and declined to look again at his visitor.

"Why are you heah?" he said after a moment's silence. "Isn't it part of the procedure for people like you to disappeah the minute they've fleeced a victim?"

Lucius chuckled. "You know, Brad, I'm very relieved to find you alive and well. I heard some preposterous tale about you threatening to do harm to yourself."

Bradford Kenyon pulled himself up to an erect stance and glared hotly at Lucius. "My deah suh, I have already done so much harm to myself, to my honuh, to my family, and to my deah friends who placed their trust in me—" His voice quivered with emotion, and he continued with difficulty, "So much harm, suh, that the only fitting thing for me now is to throw myself ovuh this railin', and hide my shame forevuh beneath the watuhs of the Mississippi!"

Lucius smiled up at the speaker. "That's a bit dramatic, isn't it?"

"It's appropriate, suh! Appropriate to the degree of my offense!"

Kenyon moved away a few steps and clutched the railing, with his back turned to Lucius. After a moment, Lucius drifted down the railing toward him.

"You asked me why I'm here, Brad. The answer is, I want to hear your story."

"I have no story that would interest *you*, suh," Brad said stiffly.

"Maybe you underestimate me. You might be surprised at the things I'm interested in."

Kenyon kept his back to Lucius, and made no response. Lucius chuckled softly.

"How do you come by all that righteous indignation, Brad? Are you really so superior to me? Didn't you have that ace in your pocket?"

386

Kenyon slumped over the railing again, and sighed heavily. "You're right. I have no one to blame but myself."

"Well, then, stop being difficult, and tell me about it."

"I do not grieve for the mere loss of money, Tom. I grieve because I betrayed a sacred trust. That money I so recklessly gambled and lost was not mine to trifle with. It belonged to an organization known as the Sons of the South Society for Texas Independence. I was proud to be associated with so fine a group, so noble a cause. I say I *was*, because I will nevuh be able to show my face among those valiant people again."

Lucius was frowning. "What is it about this Texas business that gets you so excited? Do you really care whether or not a gang of land pirates succeeds in stealing a big chunk of real estate from the Mexicans?"

Bradford Kenyon's soft brown eyes were dark with sadness. "I should have known bettuh," he murmured. "I should have known it was folly to expect someone like you to—"

"I'm asking you to explain it to me," Lucius said patiently. "I'm listening, ready and willing to be convinced."

Kenyon studied the other man's face. "Fair enough," he said, and shifted his position to face his listener directly.

"We are not interested in real estate, Tom. We are interested in the cause of human freedom. We are dedicated to doin' battle against tyranny, wherevuh it may raise its ugly head. The inhabitants of Texas are not land pirates, they are honest, hardworkin' American settlers, who have made theah homes in that region—at the invitation of the Mexican government, mind you—since the early eighteen-twenties. Ninety percent of the people of Texas are Americans, and by the sweat of theah brows, they have turned a wasteland into fields of plenty. And now, aftuh they've done what the Mexicans could nevuh dream of doin', the tyrant Santa Ana begins to reveal his true nature. He reneges on every agreement, betrays every confidence, breaks every promise—why, it's cleah as daylight, he will not rest till he has reduced our Texan compatriots to abject slavery."

Lucius was shaking his head. "When the American settlers went into Texas, weren't they required to swear allegiance to the Mexican government?"

387

Bradford Kenyon drew himself up to a towering height.

"The American settlers, suh, swore allegiance to the *Republic* of Mexico. But Santa Ana has ground the Mexican constitution unduh his heel, and turned the country into a military dictatorship. The Republic of Mexico no longuh exists, my friend, and the settlers are theahby released from all obligations."

Lucius nodded. "You're beginning to convince me. Now, what's the military situation?"

"The first clash of arms took place in Guadalupe in October. Theah was fightin' around San Antonio last month, wheah a few Texans thrashed a whole Mexican army unduh an incompetent braggart named General Cos. Meanwhile, American volunteahs are assemblin' in great numbuhs. Several companies are bein' formed in the Natchez area, includin' the Sons o' the South Brigade—"

"I'm getting the fever," Lucius said. "Tell me one more thing, Brad. When the Texans win their independence, who gets the spoils?"

Kenyon looked blank. "Spoils?"

"Surely men aren't fighting and dying over some highflown *principle*. There must be something there they can turn to *profit*."

"Well, yes, of course theah is. Land. Theah's goin' to be the greatest land rush evuh seen on this continent, Tom. Oh, I suppose theah'll be a few unscrupulous men gettin' rich at othuhs' expense, but the important thing is that a new frontiuh will be opening up. Thousands upon thousands of settlers, new towns, new homesteads, new—"

Lucius held up his hand for silence, and got it, "Thank you, Brad. You need say no more. I am now a true believer."

He had taken out his wallet, and he now extracted a thick wad of bills. "Here's six thousand dollars—the fifty-five hundred you so carelessly threw away earlier this evening, plus five hundred of my own, which I offer as a modest contribution to the cause."

Bradford Kenyon stared at the money. He gulped, he quivered, he ran his tongue over his lips.

"Tom . . . do you mean this?"

"I do."

With trembling hands, Kenyon took the money and stood with bowed head gazing down at it, blinking rapidly.

388

"Thank you, Tom. You have not only come to the aid of brave and gallant people, you have . . . you have saved my life. From the bottom of my heart, I say—"

"Don't mention it." Lucius waved a casual hand. "And may I offer you a word of advice along with the money?"

"Of course."

"Give up gambling, Brad. You have no talent for it."

Bradford Kenyon smiled—his first smile in many hours —as he pocketed the money.

"I'm delighted to accept youh advice, Tom. And could I persuade you to do likewise?"

Lucius leaned against the rail and gazed off into the darkness. "Funny you should say that. Lately I've been troubled by a feeling of . . . sort of aimlessness, as if I longed for some more important direction to take—"

"Tom, come with us. Join us!" Kenyon was clutching Lucius by the arm, and his voice was vibrant with excitement. "This is youh chance to put meanin' into youh life, to find a high purpose and—"

He stopped abruptly, and stared at the other man. "Good Lord, am I dreamin'? I thought you were redheaded!"

"That's Tom Walker who's redheaded." Lucius smiled. "When I was a little boy, my mother used to say, 'Lucius, your hair is the color of a fawn's coat.' She liked to call me her little fawn."

Kenyon was frowning in confusion. "Lucius?"

"Let me introduce myself properly," Lucius said, and stood erect. "I am Lucius Hargrave, at your service."

"Lucius Hargrave." Kenyon repeated the name in a voice soft with wonderment. "Lucius, will you join the cause? Will you walk in the company of honorable men?"

Lucius extended his hand. "I will. If you will accept the hand of a reformed gambler in friendship, I will consider it the greatest honor that has ever befallen me."

Bradford Kenyon grasped Lucius's hand in both of his own, and pressed it.

"Lucius, my friend." His boyish eyes were shining. "Welcome to a new life."

5

March 17th, 1836

Mr. Lucius Hargrave
c/o J. Knight & Company, Steamboat Lines
Number Fifteen, Merchants' Exchange
New Orleans, Louisiana

My dearest son,

I have been thinking of you almost constantly lately. It seems impossible that two weeks from today will be your twentieth birthday. You were only sixteen years old when you went away, and it stabs my heart when I realize that was four long years ago. I see you in my mind's eye, so handsome and splendid, perhaps more than reality justifies. Perhaps I would be disappointed if you stood before me in the flesh. No, I am only joking, it is the hope I live for.

Isaac says if you don't come to see us soon, we will just get on a steamboat and come to New Orleans to see *you*. Cyrus says he'd get lost in a place like New Orleans in five minutes. Isaac says (very indignantly) I beg your pardon, I'm not a child, I'm twenty-seven years old. You know Sarah is scared to death of steamboats, says Cyrus. (And there the argument ends, and Cyrus wins. I *am* afraid of steamboats.) So you don't need to worry, there is no danger of our descending upon you all of a sudden.

Our grand new home on Gilpin Street is abuilding, and Cyrus is excited as a child. He spends most of his time there, supervising every detail of construction, and making a pest of himself. It is going to be grand indeed, grander even than Cyrus first intended. In addition to our own spacious accommodations, there will be a private apartment for Isaac, and several others as well. Cyrus says he wants to have plenty of room so guests can always feel comfortable.

Lucius, we both want you to know you will always be welcome there anytime you care to come, either for a visit or permanently. I can assure you we mean it, most sincerely.

In a way I'm beginning to get a little excited about the new house in spite of myself, but it will be hard for me to leave this old place. For one brief period a long time ago, I was very happy here, and when I go away from it I will feel that I am leaving a precious part of my life behind. But Cyrus insists it is not fit for people of our prominent status (whatever that means). The ground seems to have shifted under it, and one of the walls has developed some nasty cracks. Cyrus says it will make a fine storage building for lumberyard equipment, and he intends to put it to that use. I'm sure his ideas are perfectly sensible, but I don't like to think about it.

Dear Isaac is more and more both a joy and a worry to me. It is hard to believe that such a fine young man, so well-fixed financially and so highly respected in the community, should be unable to find a girl worthy of being his wife, but that does seem to be the case. Both Anne Daniels and Penelope King eventually grew tired of waiting for Isaac to make a move, and married others, and Isaac sighs and accepts this as his rightful fate. I am beginning to think he is destined to be a lifelong bachelor. And who knows? Maybe that is best for him in the long run.

Your grandfather sends you his love. He says to tell you to remember, in whatever you undertake, that you are your father's son. (I pass the message on to you for whatever it is worth, without any comment of my own.)

Poor dear Papa. He is aging fast now, and has become so crotchety that nobody likes to have him around anymore. Rufus King and most of his other old friends are dead, and among the younger people, I am about the only one who can stand his company for longer than five min-

391

utes. One Sunday this past winter, Papa went to church (which he doesn't do very often anymore, nor do I), and afterward he marched himself up to the pulpit and in a loud voice started telling Reverend Daniels that he was not a very good preacher, nowhere near as good as Oliver Hargrave. Now, Reverend Hargrave, *there* was a preacher who could make your blood tingle—and so on and so on. I was mortified when I heard about it, and so thankful that I hadn't been there. (It was a horrid thing for Papa to do and I would never admit it to anyone but you, but in that one respect Papa is certainly right about Oliver.)

Lucius, Cyrus says to tell you that he feels terrible about all the unpleasantness that occurred between you two, and he wishes you'd come back so that you and he could start all over again, and be friends. It is a kind and generous attitude, you must admit, and I hope you can adopt it for your own.

I kiss you, my dear son, and wish you all happiness, and live in the hope that before you have another birthday we can be together again.

All my love,
Mama

6

St. Louis, Missouri
April 4th, 1836

Mrs. Sarah Thacker
River Road Route
South Bar, Indiana

Dear Mrs. Thacker,

I am writing this at the request of your prodigal son Lucius, who at the moment is much too caught up in the sweep of Great Events to have time to put pen to paper, but who wanted you to know of his present status. Not long ago I chanced to stop by J. Knight & Company in New Orleans, and found your recent letter to Lucius. It happens that we are no longer associated with that company, so I took the letter with me, and can now assure you it has been personally delivered.

I regret to report that Lucius and I have temporarily parted company. (I hope it is temporary—he has treated me shabbily and I should be glad to be rid of him, but I am not.) The sad truth is that he has become a soldier. When I saw him last, a few days ago, he was dressed in a comic-opera uniform of resplendent blue and silver, and was preparing to march off in company with other hot-heads of similar affliction to do battle with the Mexicans on behalf of independence for Texas.

He had given up his partnership with me quite abruptly

393

in January, and for six weeks I heard not a word from him. Then I received a note. In his typically dramatic fashion, he announced that all his past life was but an empty prologue to this, his first worthwhile endeavor. He urged me to come and see him, that I might absorb some of the patriotic fervor that so passionately grips him. He signed himself "Lieutenant Lucius Hargrave, Company B, Sons of the South Brigade of Volunteers for Texas."

Well, I don't care a rap for Texas, and still less for patriotic fervor, but I went (and delivered your letter at the same time). I absorbed nothing but a stiff neck, a slight case of dysentery, and severe attack of disgust. I found an appalling collection of rakes, adventurers, and ne'er-do-wells (many, like Lucius, non-Southerners), encamped on a plain directly across the river from Natchez, Mississippi. I spent a typical day with them, and it went something like this:

The early part of the morning was devoted to calisthenics, and the later part to marching up and down the field like a squad of mechanical toys, shouting, "Down with Santa Ana, Tyrant of Mexico!" After the noonday meal, the novice soldiers were instructed in how to clean and load a rifle without shooting themselves. At three in the afternoon, patriotic fervor wilted and died, and was replaced by a hunger for social diversion. The warriors bathed in a nearby stream and donned their dazzling dress uniforms (designed for them by a Natchez society lady), and piled into boats to cross the river and go to sip tea in the parlor of one of those elegant Natchez houses.

In the evening, on to a fancy ball at another residence, with much formal bowing and scraping from the young gallants, and exclamations of delight and admiration from their hoop-skirted heroines. I saw Lucius strolling in a magnolia-scented garden with an angelic young damsel. I saw him gaze longingly at a graceful, swanlike neck and a pair of lovely white shoulders. Poor fellow, I was afraid he was going to fall in love, as young men are apt to do under such circumstances, and Lucius is particularly apt. He has been violently in love not less than half a dozen times in the past four years. The first and most intense of these seizures involved a young New Orleans tart named Genevieve. When she left town suddenly, he declared to one and all that she had died of yellow fever, whispering

394

his name with her last breath. The well-known truth is that Genevieve married a wealthy Alabama planter and is now a lioness in Mobile society, but Lucius steadfastly refuses to believe it; he likes the yellow fever story so much better. He has a vivid imagination, that young man, and he makes it work for him.

So the long evening wound itself tediously down, and back to camp we went, finally, to catch a few hours' sleep before morning calisthenics. Instead of sleep, I caught a cold. There are no beds in military fields camps, it seems. They expect one to sleep on the *ground!*

In the morning I tried to draw Lucius aside, hoping to have a few minutes alone with him, so we could talk. There was nothing to talk about, he said. He had embarked on a course of action from which nothing could divert him. I bade him goodbye, then, and watched him race off across the field to join his shouting fellows in some idiotic game. With a mingling of sadness and relief, I took my leave and returned to my familiar world.

I should take the time to name for you the idler who seduced Lucius into this Texas-madness in the first place. He is a shallow young gigolo by the name of Bradford Kenyon, the darling of one of those decadent Southern families. He is so childishly silly that I found it hard to believe Lucius could abide his company for ten minutes, let alone constantly. Kenyon is unspeakably vain, and preens himself without cease in his gaudy uniform. (Absurdly, he holds the rank of captain, though he is hardly old enough to show a beard.) I disliked him thoroughly.

When I left New Orleans, the newspapers there were making a great to-do over reports of some dreadful disaster suffered lately by the Texans at a place called the Mission of San Antonio de Valero. (The Texans call it the Alamo.) I expect you have heard of it by now. Pray, madam, do not be alarmed for Lucius when you hear such horror stories; rather take heart. It is abundantly clear that the Texas rebellion will be over—crushed and forgotten— long before he gets within a hundred miles of hostilities.

That, for the present, is all I know. I cannot provide you with an address for Lucius, because at the time I was with him, the brigade was planning to break camp in a day or two and start west. By now they are doubtless

395

trudging through the tangled wilderness of central Louisiana, trying to find their way to Texas.

But I am optimistic. I feel sure that Lucius' current venture will prove to be just another boyish lark from which he will shortly return, bored with the dust of Texas and the grimy sterility of military life, fully recovered from his temporary lapse into insanity, and ready to start living normally again.

Join me in that pleasant expectation, I remain, madam

Your Most Obedient Servant,
Albert Pettingill

P.S. I have been more candid than I had intended, speaking so freely of certain of Lucius's foibles. From this you may have concluded that I have a low opinion of him. Far from it, dear lady. His flaws are many, I must admit. He is headstrong, opinionated, opportunistic, selfish, simultaneously cynical and sentimental, and profoundly deceitful (though, of this last, it must be said he is more given to self-deception than to the deceiving of others). There was hardly a day in our four years of association that he did not manage to exasperate me in one way or another. Yet he filled my life with more verve and sparkle than I have ever known before, and I shall miss him acutely while he's gone. I love him like a son and brother, and always will.

7

Excerpt from the daily log, Sons of the South Brigade of Volunteers for Texas:

Old Ford Natchez, Arkansas
Wednesday, April 6th, 1836

This day brigade broke camp and departed for Texas. Organizational strength, 21 officers, 183 men, 1 slave (Colonel Hurley's orderly). Total, 205.

Departure scheduled for 9:00 A.M. Delayed by late arrival of Colonel Hurley from Natchez. Colonel arrived 9:45 A.M., immediately called for full-dress inspection. Much grumbling in ranks. Colonel himself already in fine spirits.

More delay. Quartermaster failed to procure Colonel's silver-studded saddle, made especially for this campaign. Colonel furious. Detail of men sent across river to fetch saddle. More grumbling in ranks.

March under way at noon. Proceeded north parallel to river six miles, thence westward. Passed numerous plantations and cotton fields. In late afternoon, entered region of dense forest. Recent heavy rains made ground miry. Slow going.

Colonel Hurley ordered forced march until 10:00 P.M., hoping to exit forest and find suitable campsite. No end to *forest. Bivouac in woods. No dry firewood. Cold supper. Much grumbling in ranks. Colonel in fine spirits.*

Progress today—approx. 20 miles.

> Maxwell Eades, Captain
> Brigade Historian

Captain Bradford Kenyon of Company B hung a lantern on the trunk of a gnarled and ancient tree, and called for reports from his platoon commanders.

"Lieutenant Dantley?"

The leader of the First Platoon saluted sharply. "First Platoon in good shape, suh."

"Very good. Lieutenant Stiles?"

"Second Platoon in fair condition, suh. Two men ailin' a bit, and one lame horse. Nothin' serious."

"All right. Lieutenant Hargrave?"

"I've never seen such a goddamn mess in my life," Lieutenant Hargrave growled.

Captain Kenyon sighed. "Lieutenant Hargrave, could you couch youh report in terms more in keepin' with military dignity?"

"Military dignity be damned. We have no dignity, military or otherwise. We're a disorganized rabble, and we're being led by a drunken jackanapes who doesn't know—"

"Lieutenant Hargrave, what is the condition of youh platoon, please?"

"Rotten. Half the men are sick, and the other half are wondering why they ever came on this damn fool expedition."

"Thank you, Lieutenant. Gentlemen, dismiss youh men for the night. Reveille's at six o'clock."

Lieutenants Dantley and Stiles saluted and moved off into the darkness. Lieutenant Hargrave stood his ground.

"Brad, you're going to have to talk to that idiot Hurley, and tell him—"

"Shhh! Watch youh language, Lucius!"

"Well, goddamn it, this is not the way to Texas!"

"It's *one* way. Colonel Hurley considuhed all possible routes, and chose this one."

"The worst possible!"

"It's Colonel Hurley's decision. He's the commanding officuh."

398

"He's also an arrogant pipsqueak, and a drunk to boot."

"Just the same—"

"You know how Max Eades indicates in the brigade log that Hurley is drunk again? He writes, 'Colonel Hurley in fine spirits.' "

Captain Kenyon smiled and grasped his lieutenant by the arm. "Come on, Lucius, relax. This is goin' to be a long, hard road. We don't want to get all riled up the first night, do we? Come on, lay youh bedroll ovuh heah next to mine, and let's talk about somethin' pleasant."

Lieutenant Hargrave was fuming. "There *is* no such thing. In all this stinking world, there is nothing *pleasant!*"

"Let's talk about the beautiful girls at the balls in Natchez."

"Boring. Nothing but fluff. No substance."

"Well, then, let's talk about the whores in Natchez-Under-the-Hill. The girls at Cap'n Joe's, the girls at Mike's Bar—"

"Sick of 'em," Lucius snapped. "Sick to death of all of 'em."

"All right, then—let's talk about the Mexican girls in Texas. Gorgeous black-eyed beauties. How they'll fall into our arms, and eaguhly give themselves to us, because we're beautiful white-skinned Americanos."

Lucius's interest was piqued. "You think they will?"

Captain Kenyon chuckled. "Well . . . we can dream."

"Yes." A bleak look came into Lieutenant Hargrave's eyes. "That's *all* we can do now."

Excerpt from the daily log:

On the trail to Texas,
Thursday, April 7th, 1836

Roll call 6:30 A.M. Men slept little, look weary, complain of aches and pains. Colonel Hurley furious. Delivered stern lecture on soldier's obligation to be physically tough.

March underway 7:30 A.M. Emerged from forest about noon, into swamp. Men tried to remount, but horses sink into soft muck. Hard going. Weather cloudy but hot. This afternoon heavy rainstorm, everybody soaked. Progress halted at 4:00 P.M. Encountered deep, swift stream, un-

expected—not on Colonel Hurley's charts. Tow lines used to effect fording. One pack mule swept away in current, 250 lbs. of foodstuffs lost. No suitable campsite by night-fall. Bivouac in grassy field. Mosquitoes severe problem, campfire impossible, cold supper again. Much grumbling in ranks, but Colonel Hurley in fine spirits.

Progress today—approx. 16 miles.

> *Maxwell Eades, Captain*
> *Brigade Historian*

At midnight, Lieutenant Hargrave lay wide awake in his bedroll, staring into the murky blackness of an overcast sky. Next to him, Captain Kenyon stirred and mumbled in his sleep. Lieutenant Hargrave raised himself on an elbow.

"Brad?" he whispered. "Brad, are you awake?"

Brad started. "Wh—what? What is it?"

"What was the date today?"

Brad rubbed his face with his hands and frowned. "Uh . . . Thursday, the seventh."

"Good Lord! My birthday was a week ago today, and I forgot all about it."

"How old?"

"Twenty."

Captain Kenyon yawned. "My belated congratulations," he mumbled, and turned away.

"We'll have a little celebration tomorrow night, Brad. I'll break out some special whiskey."

"Fine." Brad was drifting back toward sleep. Suddenly his eyes flew open. "Wheah you goin' to get any whiskey, Lucius?"

"Never mind," Lucius said. "I'm having a party, and you're invited."

"I'll be theah," Brad said. He yawned again, and went back to sleep.

On the trail to Texas,
Friday, April 8th, 1836

Roll call 6:30 A.M. 37 men reported sick. Colonel Hurley livid. Issued order: any man on sick call without good reason will receive no pay for that day. Immediately, 32 men recovered good health.

400

March resumed 7:45 A.M. Emerged from swamp shortly before noon. Cheers from men. Moved into dry, rolling country with scraggly pitch-pine woods. Very poor soil in this region. Progress much more rapid now. Found good campsite on high ground. Firewood plentiful. Hot supper. Men more cheerful. Colonel Hurley in extremely good spirits.

Progress today—approx. 28 miles.

> *Maxwell Eades, Captain*
> *Brigade Historian*

Jasper, Colonel Hurley's slave and orderly, was a middle-aged black man with a large bald head and bulging eyes. His duties in the brigade were directed entirely to the personal comfort of his master. At ten o'clock, having been dismissed for the night, Jasper closed and fastened the flap on the colonel's tent, took a lantern, and moved off a short distance to prepare his own sleeping place. As he worked, someone came out of the darkness and stood over him. He glanced up. Lieutenant Hargrave nodded and smiled.

"You got the whiskey for me, Jasper?"

Jasper winced. "Shhh! Not so loud, suh!"

Lieutenant Hargrave lowered his voice an almost imperceptible amount. "Have you got it?"

"Why, sho', I got it," Jasper whispered. "I'm in charge of it, ain't I?"

"I want the good stuff, mind," Lieutenant Hargrave said. "The colonel's private stock."

Jasper became slightly indignant. "Why, suttenly! Dat's de only kind we carry. Colonel wouldn't tetch no othuh kind . . ."

"How many bottles can I have?"

"Show me yo' money," Jasper said. "Then I'll tell you."

Lieutenant Hargrave held out several bills. The orderly glanced at them and shook his head.

"Papuh money no damn good, Lieutenant, suh."

"Don't be a fool, man," Lieutenant Hargrave said impatiently. "These are New Orleans banknotes. Fine money. Best there is."

"I lak gold pieces," Jasper said.

The lieutenant swore softly, fished in his pocket, pro-

401

duced a gold coin, and handed it to Jasper. The black man examined it, rubbed it, tested it with his teeth, and smiled.

"Tha's good fo' three bottles, suh."

"Fine!" the lieutenant said eagerly. "Let's have 'em."

Jasper stood very still for a moment, listening. The camp was quiet. Lieutenant Hargrave waited, twitching with impatience. Jasper gave him a curt nod.

"Wait heah," he said, and melted away into the darkness.

On the trail to Texas,
Saturday, April 9th, 1836

Roll call 6:45 A.M. Colonel Hurley not present. Major Barnett, Deputy Commander, presided. Men anxious to get started, anticipating reaching Alexandria today. Must cover close to 35 miles to do it. Colonel Hurley finally appeared at 7:30, in terrible temper. Called Captain Kenyon, demanded to know meaning of disturbance in Company B last night. Drunken laughter, singing, etc., long past curfew. Captain Kenyon very apologetic. Occasion was birthday celebration for one of platoon commanders, Lieutenant Hargrave. Colonel Hurley furious. Ordered Lieutenant Hargrave forward, demanded to know how Lieutenant came to be in possession of alcoholic drink, in direct violation of brigade regulations. Lieutenant expressed ignorance of said regulation. Colonel Hurley observed that brigade policy had been relaxed to allow admittance of Lieutenant Hargrave, a non-Southerner. Perhaps that had been a mistake, Colonel remarked. Perhaps so, Lieutenant agreed. Colonel flew into great rage, demanded apology. Lieutenant apologized, but very surly. Captain Kenyon and Lieutenant Hargrave both given official reprimand. Captain Kenyon ordered to tighten up discipline in Company B. Captain Kenyon properly repentant. Lieutenant Hargrave remained surly. Appears to be potential troublemaker.

March underway at 8:45 A.M. No impediments today, good progress made. Bivouac at sundown in field two miles from town of Alexandria. Men excited, expecting leave to go to town. No leave, Colonel Hurley announced. Can't afford to alienate people of Alexandria by turning 200 men loose on town. Grumbling in ranks so severe that Colonel

Hurley obliged to demand silence. General discipline problem seems to be developing.

Progress today—approx. 34 miles.

Maxwell Eades, Captain
Brigade Historian

On the trail to Texas,
Sunday, April 10th, 1836

Roll call 8:00 A.M. Men allowed to sleep late today. Major Barnett presided over assembly. Explained that Colonel Hurley went into town last evening to confer with local officials and military authorities. Did not return until nearly dawn. Will remain in seclusion today. Therefore, brigade will not move until tomorrow. Men to busy themselves with useful work, such as calisthenics, close-order drill, and weapon cleaning.

Major Barnett announced that Sunday services to be conducted at 11:00 A.M. by Major Osborne, artillery commander, who has kindly volunteered to act as brigade chaplain. Attendance at services mandatory, Major declared. Needless to say, much grumbling in ranks.

Maxwell Eades, Captain
Brigade Historian

Colonel Ashton Hurley was forty years old, and a handsome man. His lean, strong, finely chiseled face was clean-shaven and smooth as a boy's, but healthily ruddy, and his thick, silvery hair swept in great dramatic waves from his high forehead to the nape of his neck. He would have been an imposing figure indeed, but for an unfortunate lack of height; he stood five feet four inches in his stocking feet, a measurement he managed to improve on slightly by means of specially built boots with two-inch-thick soles.

Late Sunday afternoon, Colonel Hurley lay on the cot in his tent and sipped from a glass of whiskey. It was warm and stuffy in the tent, and the colonel was bare-chested. His eyes were half-closed. When someone pulled back the flap of his tent and stepped inside, he was not immediately aware of it.

403

"Good afternoon, Colonel," a soft voice said.

Colonel Hurley's eyes flew open. He sat up quickly and glared at the intruder. "How dare you, suh! Don't you ask to be announced, befo' you barge into private quartuhs?!"

"May I sit, sir?" Lieutenant Hargrave asked coolly.

The Colonel quivered with indignation. "What's that?!"

"All I need is a few minutes of your time. You'll be grateful, I promise you."

The Colonel gaped, speechless.

"May I sit, sir?" Lieutenant Hargrave said again.

Colonel Hurley waved a hand toward a small canvas stool. "Sit!" he snapped.

"Thank you, sir." Lieutenant Hargrave pulled the stool forward and sat down.

The Colonel was glowering. "I'm glad you're heah, Lieutenant Hahgrave," he said stiffly. "It affords me the opportunity to remark that so far I am not impressed with your military performance. During our training period, you and Captain Kenyon were more interested in the fleshpots of Natchez-unduh-the-Hill than in youh work. And when I was planning the route of march, you undertook to impose upon me youh quaint theory that we should hire boats and *sail* to Texas. Not only a wuthless piece of advice, suh, but entirely uncalled for. Then you bring liquor on the march, in defiance of regulations, and disturb my rest with youh drunken revelry. Finally you thrust yourself into my tent without so much as a by-youh-leave, and—"

"How much did you lose last night, Colonel?" Lieutenant Hargrave put the question casually.

The colonel's mouth dropped open. "Suh?!"

"You were playing poker at the hotel in Alexandria last night. How much did you lose?"

The veins in Colonel Hurley's forehead throbbed with fury. "How *dare* you, suh! Did you heah this from Jaspuh? If that black bastard's been telling tales about me, I'll skin 'im alive!"

"You'll thank him, that's what you'll do. Because I'm going to get it all back for you, and more besides."

The Colonel had started to rise. He sat down again abruptly. "You're going to do what?"

Lieutenant Hargrave smiled. "For a consideration, of course."

404

"I'm afraid I don't quite unduhstand."

"I'll explain." Lieutenant Hargrave had produced a deck of cards, and was idly shuffling them.

"I had an uncle who was a professional gambler. Spent twenty years at his trade, then reformed and spent the next twenty years warning people about it. He taught me all the tricks. Not so I'd use them, but so I wouldn't become a victim."

"I see." Colonel Hurley was leaning forward, intently watching the silky-smooth flash of the cards in Lieutenant Hargrave's hands. Suddenly the lieutenant dealt the colonel a poker hand, tossing the cards on the cot.

"Look at your hand," he said.

Colonel Hurley picked up the cards and examined them.

"Shall I tell you what you have?" Lieutenant Hargrave said. "Four aces and a queen."

Colonel Hurley lifted his eyes to the junior officer, and gazed at him for a long moment. "You're very good, Lieutenant," he said quietly. "Very good, indeed."

The lieutenant gave a modest little shrug. "It's not me, Colonel. It's the cards."

"What are you suggesting, suh?" The colonel's manner had gone mild, almost deferential.

"I'm suggesting that we go cardplaying tonight, you and I. You rent a room at the hotel, and invite your friends in for a return match. They won't mind if you bring along your, uh . . . aide."

Colonel Hurley pondered the idea. "Only thing is, they wouldn't let you use youh own cahds."

"No, of course not. But when you, as host, ring for the hotel clerk and order a brand-new pack from the bar—" From an inside pocket the lieutenant had brought forth another package of cards, still in the original wrapper. "These are the ones he'll deliver."

"How so?" asked the Colonel.

"What do you suppose a small-town hotel clerk's wages are, Colonel? Two dollars a week? Three dollars? Do you have any idea how easy it is to bribe people like that?"

The lieutenant put away his cards and leaned back, waiting for an answer. The colonel stared fixedly at him.

"You mentioned a consideration," the colonel said. "What did you have in mind?"

Lieutenant Hargrave looked suddenly humble. "I spoke

405

in jest, sir. The truth is, I'm a great admirer of yours—that's principally why I joined the Volunteers in the first place. The consideration I seek? Merely your esteem, Colonel. Nothing more."

The colonel stroked his chin and reflected upon this at some length. Then he reached under the small table by his cot, and brought out a bottle of whiskey and a second glass. He smiled.

"Will you do me the honuh of having a drink with me, Lieutenant?"

Lieutenant Hargrave returned the smile. "My pleasure, sir."

8

On the trail to Texas,
Monday, April 11th, 1836

No early roll call this morning. Colonel Hurley absent from camp again last night. Returned to Alexandria for further discussions with local authorities. Took with him Lieutenant Hargrave of Company B. Very mystifying. Colonel thought to have low opinion of Lieutenant H. Several rumors making the rounds. (1) Lieutenant H. is special agent from Washington, reports directly to President Jackson. (2) Lieutenant H. is under investigation, suspected of being secret agent of Mexico. (3) Lieutenant H. is Colonel Hurley's illegitimate son.

Colonel Hurley appeared at 9:00 A.M., ordered general

assembly. Announced Lieutenant Hargrave appointed his special aide, promoted to Captain. Instructed Captain Kenyon of Company B to select new platoon commander from ranks. Much amazement among men. Colonel not in good spirits, but very cheerful.

Broke camp 10:00 A.M., march resumed. Progressed in northwesterly direction along banks of Red River, after which left river and turned westward. Plan is to intercept road to Texas in vicinity of Fort Jesup. Bivouac on banks of small stream. Captain Hargrave dined with Colonel Hurley. Captain H. now has his own private tent and is attended by the slave Jasper, who now seems to have two masters. Colonel and Captain both in very good spirits. Amazement grows in ranks.

Progress today—approx. 26 miles.

Maxwell Eades, Captain
Brigade Historian

On the trail to Texas,
Tuesday, April 12th, 1836

Roll call 6:00 A.M. Colonel Hurley orders early start. Anxious to get to Texas. Complains brigade moves too slowly. Roll call reveals 5 men missing from ranks. Whereabouts unknown. Presumed deserted in Alexandria. Colonel Hurley very angry. Reprimands Major Barnett for failure to maintain tight discipline in camp. March underway 7:30 A.M. Good speed today over rolling hilly country. Very hot, but cooling afternoon shower. Bivouac in piney woods. Supper somewhat meager. Quartermaster reports provisions running low. Much grumbling in ranks over scarcity of fresh meat and vegetables.

Progress today—approx. 32 miles.

Maxwell Eades, Captain
Brigade Historian

On the trail to Texas,
Wednesday, April 13th, 1836

Roll call 6:30 A.M. Three more men missing. Major Barnett says you must expect some deserters as going gets

407

rougher. Colonel Hurley furious. Appoints Captain Hargrave special intelligence officer in charge of camp security. Utter consternation in ranks.

. . March underway 8:00 A.M. Around noon, came to area dotted with small farms. Rather poor looking. Colonel Hurley ordered early camp here, afternoon to be spent in purchasing local farm produce. Several farm folk came to camp, offering foodstuffs for sale. One attracted particular attention. Young woman named Mrs. Hawkins, a widow. Driving donkey and cart, selling potatoes, accompanied by her son, small boy of six or seven. Men gathered round her, joking and flirting. Some made lewd suggestions. Captain Hargrave took charge. Castigated men severely and sent them off, extended apologies to woman. Personally negotiated purchase of potatoes, and escorted woman from camp. Much grumbling among men. Appears to be considerable jealousy and resentment of Captain Hargrave. He is youngest, least experienced officer in brigade, yet has surpassed all others in winning recognition and special privilege. However, inappropriate for me to comment on this.

Altogether good success in replenishing provisions through local purchase. Colonel Hurley says we resume march early in the morning.

Progress today—approx. 22 miles.

*Maxwell Eades, Captain
Brigade Historian*

408

9

THE DOG on the stoop of the tiny hovel of a house set up a clamor of barking when the lantern came into view down the narrow dirt road. By the time the man had opened the front gate, the door of the house was open, the dog had been hushed, and the woman stood waiting in the doorway.

She peered into the darkness. "Is it Captain Hargrave?"

"Yes, ma'am." Lucius held the lantern up to reveal his face as he stepped up onto the stoop.

The woman smiled and inclined her head in a charming gesture of greeting. "Well, good evenin', Captain. You didn't have no trouble findin' the place, did you?"

"None at all, ma'am. Your directions were perfect."

"Well, that's fine. Won't you come in, Captain?"

Lucius followed the woman into a large, high-ceilinged room, plainly meant to function as both bedroom and parlor. To the left was a stone fireplace, around which were grouped several homemade chairs. In the far right-hand corner was a large bed.

The woman took Lucius's lantern, and stood for a moment gazing in admiration at his dress uniform of gaudy blue and silver. "My, my, you got all dressed up, Captain! You needn't have, jes' for me."

"Well, so did you," Lucius said. "And you look mighty nice."

The woman blushed faintly. "I like to git dressed up for company," she said. "I don't have company very often."

She was wearing a soft white dress, with lace at the sleeves and around the neck. Her dark hair was pulled back and tied with a piece of red ribbon. Her face was deeply tanned and lined from an outdoor life, but still youthful and, in the soft evening light, almost pretty.

"But I jes' can't git over how handsome you look in that uniform!" she exclaimed. "You're so young to be a captain!"

"In our brigade," Lucius said with a trace of pomposity, "a man is promoted strictly according to merit, without regard to age."

"Well, I think that's jes' admirable!" The woman's bright social smile seemed to be fixed permanently on her face.

Lucius was looking around at the rough-hewn plank walls and the exposed roof-beams. "I'm interested in your house," he remarked. "Reminds me of my grandfather's house, in Indiana."

"Cal built it," the woman said. "That was my husband, Calvin Hawkins. We come here from Tennessee several years ago, when Cal Junior was jes' a baby."

She moved to the side of the room near the bed, opened a narrow door there, and looked in. She smiled back at Lucius.

"This here's Cal Junior's room," she said in a whisper. "You want to see?"

Lucius went to the door and looked into a tiny room. In the darkness he could just make out a quilted pallet on the floor, and on it a small boy curled up tightly, fast asleep.

"He's a fine-looking fellow," Lucius whispered.

The boy's mother beamed. "He's the spittin' image of his daddy." She closed the door softly.

Lucius accepted the woman's suggestion that he take off his jacket and be comfortable, and allowed her to serve him a large piece of sweet potato pie. He dispatched it with ease, pronounced it excellent, and accepted a second serving. After that, he leaned back in his chair and studied his hostess. She was seated now, with her hands folded in her lap, and smiling at him.

Lucius smiled back. "Sure nice of you to ask me in, Mrs. Hawkins."

She developed a hint of coyness. "You kin jes' call me Jane, Captain."

"Fine. That's a nice name. And you can call me Lucius."

"Why, thank you, Captain." She laughed with a trace of embarrassment "That is . . . Lucius."

He went on studying her with a frankness that made her lower her eyes. "What happened to your husband, Jane?"

"Died o' the fever. Two years ago." Her reply was casual and unhesitating.

"That's too bad. I guess you have a hard life here."

"We're poor. But I was raised on a farm, and I know how to work the land. Little Cal and me, we won't starve."

"Still, it's a tough life for a woman by herself. Like my mother—she raised my brother and me without a lick of help from anybody."

"I reckon she did a good job, Lucius," the woman said. "You're a mighty fine young man." She blushed at her own words, and lowered her eyes again.

Lucius smiled. He leaned back in his chair, stretched his legs, and sighed contentedly. "I feel good here, Jane. Comfortable. If I had the opportunity, I believe I might come a-courting you."

"I'd be pleased to have you," Jane said with careful decorum.

"But I'm afraid there's no time for it. I'm off to war instead."

Jane examined her fingertips and frowned. "I don't understand men," she said. There was no bitterness in her voice, only resignation. "Always shoulderin' their arms and rushin' off somewhere to do battle. What do they ever accomplish, in the long run?"

"The Texans are fighting for their freedom, Jane. It's our duty to help 'em."

"You're from Indiana, you said. What do you care 'bout them people in Texas?"

"They're Americans, just like us."

"No they're not. When they went to Texas, they promised to become Mexican citizens. That was part o' the agreement. If they made an agreement, they ought not to go back on it."

Lucius blinked in surprise. "How come *you* know so much about it?"

411

"Tha's why we came here, Cal and me. We were goin' to Texas. We got all the way to Nacogdoches 'fore we found out we'd have to give up American citizenship, an' give up our religion and become Catholics, an' all that. We knew we couldn't do it, so we came back and settled here. But lots of others were goin' right in, swearin' allegiance to Mexico and joinin' the Catholic Church and everything, an' they didn't mean a word of it. And I think that's wrong."

"Well, I'll be damned!" Lucius said, smiling. "I guess you're the only woman I ever saw besides my mother who just comes right out and speaks her mind, and to hell with everybody."

"Thank you, Lucius. I take that as a compliment."

Lucius beamed at his hostess. "Yes, it's nice here, Jane. *You're* nice. I wouldn't at all mind coming to court you."

She looked away from him. "But you can't. You ain't got the time. You've got to go to Texas and stick your nose into a lot of other people's business."

Lucius chuckled. Then his face went solemn, and his eyes took on a distant look.

"But there's more to it than that, Jane. I'm not just off on an adventure. I'm looking for something. Been looking ever since I was sixteen years old. I spent years on the big river, looked in every nook and cranny from New Orleans to St. Louis. Didn't find it. Now I'm moving on. I'll never stop looking."

"For what, Lucius?"

"Some news . . . some trace . . . some shred of information of any kind . . . about my father."

"What happened to him?"

"He was a traveling minister. He went down the river once, when I was a baby. He never came back."

"Killed by Indians, maybe. Or bandits."

"Not him. Not Reverend Hargrave."

"How do you know?"

He looked at her with calm patience. "I just know."

"Well . . . hope you find him someday."

His eyes were on her, steadily, penetrating. "Looking for something else too."

"What?"

"A good woman. And a place to call home."

Her smile returned, faintly, and the color rose again in

412

her cheeks. "That might be a little easier. Jes' look around you."

"Not so easy, Jane. I couldn't settle down anywhere, without giving up the search for my father."

"And is *that* the most important thing?"

"Yes. It is."

"Oh. Well, I reckon you have to keep movin', then. No time for courtin' and things like that."

" 'Fraid not." He sighed heavily. "No time. No time at all."

Her dark eyes came up and turned full on him. "There's tonight, Lucius."

A hush came over them. He leaned forward, staring at her intently.

"You're a good woman, Jane. I know you are. Would you take a man for one night? Even if you might never see him again?"

"Not any man. But you I would." She looked away from him and gazed dully into the dark fireplace. "Yes, I b'lieve I'm a good woman, Lucius. I'm a lonesome woman, too. An' if one night is all we can have . . ."

She got up and moved away a few steps, and stood with her back to him. He followed her. He touched her arm with his fingertips, and put his face close to the hairline at the back of her neck.

"Jane . . ."

She turned her head partly toward him. "You think I'm cheap, don't you, Lucius?"

"Of course not. I think you're a wonderful woman." His lips lightly brushed her cheek.

She smiled a sad little smile, empty of joy. "S'posin' we were jes' livin' regular, normal lives," she said. "S'posin' you were my neighbor, jes' lived down the road a ways. If you came a-courtin' me, I'd be very formal and ladylike the first two or three dozen visits. I wouldn't let you even start to *think* about gittin' familiar until I was absolutely sure—"

"You're beautiful, Jane," he whispered. His lips were on her ear, his hands grasping her by the shoulders.

She was unresponsive. "But this ain't a normal life. It's a bad, messed-up, horrible life. I'm all by myself and I don't know what to do. You're here tonight, and I feel all

413

excited like a young girl in love, but you'll be gone tomorrow, and I'll be all by myself ag'in. It's awful—"

"Let's not think about tomorrow, Jane. Just tonight." Lucius was planting little kisses up and down the curve of her neck.

She stiffened slightly. "This is all wrong. Tha's why you'll be gone tomorrow, 'cause it's all wrong."

"No, Jane, it's not wrong. You said it yourself, if this is all we can have—"

"Unless . . ." Suddenly she turned to face him. Her eyes fastened on his mouth as she leaned toward him. "Unless . . ."

With a long sigh, she slid her arms around his neck. He inhaled deeply as their lips came together, and was intoxicated by a faint, mysterious fragrance of earth and woman-flesh and wildflowers of the woods. For a long time she clung to him, while his hands moved over her back, pressing her close.

Then they were beside the bed, and with a movement too deft for him to follow, she had slipped out of the thin white dress, and her bare arms and shoulders gleamed like burnished gold in the lamplight.

Eagerly he reached for her, and as they sank down together on the bed, she whispered in his ear, "Maybe you'll like me so much you'll stay."

At five o'clock in the morning, the blackness of night was paling to a cold gray. A mist hung over the quiet land, and crept between the trees of the piney woods.

Lucius raised himself on an elbow and looked at the sleeping woman beside him. She was lying on her side facing him, her long black hair spread in beautiful disarray around her head. Lucius pushed the hair back from her face and ran his hand beneath the tresses, along her neck and bare shoulders. She shivered and stirred, and opened her eyes. She blinked at him without recognition for a moment. Then a soft smile played at the corners of her mouth. She reached up and put a hand behind his neck, and pulled him down toward her.

His eyes crinkled with amusement. "Let me go, Jane."

"Not yet."

"It's getting late."

414

She tightened her grip. "One more time," she said, and kissed him on the nose.

"It's getting late, I said!" Even as he protested, his hands were moving under the covers, tracing the soft contours of hip, waist, and breast. He drew in a long breath, savoring again the mysterious fragrance.

"One more time," she murmured. She moistened her lips and opened her mouth to receive him.

Then, when the morning sunlight began to slant through the misty depths of the woods, Lucius pulled away from the woman and left her lying limp and quiet and empty-eyed. He picked up his pants and went out to the back of the house, and when he came in again, he looked scrubbed and fresh. The woman was sitting on the side of the bed, staring at the floor. She was wearing a loose-fitting garment of coarse homespun material, which hung shapelessly on her shoulders.

As he finished dressing, Lucius stood looking down at her. "I liked you better in the white dress," he said casually.

"That was my wedding dress," she said. Her voice was lifeless.

After a moment, she glanced up at him. "You want some breakfast?"

"No time." Lucius chuckled. "This time I really mean it."

She watched him as he laced up his boots. "You're goin', then."

He shook his head glumly. "Sure wish I didn't have to, Jane."

"You don't have to."

"What would you have me do?"

"Let the damned ol' Texans and Mexicans fight it out among themselves."

"You want me to be a deserter? Could you love that kind of man?"

"Yes," she said firmly. "I could."

He laughed. "You don't mean that." He buckled on his jacket and came to her, leaned down and kissed her lightly on the forehead.

"G'bye, Jane. I sure hope I see you again."

"You won't." She did not look at him.

415

"What makes you say that?"

"You won't ever come this way agin."

"Oh, don't be too sure about that. One of these days, I just might—"

"And if you do, I won't be here."

Lucius looked faintly injured. "Well, all right. If that's the way it is . . ." He was moving toward the front door.

"Gim me some money," she said abruptly.

Lucius stopped short, and a stricken look came over his face. "What?!"

"Gim me some money, I said. You had your fun, didn't you? Wasn't it worth a little somethin'?" She was staring at him now, and her eyes had gone hard.

"Well, I'll be damned," Lucius said softly. "I'll just be goddamned. You sell yourself to any passing stranger don't you? *That's* how you make your living, not selling potatoes. Just like any Mississippi River whore, no damn difference."

"That ain't true."

"Just another whore, just like all the rest—"

"Lucius, I'm *poor*. Do you know what it means to be poor?"

"I don't know. Maybe I do, maybe I don't, all I know is you're just a—"

"Lem me tell you what it's like, Lucius." Her hands went out to him, beckoning him to her. "Come sit down, le' me jes' tell you."

"I don't have time, Jane, I've got to—"

"One time I took little Cal Junior to Nachitoches with me, Lucius. I had two dollars to buy supplies, and I was hopin' I could spare a few pennies to buy Cal somethin' with, but I couldn't, I jes' couldn't. Well, he looked all around in that big store, and his eyes got big as saucers. One thing caught his fancy. It was a cap. Kind of a sailor's cap, dark blue with bright yella stars on it. He jes' stood there starin' at that cap till I thought my heart would break, but he never said a word. It wasn't till 'bout a week or two later, one day he said to me, 'Mama, maybe sometime when my daddy comes back, he'll buy me that blue cap with the yella stars on it.' "

Jane pushed her disheveled hair back and took a deep breath. "Well, don't you worry 'bout us, Lucius, we're jes' fine. Little Cal don't need no blue cap with yella stars,

416

he'll grow up all right without that. I jes' want you to know if I beg, if I steal, if I humble myself to a man, it ain't for me. It's for him."

Lucius had moved to the side of the bed and was frowning down at the woman. "I don't understand all this. Doesn't little Cal know his father's dead?"

"Cal ain't dead. He run off and left us." Jane sat motionless, her eyes fixed on a tiny patch of morning sun creeping across the rough boards of the floor.

Lucius sat down beside her. "Why didn't you tell me?"

"A woman don't like to admit a thing like that. It makes her feel bad. It makes her feel like . . . dirt."

There was a long silence. Then Lucius got up and went to the door to the child's room, and opened it a crack. The boy was still asleep, sprawled now on his back on the floor pallet. Lucius went in quietly, and knelt and studied the small face. A lock of brown hair lay across the boy's closed eyes. Lucius gently pushed it back, and ran his fingertip with a feather-light touch over the smooth cheek.

"Good luck, Cal," he whispered. "You're a fine little fellow. And you're going to be a good man too, I know."

After a moment, he stood up and went back to the front room and closed the door. Jane was still sitting on the bed. She glanced at him, and looked away again.

"You better go on, then, if you're late." Her voice was flat and impersonal.

Lucius stepped close to her and dropped several gold pieces on the bed. She looked down at the coins, and touched them lightly with her fingers.

"That's too much," she said. "I ain't all that good."

"I'm not paying you, goddamn it!" Lucius snapped. "Just get that through your head, will you? I'm not . . . *paying* you!"

"All right, Lucius." She kept her eyes away from him.

He crossed to the front door and opened it. The dog on the front stoop scrambled up and began to whine. Lucius looked back at the woman. Still she would not look at him.

"Buy him the blue cap with the yellow stars on it," he said. He went out and closed the door behind him.

The dog kept whining until the man had disappeared from sight down the little road. Then he lay down again, licked his chops, and went back to sleep.

417

10

On the Trail to Texas,
Thursday, April 14th, 1836

Roll call 6:00 A.M. Major Barnett in charge. Colonel Hurley evidently suffering from too much good spirits yesterday. Captain Hargrave not present, whereabouts unknown. Captain Hargrave bad apple, Major Barnett declares. Directs me to record him as a deserter. Captain Kenyon of Company B sharply disagrees. Says Captain Hargrave is a dedicated soldier who would never desert. Just then, Captain Hargrave walks into camp. He is in dress uniform. Major Barnett demands explanation. Captain Hargrave gives Major Barnett haughty look. I am special intelligence officer, he says, I report only to Colonel Hurley. With that he walks away. Much amazement in ranks. Major Barnett furious, but says nothing. Considerable grumbling among men. Resentment of Captain Hargrave grows.

March underway 7:15 A.M. Good speed over open country. Intercept Texas road about sundown. Great amount of traffic on road. Many refugees coming out of Texas, on horses or mules, in oxcarts, in wagons, on foot. We hear latest war news. Some say General Houston maneuvering his troops cleverly, keeping just out of reach of Mexicans and waiting for Santa Ana to make careless move. Others say General Houston afraid to fight. Who can tell? In any case, showdown cannot be far off.

Bivouac on hillside near Fort Jesup, a short distance from road. Fort Jesup commands crest of high ridge on watershed between Red and Sabine Rivers. Guards Louisiana-Texas frontier and serves as part of Indian control system.

Colonel Hurley calls general assembly. This is last night on U.S. soil, he reminds troops. Tomorrow we cross Sabine River, enter Texas. If there are any boys remaining in brigade, Colonel says, they should leave tonight. This mission is for men only. Colonel in such extremely good spirits he can hardly stand, but somehow very dignified. Men inspired.

Progress today—approx. 34 miles

P.S. Men very serious and subdued tonight. Usual horseplay noticeably absent. Grumbling about petty things also sharply reduced. As soldiers move toward battle, they become philosophical. That is the way of war.

Maxwell Eades, Captain
Brigade Historian

11

FROM THE JOURNAL of Lucius Hargrave:

A young man's physical body grows visibly, and its increasing dimensions can be readily measured; the growth of his mind is far more subtle, infinitely more difficult to

419

trace. In the formative years, the mind is hardly more than a mental warehouse wherein new ideas are stowed away without much critical examination. But at a certain moment, a mysterious change quietly takes place. A man begins to reflect, to wonder, to judge, and to question. And suddenly, many of the items in his warehouse appear to be shoddy goods at best, not worth the sheltering. Confidence and certainty are shattered, and replaced by confusion, disenchantment, and depression.

It was about the time that our volunteer group marched off to Texas that I entered this unsettled and unsettling condition, and in retrospect it appears that the phenomenon was triggered by the brigade's commander, one Colonel Ashton Hurley. Gradually it dawned on me that the fate of several hundred brave men was in the hands of a vain, dictatorial, self-indulgent, fuzzy-minded, drunken amateur, and a hopeless incompetent. He needed help and needed it badly, yet in his monumental arrogance, he stubbornly refused to admit the need, or to accept assistance when it was offered.

I sought to confer with my fellow officers to see what could be done, and was dismayed to find them, to a man, cowed and timorous. Though clearly aware of the disgraceful situation, they were meekly resigned to it. Then it was that I learned something new about myself: I was not cut out for a military career.

Nevertheless, I was determined to do what I could to set matters aright before disaster occurred, so I made a careful study of Colonel Hurley, noted his weaknesses, played delicately upon them, and insinuated myself into his good graces. My efforts were more successful than I had dared hope; the colonel was soon heavily dependent on me (much as Albert Pettingill had been, I wryly noted), and I was appointed his special aide and promoted to the rank of captain. I would be loath to suggest that this minor change in organizational structure had a significant effect; I can only report it as a fact that from that moment on, the brigade functioned with smooth efficiency. Could I likewise report that my fellow officers and the men in the ranks were grateful for the service I had rendered them? Perish the thought—such a thing would be entirely at odds with all we know about the mean and petty nature of Man. He may be swayed by greed, driven by lust, blinded by anger or hate, but he is absolutely *ruled* by jealousy.

Colonel Hurley, however, (much to my discomfort) not only accepted my assistance, but developed a fatherly attachment to me, and began to look upon me as his protege. He confided to me that if I would stick with him, I could look forward to a brilliant career. (More echoes of Albert Pettingill!) This Texas venture is just made to order, the colonel said, and his eyes shone with glee. All we need is a touch of action—just a touch, no more—and his friends in New Orleans and Washington would do the rest. Reams of glowing publicity about his valor would be produced, and he would be a bona fide hero. At the very least, a generalship in the U.S. Army would follow, and I would be his personal aide, with the rank of colonel.

Sick at heart, I turned away from this evil man. Night after night I lay awake in my bedroll, my mind burning in torment. How could a noble cause be so basely subverted? Why would rational men willingly place their trust in a leader whose only interest was the furtherance of his own career, and the cause be damned?

And gradually, as my fevered mind seethed in this new-found questioning, it dared to probe into a hitherto sacred region.

What about this Cause, this heroic struggle for Texas independence? Somehow it had seeped into my consciousness that there was another side to the story. American settlers had gone to Texas at the invitation of Mexico, had cheerfully agreed to embrace the state religion and accept the sovereignty of the Mexican government and the conditions of Mexican life—and now, less than a generation later, they were howling in self-pity, picturing themselves as innocent, peace-loving American citizens who were being wrongfully oppressed by a foreign despot! Clearly, there was much thinking still to be done on the subject.

As often as I could, I went for long walks away from camp, desperately seeking a few minutes alone from time to time to meditate upon this roiling of doubts within me. And as I did so, I felt more feeble, more ignorant, and more uncertain of myself than I had ever felt before. Oh God, I prayed, give me thy hand and lead me out of the dark wilderness into the light, that I may see to find my true way in the world. But God was a stranger to me. I

421

was alone. I yearned for the gentle sound of my mother's voice. I longed to be a child again. And I cried out to be touched by the same light of nobility that had shone down upon my poor lost father.

12

April, 1836

Fort Jesup sat grimly on its eminence, guarding the southwestern frontier of the United States. To the west, the land sloped away down to the Sabine River, and beyond the Sabine lay the country that Mexico regarded as part of its vast province of Texas-Cohuilla, and that the American settlers who lived there were hailing as the Independent Republic of Texas. Across that broad, mostly uninhabited territory, armed men stalked each other, ready to kill or be killed.

The road to Texas came from Natchitoches, Louisiana, passed southwesterly in the vicinity of the fort, then dropped down to the Sabine and on into the hazy blue distance to Nacogdoches, the first Texan town of consequence, and the westernmost reach of the Spanish-Indian culture of Mexico. There was an old legend to the effect that Natchitoches and Nacogdoches were named for the twin sons of an Indian chief. If that brotherly feeling had ever existed between the two towns, it was gone now. The white man had come, and brought with him the passion called nationalism, and divided the continuous land into armed camps bristling with rivalry and suspicion.

Imbedded in the hard-packed ruts of the Texas Road were the imprints of centuries: the hooves of the buffalo, of the horse, of the ox; the moccasin of the Indian; the homemade shoe of the pioneer; the boot of the soldier; the long, grinding lines of the wagon wheels. Life moved here, and death; hope and despair; ambition and fear; purpose and aimlessness. The traffic was heavy now, with the flood of volunteers rushing to join the fight, and the tide of refugees moving eastward, seeking to escape it. Destiny beckoned. Some responded with eagerness, some fled. Two streams of humanity flowed past each other in opposite directions. There were heroes and cowards in each.

Late in the night, Jasper stuck his head into Captain Lucius Hargrave's tent and said, "Cap'n, suh? You awake?"

Captain Hargrave was lying on his cot with his eyes closed. His left hand cradled a whiskey glass, perched precariously on his stomach. His right hand hung over the side of the cot, and an open bottle stood on the ground beside him. A lantern hanging from the apex of the tent roof was turned down low, providing a dim light. Captain Hargrave opened his eyes lazily.

"Cap'n Hahgrave, suh, Cap'n Kenyon's heah to see you," Jasper said.

"Business or pleasure?" Captain Hargrave mumbled.

"He say jes' a social call, suh."

"In that case, show him in."

Jasper pulled the tent flap back. Bradford Kenyon stepped inside, and Jasper withdrew. Captain Hargrave raised a limp hand and indicated a tiny canvas stool.

"Nice to see you, Brad. Sit down and pour yourself a drink."

Captain Kenyon accepted both invitations, and smiled in good-natured astonishment at Captain Hargrave.

"Good Lord, Lucius! How do you do it? The first officer in the brigade to be promoted. Youh own private tent, unlimited access to Colonel Hurley's liquor supply, and now, as I live and breathe—valet suhvice!"

"Colonel Hurley and I have entered into a mutual-assistance pact," Lucius said.

423

"Well, I can easily see the evidence of the colonel's assistance to you. What do *you* do for *him?*"

Lucius smiled mysteriously. Brad became embarrassed.

"But I'm gettin' too personal. I withdraw the question."

Lucius chuckled. "Don't be silly, Brad. You're the only friend I've got around here; I keep no secrets from you." He reached for the bottle and poured himself a refill.

"What I contribute to Colonel Hurley's welfare is a very simple thing. It comes under the heading of social felicity. He likes to go cardplaying with me. He's noticed that when we play together, he develops the most uncanny knack for winning."

Brad groaned. "Oh no, Lucius!"

"You remember when we spent the whole night long 'conferring with the local authorities' in Alexandria? Colonel H. won thirty-eight hundred dollars that night. And did you know that he and I had dinner this evening with the command staff at Fort Jesup?"

"Yes, we heard you were goin' to be briefed on the military situation along the frontiuh."

"That's right. The colonel won eight, nine hundred, thereabouts. We quit and came back early, because there's not much loose money in an isolated army post. Hardly worth the trouble."

Bradford Kenyon's face was clouded. "Well, I'm disappointed, Lucius. You told me you'd given it up, and I thought you meant it."

"I did mean it. I'm just having a last fling. And I'm not playing for money, I'm playing for special privilege."

"Next time you'll be playin' for some othuh reason."

"No, Brad. Tonight was my last game. This time tomorrow we'll be in Texas, and from then on, I won't need to curry favor from our little stuffed-shirt Napoleon."

"What do you mean, Lucius? What are you goin' to do?" Brad was staring in dismay at his friend. "Aren't you still dedicated to the cause?"

"Cause? What cause?"

"Why, the noble cause of Texas indepen—"

"Oh, come *on*, Brad! When are you going to stop talking like a recruitment poster?"

"But that's why we're heah, isn't it? To help the Texans?"

424

Lucius sat up and swung his legs over the side of the cot. "Let me tell you about Texas. We really did get a military briefing over at the fort—it only took a few minutes, and didn't interfere with our card game at all. The situation is this: Sam Houston has collected himself a gang of killers that could probably take on the whole U.S. Army if it were of a mind to. Most of his men aren't Texans at all; they're adventurers from here, there, and everywhere, spoiling for a fight. The Mexicans, on the other hand, aren't real interested. Most of 'em figure Texas isn't worth interrupting a siesta over, much less dying for. Santa Ana spends half his time dallying with a slave girl he carries around with him—that's how interested *he* is. In other words, the show's almost over. Now Hurley's in a panic to get there, afraid he'll miss his big chance to become a hero. Me, I'm just biding my time, because I know that Texas independence is just about an accomplished fact, and it's surely going to be the land of opportunity if there ever was such a place."

"What kind of opportunity do you mean?" Brad Kenyon asked warily.

"I don't know yet. But whatever it is, I'm going to grab it. I'm looking to advance the fortunes of Lucius Hargrave —that's the cause *I'm* dedicated to."

Brad turned his whiskey glass in both hands, and gazed sadly into it. "You've changed, Lucius. I feel I hardly know you anymore."

Lucius's reply came back quickly, in a hard voice. "Yes, I've changed. Thank God. I hope I go on changing until I'm old enough and smart enough to recognize the difference between real things and fanciful things—to take hold of the one and let the other go."

For a little while they sat in silence. Brad sipped his whiskey thoughtfully.

"Well, wherevuh you're goin', Lucius, I wish you Godspeed. I jes' hope you don't progress so far and so fast you leave youh pore little ol' fun-lovin' friend behind."

Lucius's grim face softened. "No chance, Brad. You'll come with me, I'll see to that."

Brad smiled suddenly. "Speakin' o' fun—let me tell you what I did tonight, Lucius. Some o' the troops were out patrollin' this afternoon, and they said theah was a fortune-telluh's wagon parked up the road, 'bout two miles

425

on the othuh side o' the fort. So aftuh super, Jim Stiles and I went to take a look. Theah was this tall, strange-lookin' man, all dressed in long, silky robes, with a turban on his head. He's in a big covered wagon that's all painted up with signs and symbols, and he calls himself some crazy name—the High Priest of somethin' or othuh. Funniest thing you evuh saw."

Lucius had replenished Brad's drink and his own with what remained of the whiskey, and was now frowning at the empty bottle. "That's the last of Hurley's private stock. Sure hope we can get some decent whiskey in Texas."

"Listen to this, Lucius," Brad said. "I had my fortune told, just for the fun of it. And I was both amazed and amused by how frank this fellow was, tellin' me things about myself."

"Like what?"

Brad chuckled. "He told me I was the spoiled and pampuhed son of a wealthy Southuhn family."

"Anybody could look at you and know *that*."

"He said I'd nevuh done a lick o' work in my life, that I was goin' off to Texas because I was tryin' to find a way to prove my manhood. He told me all sorts of funny things like that. He told Jim Stiles things about himself that even Jim didn't know. He's an absolute magician."

"No he's not. He's a shrewd judge of character and a skillful fabricator. And you're a fool for wasting your time like that."

"Well, I thought it was fun."

"He insults you, and you think it's fun?"

Brad gave a modest shrug. "I don't have any illusions about myself, Lucius. I think the man told me the truth, mostly. Anyway, he only chahges two dolluhs, and he puts on quite a show. Very entuhtaining."

Lucius dropped the empty whiskey bottle on the ground and kicked it. The bottle rolled into a corner. He scowled at it.

"Goddamn! Wish we had some more whiskey."

"You're drinkin' too much, Lucius. You didn't used to do that."

"What else is there to do?"

"Go see the fortune-telluh. Listen, the Nigra slave who travels with him is wuth two dolluhs by himself. He

426

weahs the same kind o' silky robes his mastuh does, and he smiles and bobs his head up and down and talks like a maniac. Funny."

Lucius did not appear to be listening. "Not another drop for a hundred miles around," he muttered. "Not a decent meal, or a clean bed to sleep in."

Brad sighed, put down his glass, and got to his feet. "Well, I guess I'll tuhn in. Hope you'ah feelin' bettuh tomorrow, Lucius. It's gonna be a big day."

Lucius was still staring moodily at the empty whiskey bottle. "What the hell am I doing here?" he said in an almost inaudible voice.

Brad put a hand on his friend's shoulder and leaned down close. "Lucius? Are you all right? I worry about you."

Lucius glanced up briefly. "Oh sure. Sure, I'm all right."

"Well . . . good night, then." Brad gave him a pat on the shoulder and went out.

Lucius sat for several minutes with his elbows on his knees, gazing at the whiskey bottle in the corner. Then he began to talk to himself in an undertone.

"Long, silky robes," he mumbled. "Bobs his head up and down. Talks like a maniac."

After another minute, a faint smile crept over his face. He got up and threw open the tent flap.

"Jasper!"

"Yes, suh, Cap'n?" the attendant answered from somewhere in the darkness.

"Get my horse saddled up. I'm going on patrol."

427

13

THE ROAD twisted downhill like a piece of string, shining under a full moon, and at the bottom of the slope it plunged into a path of darkness around a broad and ancient oak. This was the fording place across a small stream, which flowed inches deep over the roadway.

Captain Hargrave's horse plodded without enthusiasm down the road, and when it came to the water, it stopped and lowered its head to drink. The rider made no move to prod it onward. He sat quietly in the saddle and peered through an alcoholic haze into the deep shadows beneath the big oak tree. There was a faint amber light there, glowing dully behind canvas, fifty feet from the road. All else was obscure.

Then there was a quick movement in the moonlight. A man had stepped out of the darkness. He took hold of the reins of Captain Hargrave's horse, causing the animal to neigh in alarm and toss his head. Captain Hargrave drew the reins tight, and glared down at the intruder.

"Goddamn you! What are you doing?!"

There was a shrill laugh, and a flash of white teeth against black skin. "Evenin', sar, evenin'." The voice was genial. "You be out alone, sar. Dat's bad. De debbil will git you, sar." Again the laugh.

"Who the hell are you?" Captain Hargrave demanded.

"Sancho, sar. Sancho, servant to de High Priest of de Temple of Eternal Light."

The black man was tall and broad-shouldered and dressed in a loose, multicolored robelike garment that reached to the ground. His head was wrapped in a turban of the same material, and bobbed repeatedly as he smiled up at the man on horseback. He continued to hold onto the horse's reins.

"You come to see de High Priest, sar?" Either the man's pleasant expression was a mask, or it reflected an innate cheerfulness, or both.

Captain Hargrave was leaning forward, studying the black man's face. "Hmmm. Thought so. I've seen you before. In New Orleans, several years ago."

"Maybe so, sar. We be in N'Orleans sometime."

"And you're servant to no priest. You're a seller of women."

Sancho's shrill laugh rang out again.

"You got a woman here?" Captain Hargrave asked gruffly.

"No woman here, sar. Very sorry. Had nice woman in Texas. Injun woman. But she run away. We run away now, too."

"Why's that?"

"Texas no good, sar. Bad war dere. Shooting, killing— no good. We go back to de States now."

Captain Hargrave squinted at the dim outlines of the big canvas-covered wagon beneath the tree. "Who is this so-called High Priest?"

"He very holy man, sar. Great man. He talk wid de debbil, sar. Know many t'ings, 'bout life an' 'bout death. 'Bout de earth above, an' hell below. He tell yo' fortune, sar. Only two dolluh."

"He's a fake," Captain Hargrave snapped.

Sancho recoiled. "Oh no, no, you mistake, sar! Don' let de debbil hear you speak so! De High Priest great man, sar, he tell you many t'ings. You go visit, you see. Only two dolluh, sar."

Captain Hargrave laughed, and Sancho bobbed his head and joined in.

"You're a damn fool," Captain Hargrave said abruptly. "And so's your master."

Sancho's laughter died. "Why you call us fool, sar?" His voice was almost plaintive.

"Because two dollars is no price for anything. Either the

429

man's a fake and his words are worth nothing, or he has some genuine power, in which case they're priceless, they're worth a for—"

"Suppose you come and visit awhile, and judge for yourself." A deep, quiet voice sounded startlingly from the darkness beneath the oak tree.

Captain Hargrave twisted in his saddle and stared in that direction. The flap of the wagon was open, and a tall man stood there, dimly silhouetted against candlelight.

"Come, sir," the deep voice said coaxingly. "You may pay whatever you thing it's worth. Nothing, if you like. You are welcome in any case."

Captain Hargrave dismounted and took a tentative step forward. He strained to make out the face, but it was hidden in shadows.

"Sancho!" the voice said with sudden authority. "Look after the gentleman's horse."

"Yas, sar."

Captain Hargrave moved toward the wagon. The man stepped back into the interior, but continued to hold the flap open. Captain Hargrave climbed a set of wooden steps to the entrance of the wagon, and peered inside.

"Come in, come in," the voice said.

Captain Hargrave entered.

The man was perhaps fifty years of age. His face was long, thin, and bony, with an aquiline nose and piercing eyes. He seemed grotesquely tall in a huge, bejeweled turban that almost touched the curved wooden roof staves. He was dressed in a long robe of silver and purple. He stroked his chin as he looked his visitor up and down, and his expression, his stance, and his long, delicate fingers exuded an air of lofty elegance. He smiled, but his eyes were as hard as the jewels on his turban.

"Welcome, sir," he said. "Won't you sit down?" He gestured toward a small chair beside an even smaller table.

Lucius looked around. In the murky light of a single candle, he could make out little detail in the cavernous wagon interior. He sat down.

As soon as his visitor was seated, the robed man took a chair opposite him. A thin smile played on his lips.

"I am glad you are here, sir," he said. "I am a mystic, and you are a cynic. It is the kind of confrontation that delights me."

430

Lucius snorted. "I'm no cynic. I just happen to be experienced in the ways of fakery, having spent a number of years at it myself, preying on other people's foolishness."

The robed man's eyebrows went up slightly. "Indeed? In what profession, may I ask?"

"I was a riverboat gambler, and a good one. To be good at that kind of work, you not only have to read cards, you have to read men's faces. You have to look right through their eyes and read the fine print in the backs of their minds. And when I look into *your* eyes, mister, I know I'm in the presence of a master of fakery."

Lucius's shoulders shook as he laughed in appreciation of his own cleverness.

His host leaned toward him, still smiling. "How interesting. Tell me more."

Lucius waved a hand at his surroundings. "All this—the High Priest of something-or-other, the robes, the fancy headdress, the fortune-telling—the only thing I can't figure is how you make a living at two dollars a head."

The robed man's cold smile was lit with something akin to amusement. "My, my, what a bright young man you are! How refreshing, after all the dullards I usually encounter."

"Thanks." Lucius accepted the compliment with a nod. "So, would you care to share your secrets with me? As one professional to another?"

"I have no secrets," the robed man said with a shrug. "I make a modest living, and that is enough; I'm a modest man. I enjoy this vocation. It amuses me to play upon one of my fellowman's deepest yearnings—his hunger for mystery."

Lucius was chuckling again. "Hey, that's pretty clever. Too bad we couldn't put our acts together; I'll bet we'd make good partners." He produced a mighty yawn. "But, no time for that. I'm on my way to Texas, and you're on your way out."

"Yes. Ships that pass in the night, as they say. Too bad." The robed man reached into some hidden crevice behind him, and brought forth a bottle and two glasses. "My young friend, I can see you've had quite a lot to drink tonight already, but . . . would you feel up to having a drink with me?"

431

Lucius was insulted. "What d'ya mean, I've had a lot to drink?! I'm as dry as the dust of Texas! Pour it!"

The man poured a milky liquid into the glasses. Lucius leaned forward and watched.

"What the hell *is* it?"

"It's called mescal. It's what they drink in Texas when they can't get whiskey. I've grown quite fond of it." The man handed Lucius a glass, and raised his own. "To your future, sir. May you know nothing but success and happiness."

They sipped in silence. Lucius smacked his lips thoughtfully.

"I could get used to this," he said. "If I had to."

"The Mexicans make it from some cactuslike plant," his host said. "It's surprisingly potent. You have to handle it with care."

"I can handle my liquor, mister," Lucius said cockily.

The older man smiled. There was another short silence, while Lucius worked on his drink with appreciative interest. His host watched him.

"Tell me about yourself," the robed man said finally. "Why are you going to Texas?"

Lucius gave a careless shrug. "I don't know. Why are you leaving?"

"The Mexican government is very inhospitable toward people like me. Catholicism is the state religion, you know, and the church fathers are very stiff-necked about anyone infringing on their territory. They have no enthusiasm for that old Yankee custom called religious freedom."

Lucius was frowning. "What's that got to do with you?"

"As I said, I'm a mystic. Religion is just organized mysticism, is it not?"

Lucius drained the last drop of his drink. "Wouldn't know," he said flippantly. "Never thought much about it." He held up his empty glass and winked at his host.

The robed man quickly filled the glass, and went on, "Well, I can assure you, the Mexicans have thought about it. For a time I was doing very well, running my old Protestant evangelism show, but then the authorities cracked down on me. So I switched to this fortune-telling thing, but they still wouldn't leave me alone. When the fighting started, I said to myself, enough, I'm moving out."

Lucius was sipping his mescal and gazing over the rim

432

of his glass at his host, and his face was twisted in a sardonic grin. "Funny," he said. "Mighty funny, what a multitude of sinners can hide under the cloak of religion. It's one of the many things that made my father's life so miserable."

"Your father?"

"He was a minister of the gospel. Traveled around for years, saving souls."

The robed man nodded. "Well, it *can* be a profitable business, if the conditions are right. For a number of years, I was—"

"Just a goddamn minute, mister," Lucius said with sudden belligerence. "Get one thing straight in your head. My father was a *real* minister, he was *nothing* like you. He was truly dedicated to doing the Lord's work, and he was a great man."

"My apologies," the fortune-teller said mildly. "I did not mean to be disrespectful. You say 'was'—is he not still living?"

Lucius took a long time to answer. He was becoming bleary-eyed, and he stared vacantly into a dark corner of the wagon chamber.

"He disappeared when I was a baby," he mumbled. "I never knew him. To me he's a legend. A living legend."

The fortune-teller was leaning forward, observing his guest with intense interest. Quietly he picked up the bottle of mescal and refilled Lucius's half-empty glass. Lucius seemed unaware of it. His head sagged toward his chest as he continued to gaze dumbly into space.

"Where are you from, may I ask?" the robed man said.

"Little village in Indiana, called South Bar," Lucius said. After a moment, alertness returned. He looked quickly at his host, as if in surprise. The man's eyes were burning into him, piercing him like daggers. Lucius grimaced.

"What the hell's the matter with you?" he growled. "You crazy or something?"

"I beg your pardon," the man said hastily. "It's nothing." He pulled his eyes away from Lucius, picked up his glass, and gazed into the milky liquid. After a moment he spoke again, with careful casualness.

"Would you mind telling me your name?"

Lucius's spirits were picking up again. He took another long pull on his drink, and grinned.

433

"My name? Lucius Hargrave. You want my full official title? Captain Lucius Hargrave, of the Sons of the South Brigade of Volunteers for Texas. I qualify because I'm from South Indiana, y'see." He giggled. "I'm special aide to the commanding officer, in charge of intelligence operations and gambling parties."

Lucius stopped and regarded the other man with a sudden frown. "Hey—are you there?"

The robed man had put a hand over his brow, covering his eyes. He started slightly at Lucius's sharp tone.

"Forgive me. I'm afraid my mind was wandering." He set his glass on the table and studied it, running his finger around and around the rim.

"How strange," he murmured. "How very strange . . ." He seemed to be talking to himself.

"What do you mean, strange?" Lucius demanded irritably. "The only thing strange around here is you."

"I'm a mystic, sir, don't forget," the other man said. "Mystics are seized with sudden visions from time to time, and on such occasions, they are apt to seem strange to—"

"Don't give me that!" Lucius snapped. "We both know damn well we're human parasites, living off others. So why don't you just talk straight?"

The robed man leaned forward suddenly, and impaled Lucius again with the piercing eyes, and his gaunt face was dark and grim. "Tell me, Captain Hargrave, what do you know about that father of yours?"

"I know he was a saint, living among devils. A good, kind, gentle, loving man, surrounded by envy and hatred and viciousness."

"A tragic portrait you paint, Captain."

"Well, isn't that the way of the world? Men hate what they can't understand, and the one thing they absolutely can't understand is perfect, total *goodness*."

Incongruously, behind his grim visage, the robed man chuckled.

"What's so goddamned funny?!" Lucius barked.

"Captain, how is it possible you can draw such a vivid picture of a man you never knew?"

Lucius huffed with anger. "How is it possible you can ask so damn many stupid questions?"

"Professional curiosity. Your father and I have certain things in common, I'm sure you'll agree."

434

Lucius's hand slammed down on the tabletop. He fixed the other man with a look of wrath, and his voice rang with vehemence.

"You bastard! You don't come within a million miles of being in a class with my father, and I'll thank you not to mention him in the same breath with yourself. He was a saint, and you're a two-dollar fortune-teller!"

The fortune-teller was properly contrite. "Again, my apologies, sir. I do seem to have trouble at times, remembering my humble station."

Lucius laughed. His mood was shifting with mercurial ease from gaiety to despondency to belligerence. Now he was abruptly cheerful again. He drained his glass and slammed it on the table with a loud slap.

"Good stuff!" he bellowed. "How about another one?"

The other man observed him calmly. "You're drunk, Captain."

Lucius's raucous laugh pealed out again. "The hell you say!"

The host picked up the mescal bottle, refilled both glasses once more, and smiled. "But I appreciate your generous spirit. Being willing to drink with a two-dollar fortune-teller—most democratic."

"S'all right, don' mention it. When I feel like drinkin', I don' give a damn *who* I drink with!" Lucius was still shaking with mirth as he put his glass to his lips again.

The fortune-teller continued to watch him, with eyes narrowed shrewdly. "Tell me about the rest of your family," he said after a moment. "Tell me about your mother."

Lucius leaned back in his chair, and gazed fuzzily into the dim recesses of the wagon. His mood was changing again.

"My mother," he mumbled. "A good, good woman. Best damn woman who ever lived. She loved my father dearly, and she absorbed a lot of his qualities. But, hell, she loves everybody. Has more love to give than any other ten people I ever met. And strong. She raised my brother and me all by herself, and took care of her parents' place, besides."

"Her parents still live?"

"Her mother is dead. Her father was alive, last I heard."

"Your mother . . . never remarried?"

"Oh yes, she remarried. Her second husband's an illiterate woodchopper."

435

The fortune-teller grimaced. "What a shame."

"She jus' did what any woman'd do under the circumstances—marry whoever's available. Cyrus was available."

"Cyrus?!"

"That's right. Man named Cyrus Thacker." Lucius blinked several times, and made an effort to focus his eyes on the other man. "I still can't figure out what makes you so goddamned inquisitive."

"I'm a lonely man, Captain. Do not begrudge me a little social contact." The fortune-teller took up the bottle, and again replenished Lucius's drink. "Please go on. What about your brother?"

"Good fellow, but weak. No spunk. Became a woodchopper too."

The fortune-teller waited. "Any other children? There must have been one more."

Lucius frowned at his questioner. "What the hell makes you say that?"

"I'm a mystic," the fortune-teller said with a small smile.

"Well . . . there *was* one other," Lucius conceded. "A girl. She died young."

"I'm sorry to hear that," the fortune-teller said in a soft voice.

Lucius sipped his drink and grew pensive. "Little Martha," he murmured. "Haven't thought about her in a long time." He let his eyes wander off again into the hazy distance.

"She loved clover blossoms. Used to bring home bunches of 'em. Strewed 'em all over the house. Used to drive us all crazy with those damned clover blossoms . . ."

Lucius's voice trailed off. In the silence that followed, the fortune-teller leaned far across the table and looked hard at his guest.

"Who were your father's enemies?"

Lucius was drifting in an alcoholic mist. "Yes . . . my father's enemies."

"Who were they?"

"Many of 'em. But only one really mattered. My mother's brother, George Gilpin."

"What about George Gilpin? What became of him?"

Lucius shook his head, and blinked, and again tried to bring the other man into focus. "What'zat?"

"I said, what happened to George Gilpin?"

436

Lucius frowned as if befuddled. He emptied his glass in one gulp, and winced as the fiery liquid burned his throat. Then he glared at his interrogator.

"Goddammit, I'm sick of your everlastin' questions. I'm gettin' out o' here." He slapped his glass down on the table and made a concentrated effort to get up.

"No, no, wait." The other man rose hurriedly, hands outstretched. "Don't go yet, Captain. Tell me more, just a little more."

Lucius's head wobbled drunkenly. "Why the hell should I?"

"Because I think the moment may be near when *I* can tell *you* something."

Lucius allowed himself to be pushed gently back down into his seat. His host filled his glass again, and handed it to him.

"Here. Have another drink. The evening is young yet."

Lucius stared stupidly into his glass. His hand shook; the liquor trembled precariously. The fortune-teller sat down again.

"Now, then. What happened to George Gilpin?"

"Dead," Lucius mumbled.

"Dead! George Gilpin is dead?!"

"Yes, goddamnit, dead!" Lucius answered with an angry shout. He tilted his head back and tossed down the drink. Half of it rolled down his neck and chin.

"Twenty years too late, the bastard's dead. He destroyed my mother's life and forced my poor tormented father into exile. A man whose shoes he wasn't fit to shine, he drove to ruin!"

"Really," the fortune-teller said dryly. "How regrettable." He picked up the bottle and filled his guest's glass yet again.

"My father was a great man," Lucius said. His eyes were vacant, and wandering aimlessly. "Great man. His very presence filled lesser men with envy, wherever he went. And I can tell you, my friend, of all the lesser men in the world, the least, the meanest, the most contemptible . . . were the lesser men of South Bar, Indiana. From the first day my father stepped ashore there, they were after him. Hounding him, spying on him, waiting for him to lift a careless finger or speak a careless word—anything they could grab and use against him. A pack of jackals, tor-

437

menting a noble lion. Well, they succeeded, by God, the sons o' bitches succeeded. They drove the lion away. And their leader, the meanest jackal in the pack—George Gilpin!"

Lucius's speech had grown thick, slurred, almost unintelligible. Once more he put his glass to his lips, and spilled the liquid. He reached for the mescal bottle, and knocked it over. The fortune-teller quickly retrieved it.

"Allow me," he said gently. He held Lucius's trembling hand steady with his own as he poured, this time emptying the bottle.

Lucius's head sank toward his chest. He stared unseeing at the wagon floor, and spoke in a thick-tongued mumble that caused the other man to lean down close and strain to hear.

"Twenty years late. But at least the bastard's gone. And I won't rest until I've found my father and brought him back, and cleared his good name, once and for—"

He swayed. Perspiration stood on his forehead. He tried to bring his drink up to his lips again, but his hand trembled violently and lost its grip. The glass fell to the floor with a clatter. Lucius leaned back, closed his eyes, and heaved a long sigh.

The fortune-teller was bending over him, slipping a hand behind his neck and lifting his head. "Captain Hargrave, can you hear me?"

"Uhhh," Lucius said. His eyes remained closed.

The fortune-teller's face was very close. "Captain Hargrave. What about . . . Emily?"

Lucius opened his eyes. He blinked rapidly several times, trying vainly to focus. He opened his mouth to speak, choked momentarily, gulped, and tried again.

"Who . . . are . . . you?" he whispered.

"I told you, I am a mystic," a voice close to his ear said. "And this night I have been visited by a vision."

Lucius's voice returned as a snarl. "You've been visited by no vision, you bastard! You're a fake! Just as much of a fake as I am!"

"Very well, Captain," the voice said coolly. "You don't like my answer, let me see if I can think of another."

The voice came closer, so close that Lucius shuddered from the cold intimacy of it. *I am your father.* Do you like that one any better?"

438

Lucius closed his eyes tightly and gritted his teeth and shook his head frantically, as if trying to elude some hideous pain. "No! *No!!*"

"Well, I'm sorry, Captain, those are the only two possibilities that occur to me at the moment. I am a mystic, or I am your father. Choose."

Lucius kept his eyes shut tight, and forced his words between his clenched teeth. "No, I said. You're a goddamned liar!"

"Choose, Captain Hargrave." The voice beside his ear was stone-hard.

Lucius lurched forward and buried his face in his hands. A muffled sob escaped him. "All right," he mumbled. "You're a mystic."

The fortune-teller stood, and looked down from a great height at the younger man. "Thank you for making a practical choice, Captain. It speaks well for your good instincts. Now then—Emily. What about her? Very briefly, if you please."

Lucius's face remained hidden in his hands. His voice was barely audible.

"She survives. She's the toughest one of all. She survives everything."

"Good."

After a moment, Lucius slowly lifted his head and peered up at the face of the fortune-teller, far above him. Perspiration rolled down his forehead, and dripped off his eyebrows and into his eyes. He blinked and wiped at his face with his hands.

"What am I to believe?" he asked in a tremulous whisper.

The fortune-teller appeared as a towering god, looking down through a veil of soft clouds. "Captain Hargrave, I will now give you my advice, the brief consultation for which I usually charge the modest fee of two dollars, but which, for you, will be a gift."

Lucius nodded, unable to speak. The fierce god-face came a little closer, but remained suspended and lofty.

"You're a dreamer, Captain Hargrave. You are a spinner of tales, which you carefully weave into a cocoon of silken smoothness and use to shut yourself away from reality like a sleeping moth. You sing sad songs of innocence wronged, and weep into your pillow. You are an indulger

439

in fantasies of sentimental self-delusion, which grow upon you until you are no longer able to bear their sullen weight. You are, to put it bluntly . . . a rather pitiful fellow."

Lucius stared up at the speaker. His mouth was open; he was panting.

"I don't . . . I don't understand . . ."

"On the other hand, Captain, you are splendidly endowed with the attributes of worldly success. Strong, intelligent, handsome, articulate, personable—there should be nothing to prevent you from rising to great achievements. Except, perhaps . . . yourself."

"Yes," Lucius breathed weakly. "Myself . . ." He closed his eyes again. His head began to sink.

Long, lean fingers grasped his chin and lifted it, tilting his face upward. His eyelids fluttered. He drew a long, peaceful breath. The voice was close again, and strangely soft, caressing his ear.

"Forget about all those ghosts of the past, Captain. Be your own man. Be Lucius Hargrave. That is all the identity you need."

Lucius opened his eyes. He frowned, and the frown turned to a ferocious scowl.

"Goddamn you!" he growled. "What the hell do *you* know? You cheap two-dollar fake! I ought to—"

With a sudden, half-choking cry, he lunged forward and upward, swung wildly at the man leaning over him, and went reeling into space. The chassis of the wagon shuddered and creaked as his body struck the floor. He lay flat on his back. His vacant eyes stared up at the canvas ceiling, and his lips moved soundlessly.

The black man stuck his head in the doorway. "Is anyt'ing wrong, sar?"

"Sancho," the fortune-teller said, "put Captain Hargrave on his horse, will you, and see to it that he gets safely back to his camp? He's had a little too much to drink."

The moon was almost down; the night would become darkest just before dawn.

Sancho half-coaxed, half-pushed the drunken man up into the saddle. "Tha's fine, sar," he said soothingly. "You jes' sit still, now. Sancho lead you home."

440

Lucius sat like stone, gripping the saddle horn. His head drooped on his chest. He was muttering under his breath.

"Damnable fake. Low, disgusting, cheap, two-dollar, scum of the—"

"Lucius!" The fortune-teller called to him from the shadows beneath the tree.

Feebly, Lucius raised his head and peered in that direction. The man's erect form was again silhouetted against the candlelight at the door of the wagon. The deep voice rang in the still night air.

"Be your own man, Lucius," the fortune-teller said. "Don't spend your life chasing after phantoms."

Lucius stared dumbly. The black man grasped the reins and pulled, and started the soldier's horse plodding listlessly up the rutted road.

14

THE FORTUNE-TELLER lay on his bed in the forward end of the wagon, and with half-closed eyes watched the flickering flame of the candle on the table beside him. He had laid aside his turban, uncovering a shock of straight black hair, lined with gray. He took no notice when his black servant stuck his head in the doorway.

"Rev'rend, sar? De young cap'n's back to camp, safe and sound."

With an effort, the fortune-teller drew his eyes away from the candle and looked at his servant. "Thank you, Sancho."

The black man came inside the wagon and squatted beside his master's bed. "He mighty drunk man, sar."

"Yes, wasn't he? Young men can't hold their liquor nowadays. Shameful."

Sancho inched a little closer. "Rev'rend, sar?"

"What is it, Sancho? Something bothering you? Speak up, man."

"Rev'rend, sar, I was listenin' right outside."

"Why, of course you were, I know that. You've always been incurably nosy, haven't you?"

"I heard de young cap'n tell his name, an' where he from."

"So you did. And?"

"But den', when you tell 'im who *you* was, he don' b'lieve you."

The fortune-teller's eyes crinkled with amusement. "That's right."

The black man's face was grave and thoughtful. "How come he don't b'lieve you, sar?"

The fortune-teller sat up. He let his eyes wander idly around the dim confines of the wagon's interior. The amusement had gone from his face. He suddenly looked old.

"Because *this* is all I am," he murmured.

The black man frowned and shook his head. "I don' understand, sar," he said earnestly. "You very great man."

The fortune-teller looked at Sancho, and a softness akin to affection came over his face. He reached under his bunk, pulled out a fresh bottle of mescal, opened it, and poured small portions into two glasses. With a gentle smile, he handed one glass to the other man.

"And *you* . . . are a good and faithful servant."

"Thank you, sar!" Sancho said breathlessly. He took the glass with both hands, and watched his master, and when he saw the white man begin to sip, did the same.

"It sho' do seem funny, though, sar," he said after a moment, "bout de young cap'n. Mighty funny."

The fortune-teller chuckled. "Why, yes, it *is* funny, Sancho. Life is altogether funny. We know that, don't we?"

The servant looked up quickly, his eyes bright with a brand-new thought. "Are we goin' back to N'Orleans, sar?"

"Perhaps. For a while, at least."

442

"Then where, sar?"

The fortune-teller shrugged. "I don't know, Sancho. We're wanderers, you and I. Wanderers don't know where they're going next. If they did, there would be no excitement in it."

The black man edged a little closer still. "Sar? Now we back in de States, can we go back to my old name? Sancho no good no more."

The master laughed aloud. "Why, of course!" With a bright smile, he clinked his glass against the other man's. He looked young again, and almost handsome.

"Cheers, Camus. Here's to our next adventure."

Camus grinned, and gulped his drink.

15

FROM THE JOURNAL of Lucius Hargrave:

Dawn comes at last. My fevered brain has burned in the darkness, seeking repose, but finding nothing but torment.

I have dreamed, and my dreams have turned to nightmares. Kind faces have smiled at me, and the smiles have whispered treachery, the faces have become the grinning masks of friends. Cruel talons clawed at me, and ripped my soul to shreds. The night is over, and though I lie limp in exhaustion, I welcome the morning light.

I dreamt of my mother. Sarah Gilpin, daughter of a

pioneer. Sarah Hargrave, loving wife. She is kind, she is beautiful, and my heart aches for the sound of her voice, yet I fly from her. Why? Because she gave herself to my father's enemy.

I dreamt of that man who calls himself her husband. He beckons to me, pretending to be my friend. I pay him no attention, for he lies. I am Oliver Hargrave's son, and well he knows it.

I dreamt of my grandfather, Samuel Gilpin. Stern, rigid, forbidding. I grew up thinking we hated each other—only now do I know it was respect between us, and a kind of guarded love, for he saw in me the qualities of his friend, my father, and strove to make me worthy of his vision. Dear old man, forgive me for not responding to you.

I dreamt of George Gilpin. He never knew me, yet he dogs my footsteps every day of my life. Even in death, he follows me. Someday, somehow, I pray to God I will be done with him.

I dreamt of my brother Isaac. Only half a brother; his mother is known to none of us, and he has taken my mother for his own. Only half a man, as well. He is prosperous and respected, but he has so little life that he is hardly more than a name and a shadow. I pity him. And yet I am eaten with envy, for he once had something precious that I never had—years with our father.

I dreamt of my little sister Martha. Dead at seven, she is blessed, for she never knew a moment of grief, was never touched by anything but love, purity, innocence, and joy. One day I will go and lay an offering of clover blossoms on her grave.

And I dreamt of my father. But it was anguish—I could not see his face. It was floating in a dismal cloud, hidden from my sight. He was a commanding figure, nevertheless; he stood tall and erect, silhouetted dimly against some feeble illumination and, curiously, garbed in long flowing robes. I held out my hands to him, cried out his name. He did not respond, nor did he come closer. Once I thought I heard his voice, from a distance, echoing along some timeless corridor.

"Be your own man, Lucius," he seemed to say. "Do not spend your life chasing after phantoms."

What does it mean?

The dream ends, the nightmare mercifully vanishes. The

morning comes now, washing those sounds and images away, and I am left bewildered and desolate.

There is a vast silence in camp, here in this wilderness place, before the first bugle call. In the dim light I bend over my task, writing the final lines in this first volume of my Journal, the chronicle of my total experience. Is it mindless chance, or by profound and fateful purpose, that I arrive at the last page of this well-worn notebook precisely at the moment when I come to the end of a major part of my life, and enter another? Who can say? Perhaps, some day far in the future, if I survive, I will look back and see beautiful design where now I can see only chaos, ugly and meaningless.

Meanwhile, I think it is good to close this Journal for a time and put it away. There are tremendous years ahead, to dwarf the puny ones through which I have passed, and I await them eagerly, I need them. There must be time to live, grow, think, feel, act, experience, meditate, and mature. And somehow, there must be a way to follow the advice of that disembodied voice, speaking to me with wisdom and love from the veiled realm of dreams.

Yes, Father, I will try to be my own man. I will try to banish all phantoms from my life. Forgive me if I refuse still to count you one of them.

The bugle sounds. It is time to go.